CHRISTMAS IN CORNWALL

CHRISTMAS IN CORNWALL

MARCIA WILLETT

Thomas Dunne Books
St. Martin's Press
New York

THOMAS DUNNE BOOKS.
An imprint of St. Martin's Press.

CHRISTMAS IN CORNWALL. Copyright © 2011 by Marcia Willett. All rights
reserved. Printed in the United States of America. For information, address
St. Martin's Press, 175 Fifth Avenue, New York, N.Y. 10010.

www.thomasdunnebooks.com
www.stmartins.com

ISBN 978-1-250-00370-6 (hardcover)
ISBN 978-1-250-02357-5 (e-book)

First published in Great Britain by TRANSWORLD PUBLISHERS,
a Random House Group Company

First U.S. Edition: November 2012

10 9 8 7 6 5 4 3 2 1

To Evelyn

EPIPHANY

The Holy Family live in an old linen shoebag. The bag is dark brown, with a name-tape sewn just below its gathered neck where a stout cord pulls it tight, and each year on Christmas Eve the bag is opened and the Family, along with its attendant Wise Men, shepherds, an angel with a broken halo and various animals, are set out on a table beside the Christmas tree. They have their own stable, a wooden, open-fronted building, which has once been part of a smart toy farm, and they fit perfectly into it: the golden angel standing devoutly behind the small manger in which the tiny Holy Child lies, swaddled in white. His mother, all in blue, kneels at the head, opposite a shepherd who has fallen to his knees at the foot of the crib, his arms stretched wide in joyful worship. Joseph, in his red cloak, with a second shepherd – carrying a lamb around his neck as if it were a fur collar – stand slightly to one side, watching. A black and white cow is curled sleepily in one corner near to the grey donkey, which stands with its head slightly bowed. And here, just outside this homely scene, come the Wise Men in gaudy flowing robes, pacing in file, reverentially bearing gifts: gold, frankincense and myrrh.

Jakey stands close to the table, gazing at the figures, his eyes just level with them. Occasionally he might pick up one of the figures in order to study it more closely: the angel's broken halo; the lamb curled so peacefully around the shepherd's neck; the tiny caskets carried by the Wise Men. Once he'd dropped the Holy Child, who rolled under the sofa. Oh, the terror of that moment: lying flat on his face, scrabbling beneath the heavy chair, hot with the frustration of being unable to move it – and the huge relief when his fingers had closed over the little figure, and he'd drawn out the Baby unharmed and placed Him back in His blue-lined crib.

Now, as he stands by the crib, Jakey grows slowly aware of the sounds around him: the clock ticking weightily, its pendulum a crossly wagging finger; the sigh and rustle of ashy logs collapsing together in the grate; his father talking on the telephone next door in the kitchen and the monotonous quacking of the radio turned down low. Today the decorations must be taken down because it is Twelfth Night: the last day of Christmas.

Jakey begins to sing softly to himself: '"Five go-hold *lings*. Fo-our calling birds, thlee Flench hens, two-hoo turtle doves, and a partdlige in a pear *tlee*".'

He feels restless; sad that the tiny, sparkling lights and the pretty tree will no longer be there to brighten the short dark winter days. Still singing just below his breath, he climbs onto the sofa and tries to balance on his head on the cushions, his legs propped against its back, until he falls sideways and tips slowly onto the floor. He lies with his feet still on the sofa, his head turned sideways on the rug, and regards

Auntie Gabriel who stands on the bookcase presiding over the Christmas festivities. The angel is nearly two foot tall with clumsy wooden shoes, a white papier-mâché dress and golden padded wings. Her hair is made of string but her scarlet, uptilted thread of a smile is compassionate; joyful. The clumpy feet might be set square and firm on the ground but when the golden wire crown is placed upon the tow-coloured head then there is something unearthly about her. Held lightly between her hands is a red satin heart: a symbol of love, perhaps?

There are several other, smaller, angels strung from convenient hooks about the room; but none has the status of Auntie Gabriel. Not as fierce and cold and glorious as the Archangel himself, flying in from heaven in all his power and majesty, and trailing clouds of glory; she is, nevertheless, a distant relation: the human, fallible face of love.

With a mighty heave, Jakey rolls head over heels and stands up. He goes over to the bookcase and stares up at Auntie Gabriel, who beams sweetly at him with her lop-sided silk-thread smile. He doesn't want her to be packed away in the soft roll of material that protects her fragile dress and padded wings, her gold crown wrapped separately, before they are all put into a large carrier bag and tucked into the drawer in the old merchant's chest. He doesn't want Christmas to be over. Jakey is utterly miserable. Deliberately he kicks out and stubs his toe in its soft leather slipper against the corner of the bookcase, hurting himself, and his mouth turns down at the corners. He decides to let himself cry; he's just going to, even though he knows that he's a big boy now; that next birthday he will be five. He experiments with a sob, listens to it with interest, and squeezes his eyes shut to force out a tear.

*   *   *

Clem watches his small son from the doorway, his heart twisting with a mix of compassion and amusement.

'Listen,' he says. 'Guess who that was on the phone.' And at the sound of his voice, Jakey jumps and turns quickly. 'It was Dossie,' Clem says. 'She's on her way over and she's bringing something special with her.'

Jakey hesitates, head down, his lower lip still protruding, not quite willing yet to be jollied out of his self-pity.

'What?' he asks, pretending not to care much. 'What is she blinging?'

'It's a secret.' Clem sits down and scoops a long-eared, long-legged brightly knitted rabbit onto his knee. 'Isn't it, Stripey Bunny? It's a Twelfth Night present. Something you have when all the decorations have been taken down.'

Jakey looks around the room: at the Holy Family; at the glittering tree; at Auntie Gabriel. He hesitates, debating with himself, but Clem senses signs of weakening and blesses his mother for the idea.

'He's utterly miserable,' he told her on the phone. 'He can't bear the thought of Christmas being over and I can't really explain to him why we have to take all the decorations down. It's going to be a bad evening.'

'Poor darling,' she said. 'I couldn't sympathize more. I hate it too. Now here's a plan. Why don't I bring over the chocolate cake I made this morning and something out of my present drawer? I've got one of those *Thomas the Tank Engine* thingies. James, I think it is. Or is it Edward? Jakey will know. We were reading a story about them all.'

Clem hesitated. 'He's had so much for Christmas, Dossie. I don't want to spoil him.'

'Oh, darling. One little truck. Remember how you used

to feel? Anyway, we couldn't spoil Jakey. He's much too balanced. A Twelfth Night present. What d'you think?'

'OK. Why not? Do I get one too?'

'Certainly not. You're not nearly as balanced as Jakey is and I can't risk spoiling you at this late date. But you shall have some cake. See you soon.'

Now, Jakey wanders over and leans against Clem's knee. He twiddles Stripey Bunny's long soft ears and allows himself to give in.

'When will Dossie be here?'

'Soon.' Clem glances up at the clock: the drive from St Endellion to Peneglos should take about half an hour. 'Let's have a quick walk before it gets dark and you can ride your new bike. Stripey Bunny can go in the back.'

Jakey runs shouting to the door, high spirits restored.

'Boots on,' calls Clem. 'And your coat. Wait, Jakey. I said, *Wait . . .*'

Presently they go out together into the wintry sunset.

Frost lies thick in the ditches, crisping the bramble leaves, scarlet, yellow and purple, that trail over the bleached, bent grass and frozen earth. Dossie drives carefully in the winding lane, watching for icy patches unthawed by the day's sunshine. A flock of starlings rise from a field beyond the bare thorn hedge; they swoop and dive, as sleek as a shoal of fish swimming in the cold blue air, settling randomly on the telephone wires like notes of music scribbled on a score.

At the A39 she turns westwards towards Wadebridge. She is filled with joy at the glory of the sunset – gold and crimson clouds streaming out across the rosy sky – and at the sight of a half-moon, already well risen, trailed by one great star. She hopes that Jakey can see the star; he loves the firmament at night. At this time of the year they are able to star-watch together before his bedtime; and she made him a stargazy pie for his fourth birthday. The memory of his expression at the sight of all the little pilchards staring skywards makes her smile, but with the smile comes the familiar twist of pain. How sad it is – how cruelly sad – that fate should repeat her wicked little trick, so that, just as Clem never knew his father, so Jakey's mother died of post-partum haemorrhage just hours after his birth. Dossie heaves a great sighing breath: oh, the shock and the pain of it, still fresh. At the time she tried so hard to persuade Clem not to give up his theological training, just begun at St Stephen's House in Oxford, offering to make a home there for all of them until he was ordained, pleading with him to allow her to look after Jakey, either in Oxford or at the family home in Cornwall.

'Mo and Pa would love to help,' she said. 'He's their great-grandson, after all, Clem. They helped me bring you up; now they could do the same for Jakey.'

It was quite useless. Politely but steadfastly he refused to listen to his tutors and his spiritual advisers, who tried to convince him of his vocation, telling him that his grief was blinding him to his true calling. He returned to his lucrative job in IT in London, working from their little flat whilst paying for a nanny to take care of Jakey, and doing as much as he could for his baby son.

Dossie knew very well that Clem hadn't wanted her to give up her own work as a self-employed caterer or to lose the contacts and reputation she'd spent so many years cultivating on this high windswept Atlantic coast; and Mo and Pa were no longer young. He must fend for himself and for Jakey, he said. But she knew he hated returning to that place where first he'd felt what he'd once described, with a kind of disbelieving awe, as 'the pressing in of God'.

Now, ahead, Dossie can see the New Bridge striding across the River Camel. The tide is out and only a silver trickle marks the water's course. Little boats lie lifeless at their moorings on the pale shining mud, waiting for the sea's pulse to lift them again into life. She drives across the bridge, past Wadebridge and the old bridge upstream, turning off the A39, taking the road towards Padstow, remembering Clem's phone call just over a year ago.

'There's this job advertised in the *Church Times*,' he said. 'It's somewhere near you at a place called Peneglos. It says: "Strong person required to work six acres of grounds plus some house maintenance. Small salary but a three-bedroom lodge house comes free with the post." It's an Anglican convent.'

His voice, abrupt but oddly eager, almost daring her to comment, silenced her for a moment. She had no idea that he still read the *Church Times*.

'That must be Chi-Meur,' she said lightly. 'It's a lovely old place. A little Elizabethan manor house that was given to the nuns by an elderly spinster of the Bosanko family who owned it at the time. And Peneglos is the tiny village running down to the sea between Stepper Point and Trevose Head. The convent sits up above it in the valley.'

She waited; the silence stretched interminably between them.

'I'm thinking of going for it,' he said at last, challengingly. 'I can sell the flat and invest the money and then see how we get on. After all, Mo always used to make me work like a slave in the garden and Pa made sure that I'm no stranger to a paintbrush.'

13

Dossie's excitement was so intense she hardly dared to breathe.

'Sounds great,' she said casually. 'Nothing you couldn't handle, I'm sure, and fantastic for Jakey. A perfect place for a little boy to grow up, so close to the sea.'

Once again she waited: she would not question him or ask how he'd manage with Jakey while he was working.

'I'll have to find out about childcare,' he was saying. 'It'll be easier when he starts school, of course, but there should be a nursery in Padstow. And you're not far away.'

'Half an hour at the most, I should say. We can all help till you're settled.'

'OK.' He sounded excited; hopeful. 'If they give me an interview we could stay at The Court for a few days. That'd be OK, wouldn't it?'

She laughed then. 'Of course it would. Let me know what happens.'

'"Ch'Muir?"' Clem repeated thoughtfully. 'Is that how you pronounce it?'

'More or less,' she replied. 'It's Cornish for "the big house". Something like that.'

'Sounds good. There was suddenly a wistful longing in his voice.

Dossie saw in her mind's eye his tall, lean form; the silvery-gilt blond hair, the same colour as her own, cropped close to his head. She remembered how happy he'd been in the discovery of his vocation, in the love of his pretty French wife and the prospect of their baby, and her heart ached for him. No point in asking if he found his present work empty; she knew the answer.

'If it's right then it will happen,' she said, suddenly cheerful; some sixth sense prompting her to confidence.

And it had happened. The Sisters of Christ the King at Chi-Meur Convent and their chaplain and warden, Father Pascal, had taken Clem and Jakey to their hearts and Clem was offered the post and the sturdy little lodge house with it.

Now, as Dossie turns into the lane towards Peneglos, her heart is glad with gratitude. Clem is healing, and Jakey is growing – and they are happy. She passes in through the convent gates and there is the Lodge, light streaming out across the drive, and Jakey at the window, waiting for her.

'I was wondering,' says Clem, watching as Dossie puts the remains of the cake back into its Raymond Briggs Father Christmas tin, 'whether to leave the decorations until he's gone to bed. You know? Do them when he's asleep.'

They had tea in the big, square, cheerful kitchen and now Jakey is next door in the sitting-room watching a DVD: *Shaun the Sheep*. With Stripey Bunny curled under his arm he is engrossed by the flock of amiable sheep and the antics of the idiotic sheepdog.

'No, no.' Dossie is very firm. 'He'll enjoy it in an odd kind of way. It's important, isn't it, to learn to finish things as well as to begin them? It'd be a terrible anticlimax for him to wake up to find it all packed away. It's like grieving. It has its own pace and its own rituals. He was too little last year to do much but this year he can be helpful. He'll like that.' She glances at Clem. 'Am I being bossy, darling? You must do what you think is best.'

'I expect you're right.'

He turns away and stands for a moment, leaning against the sink, staring out into the darkness. The convent lights shine out between the bare branches of the trees but Dossie knows that he is thinking of Madeleine; of how Jakey's

15

mother might have dealt with the situation. She reflects that there isn't much that Clem doesn't know about grieving.

'He can pack up Auntie Gabriel,' Dossie says cheerfully, hiding her own anguish. 'He loves Auntie Gabriel. And the Holy Family. He can be responsible for them. And afterwards he can have his present and we'll play with the trains before he has his bath. What d'you think?'

Clem turns back and smiles at her. His smile frightens her; there is an empty quality about it, a determined stoicism. She wants to put her arms round him but she knows that her desire to comfort will merely be a burden to him; he'd be obliged to bury his pain more deeply in order not to worry her.

Jakey comes into the kitchen with Stripey Bunny still under his arm.

'*Shaun*'s finished,' he says. 'Are we going to take the decolations down now?'

He is still slightly reluctant to abandon his air of sadness, which has so far earned him a big slice of cake and the present to come, and Dossie watches him, amused. Showing great restraint, he hasn't asked about his Twelfth Night present but clearly he guesses that it is contingent upon the decorations being packed away and is now quite ready for this next step. She raises her eyebrows at Clem, who nods.

'Could you deal with Auntie Gabriel? And the Holy Family? The tree takes a bit of time so it would be a great help if you could manage them.'

Jakey's eyes open wide with importance; he grows visibly. He nods. 'But I can't leach Auntie Gabriel unless I stand on a chair.'

'I'll come and help,' says Dossie. 'I'll do the tree and then Daddy can take it out.'

They go together into the sitting room and she opens the heavy bottom drawer of the merchant's chest. Out come the empty boxes and bags and she puts them on the sofa. Jakey seizes the linen shoebag and studies the name-tape with its red stitched letters: C PARDOE. He knows that the letters spell Daddy's name and his own name, and that the shoe-bag belonged to Daddy when he was little and at school. He opens the neck of the bag as wide as he can and carries it over to the low table beside the tree.

Which to take first? He puts the cow in, and then the donkey, laying them right down into the bottom of the bag, and then peeps in at them to see if they are all right. They look quite happy, resting in the slightly musty interior. Next come the kneeling shepherd, arms stretched wide, and the Wise Men: one, two, three. Once again he peers into the bag where they all loll together.

'They're having a lest,' he tells Dossie. 'They like it.'

'Of course they do. They've been standing or kneeling there for twelve days. You'd need a rest if you'd stood up for twelve days.'

Jakey reaches for the second shepherd and Joseph, feeling happier. Joseph settles comfortably at the bottom of the bag, and he puts Mary beside him. The angel Gabriel, staring loftily at nothing, wings unfurled, halo broken, goes in next and, last of all, the little crib and the Holy Child. He puts the manger in but continues to hold the sleeping baby.

'Baby Jesus doesn't need a lest,' he says, almost to himself. 'He's been lesting all the time.'

'But he wants to be with his family,' answers Dossie. 'He'd miss them otherwise.'

Briefly he wonders whether to make a little fuss, to argue,

but then he thinks about the present to come and decides not to. 'OK,' he says cheerfully.

He puts the Holy Child into the shoebag, takes one last look at them all, and with some difficulty pulls the drawstring tight.

'Well done,' says Dossie. 'We'll put the stable in the drawer separately. Now can you pack up Auntie Gabriel?'

She takes the large bulky figure from the bookcase and props her against the cushions on the sofa beside the soft wrappings. Jakey studies her regretfully: he'll miss her smile and the comforting feeling that she is watching over him. A memory of a dream he's had several times flickers in his mind: the still, silent figure, wrapped in pale shawls, standing amongst the trees across the drive from the Lodge, watching. Jakey can't remember now whether he's actually climbed out of bed and seen the figure from his window, or merely dreamed it. He fingers the heavy blocks on Auntie Gabriel's feet and the soft padded wings, and touches the red satin heart, which she holds between her pudgy hands.

'Don't forget to take her crown off,' says Dossie, 'and wrap it separately. Poor old Auntie Gabriel. Now she *really* needs a rest. She'll be all ready, then, to come out again next Christmas.'

Reverently, Jakey takes the gold wire crown from the thick string hair; he bends forward so that his mouth is close to the silk thread of a smile.

'See you next Chlistmas,' he whispers. 'Have a good lest.'

He lays her on the soft piece of material and wraps her in it as if it were a shawl. He doesn't want to cover her face so that she can't breathe. He puts her very carefully into the big carrier bag and then wraps some tissue paper round the crown and puts it in after her. All at once the sadness overcomes him again: he hates to see Auntie Gabriel hidden in a bag as if she were some ordinary old shopping. Before he can speak, however, Dossie is talking to him.

'Could you help me, darling?' she says. 'I've been so silly. I've taken these things down and I can't find the box they go in. Is it there on the sofa? Oh, yes. That's the one. Come and see these little figures, Jakey. Daddy loved these when he was your age.'

And he goes to look at the little carved wooden figures – a drummer boy, a snowman and a small boy with a lantern – and helps Dossie to put them into their little green box; she shows him the fragile glass baubles, an owl, and a clock and a bell, and the moment passes.

That night he has the dream again of the figure, wrapped in pale clothing, standing amongst the trees, watching. But he isn't afraid: he knows now that it is Auntie Gabriel.

The drive passes in front of the house, with its stone-mullioned windows and stout oaken door, and curves round to the open-fronted stables, which are used as a garage, and to the Coach House. This has been converted to a guesthouse for those small groups of retreatants who prefer to cater for themselves, rather than stay in the house and eat in the guests' dining-room, and who like to walk the coastal footpath and visit Padstow, as well as attending some of the Daily Offices in the chapel. It's an attractive building looking north-west across the Atlantic coast to the sea and south-east towards the orchard where the caravan stands amongst the apple trees.

Once the caravan was a hermit nun's refuge: now it is Janna's home. She comes down the steps, tying a bright silk scarf over her lion's-mane hair, bracing herself against the cold air. Inside, with the low winter sun streaming in through the caravan's windows, it's cosily warm; the dazzling light shining on her few precious belongings, glinting on the little silver vase that Clem and Jakey gave her for Christmas. She's found some pale, green-veined snowdrops under the trees to put into it and she looks at the fragile blooms with pleasure when she sits at the small table each morning to eat her breakfast.

The vase is real silver, and she was both shocked and gratified by this expensive token of their affection for her. She opened the present carefully, aware of Jakey's excitement and Clem's faint anxiety. Her delight pleased them both and they exchanged a man-to-man look of relief, which amused her.

'I love it,' she said. ''Tis really beautiful,' and she stood it on the table, tracing the swirling chasings with a finger, and then hugged Jakey. She didn't hug Clem: Clem isn't the sort of person you could hug just casually; not like his mum, Dossie, or like Sister Emily, for instance. Clem is very tall, for one thing, and very lean, and there is an austerity about him – Dossie said that once, used that word: 'Old Clem's a touch austere, isn't he?' – which is rather like Father Pascal. She loves Father Pascal because he never questions her or judges her, and so, after a while, she's told him things: things like her dad disappearing before she was born and her mum being barely more than a child herself. About being on the road, and then, later, being fostered because her mum drank too much and how she'd kept running away from her foster homes trying to find her mum.

'We missed the travelling,' she told him. 'Always being on the move. Going places. She couldn't bear it at the end when she was in a wheelchair. I'm the same. "Trains and Boats and Planes . . ."' She hummed the tune. 'Don't know why.'

'We're all pilgrims,' Father Pascal said thoughtfully. 'One way and another, aren't we? Always searching for something.'

Janna finishes tying the scarf at the nape of her neck and pauses to do homage to the large pot of winter pansies that stands beside the steps: creamy white and gold and purple, they turn their pretty silken faces to the wintry sunshine. She shivers, wrapping her warm woollen jacket more closely round her. Dossie gave her the jacket. It is almost knee length, soft damson-coloured wool, and elegant, but oh! so warm. This time, when she opened her present, she was unable to hide her emotion, and she and Dossie hugged each other, and Dossie's eyes shone too, with tears. It was what she calls 'having a moment'; but Dossie has many such moments: having chocolate cake with your coffee might be having a moment: or dashing into Padstow for an hour in the sunshine and then eating fish and chips by the sea wall: 'I think we need a moment, darling.' She celebrates life with these moments and Janna accepts them with joy: she understands this. She, too, has a passion for picnics, for impromptu meals and sudden journeys.

Her Christmas gifts to them were much more simple: a *Thomas the Tank Engine* colouring book for Jakey; two spotted handkerchiefs for Clem; a piece of pretty china from the market for Dossie. Janna's work is not highly paid, though her caravan is rent-free, but she eats well in the convent kitchen and counts herself lucky: much better than working the pubs in the summer season and taking anything she can find during the winter months. She heard about this job when she was working down in Padstow at the end of the season and she wandered up from Trevone

one windy afternoon, leaving the surfers she was hanging out with down on the beach, walking over the cliffs in the late September sunshine. She came by the cliff path with the gulls screaming above the ebbing tide and the wind at her back.

'Blown in on a westerly,' Sister Emily says, beaming, 'and what a wonderful day for us it was.'

It's odd, thinks Janna, how quickly she felt at home. Even as she walked between the two great granite pillars, passing the little lodge house and wandering along the drive, she was aware of a sense of homecoming. The granite manor, set amongst its fields, looking away to the west, with its gardens and orchard surrounding it, was so beautiful, so peaceful. Yet even with the warm welcome she had, and that strange sense of belonging, nevertheless she chose the caravan in the orchard rather than the comfortable bed-sitting-room in the house that they offered her. The caravan is separate; it offers privacy and independence.

'It reminds me of when I was a kid,' she told the kindly Sisters, eager to welcome her and to make her feel at home, 'when we were on the road.'

If they were surprised they showed no sign of it. Warmly, courteously, they gave her the freedom of the caravan and outlined her duties, which are simple: to keep the house clean and the washing and ironing done; and, if necessary, to sit with Sister Nichola who, at ninety-two, is failing.

'We used to be completely self-sufficient,' Mother Magda told Janna rather sadly. 'Inside and out. But there were many more of us then, and we were young. We always had a couple in the Lodge that helped us, but the husband died and his wife went to live with her daughter. Now we have Clem, who is a true blessing.'

'And Jakey,' Sister Emily added, twinkling.

'I'm not certain,' Sister Ruth said, rather coolly, 'that Jakey is a great help to us.'

'He makes us feel young again.' Mother Magda spoke firmly. 'And he understands reverence.'

Now, Janna passes beneath the apple trees and crosses the yard, the pretty little bantams, soft grey and warm gold, scattering and running before her. The Coach House is empty; no guests this week. She is glad. It is good just to be themselves. She loves it when they are just family; the family for which she's always longed. Mother Magda, Father Pascal, Sisters Emily, Ruth and Nichola; and Clem and Jakey and Dossie. How strange it is to find them here, unexpectedly, in this high, tiny valley that tips and tumbles its way down to the sea. She goes in through the back door and into the kitchen.

In the chapel the Sisters are at Morning Prayer. Sister Nichola sits with her eyes fixed on the mullioned window and the bare, frost-rimed branches of the lilac tree beyond it. Her thoughts are not always clear and she fancies that if she were to breathe in she might smell the heady scent of the lilac blossom drifting in through the open window; and she will hear the blackbird's song as he perches amongst its branches. This morning the window is closed against the winter's chill and the spring is yet some way off. Beside her, Sister Ruth stands up to go out to the lectern; Sister Nichola watches the tall, spare figure, trying to remember her name. She looks around the chapel, seeing long-gone faces and quiet, attentive forms sitting in the empty stalls, observing Mother Magda's thin, fine-drawn face and serene blue eyes, and Sister Emily's intelligent, direct look and her half-smiling mouth. They are watching Sister Ruth – yes; that's her name; Sister Nichola gives a delighted little nod as she remembers it – who is now opening the Bible and is beginning to read.

'"Arise, shine; for your light has come, and the glory of the Lord has risen upon you."'

Isaiah: Epiphany. The familiarity of the Church year, turning and turning in its endless dance, comforts Sister Nichola. This remains whilst so many other things fall away from her. Her head droops a little but she does not sleep.

Clem arrives in the kitchen before Janna, emptying some vegetables from a basket onto a newspaper on the big, scrubbed table. A pan containing stock simmers on the Aga but there is no sign of Penny, who comes up from the village to cook. Janna and Clem smile at one another. In the few months that she's been at the convent Janna has learned to move softly, to speak very quietly: the nuns value silence although here, in the kitchen, quiet conversation is allowed. To Clem silence comes naturally. She and Penny, however, often have to muffle cries of irritation or bursts of laughter as they prepare and cook food, getting in each other's way, burning a saucepan or dropping a plate. Often Sister Emily, gliding in behind them, smiles but Sister Ruth is less sympathetic to such outbursts. Her pale, level glance restores them to order very quickly, whilst Emily's dark eyes crinkle with fellow feeling.

On her afternoons off, Sister Emily often makes her way through the orchard to the caravan for a cup of tea. Janna loves these 'moments'; for they are of that order of celebration of which Dossie approves. Sister Emily has a passion for life that, at eighty-two, is unexpected: her brown eyes sparkling at the sight of a special cake or at the variety of Janna's fruit teas.

'Echinacea and raspberry,' she murmurs. 'Camomile and lemon *and* mint. How delicious. Now which shall I choose?'

For the first time for years Janna is living among women who own even less than she does: she no longer needs to justify her lack of belongings. It even seems to be a virtue. She showed Sister Emily her small store of treasures: the Peter Rabbit mug and the Roger Hargreaves *Little Miss Sunshine* book, and the threadbare Indian silk shawl.

'My mum gave them to me when I was little,' she said almost defensively. 'She loved me, see, even if she had to give me up. She bought me stuff; called me her Little Miss Sunshine. She didn't want to let me go but she was really ill.'

The older woman looked at the treasures, nodding her understanding, her eyes thoughtful. Then she smiled at Janna.

'When you no longer need them, then you will be free,' she said. She said it encouragingly, almost exultantly, as if it were towards this exciting and rewarding goal that Janna must naturally be working, and the words took her by surprise. She was used to people being gently consoling, telling her they could believe how important these symbols were, but Sister Emily seems to be travelling a different road. Janna thinks about it quite often. Sister Emily's responses are often unexpected.

Clem is drawing her attention to a small piece of paper lying on the bread board. A note. Janna smiles involuntarily: the Sisters use notes to communicate so many things. Small hoarded pieces of paper torn from letters, backs of used envelopes, receipts; nothing is wasted: folded messages pushed under doors, left on beds and in stalls in the chapel. They read the note together, Clem peering over her shoulder.

'Penny is unwell,' is written in Mother Magda's scrawling handwriting. 'I have started the soup. Can you possibly manage, Janna dear?'

It must be hard, reflects Janna, to be so dependent where once they were so self-sufficient.

'Vegetable soup?' murmurs Clem in her ear, nodding towards his offerings: carrots, onions, potatoes, some leeks.

She nods, smiling her thanks, and he goes back to his work whilst she carries the vegetables to the sink and begins to wash them under the tap.

A week later, out in the Western Approaches, heavy grey clouds begin to pile and mass. Towering and spilling, they race in towards the coast, driven by wild winds that batter the peninsula. Ice melts, turns to water and begins to drip. The sun grows pale, a lemon disc behind the advancing veils of thin cloud, and is quenched at last. Deeply rutted tracks, which have been hard as concrete, quickly soften into thick, heavy mud; rivers and streams fill, roaring and rushing in their rocky beds.

The windows of the Lodge rattle in the gale and the trees creak and toss, bending bare wintry branches above its chimneypots. Jakey, eating his tea at the kitchen table, looks out into the dark, drenched garden. The curtains are not yet drawn and the bright scene within is reflected in the streaming black glass. He feels safe and warm, here in the kitchen, with Daddy sitting at the other end of the table with his laptop open.

Jakey carefully balances some more baked beans onto his fork and puts them into his mouth: Stripey Bunny sits beside his plate in attendance. Sometimes Daddy raises his head and says, 'OK, Jakes?' and he nods; he likes these times when

Daddy is with him but busy with something else, and Stripey Bunny is just within reach. He feels safe but free, too; free to think about things and to listen to the sounds. There are lots of sounds: long fingers of rain drumming on the window; the low hum of the laptop; the droning of the fridge; the gurgle in the radiator.

In a minute Daddy will stand up and take the plates to put in the dishwasher. He'll open the big heavy door and the dishwasher's bad breath will belch out into the kitchen. Dossie says that Daddy ought to rinse the plates first, especially if they're fishy, and Daddy says that if he were to do that, then having a dishwasher would be utterly pointless. Then Dossie rolls her eyes and gives a big sigh and Daddy simply carries on with what he is doing with a particular look on his face. Jakey picks up a piece of toast and wipes it round his plate in the beans' thick tomatoey juice, thinking about that look. It's the look Daddy has sometimes when he, Jakey, is being naughty and Daddy says, 'Don't push it, Jakes,' and then it's best to stop being silly. Jakey eats his toast happily, wondering what he might be allowed as a pudding if he eats everything on his plate.

Clem closes his laptop.

'All finished?' he asks. 'Well done.' He takes Jakey's plate and puts it in the dishwasher. 'Now what about a Petits Filous? Would you like one of those? Or some grapes?'

'Petits Filous *and* glapes,' Jakey says firmly. 'And a biscuit.'

'We'll see about the biscuit,' says Clem. Dossie, and the nanny who looked after Jakey in London, have trained him well in the matter of his small son's diet though sometimes he allows the rules to be bent a little. He reaches across the sink to draw the curtains. Janna has bought pots of cyclamen, which stand on the white-painted sill. Unobtrusively she introduces pretty, quirky, gentler things into their masculine world and Clem is grateful for it. He and she have quickly fallen into an easy, undemanding relationship; her naturalness infiltrates and warms his austerity. She makes him laugh, and Jakey loves her.

'We're the two Jays,' she says to him. 'We're a team: high five, partner,' and Jakey stands on tiptoe, reaching up high to strike his small palm against Janna's.

Even as Clem thinks about her, there is a quick little tattoo on the door and she comes in, scattering raindrops, her face screwed up against the wind and rain.

'Yeuch!' she exclaims. 'What a night! Nice and warm in here, though. Shopping!' She heaves two large bags onto the table and Jakey pushes himself up higher in his chair to peer inside.

'Thanks, Janna.' Clem takes a Petits Filous from the fridge and gives it to Jakey. 'Honestly, I'm really grateful.'

'I was going anyway. I just hope I remembered everything.'

Clem begins to take out packages: fish fingers, sausages, yoghurt.

'Good job your mum's a cook and stocks the freezer up for you with proper food,' observes Janna.

'I can cook,' says Clem, unperturbed. 'Jakey and I happen to like sausages and fish fingers.'

'I love sausages,' announces Jakey. 'Sausages are my favoulites.' He bounces in his chair, beaming at Janna, flourishing his spoon, showing off.

Clem puts a small bowl of grapes in front of him. 'Eat properly or you'll get a tummy-ache. Tea, Janna?'

'Love some.' She sits down beside Jakey. Clem switches on the kettle and begins to pile the tins and packets into the cupboard. Janna looks at Jakey; gives him a tiny wink.

'So what have you had for supper, my lover?' she asks. 'Don't tell me. Beans on toast with sausage.'

'He likes beans on toast with sausage.' Clem shuts the cupboard door. 'It's very nourishing. He gets a good lunch at school and Dossie's here often enough to make sure he has a balanced diet.'

Jakey knows that Janna is teasing Daddy and that Daddy doesn't mind; he's smiling as he puts a tea bag into the mug. Jakey eats some grapes. He wrinkles his nose and wriggles. He is deciding whether to demand Janna's attention: ask her to play with him or read him a story. But a bit of him knows that when other people come and talk to Daddy, then this is a good time to ask if he can watch the television. Usually, he'll be allowed some extra watching time while the grownups talk. He finishes his grapes and picks up Stripey Bunny.

'Can I get down, Daddy? Can I watch television?'

'"*May* I get down?" OK, yes. Just for a bit. Hang on a sec; let me wipe your face.' The kettle boils. Clem makes Janna's tea, puts the mug beside her and goes with Jakey into the sitting-room. She can hear them arguing about who should press which buttons, and what and for how long Jakey will be allowed to watch. Presently Clem comes back and sits down at the table. He pushes the laptop to one side and picks up his half-drunk, nearly cold coffee.

'It's keeping one step ahead that's so exhausting,' he says. 'I had no idea that the mind of a four-year-old was so devious. He can argue for hours and the scary thing is that his arguments are very logical. I get to a point where I want to shout, "Just because I say so!" but I'd feel he'd outwitted me. It's like living with Henry Kissinger. Dossie's better at reasoning with him than I am.'

'She had all those years of practice with you. Anyway, she's a woman. She's more devious than Jakey can ever hope to be.'

They sit together companionably, talking over the day. Janna has a second mug of tea.

'There was a chap round earlier,' she says. 'Funny bloke. Just wandering about. Did you see him?'

Clem shakes his head. 'I've been decorating the little West Room. No chance of getting anything done outside this last couple of days, and there are no guests in at the moment. When you say "funny" what do you mean exactly?'

Janna frowns. 'He seemed a bit shifty when he saw me. I was going down to the village the back way and he must have come up that way because he was round the back of the Coach House, just peering around. So I asked if he wanted anything and he said no, and that he hadn't realized that the lane led straight into the grounds. "So this is the convent?" he said, all bright and interested. And I said that it was. And he said something about it being rather smart having your own private road into the village. Then he said, "But then, of course, they owned the village too in the old days, didn't they?" After he'd said that he looked awkward and I didn't know what he was talking about so I just left him to it. I didn't want to walk down with him, see. I felt uncomfortable with him. Afterwards I wondered if it had been right to leave him but he didn't look rough or anything like that. He was quite smartly dressed. What did he mean about owning the village?'

'Before it became a convent, Chi-Meur and Peneglos, the church and all the farmland around here belonged to the Bosanko family. When Elizabeth Bosanko willed Chi-Meur to a small community of nuns, the village and most of the farms were sold off. Obviously this fellow has been studying the local history but even so I'd have thought he would've seen the notice at the back entrance that says "Private".'

'That's what I thought, but I didn't quite like to be rude. You know – he might've been a visitor that the sisters were expecting. After all, we do get some odd people turning up.'

Clem shrugs. 'Well, he clearly knew the history of the place. Perhaps he was just a nosy visitor staying down in the village.'

Janna finishes her tea, glances at the clock. 'I'd better dash. Vespers will be over in ten minutes and Sister Ruth'll be needing help with supper. I've left your change on the table. Thanks for the tea.'

'Thanks for the shopping,' Clem answers.

He pockets the pile of loose change, scrumples the till receipt and puts it in the bin. Part of him wishes that he'd asked Janna to come back later and have supper with him, but he knows that once he's finished Jakey's bath-and-bed routine he'll be quite happy simply to slump in front of the television with a sandwich. It's hard physical labour, keeping the grounds and the house maintained, as well as making certain that Jakey's needs are answered. Dossie and Janna are a terrific help, but the aching emptiness remains: he misses Madeleine, and he misses the peace he once knew: the deep-down peace of recognizing his vocation and committing to it.

He stands beside the table, hands in his pockets, head bent. The shock of Madeleine's death threw him off track. He utterly lost his bearings. A few things were clear: she'd want his first care to be for their child and he couldn't possibly have managed that at Oxford. Her parents lived and worked in France and so were unable to be of any great help to him, and although Dossie offered, even begged him to allow her to move to Oxford to make a home for them, he couldn't have been responsible for the fact that the move would be such an upheaval for her. After all, she went through all this before: the loss of her beloved young husband in a car smash and the prospect of bringing up their child without him. Back then, she was in the last year at catering college and she used all her new-learned skills to start up a business immediately so as to earn a living whilst looking after her baby. How could he possibly have asked her to give up her clients, her contacts and all her other commitments? Impossible. Clem shakes his head. The other alternative, of Dossie taking Jakey back to Cornwall while he continued his studies in Oxford for the next three years, was also out of the question. Jakey had lost his mother; he needed his father. Back in London Clem could earn good money to pay for a full-time nanny and he'd have the network of his friends to support him. The prospect was a bleak one in contrast to all that he'd looked forward to but, anyway, how could he trust that his sense of vocation was a true one? Why should this tragedy have happened within the first few months of his training if he had indeed been called to the priesthood? For a long while he railed against God: angry, despairing, in pain.

In retrospect, he sees that all his decisions were driven by guilt and grief – and yet, three years later, he found his way to Chi-Meur. And now there is a sense of healing and a measure of peace to be found working in this magical place so close to the sea, or slipping into the chapel for the Eucharist at midday, or to listen to Terce or Vespers or Compline. And talking to Father Pascal in his tiny cottage down in the village.

Slowly, reluctantly at first, Clem talked to the old priest

about his confusion and his anger: how he believed that finding the job at Chi-Meur and the kindness of the Sisters, as well as Janna's friendship, were healing him. But to what purpose? What of the future?

'Signposts?' Father Pascal suggested on one of these occasions. 'The generosity of strangers, the love of friends. Don't you think that these might be signposts on the road to God? The promises of God, who is on the road ahead of you. He will meet you there.'

'Where?' Clem asked wearily. 'I thought I'd already got started on that road and then it blew up in front of me.'

'But you found Chi-Meur. You are on the road again, perhaps even a little further on. But the initiative is with God.'

Now, Clem takes his hands out of his pockets and glances at his watch: nearly bath-time; and Jakey has been watching television for much longer than his usual allowance and won't want to stop. Clem breathes deeply and braces himself for battle.

In his bedroom in a farmhouse further along the coast, Janna's stranger crouches over his mobile.

'It's all in pretty good shape,' he's saying. 'Lovely house. Young feller in the lodge house looking after the grounds. He's got his work cut out. And a girl in a caravan. Chief cook and bottle-washer, I should say. Bit of a looker . . . No, no. Don't get out of your pram. There's nothing like that going on. But I'm picking up information in the village. Four nuns. Sisters, they call them. Elderly. One of them a bit ga-ga. Can't see how they can hope to carry on myself, though they're very popular with the locals . . . No, I'm not staying in the village. I'm at a bed and breakfast up the coast a bit. It's a farm. Nice and quiet. Pretty basic, touch of the Worzels, but it suits. I've told them I'm writing a book about the north Cornish coast and its history. They're thrilled about it . . .

'So we put in our offer and wait? And, if they accept, then it can be proved that the house is no longer going to be run as a convent and you can appear waving your bit of paper and say that, under the terms of the old will drawn up hundreds of years ago, you, as the last descendant of these particular Bosankos, are entitled to inherit . . . Yeah, I know that's a bit garbled but that's where we are. Right? . . . No, nobody can hear me. Don't be so twitchy. I told you, the dit is I'm researching a book. It might be televised. I've dropped a few well-known names and the locals can't wait to be in it. Everyone wants to have a say. I've got Phil Brewster lined up, ready to go when you say the word . . . OK, I'll have another look around. Same time tomorrow? OK.'

He switches off and stares around the tidy, comfortable room and then out into the wet, dark night. There is no sound, no streetlights. He shivers, makes a face, wonders how people can stand living in all this quiet. He drags the curtains across and stands for a minute, thinking. Seems a crazy scheme, this one, but Tommy's got them through a few deals, right on the edge, bit dodgy, but lucrative. He's a bright boy, is Tommy; old school tie with a lot of upmarket contacts, but he keeps you on your toes, chin on shoulder. He was excited at that last meeting, really buzzing with it.

'Now listen,' he said. 'A friend of mine down in Truro, a lawyer, has turned up something rather interesting on the old family estate. I want you to go down and have a look around. It's been a convent for nearly two hundred years but if we can get proof that it is no longer viable then, according to this document, it reverts to any surviving descendant of this particular branch of the family. We've checked it out and that's me. Seems there's only a couple of the nuns left and they might be thinking of joining other larger communities. Now we don't want to alert them, d'you see? We're working on the fact that nobody's been looking at the small print. Just get down there and check it out.'

'I don't get it. If it's yours by right anyway—'

'Look, old chap,' Tommy let him see he was being patient with him, 'you discover that the old dears are thinking of moving on. You give the OK to Phil Brewster. He does his hotelier act and puts in a very nice offer, which they'll imagine tucking into the coffers of their religious society to secure their futures. "Oh, yes," they say. "Thank you very much." He gets some positive proof of their intention to accept the offer, passes it on to you and then – wham, I turn up with a copy of the old will. Deal falls through, the place is mine. I know someone who would pay very, very serious money for a place just there.'

'But what do they get out of it?'

Tommy laughed then; really laughed. 'You just don't get it, do you?' he said. 'They don't get anything. I get the ancestral home back and sell it to the highest bidder and they have their treasure in Heaven where moth and rust don't get a look in. Now, you get the proof and I move in. Usual pay and expenses.'

Caine raises his head. The wind is rising and the rain slaps against the window. He's been offered supper and he's accepted gratefully. He'll spin a story about the book, talk about a television series and mention a few names: Simon Schama, Dan Cruikshank. What's the name of that bird who does *Wainwright Walks*?

He hears a noise. The farmer's wife is on the stairs and he goes out quickly to meet her, shutting his door behind him so that the sharp black eyes can see nothing in his room.

Nosy cow, he thinks, but he smiles at her, turning on the charm.

'Is that supper ready, Mrs Trembath? Goodness, I'm hungry after being out all day.'

''Tis all waiting, Mr Caine,' she says, and he follows her down the stairs.

Dossie puts down the telephone and makes a few notes on her laptop. She's working in the kitchen this morning, it being a much warmer room than her tiny, north-facing study upstairs; but at least, these days, she has a study all to herself. Things have changed since she came back home all those years ago as a very young widow, to have her baby and try to make a career. It was her parents who, in between running their own rather off-the-wall bed-and-breakfast business, looked after Clem whilst she organized lunches and dinners, cooking up special-occasion feasts in other people's kitchens.

'Of *course* we can manage, darling,' her mother said. 'And we know lots of people who will simply leap at the chance of having you catering for their parties.'

She was right. Her parents had a great many connections all over the peninsula who were very willing to help out the widowed daughter of their friends. Gradually she built up a very solid client base and, with Pa and Mo as resident baby-sitters, she travelled the length of the county from Launceston to Penzance, and from Falmouth to St Ives. Sometimes, now, Dossie wonders whether it was fair to allow herself and Clem to be a burden to two middle-aged people who were trying to earn their own living. Yet, somehow she didn't think about it quite like that. Pa and Mo were so all-embracing; so capable and so laid-back. Their guests, mainly friends of friends and parents of friends, who all seemed to become dear old chums after the first visit, would arrive with dogs – or even with a grandchild – in tow and the elegant grey stone house – The Court – was always full of people. She'd come in from doing a lunch in Truro to find two old fellows having a quick pre-dinner drink with Pa in the drawing-room before they set out for the pub, their wives chatting to Mo in the kitchen whilst they ordered breakfast. A dog or two might be stretched out in the hall or in the little television parlour where someone would be catching the news.

Clem loved it. They brought him little presents when he was small, agonized with him through GCSEs and A levels, cheered him on to university, whilst Pa and Mo gave him exactly the kind of loving neglect that worked so well for his independent character. And now she is able to make some kind of return for all that love and generosity. The roles are reversed, and she can support them as once they supported her and Clem. It took Pa's stroke, collapsing all among the debris of the full English breakfast, to persuade them both that perhaps they should give up their 'B and B-ers', as they called them, but she still has a few of the specials to stay. Pa and Mo still behave like the good old-fashioned hosts that they were, and everyone has a lot of fun.

Dossie makes some notes on the big calendar on the fridge so that Pa and Mo will know where she'll be and what is happening workwise. When it comes to a social life not much is going on at the moment. There have been relationships, of course, one or two more serious than others, but some of the men involved were rather cautious about taking on a young boy, as well as the possibility of Pa and Mo at a future date.

'You're crazy,' her younger brother, Adam, would say. 'Get a life. You're still young and they'll manage perfectly well on their own. They're indestructible. I don't know how you bear it. I couldn't get out quick enough.'

Just recently, since he's moved in with Natasha and her two teenage daughters, Adam's words have changed. 'They should have downsized ages ago when the market was still strong. You shouldn't have encouraged them to stay on. What are you going to do when The Court has to be sold and they go into a home?'

Dossie always feels a little chill of fear at these words. She can't quite imagine herself anywhere else but in this pretty, gracious Georgian house, with its elegant sash windows and perfect proportions, which has been in the family for generations. Even worse, she can't picture Pa and Mo in sheltered accommodation amongst strangers. After all, they are still quite fit even if Pa tires very quickly since his stroke and Mo struggles with arthritis and is rather deaf. And, oh, how they'd miss the dogs if they were to be separated from them.

'Are they crazy?' Adam demands, when Pa and Mo adopt a Norfolk terrier as a companion to their old black Labrador. 'How old is it? They're far too tottery to be having puppies around.'

'Wolfie is six,' Dossie answers. 'He's not a puppy. His owner died very suddenly. He was one of Pa's old mining friends. Wolfie's an utter sweetie and no trouble at all, and John the Baptist loves having him around. He lets Wolfie share his basket and he's got a new lease of life.'

'And if they have to go into a home? Pa and Mo, I mean. Are you going to be able to afford a place where you can have two dogs and keep working? Especially an elderly lab with a predilection to submerge himself in any kind of water at every opportunity. Try to think ahead, for God's sake!'

'Is it permissible to dislike one's brother?' she asked Clem furiously, later that afternoon at the Lodge. 'He is just so bloody selfish! He's so afraid that I might think that I can stay on at The Court when Pa and Mo have to leave it.'

She didn't want to use the word 'die' but she saw that Clem understood her. His half-smiling, half-frowning expression was a familiar one: compassion mixed with an instinctive need to keep a balance, which was oddly comforting. If he'd raged with her she'd have contrarily felt obliged to be reasonable. Clem's calm but sympathetic response always gives her full scope for her fury when she feels like it: he is on her side.

'It's not just Adam, is it?' he answered. 'Natasha eggs him on. She sees The Court as a nice little pension plan for them both. After all, Adam didn't have much left after his divorce, did he? It was Maryanne who brought the money with her, and the flat, wasn't it?' He hesitated a little. 'If it came to it, you and the dogs could always come here. You could cook for the Sisters. Think what a treat it would be for them. We'd manage somehow.'

She wanted to cry, then. Instead she put her arms round him and hugged him tightly; and he patted her shoulder blades comfortingly, which is as close as Clem comes to the act of hugging.

Now, Dossie thinks about the recent phone call. A party of people coming down for a week to one of the self-catering cottages at Penharrow, near Port Isaac, have asked her if she would prepare some meals for them to put into the freezer. This is her new project. Friends and clients with holiday cottages are recommending her in their brochures and on their websites to self-catering holiday-makers who can't afford to eat out all the time but don't want the bother of cooking for themselves; it's picking up very well. She sits down, studies the notes she's made about possible menus and begins to make lists. The telephone rings.

'Hello?' A man's voice. 'I wonder if I could speak to Dossie Pardoe?'

'That's me.'

'Oh, great. You don't know me at all but I've been given your number by the people who own the holiday complex at Port Isaac . . .'

Dossie begins to laugh. 'What a coincidence. I've just been asked to supply a week's meals for one of their visitors.'

'Oh, well now.' His voice is eager. 'That's exactly it. It's an absolutely brilliant scheme and I wonder if I can join it. I've got quite a few holiday properties, though they're more to the south – on the Roseland Peninsula around St Mawes – but I'd like to offer a freezer full of food as an added attraction, if you're prepared to travel that far.'

'I can't see why not.' She likes the sound of him. 'I'm used to driving all over Cornwall.'

'Fantastic. So I can sign up for it, then? How do I start?'

'It's not particularly complicated but I usually like to check up a bit first.'

'Well, of course. How does it work? You could look at my website . . .' A hesitation. 'Or perhaps we could meet . . . ?'

'We could.' She tries not to sound too keen. 'Look, give me your website details and then I'll phone you.'

'Fine. And you can check with Chris at Penharrow. I don't want to mislead you; he isn't a friend. I just know him slightly through the trade, but it's a reference of a kind.'

'I'll do that.'

'Right. Got a pencil . . . ?'

As Dossie puts the phone down, Mo comes into the kitchen, a big black Labrador shouldering ahead of her. For once, John the Baptist is quite dry, and Dossie bends to caress him, murmuring approvingly to him.

'The rain has stopped at last,' Mo says. 'We've had a lovely walk across the fields. Pa's getting his boots off and giving Wolfie a good towelling. He found a badger's sett. You're looking very cheerful, darling.'

'I feel very cheerful. Looks like I've got a new contact, as well as an order for a week's meals at Penharrow.'

'That's wonderful.' Mo's ashy fair hair fluffs up like feathers around her head as she pulls off her fleecy hat. Even in her middle seventies she is a force; there is strength and determination in her small figure. She warms her hands on the closed lid of the range and smiles over her shoulder at her daughter. 'I think Jonno deserves a biscuit, don't you? He's been such a good fellow. He's resisted all sorts of watery temptation, haven't you, Jonno? I think he's feeling his age, and getting soaked to the skin doesn't appeal quite so much any more.'

The old dog presses close against her, settling down beside the range, and Dossie brings him a few biscuits, which he crunches gratefully. Wolfie bustles in importantly and hurries to see what goodies are being given out. Pa follows him. Hardly taller than Mo, upright, though slightly less brisk since the stroke, he sits down at the table looking rather strained and tired. Nobody except his doctor ever

41

refers to the stroke. 'Don't mention the s-word' has become the family's motto.

'Dossie's got a new client,' Mo tells him. 'And another Fill the Freezer order. Isn't it great?'

They've dubbed Dossie's newest idea 'Fill the Freezer' although, as well as the week's food, she nearly always makes up a separate meal to be eaten on arrival: soup, a casserole, fresh rolls and fruit and cheese, depending on the client's requirements.

Pa beams his delight. 'It's a brilliant scheme. Just the thing now, with the credit crunch. Visitors can't afford to eat out all the time, and takeaways can be almost as expensive. You're onto a good thing, Doss.'

As usual, she is warmed by their response and encouragement. She knows that some of her friends find it extraordinary that she continues to stay with Pa and Mo, especially now Clem has grown up, but then she's never known an ordinary family life. Pa's expertise as a mining engineer meant that in the early years of her childhood they moved from one country to another, and then, after Pa's widowed mother died and they settled at The Court, there was the continual stream of 'B and B-ers'. She managed to have quite enough privacy, quite enough scope, to live her life very happily; and it was much better for Clem to be amongst this kind of extended family than in some tiny flat alone with her whilst she strived to earn their living. In an odd kind of way, Clem is repeating the pattern with Jakey, surrounded by the Sisters and Janna and Father Pascal.

Dossie knows that Pa and Mo miss the B and B-ers and she sometimes wonders how they'd manage if she ever decided to move away. Up until now, she's never met anyone about whom she's felt strongly enough to make the question a serious one. For some reason she finds herself thinking about the man who telephoned earlier. She picks up her laptop.

'I've got some work to do,' she tells them. 'I need to check out this new client. See you later.' And she goes out into the hall and up the stairs into her little study, and closes the door behind her.

CANDLEMAS

It is Sister Emily's first thought on waking: Candlemas! Goody! I wonder what we shall have for lunch! Her Novice Mistress taught her to say the Gloria first thing each morning but Feast Days are special occasions and the words 'Glory be to the Father . . .' are more heartfelt when prayed *after* the goose, say, at Michaelmas, or a delicious rack of lamb on Easter Sunday. And anyway, these days, the waking thought is more likely to be, Oh dear. Here we go again . . .

Pulling off her nightgown, running water into her wash basin, she wonders whether Janna is capable of producing a special feast. After all, she hasn't come here to be a cook. Since Penny has not yet recovered from her bad attack of shingles, poor Janna has been cast unceremoniously into the role and is struggling to cope with the extra work. Well, they are all struggling.

She glances at her little bedside clock. Eighteen minutes past six. At this moment, Ruth – the youngest of them all at a mere sixty-eight – will be washing Nichola and then helping her into the chair, where she spends most of her time, whilst

44

Magda makes tea and coffee and Nichola's breakfast in the little kitchen at the end of their corridor. These days they all have a hot, comforting drink before Morning Prayer, which has been moved from seven o'clock to half-past to give them all a chance to get ready and finish their early morning tasks. Sister Emily sighs: she could remember the days when she'd risen at dawn for Lauds, and even earlier for the long night vigil of Matins: but now they are too frail to test their small stores of strength.

As sacristan it is her job to set up in the chapel and prepare for the Daily Office, and as she begins to dress she considers the familiar routine of the day ahead: Morning Prayer and then Terce after breakfast at a quarter to nine – and then Father Pascal will arrive to celebrate the Eucharist at midday. Although he is their chaplain, there is a small group of priests who share the rota with him. He'll stay to lunch today, and so will Clem and Janna. She pauses, sitting on the edge of the bed to put on her shoes, to give thanks for Janna and Clem: how could they manage without them? Chi-Meur has many good friends, as well as alongsiders and oblates, who help in many different ways, but Clem and Janna are part of the bones and blood of the place now. They work and strive alongside the community; and each is on a particular path of discovery.

Pilgrims, she thinks. We are all pilgrims.

She senses Janna's inward struggle between her need to belong and her fear of commitment; soon, very soon, she might be required to face up to this conflict more directly. Clem's is a different pilgrimage. Clem responded to a call, to a vocation to serve God as a priest, but has swerved aside from it. He's questioning that decision now, whilst yet being unable to contain the resentful thought that his bereavement forced it upon him. Meanwhile Chi-Meur embraces them both, and little Jakey, and holds them in safety and in love. But for how much longer? In Chapter, Mother Magda talked about the difficulty in continuing to sustain their life at Chi-Meur: the financial commitments, their vulnerability. She'd been approached, she told them, by someone who was very ready to buy the estate. He'd asked if there were a sister community somewhere that they might join with; he was prepared to be generous.

'Sell? Sell Chi-Meur? Are we allowed to sell it?' The Sisters looked at one another anxiously.

'I think we are allowed to sell. We are all trustees, after all, and are allowed to dispose of its assets. Chi-Meur belongs to the Society of Christ the King, and I imagine the money simply goes into the Society's bank or towards our support in another House,' answered Magda.

'But to leave Chi-Meur.' Emily was shocked. 'I have been here for more than sixty years. You, too, Magda.'

'I know that none of us wants to do this,' Magda said almost desperately, 'but things are very hard now. Even with Clem and Janna we are barely managing, and if any of us should become seriously ill . . .'

None of them looked at Nichola who sat smiling, gazing at nothing. Ruth made sure that she was fresh and clean but it was hard graft keeping an eye on her, and what if one of the others should fail? Fear crept like a chill miasma between them, and she, Emily, had drawn a little closer to the fire.

'Where might we go?' she asked bravely.

'There are the Sisters at Hereford,' Ruth suggested. 'They are a small community, but larger than us and with a very good support network.'

'That's true,' agreed Magda, 'though I know that they have

their share of sick and elderly Sisters. They might not feel that they can manage Nichola.'

Ruth instinctively stretched a protective hand to the immobile form beside her; her care for Nichola had brought a special love with it, such as a mother might care for a weak child. Tenderness came late to her, and she remains sharp-tongued and touchy, but Nichola's helplessness, her gentleness and gratitude, have touched Ruth's jealous, fearful heart.

'Shall we pray about it? But please say nothing about it to anyone else.' Magda closed the meeting and they got up, feeling frightened; Ruth helping Nichola, shuffling slowly with the aid of her stick, and the rest of them going back to their tasks.

Now, Sister Emily stands up and pulls back the curtains: it is still dark outside. The long wing in which the community lives faces south, across the kitchen garden, and she can just glimpse a light in the caravan in the corner of the orchard. Janna is already awake. Perhaps she is planning lunch. Sister Emily arranges her veil, smiling to herself, and goes out into the corridor.

Janna is propped in her bunk, wrapped in a shawl, drinking tea and brooding on the day ahead.

'We'll do this together,' Dossie promised, when Janna admitted her fears. 'And while we're at it, we'll fill the freezer. You need some meals to fall back on if you're going to have to cope with cooking as well as everything else. You can tell me your budget and we'll go shopping together. It's not a problem. I expect they don't eat much, do they?'

'Sister Nichola and Sister Emily love their food, though Sister Nichola doesn't really have a clue what's she's eating,'

Janna told her. 'Mother Magda is diabetic and Sister Ruth is picky because she's got a bit of a tricky tummy.'

'So it's hardly a big lunch, then. Just the four of them.'

'Father Pascal will stay on after the Eucharist. And they invite me and Clem to share with them on Feast Days in the refectory.'

'OK. Who does the actual shopping?'

'Mother Magda used to but she's been quite happy to let me do it for them lately. I pick up their pensions and prescriptions and stuff like that. She makes a list for me. Of course, Clem grows most of the veggie stuff and we've got eggs from the banties.'

'OK,' Dossie said again.

Janna watched Dossie, head bent, calculating what menus she might prepare, and she thought how much Dossie was like Clem and Jakey: the silvery-gilt blond hair; the narrow dark blue eyes that sometimes looked brown; smiling eyes but a serious mouth. Mo looked like that too.

'Why do you have such funny names?' she asked Dossie. 'Mo, Pa, Dossie. Even Jakey and Clem use them. Not Mum, or Grandma or Grandpa. I've got a friend who always calls his dad by his name because he hated the way his mother used to refer to him as "your father" but they were divorced. Yours are all such funny names.'

'I was called Theodosia after my granny, who died very young,' she answered. 'But I've always been Dossie, even at school and college, and then Clem just picked up on it when he was little because it was what the B and B-ers called me. Mo is Mollie and Pa is Patrick. Pa trained at the Camborne School of Mines; he's a mining engineer. They married very young, when Pa was still at Camborne, and they had a little flat in the town. It was a kind of tease by Pa's friends, as if he and Mo were more responsible and grown up because they were married. His friends would go round for supper and treat it like home and they just became Pa and Mo. It was just a joke to begin with but it caught on. We rather like it, though some people think it's a bit odd. Perhaps we're just natural nickname people.'

Janna finishes her tea and climbs out of her bunk, shivering. It is very cold, the wind in the north-east. Even with her little gas fire full on, the caravan suddenly feels rather flimsy. She dresses quickly: thermal underwear, a long thick cord skirt the colour of crushed raspberries, several jerseys. Dossie has made a delicious concoction with duck breasts and a rich sauce for the Candlemas feast; all quite ready for Janna to pop into the oven. She'll roast potatoes and parsnips, and Clem has promised broccoli; Pa donated a case of wine at Christmas. Should it be white or red with duck? She'll have to ask Clem.

Clem has already lit the fire in the library where the Sisters hold their Chapter meetings and have tea in the cold winter afternoons with any visitors who venture out to see them. The big room on the north-west corner of the house takes a long time to warm up and at present, with no guests to consider, Mother Magda refuses to waste the precious central heating oil. She is a worrier; her brow permanently creased, her slight frame tensed against criticism, braced for disaster. Jakey can make her laugh, though, so that the worry lines seem to disappear into a wide delighted smile and her still beautiful dark blue eyes shine with joy.

Clem's allayed any anxiety about logs. His predecessor left a barn full of them, chopped up and piled there over a period of years, unused because the Sisters consider log fires a luxury. He didn't ask permission the first time but simply lit it one Friday morning before their Chapter meeting. He saw their instinctive delighted reaction – their looks of pleasure and surprise – though Sister Ruth bridled at his temerity and Mother Magda quickly began to look anxious.

'Just while the weather is so cold,' he explained quickly. 'And the room needs airing, especially with all these books. It would be a pity if they got damp and musty and we've got so many logs.'

'Oh, yes.' Mother Magda was relieved at this rational explanation. 'And Sister Nichola might like to sit here for a while after lunch,' she suggested placatingly to Sister Ruth, sensing her indignation. 'Just for a change.'

Clem could see that Sister Ruth was torn between wanting to voice her disapproval and acknowledging the pleasure the fire would give. Sister Nichola was already advancing towards it with little murmurs of delight.

'Just while the weather is so cold,' Sister Ruth agreed reluctantly.

Now, he builds the fire up and puts the guard in front of it. At the window he pauses. The fields slope steeply to the cliff's edge and he can see away across the sea to Cataclews Point and Trevose Head. The silvery water, fretted by the sharp north-easterly wind, churns restlessly, chopping and changing – now azure, now grey – beneath the cold clear blue sky and snow-charged clouds. In the clump of ash trees just below the house Clem can see a quarrelsome party of rooks balancing amongst the bone-white branches; their bulky, twiggy nests being bargained over and refurbished. Suddenly one of the rooks takes to the air, swerving and diving, showing off to his mate and rivals alike as he exults in the strengthening breeze. Others follow him, challenging him, their harsh voices tossed and lost in the wind.

Clem likes the rooks: he senses their joy in their connivance with the elements, their bravado, and their instinctive one-upmanship battling with their need for community.

'Like us, don't you think?' Sister Emily is at his shoulder: 'Argumentative, difficult, but needing one another.'

Clem, who has just been thinking that very thing, bites his lip. 'I expect,' he says awkwardly, his eyes still on the rooks, 'that living in a community probably makes you better people in the end.'

'But we're not here to be "better" people. Or even "nice" people. We're here to try to be God's people, wouldn't you say?' She touches him lightly on the shoulder with the sheaf of papers she is holding and glides quietly away, pausing at the door. 'How inviting that fire looks. Thank you, Clem.'

He follows her out and goes back to the Lodge to waken Jakey and give him breakfast.

The snow begins to fall later that afternoon. The duck is finished, and the remains of the feast are cleared away. The Sisters are having tea in the library and Jakey has just arrived home on the school bus.

'Bad weather setting in,' shouts the driver to Clem. 'Snow's forecast. Doubt I shall see you tomorrow.'

He pulls away up the narrow lane and Clem catches Jakey's hand and hurries him into the Lodge out of the cold wind.

'Snow!' Jakey struggles out of his coat; his eyes shine in expectation. 'We can make a snowman.'

'If there's enough of it.' Clem hangs the coat up on the row of pegs in the hall. 'We don't usually get very heavy falls down here in Cornwall so don't count on it. It'll probably be gone by morning. So have you had a good day? What did you do?'

'Nothing.' Jakey goes into the sitting-room and through to the kitchen.

'That must have been interesting then,' Clem says, sighing inwardly, recognizing the mood, knowing he should have been more upbeat about the snow. 'So you all sat in rows not doing anything all day. I thought it was Show and Tell today. You took your pirate book that Mo and Pa gave you. That must have gone down well.'

Jakey leans against the table, puts his thumb into his mouth and nods slowly; he is finding his first term at school very tiring. He looks exhausted, with dark circles under his eyes, and Clem is filled with the familiar ache of love and compassion for him.

'What would you like to eat?' he asks. 'Just a little something to keep you going until supper time. There's still some of that Smartie cake. Would you like some milk? Or juice?'

Jakey takes his thumb out. 'I'd like a cup of tea.'

'Tea?' Clem's mind jumps to and fro. Is it OK to give tea to a four-year-old? What about tannin? And caffeine? He hesitates and Jakey looks mutinously at him.

'The Sisters give me tea,' he says. 'And sometimes coffee, if they're having it. I like it.'

Clem begins to laugh. 'The Sisters are naughty,' he says – and Jakey laughs too, at the idea of the Sisters being naughty.

'Sister Emily is naughty,' he says thoughtfully, 'but Sister Luth isn't.'

'OK,' says Clem. He'll make it nearly all milk with just a dash of tea: surely it can't hurt him. 'Tea it is. Now let's hear about Show and Tell.'

Jakey scrambles up onto his chair and reaches for Stripey Bunny, eager now to tell. Outside the snow whirls. It flutters past the window and begins to settle on the fields.

'I'm outa here,' says Mr Caine, mobile clamped between ear and shoulder as he packs. 'The weather forecast is snow and more snow. I'm getting back to civilization while I can . . . No, Tommy, I'm not ratting out. I'm just biding my time. I'll come back when it's clear . . . Phil is holed up in Plymouth, waiting by the phone . . . No, they haven't come to a decision. I've told you. These old dames don't work like we do. Their time frame is different. We want everything yesterday and their eyes are fixed on eternity . . . Yeah, I know it sounds fanciful but I tell you, a few weeks on this godforsaken peninsula, you get fanciful. It's enough to drive you crazy. A load of Worzel Gummidges drivelling in your ear all day about farming and fishing . . . Yeah, yeah, I know the stakes are high but Phil's on the case. If they accept the offer he'll be right on to it . . . No, he can't just frighten them into signing a bit of paper saying the convent's done for and they'll accept his offer. He's got to keep cool. They're thinking about it . . . OK, but nobody else is gonna come charging in, are they? Why would they? Nobody's gonna be thinking about it, are they? . . . Yeah, I know we don't want to give them time to start looking at that old covenant saying it's got to be a convent or else, but we don't want to make them nervous either. You said not to make them suspicious. I hope that mole solicitor of yours is right about it, that's all. He's probably as crooked as you are. Can it be proved, that's the real question? . . . OK. OK. I'm off. I'll speak when I get to Exeter. If I get that far. I've told the Worzels I'll be back in a few days. They're holding my room. Like they need to!

Nobody else is crazy enough to want to be here in bloody February . . . Yeah. Be in touch.'

He crams the last of his clothes into his bag, glances round. He can hardly wait to be out and driving up the A39 towards civilization. It gives him the creeps, all this emptiness, the steep cliffs, the awful relentless sound of the sea. He's always hated the sea: feared it, even. It's so uncontrollable, indifferent, vast. He likes to be in control and here, on this wild north coast, he feels helpless. These poor sods spend their whole lives in one long battle against the elements.

He checks the tiny bathroom, comes out and here's Mrs Trembath in his room. He swallows down a surge of irritation – everything's packed, there's nothing to see – but he allows a suggestion of surprise to creep into his smile.

'Didn't hear you knock,' he says pointedly.

She ignores it. Well, what do you expect from yokel locals? He picks up his bag.

'I'm off then. See you as soon as this passes.'

'There was a phone call,' she says – and he tenses. What phone call? Who'd try to get him here? Tommy and Phil use only mobiles.

'Who was it?'

She shakes her head. 'Woudden leave no name. I told 'en you was packing. Said 'e'd try another time.'

He wants to shout at her; give her a good shaking. Why didn't the silly cow simply come and get him? He hides all these reactions, and smiles.

'Can't have been important then.'

She watches him, saying nothing.

'Well, then.' His joviality sounds forced. 'Thanks for holding the room for a few days,' he gives a little chuckle, 'though

I'm not sure it's really necessary. Can't see people beating down the door exactly, can you? Not in this weather.'

She continues to stare at him. 'We gets all sorts,' she answers. 'All weathers.'

His smile fades. 'Yes, I'm sure you do.'

He can't wait to be away; it's really getting to him now. He's wasting time and it's still snowing. He edges past her and hurries down the stairs.

''Bye, then,' he shouts. 'I'll be in touch. Thanks,' and he goes out into the whirling snow, slings his bag into the car and then he's away down the track as fast as he dares.

Janna wakes in the West Room above the porch. The little room, recently painted by Clem, is full of a chill, unearthly light. Janna lies quite still, accustoming herself to strange new sensations: the softness of the bed, the low beams and the silence.

Mother Magda and Clem persuaded her from the small, cosy security of the caravan early in the evening after Clem heard the weather forecast. Like an unwilling animal coerced from its lair, she reluctantly stumbled through the already thick snow, clutching her tote bag full of the things she'd need for this sojourn in the house. Her protests fell on deaf ears. She had no fears of the snow or of being cold, she said, but it was the sight of Mother Magda, frail and anxious at the caravan door, that made her give in. Clem wore his usual, secretly amused, half frowning expression, which always gave the impression that he utterly understood everything but was saying nothing.

Janna slides out of bed, pulls her shawl closer around her and goes to the window. She gives an involuntary gasp of shock. Snow is falling so thickly that she can barely see further than the window. The lawn below the house is indistinguishable from its surrounding wall and the fields beyond. The cliffs and the sea are swallowed by this dazzling, dancing cloud of snow.

Recovered from the shock, her first thought is: Thank goodness Dossie filled the freezer with all that food. Her second thought sends her reaching for the light switch. With relief she sees that the electricity hasn't been cut off.

She dresses quickly, staring at herself in the small square mirror above the little basin in the corner. Her untameable lion-mane hair clings to the brush and stands out about her small thin face. Someone once told her that her eyes were the colour of clear honey and she peers into them, trying to see herself as others see her, wondering if she is attractive.

Passing out of the room, she pauses in the corridor to listen to the silence. No visitors to fill up the empty bedrooms, nobody hurrying to the bathroom, or down the stairs to breakfast in the guests' dining-room next to the refectory. Standing outside her bedroom door she is aware of the spaces of the house all about her, used now only by retreatants, and of the nuns tucked away in their private wing. She goes down into the hall and through to the back of the house to the kitchen. How warm it is in this long, low room; how welcoming.

Slipping between the kitchen and the refectory, she makes porridge, and puts bread in the toaster; assembles cereals, butter and marmalade and lays places for the Sisters. There are voices in the back hall and Clem and Jakey come into the kitchen. Jakey's cheeks are poppy red, his eyes bright. He is trussed up like a parcel in his warm, padded jacket and he wears a woolly knitted hat with earflaps.

'We shall be able to make a snowman,' he says to Janna.

'And the bus won't get up the hill so I can't go to school. We've come to have bleakfast with you.'

'That's great,' Janna says, and Clem says, 'Remember that you must talk quietly, Jakey.'

Jakey makes a face; he presses his lips together and puts his hand in front of his mouth. His eyes beam at Janna above his fingers and she grins back at him.

'I'm going to check the banties,' Clem says. 'They'll have to stay in their house today. I'll clear a bit of a path and then I'll light the fire in the library. You stay here, Jakey, and no nonsense. Janna's got to get everybody's breakfasts. Make sure you help her.'

Jakey wrestles the small rucksack off his back, opens it up and sits Stripey Bunny on a chair at the table. He hangs the rucksack on the back of the chair and looks round as he struggles out of his coat. He loves the kitchen, with its huge ancient inglenook fireplace, which now houses the big four-oven Aga, and the low-beamed ceiling. Along the deep-set stone windowsills Janna has put pots of hyacinths and cyclamen and there are some special pretty pebbles and stones too, which he and she collect down on the shore. He goes to stand beside her at the Aga as she stirs the porridge.

'Daddy got his shovel out,' he says to Janna, 'and dug a path for us. Can I have sausages?'

'Not for breakfast.' She looks down at him, touches his blond hair very lightly. 'Maybe for lunch. How about porridge? And then toast and honey?'

He considers and then nods: if he'd been at home he might have argued about which cereal he wants but he remembers that he is supposed to be helping Janna. And, anyway, he likes porridge and toast and honey.

'Get some spoons out of the drawer there,' she tells him.

'Three spoons, one each for you, me and Daddy, and put them on the table. Can you do that? Listen. I think the Sisters are coming out from Morning Prayer.'

He puts the spoons on the table just as Mother Magda comes into the kitchen. She raises her eyebrows at him in a kind of smiling surprise and makes him a little 'Good morning' bow. He is quite used now to this form of silent greeting and he bows back to her, very seriously, and then picks up Stripey Bunny and makes him bow too with his long floppy ears falling forward. Mother Magda's smile becomes a wide beam and he laughs with her, sharing the joke.

She and Janna speak softly together and Janna takes the bowls out of the lower oven and begins to fill them with porridge. He watches Janna put four bowls on the tray with a jug of milk and carry them into the refectory; Mother Magda follows her. The toast pops up; four pieces in the long silver toaster and, as he stands beside his chair, the room grows brighter and is suddenly filled with light; long fingers of sunshine reach through the windows and touch the flowers and the pebbles.

Janna comes back. She fills a bowl with porridge for him, mixes it with some cold milk, sprinkles sugar over it and puts it at his place. He scrambles onto his chair, still watching her as she puts the toast into the rack. She is like nobody else he's ever known, with her wild lion hair and thin brown face and bright strange clothes. Beside the elderly sober-clad nuns she is vivid and exciting. Today she's wrapped herself in the apron that has words printed on it: 'SAVE WATER. DRINK WINE.' She'd read them to him and even then he hadn't understood, but Sister Emily said, 'Now I think that is *such* a good idea.' And they laughed together, silently, bending close, with Sister Emily's wrinkled, thin hand on Janna's warm, strong arm. Sister Ruth came in and paused, looking at them both, her chin high and forbidding, and Janna moved away, still smiling secretly to herself.

Now she turns suddenly, holding the toast rack, and catches his stare.

'OK, my lover?' she asks, and there's a tenderness in her voice and in her look that makes him feel a bit odd: shaky and upset, and wanting to run over to her and bury his face in the warmth of her body and snuff up the scents of her skin. He has a little pain in his chest, as though something is missing, that he's lost something really important, and he wants to hold on to Janna. He feels as if he might cry and, as if she understands, she puts the toast on the table and comes swiftly round to him. She kneels beside his chair and puts her arms round him, and he buries his face in her warm breast and cries without knowing why, although Daddy has explained that it happens because he lost Mummy just after he was born and it's all quite natural and nothing to be worried about, and that Daddy feels the same way too, sometimes.

Gently Janna smooths his hair and wipes his cheeks with her fingers. 'Poor Stripey Bunny needs some porridge,' she whispers to him. 'Poor old Stripes. He's all thin, look.' And she squeezes his middle so that he flops about and looks funny, and Jakey manages a smile and takes up his spoon. And then Daddy comes in saying how cold it is and they'll build a snowman after breakfast, and suddenly everything is quite all right again.

Clem eats his porridge gratefully. He knows he's lucky that the Sisters are prepared to stretch a point with Jakey so that he is allowed into certain parts of the house and the grounds as long as he is quiet and good. It had to be part of the contract and Mother Magda was quick to see that there needed to be a readiness to adapt on both sides. It's odd, actually, how readily Jakey has accepted convent life. He seems to understand the reverence required and even enjoy it. Of course, he got used to going to church in London but even so it's a great deal to ask of a small boy. He remembers, when he brought Jakey to be introduced to the Sisters, how Sister Emily shook his hand and then asked to be introduced to Stripey Bunny.

'How do you do, Mr Stripey Bunny,' she said gravely, shaking his paw, and Jakey gazed at her for a moment in surprise, and then they chuckled together, sharing the joke. Mother Magda laughed too, and took Stripey Bunny's paw but Sister Ruth watched with her hands hidden in her sleeves, not reacting when Jakey looked hopefully towards her, inviting her to share in the game. Clem could tell by her expression and body language that here was a woman who feared any kind of loss of control; who instinctively disliked any relaxation of the rules. He stiffened a little, anxious for Jakey lest he was hurt by the rebuff, but Jakey was already turning back happily to Sister Emily and Mother Magda – his new friends.

Clem finishes his porridge and puts his bowl aside, still brooding on the oddness of bringing up a child in such a place as Chi-Meur. The point is that they are all bringing Jakey up: Janna, the Sisters, Father Pascal, Dossie, Mo and Pa. Clem watches Janna cutting soldiers of toast and spreading honey on them. She puts them on to Jakey's plate and he eats them, relishing them and offering bites to Stripey Bunny at intervals.

It is as if we are a family, Clem thinks. And I'm sure Jakey is happy here.

Janna smiles at him and pushes some toast towards him and he thinks: If only I could fall in love with her, how simple life would be.

The snow falls, freezes, and falls again: in Cornwall the schools are closed and roads are blocked with drifting snow.

'Unheard of down here,' Pa says crossly, staring disconsolately from the bedroom window. 'Climate change. We can look forward to this kind of thing now: floods, snow, heat waves. All this energy in the atmosphere; that's what's causing it. Tsunamis, volcanoes erupting. How am I supposed to get the dogs out in this?'

Straight-backed, one hand clenched in a fist behind his back, he raises his coffee mug and drinks. Mo watches him from the bed. His intensity, his high-octane energy, has always been slightly exhausting, even when they were both young; now it is poured out in tirades against the government, roaring at the television, raging at newspaper articles. She is terrified that these storms will cause another stroke. Their GP has been understanding about her anxiety but realistic about Pa's character.

'We know him,' he says, resigned. 'And it's no good trying to change him at this late date. He'll probably crash down with another stroke, just like he did before, and it might be worse next time, but can you honestly imagine him sitting quietly on the sofa with a tea cosy on his head? Might as well let him get on with it, Mo. I know it's hard for you . . .'

And it is hard. At first she watched anxiously as he bellowed down the telephone at an unknown voice trying to sell him double glazing – 'Can't you understand what I'm *saying*?

This is a grade-one-listed *property*. We can't *put* in double glazing. Why don't you check your facts before you waste people's time?' – or she'd keep an eye on the clock whilst he spent an hour digging a trench for the runner beans, popping down the garden at intervals to make sure that he hadn't collapsed again. Gradually she built up a defence against the fear, knowing that her anxiety added to his awareness of his vulnerability and weakness, and by degrees they'd fallen back into their old cheerful ways.

'If you could get the ride-on mower out of the barn some-how,' she says now, 'you could fix something on the back and make a path through the snow to the lane. They'll have the tractors out soon, so as to get to the stock. The dogs will enjoy it. Wolfie can ride on the mower with you.'

She can see by the alert tilt to his head that he is thinking about it. She stretches her hand to Wolfie, curled on the quilt by her knees and, at the bottom of the bed, John the Baptist beats his tail on the rug. He's always been sensitive to Pa's occasional outbursts – ears flattened, an eye rolled backwards to glance at his master whilst he laid a conciliatory head on Pa's knee – and even in his most fiery moments Pa's hand is tender on the black head, gently pulling an ear, smoothing the soft coat. John the Baptist understands all about barks being worse than their bites and he adores Pa.

Mo finishes her tea. She watches Pa's shoulders shrugging inside his disgraceful old dressing gown, his fingers clench-ing and unclenching, as he plots and plans and works things out.

'*If* I can get it out,' he says, with a kind of gloomy relish, 'I suppose it might work. The snow's drifted across the barn doors again. It'll be hell's own delight shifting it.' But when he turns to look at her, his face is bright with intent, concentrated with purpose. 'All right, Mo?' he asks – and she smiles as she nods her 'yes' to the old familiar question. He's asked it all their lives together: speeding along in his Austin Healey Sprite; racing before the wind in sailing boats; walking on the cliffs; lying on beaches in the sun. At all the crucial moments, birth and death and celebration, there has been the look and the question: 'All right, Mo?' like an arm around the shoulder, an embrace.

John the Baptist gets up and goes to him, tail wagging, and she looks at them both with love and sudden gut-wrenching panic: how would she possibly manage without them? She pushes the quilt aside and swings her legs rather painfully over the side of the bed.

'Well, dress up warmly,' she says. 'Is Dossie up yet?'

He shakes his head. 'Lucky we've got plenty of supplies in. Good old Dossie. She'd have made a first-rate purser. She can sleep in and I'll cook the breakfast.'

But Dossie is not asleep. For once the snow has not had its usual effect upon her. She is neither delighted by its magical transforming qualities nor excited in a childish way by the white stuff. She is quite simply irritated by it: she will not now be able to keep her lunch date. She's exchanged several emails with the amusing Rupert French, whose holiday properties are mainly to the south of Truro, and it seems a natural progression to meet him for lunch.

'I buy a run-down old cottage or a barn with planning permission,' he told her, 'and live in it or in a caravan while I do it up. Then I move on to the next one. My wife and I used to do it together but now . . . well, now I'm working on my own.'

His voice changed when he said that. He sounded rather bleak and she didn't like to ask him whether his wife had died or whether they were divorced.

Chris at Penharrow is pretty certain that she died. 'I heard some rumour that she was very ill and that she went upcountry for treatment. Bristol, I think it was. It was a while ago now. I really don't know him all that well, only through the trade. He's based more on the south coast. But he sounded quite cheerful when he phoned to ask about your new scheme.'

Huddled in her duvet, Dossie wonders why she feels so disappointed that they won't be able to meet up as they've planned. After all, a phone call and a few emails are nothing to go by, though she knows that he's rather dishy. There is a photograph of him on his website with some of his clients outside one of his cottages and she's studied it closely. He is laughing into the camera and he looks quite tough and rather fun. In one of the emails he wrote:

> I'm not that far away from you at the moment, working on a little cottage up near the edge of the moor. The first one I've bought outside my usual area and it's still in a bit of a state. A cross between a builders' merchant's and a squat! I haven't had the telephone connected yet and I have to go up to the village hall to send emails. We must meet up some time and talk all this through. I've got a lot of clients I know will be really keen to try it out. How about a pub lunch?

And so it was arranged and they exchanged the numbers of their mobiles in case of some emergency, though he warned her that the signal was very patchy. Dossie wonders how he is faring, up on Bodmin Moor, and reaches for her mobile phone on the bedside table: no message. She'll get up and check her emails. Sitting up, pulling the duvet higher, she texts quickly to Clem: *Snowed in. Hope u r ok? xx*

Clem and Jakey will be quite safe at Chi-Meur: they are so self-sufficient and she knows that the freezer is well stocked up. Pulling on her dressing gown, she slips next door into her study and switches on her laptop: no emails. She glances at her watch: barely eight o'clock. It is much too early; he'll hardly manage to get up to the village hall before breakfast. Meanwhile, she can smell bacon frying. Mo puts her head in at the door.

'So you *are* up. Pa thought you were still asleep. He's got a little plan to dig us out but he might need some help.'

'I know what that means.' Dossie comes out of the study and closes the door behind her. 'It means lots of hard labour on my part and a great deal of shouting on his.'

Mo chuckles. 'It's my fault, darling, I'm afraid. I suggested it. He gets so fretful if he can't be doing. You know what he's like.'

'Don't I, though.' Dossie looks resigned. 'OK. I'll get dressed but tell him to save me some bacon.'

Back in her room she checks her mobile again. There was a message from Rupert: *Cant get car out. Gutted. How about u?*

She texts back: *Same here* – and then hesitates. Is he asking if she is gutted or merely snowed in? She doesn't want to sound too keen but she feels pleased that he is gutted. However, she wipes her message and starts again. *No luck today. B in touch*, and leaves it at that. But his message has cheered her. She feels excited, on the brink of something, and is almost glad that the meeting is postponed so that the expectation can continue to grow for a little while longer. He is disappointed: gutted. She hugs the sense of excitement to her and looks out upon the pastoral scene with equanimity now.

Perhaps he'll send another text; perhaps she'll email him later on, just something casual. Dossie begins to dress, humming beneath her breath.

'What are you doing?'

Rupert slides the mobile into a small compartment in his briefcase and zips it shut.

'Just checking messages,' he calls. 'This snow is going to be causing lots of problems. I shan't be able to get out this morning. And you won't be able to get home.'

She comes carefully down the steep narrow staircase wrapped in a thick long dressing gown, huddling the collar up around her neck. Her morning face is slightly shiny and pallid, her brow creased into an expression of faint dissatisfaction: Kitty has never been a morning person.

'Lucky I kept the wood-burner going overnight,' he says. 'I should go into the sitting-room if I were you. It's cosy in there. I'll bring some coffee in.'

She gives a little unsmiling nod and he goes back into the kitchen, slightly irritated that she's taken it into her head to pay this flying visit, but far too experienced to show it. The important thing is to keep the mood light. Kitty has a sixth sense where other women are concerned and there must be no hint of his lunch date with Dossie. Yet he can't quite keep himself from smiling as he finds the percolator and makes coffee: Dossie sounds rather fun and he is looking forward to meeting her. But not today.

Kitty turns her head as he carries in the coffee. 'I still think it's crazy that you bought this place,' she says. 'Honestly, it's miles off the beaten track.'

He passes her the mug of strong, black coffee. 'You know why I bought it,' he answers, perching on the chair opposite. 'I bought it because the owner was in trouble and needed to offload it quickly. I got it very cheap and I should be able to turn it round and sell it on and make a nice little profit.'

'In this market?'

'OK,' he says easily, smiling at her, 'then I'll rent it out until the market improves.'

She sits back in the corner of the shabby armchair, drawing her long legs up beneath her, folding her thin elegant hands around the mug. He sees that she is pulling herself together, shaking off the grumpy early morning mood that reflects the uncomfortable night on the second-hand bed. He wonders why she's made the sudden dash down to see him and hopes it isn't going to become a habit. After all, he gets up to Bristol twice a week. The truth is that he's begun to enjoy his semi-bachelor existence, though he won't let her guess this.

She makes a little face at him. 'It's just so silly to be so far apart. After all, we don't need to be, do we? There's plenty of room at the flat and Mummy would love to have you there.'

She's wheedling now, regretting her grumpiness. He watches her, still smiling, thinking, as he always does, how ridiculous it sounds to hear a grown woman calling her mother 'Mummy'. One day soon Mummy will leave her darling daughter a beautiful ground-floor flat in Sneyd Park in Bristol, some very valuable 'pieces' and a comfortable bank balance. Not that it matters: he has plenty of money of his own, though most of it is tied up in property. Still, it's a comforting prospect. One can always do with extra security. The cottage has been a bit of a bolt hole from the restrictions of the flat: a good excuse to get away from the invalid atmosphere.

'It's serving a turn,' he shrugs. 'You don't really want me in the flat in Bristol all the time while you're looking after your mother and it's keeping me busy.'

She glances around the small room, at the temporary shabby furniture, and he almost laughs aloud at her expression of distaste.

'Come on, love,' he says. 'I warned you what it was like here. Anyway, you know perfectly well how uncomfortable renovating a house can be in the early stages. We've done it often enough.'

'It's different now,' she argues. 'I've got used to the comfort of the flat.'

He shrugs, bored with this increasingly familiar argument which leads nowhere. He might point out that if she were with him they would have made the cottage much more comfortable but some instinct tells him to stay cool; not to press her. Her determination to visit despite his attempts to discourage it has surprised him – and slightly unnerved him.

'I have to finish the cottage,' he points out reasonably. 'It's my job. It's what I do.'

She sits with her head bent, watching the flames through the glass door of the stove.

'Well, you don't have to do it for much longer,' she says. 'It's time we relaxed a bit and enjoyed ourselves.'

He feels a thrill of fear at the prospect of being joined at the hip to Kitty in the Bristol flat with her elderly mother, who suffers from aortic stenosis, and no work to which he can escape, no excuses of meetings. He's done very well since he came out of the army and started his restoration company. It owns a great deal of property, including five cottages down on the Roseland Peninsula. Her father respected him, no doubt about that, though he was always slightly cautious about his, Rupert's, background: good schools, good regiment, yes, but there was something indefinable that unnerved that unimaginative old stalwart of Bristol's merchant aristocracy. He'd been wary of this ex-army officer's approaches to his little princess: he'd glimpsed that odd, passionate, creative streak that made Rupert a perfectionist in his work and meant that a beautifully finished product was much more important than simple profit.

Rupert grins to himself, remembering the predictable old fellow who was so anxious for his precious daughter's financial wellbeing. His wife – whose life was full of good works, charity lunches and photographs in *Country Life* – was an easier prospect. Flustered and flattered by compliments, charmed into approval of this young man's absolute need to create something beautiful, she'd added her persuasions to Kitty's passionate appeals and they'd carried the day.

'What are you grinning at?'

He laughs aloud. 'I was just thinking about your dear old dad. He didn't get it, did he? My theory that each old house has a soul that has to be consulted before you can start work on it? It made him nervous. He never really reckoned me, did he?'

'Of course he did,' she says quickly. 'Don't be silly.' But she smiles too, remembering those earlier days and the excitement of slowly drawing out the character of each cottage, and he sees the pretty, sexy Kitty with whom he'd fallen in love back then. With her short bed-rumpled hair and the glow of the firelight on her pale skin she suddenly looks younger, more vulnerable, and he is pricked by affection and desire.

He stands up, still laughing. 'We'd better get some clothes on . . .' He hesitates, eyebrow quirked. 'Unless you have any better ideas?'

She hesitates but glances at the window. 'I thought you said the farmer might come down to see how you're coping.'

He shrugs. An untimely visit from the farmer wouldn't faze him but Kitty is already clasping her dressing gown around her and standing up.

'I think we ought to get dressed,' she says firmly. 'Thank God you've got the shower working. I'll go first.'

'OK,' he says lightly, and follows her up the stairs.

The narrow alleyways are full of streaming golden sunlight. It gleams on old wet cobbles, slants across slate-hung walls, slides into a secret corner where a tub of pansies shelters beside a cottage door. Janna passes like a shadow down the steep hill; beneath a tiny, pointed slate roof with a crooked chimney; past uneven whitewashed granite walls; below the slits of windows peering slyly down. Far beyond the uneven, lichen-painted roof-scapes, seen in glimpses between angles of jutting walls, the sea rocks placidly, its back turned to the land as if sleeping between the rise and fall of tides.

Janna slips into a passage that leads uphill again towards gorse-covered cliffs and the small Norman church perched halfway up on a grassy plateau. Father Pascal's cottage is the last in a row of tinners' cottages, next to the churchyard wall, and kept by the Church as a 'house for duty'. He moved into it from his parish rectory near Padstow when he retired, and he takes services in the little church next door – which is now served by a team ministry and anywhere else where he might be needed.

From his upstairs study window, Father Pascal watches Janna appear from between two cottages and begin to climb the stony lane. He likes it here in Peneglos amongst the odd mix of villagers: locals, who try to wrest a living from the hostile countryside or the sea; incomers, who come looking for a quieter, more peaceful existence, and the second-homers, who appear and disappear like small bands of swallows, following the sun. He walks between them all, maintaining a delicate balance, smoothing ruffled feelings, softening antagonisms, diluting prejudices. He loves them, and despairs of them, and supports them. A Breton by birth, with an English mother, he feels at home on this rocky, turbulent coast where every other village honours a saint: a misty land, where the borders between myth and legend and reality are not distinct.

When his father, fighting with the French Resistance, was killed at the end of the war, he and his mother returned to England to live with her family between Penzance and Zennor and, ever since, he's had a deep passion for his mother's birthplace. Named for the great French mathematician and moralist, he was quite at home amongst the children of fishermen and miners, who called him 'Frenchy' but accepted him as one of their own. His black eyes, and blacker hair, were not remarkable amongst these Celtic people who lived for centuries at the mercy of Spanish invaders, smugglers and seafarers.

Now, he sets aside the homily he's been preparing and descends the narrow, steep staircase. He opens the door into his little parlour and hastens to put another log into the small wood-burning stove. The cottage has no heating, apart from this stove and the old Cornish range in the living-room-kitchen across the passage, but he is content. Between them they warm the two rooms above – his study and his bedroom – though the bathroom built over the scullery extension at the back of the house is generally freezing.

Here, close to the sea, the snow has disappeared, though there are still problems upcountry. The gullys and alleyways have been awash with snow-melt, the rivers flooding on their descent from the high moors to the sea, but now the paths are clear at last and he smiles with pleasure at Janna, as though he has been separated from his friends at the convent for many months instead of little more than a week.

As usual, she has an offering for him: a small posy of snowdrops and jonquils. He takes them with delight as she slips past him into the warmth of the parlour. He shares with her a deep joy in the wild things the countryside shelters and they spend happy moments together checking a rare flower or some small bird against one of his many reference books. He takes the posy into the kitchen, finds the little vase he uses for such a tiny bunch and brings it back to the parlour.

Janna is standing before the fire, looking round her. For once the narrow shoulders are relaxed, her face peaceful. She's told him many things in this room: about Nat, her very dear friend, who is gay and who has now found a partner so that she is a little less able to be so completely at home in his cottage as she was once. She misses Nat and the special friendship they had, though she still stays in touch and visits him and his partner. She's explained about her upbringing as a traveller; how her father abandoned her mother before she, Janna, was born, and how her mother became addicted to alcohol and drugs. He knows all about the years of being fostered and how she ran away over and over again to try to find her mother, and how her family are so scattered now that since her mother's death she's been quite alone. It was then that Janna started travelling again and came by strange ways to Chi-Meur. And now she is happier than she's ever been before.

It was he who suggested that her father might be Cornish, that she belonged here just as he did, and that it explained her love for the place and this odd feeling that she'd come home. She shook her head uncertainly. Her mother was from around Plymouth way, or so she'd been told, but it might be possible . . .

Perhaps, he said on another occasion, perhaps her father hadn't known her mother was pregnant; that he might not have gone if he'd realized. Or perhaps he'd panicked at the prospect of such responsibility. After all, they'd both been so very young and he'd probably been a wild, free spirit looking for adventure abroad and he'd had a terror of commitment. This struck a chord with Janna, just as he knew it would, and removed a little of the pain. She began to imagine her father rather differently from the heartless philanderer that had always been her concept of him, and was allowing a small area of doubt to creep around and soften that idea of him. But it would be a long and painful process.

As Father Pascal places the flowers on the small bureau he makes a little prayer for wisdom, for guidance, and turns to smile at her and gestures to one of the wooden-framed armchairs.

Janna sits down quickly, still clutching her long woollen coat around her. She loves this room: the bookcase reaching from ceiling to floor filled with the warm, glowing bindings of the books; the paintings and drawings that are fixed to every spare inch of the cream-washed walls. Everywhere she looks is colour and warmth: gold-leaf on soft brown leather, and the crimsons, greens and blues in the bookcase, where the books turn their colourful backs on the room; delicate watercolours and charcoal sketches and bold splashes of thick oil paint. Yet there is peace too.

She looks at Father Pascal with a kind of relief: his presence here all among his paintings and books is necessary to her. There is security here, but the sense of security comes from the man himself; from something he carries within himself. As usual he is all in black: a black roll-neck jersey and old jeans, and thick woollen socks on his feet. He looks like an artist or a jazz musician, yet there is this natural air of authority and of confidence.

'I've moved back into the caravan this morning,' she tells him triumphantly. 'I slept in the house when the snow came because Mother Magda was worried about me being outside but we've got guests arriving later on today so I've gone out-side again.'

She smiles a little, remembering how she panicked at the thought of being all amongst the guests, bumping into them on the landing or queuing for the bathroom. She would have felt out of place. Much better to be back in her van, hidden in the trees in the orchard, slipping quietly to and fro. So as soon as she wakened she packed up her things into her tote bag, stripped the bed, took the sheets and towels down to the utility room and put them in the washing machine. Then she let herself out into the cold, bright morning. There was still snow lying under the trees in the orchard, and the van felt chill, so she lit her small gas fire and left it to warm up a bit whilst she went to prepare breakfast. She felt an odd sense of freedom, of lightness, and it was because of that she'd picked the snowdrops and the early jonquils and decided to run down to the village to see Father Pascal as soon as breakfast was cleared away.

'How will you manage without Penny?' he is asking. 'She's still very poorly.'

''Tis difficult,' Janna admitted. 'Mother Magda has had to ask guests to bring their own sheets and towels in future. She hates it, of course, but we simply couldn't cope other- wise. There's just too much to do. 'Tis a big house, isn't it? It felt quite creepy at night being there all on my own with the Sisters shut away in their bit. Luckily there're only two people coming today so that shouldn't be too hard. Dossie's been great, though. She's made up all sorts of meals that I can just get out of the freezer. But I don't know how we'd do it with a lot of guests all at once.'

'No,' he agrees thoughtfully. 'So many people have come to depend on Chi-Meur and the Sisters have so little strength now. We must pray that some solution soon presents itself.'

He looks rather sad and she feels the stirrings of anxiety. Old fears touch her heart and she frowns at him anxiously.

'But what could happen?' she asks. 'What sort of solution?'

He shakes his head as if to dismiss his thoughts and her fears. 'Can I make you coffee?' he asks. 'Or tea?'

'No, I must get back.' She rises to her feet in one quick graceful movement. 'I only dashed down because I could.' She laughs. 'I've felt a prisoner up there with all that snow.'

He laughs too. 'A prisoner?' he teases her. 'At Chi-Meur? But I know what you mean. We hate to have restrictions placed upon us, don't we? Physical or emotional. Blaise Pascal wrote: "All the misfortunes of men derive from one single thing, which is their inability to be at ease in a room."'

She stares at him. 'What does that mean?'

'It means that we might be more content if we were to seek

75

interior freedom rather than physical escape. We can reach into ourselves and find our own freedom without having to rely on other people or external stimulation. That is true freedom.' He stands up too. 'Thank you for my flowers. I shall see you on Sunday unless the Sisters need me before that. I know Father John is looking after them this week.'

Janna hurries away, thinking about what he's said; confused. Is it wrong, then, to want to run out into the wind and the sunlight and to gulp down great salty breaths of sea-laden air? Or is he hinting at her need to escape responsibility, to panic each time she attains the security she craves because it brings with it the chains of loving and caring and obligations? Perhaps this is how her father felt. Oddly, this thought makes her feel strangely happy, almost hopeful. She no longer feels that she should despise him.

Janna toils back up the hill to Chi-Meur, her heart light and full of love.

LENT

Late March sunlight fills the little room, shining on the simple furniture and white walls. Sister Emily puts down a book, picks up her pen again and begins to write. Her small table set beneath the window is covered with sheets of paper: letters from people whom she has been spiritually mentoring over long periods of time, some relationships stretching back for nearly fifty years. She spends a great deal of time – thinking, praying, reading – before she answers any letter, and her correspondence is liable to mount rather alarmingly. Nevertheless, each letter is given its allotted time: nothing is allowed to hurry the process. This afternoon she's spent some considerable time looking for references, for certain passages that have slipped into her mind, interrupting the progress of the letter. The writer is a middle-aged man who, with his wife, started to come to Chi-Meur some ten years ago. They stayed in the Coach House, self-catering; coming into the chapel for some of the services but also walking and exploring the surrounding countryside and visiting Padstow: what she and the other Sisters call Holy Holidays. Recently his wife died and he's begun to come alone, staying in the big house on silent retreats to which she has been assigned as his mentor.

He is a good man, finding silence difficult, needing to talk. Sometimes, however, the talk becomes a block to real spiritual growth and she has to stop him as gently as she can. 'Too many words,' she says firmly, smiling at him, rising to go. He writes to her often and she's brooded long on his most recent letter regarding another lately bereaved friend whom he, in his turn, is attempting to advise and counsel. Now, she believes, she can see her way forward.

I quite understand your longing to be able to enter into your friend's painful experience, especially as you have suffered the very similar pain of loss. However, it isn't necessary to keep telling him your story. In fact, to enter properly into solidarity with him, it is far better to remain silent: your gift to him is merely to listen in silence. Total concentration is what is required; not that half state of listening we so often adopt when we are mentally deciding how we might introduce our own pain or preparing our next piece of advice ready for the minute the other person stops speaking.

There is a tentative tapping at the door. Emily puts down her pen, irritated.

'Come,' she calls, and turns on her chair to face the door. It is Janna, her face alarmed, contrite and guilty all at once. Emily rises quickly and Janna, still holding the door, begins to speak quietly but with great haste.

''Tis Sister Nichola. She was with me in the kitchen, sitting at the table, so that Sister Ruth could have a bit of a quiet moment on her own, and I was making her a cup of tea and chatting away to her and when I turned round she'd gone. I ran out in the garden but there's no sign of her . . .'

Emily goes to the door; she smiles reassuringly into the anxious face. 'Shh, now, shh. Sister Nichola has an independent streak and she likes to go off on little expeditions. She never goes very far, though. Have you looked in the chapel?'

'The chapel?' Janna's face is blank. 'But it isn't time for Vespers yet.'

'No, no, but Nichola loves the chapel. It's always been her favourite place and it's where she always went whenever she had any free time. People think that nuns spend all their time in chapel or at prayer, or dwelling on their faults and failings, but the truth is that we have very little time for such luxuries. I was telling a very intense young woman who was here on retreat quite recently that if she treasured her prayer life then it was best not to even think of becoming a nun.'

All the while she is talking she is leading the way along the corridor towards the ante-room outside the chapel. Gently she looks through the half-open heavy oaken door into the chapel, beckons to Janna, and they stand together in silence. Sister Nichola is sitting in her stall. Her round pale face glows with some internal joy; her hands are open to receive the gift, one palm cupped within the other. She seems to be listening to something that ordinary ears cannot hear and Emily's heart constricts in a spasm of delight and envy: Nichola has always been one of those few blessed souls who live in the light. She steps back, drawing Janna with her.

'I will watch with her for a short while,' she murmurs, 'and then I'll bring her back to you in the kitchen. Go along. All is well.'

Janna slips away and Emily goes quietly into the chapel and sits in the nearest seat by the door. She does not look at Nichola but is simply aware of her. Her own thoughts run on rather formlessly. She has never been as fortunate as Nichola; she has only ever seen the back of God.

> God is that great absence
> In our lives, the empty silence
> Within, the place where we go
> Seeking . . .

She can hear the words in her head and she broods on the paradox: that the awareness of that emptiness is the beginning of fullness. Her thoughts become a contemplative form of prayer and presently Nichola stirs and glances around. Emily rises up and goes to her. Nichola smiles and Emily nods reassuringly and encourages her to her feet. She picks up the stick and puts it into Nichola's hand. Quietly, slowly, they make their way to the door which, unless the Office or the Eucharist is being said or Silent Prayer is in progress, is always slightly ajar. Nichola pauses, turns aside to dip her fingers into the stoup of holy water and crosses herself; then stretches her wet fingers with a smile to Emily, who receives the drops of water as if they are a special blessing. Together they pass through the back of the house and into the kitchen where Janna is ironing.

'I think Nichola would like a cup of tea,' Emily says cheerfully. 'Would you, Nichola?'

'Yes.' The word is barely a breath. 'Yes, please. Penny . . . ?' She looks at Janna, puzzled, fumbling with the chair that Emily has pulled out for her.

'This is Janna,' Emily reminds her, helping her into the

chair. 'Janna. Penny isn't very well and Janna is doing all her work as well as her own. Will you stay with her?'

Nichola nods, quite happy again, and Janna goes to re-heat the kettle, exchanging a relieved glance with Emily who hurries quietly away, back to her room and her abandoned letter.

Dossie, driving along the lane to St Endellion, is fizzing with a wild joy. She'd forgotten what it is like to feel so madly happy. And these early days of a Cornish spring are utterly in accordance with her mood: the hot sun, the clear sky, the light north-easterly breeze tingling with energy. In the twisting, sunken, secret lanes the banks and ditches are lit with glowing pools of rich gold and pale, luminous yellow: celandines, daffodils, cowslips and primroses, all flowering in abundance. On bare black thorny branches white-tipped blackthorn buds are just beginning to show and there is a flutter of wings and a flash of bright feathers in the hedgerows.

Just round corner at farm shop. Any chance of buying u a cream t?

His text has taken her by surprise: her gut churns and she laughs at her reaction, mocking herself, as if it might make it seem less important. She feels like a girl, slipping out to meet an undesirable boyfriend; fooling Pa and Mo.

'Just dashing off to meet up with a client,' she calls to Mo, who is pruning fuchsias. Well, it's true: Rupert is a client. She waves to Pa mounted on his sit-on mower with Wolfie perched beside him, making the first cut of the year, but he hasn't heard a word and simply waves back cheerfully. 'Might be an hour, maybe longer,' she shouts, and Mo nods, smiling, and goes back to her ruthless cutting back of the dead wood. Dossie unlocks her car door, relieved not to be questioned, but the dogs come running after her and she bends to ruffle Wolfie's ears and to rest her forehead, just for a moment, on John the Baptist's wise, domed head.

'I know what you're up to,' his glance seems to say, and she laughs silently, secretly to herself as she kisses him lightly between his ears.

Hopping into her little car, whizzing out into the lane, she takes a deep gasping breath. Rupert mustn't see her excitement. She speaks sternly to herself: 'You've only met him once. You hardly know him. Act your age.'

But she simply can't. That one meeting in the pub near Bodmin was amazing. He was standing at the bar and turned suddenly as she came in blinking from the bright sunny day, into the gloom of the dark interior. She recognized him at once from the photograph on his website. He isn't particularly tall – not as tall as Clem – but he has a presence. His personality dominated that crowded bar and he waved at her, laughing, and the man behind the bar laughed with him as if he too had been waiting for this moment. She hesitated and Rupert came towards her, looking at her intently with brown eyes and holding out his hand, and she said, rather foolishly: 'How did you know it was me?' and she took his hand, and shook it, and dropped it very quickly.

'Chris described you,' he answered with a little private smile, still with that intent look, and she knew that, against her will, her lips were curling upwards too, smiling with him, acknowledging that something special was happening.

And that's the trouble, she warns herself, as she hurries along the lane listening to Joni Mitchell singing 'Comes Love'; she'd been too eager. It was if she'd known him for ever, yet there is this tingling excitement still fizzing along her veins so that her heart hammers and she feels breath-less.

He asked her questions about her work, her achievements; intelligent questions from someone who knew the business, and who clearly respected what she did. They chuckled together about the whims of clients and the precariousness of being self-employed and working alone without a back-up team.

'Though I've got Pa and Mo,' she said, and then regretted it, not wanting to bring in all the freight and baggage of their private lives just yet.

He raised his eyebrows but he didn't press it, and some-how she found herself explaining about Mo and Pa and the B and B-ers, and about her early widowhood, and Clem and Jakey. It all came out rather suddenly and unexpectedly, and he listened – really listened – to her, and she waited for the slight withdrawal of interest which had happened so often before when she talked about how she still lived with her parents. But Rupert was fascinated, asking more questions – roaring with laughter when she explained about John the Baptist as a puppy diving headfirst into his drinking-bowl – not in the least fazed by her unusual family set-up.

When she tentatively invited him to talk about his own situation he merely shook his head.

'I'm on my own at the moment,' he said.

His expression was an odd one – a mix of bleakness? a determination not to become emotional? – and she decided to respect it; not to pry, or to persuade him that he would be quite safe with her if he wanted to let it all hang out. She was used to Clem's need for emotional privacy. She'd seen how he'd dealt with Madeleine's death in this same way, and she was determined not to make Rupert uncomfortable.

Carefully she led the conversation back into its former lines and soon they were laughing again. And there was a new sense of freedom between them, as if by getting all the baggage out into the open they were free to go forward.

She drives into the farm shop car park and looks for his car: an ancient dark blue Volvo.

'It's a good old work horse,' he said affectionately after that lunch, as they stood outside the pub beside the car. The back seats were folded forwards and an old sheet was laid down across them; various tools were scattered on it. 'What do you drive?'

She pointed to her tidy little Golf. 'I have to look reasonably smart,' she said, 'but I need to be able to get trays of food in the back too. My clients like to believe that I'm efficient *and* respectable.'

'What a pair we are,' he said. He dropped a hand lightly on her shoulder and she quivered suddenly at his touch, looking quickly away and pretending to shield her eyes from the sun.

'I'd better dash,' she said. 'Let me know if you want any more information for your clients.'

'Oh, I will,' he assured her, but she saw that disturbing look in his eyes, and she smiled and said, 'Thanks for the lunch,' and hurried away before he could say anything else. Just as she was almost glad that the snow prevented their first meeting, so then she wanted to postpone any further commitment; she wanted to preserve this excitement and the sense of anticipation of what was to come.

And now she is here, staring at his battered old Volvo, and taking a deep breath to steady herself. She slants the driving mirror and stares anxiously at her gilt-fair hair, at her face with the slatey-blue dark eyes. Too late to wonder whether she should have changed; her moleskin jeans and favourite old cashmere jersey will have to do. She mustn't look too keen, as if she'd made a great effort.

She gets out and slams the door, swings her bag on its long leather handle over her shoulder and goes in, through the shop with its fresh vegetables and home-made chutneys and delicious fudge, and into the restaurant. He isn't at any of the tables at the end of the shop, so she smiles at the girl by the till and passes on into the bigger, brighter area with its high wood-framed pine ceiling and big windows. He is standing beside a table, staring out of the window across the grassy spaces towards the hills behind St Austell.

He glances round as she comes in, his face brightening with pleasure. 'Wasn't I lucky to find you at home!' he says. 'There's an old cottage for sale not too far away that I thought I'd go and have a quick look at, and I suddenly realized how close I was and it was too good an opportunity to miss.'

She is glad that he hasn't decided simply to drop in. She isn't ready to explain anything to Pa and Mo just yet.

'It was good to get out into the sunshine,' she says lightly. 'I've been cooking all morning for a dinner this evening, so I can't be too long.'

'It's incredible, isn't it,' he says, gesturing to the view, 'that those amazing-looking hills are simply spoil heaps from the china clay industry? How quickly old Mother Nature would obliterate us if she could! So are you up for a cream tea?' He looks at her with an almost intimate all-appraising stare. 'You're not a calorie counter, are you?'

She laughs then: challenging his disturbing glance. 'Do I look like one?'

He shakes his head delightedly. 'Thankfully not. I can't abide skinny women. I'll go and order.'

He leaves her standing by the table and goes out to the bar. She watches him go, liking his casual, elegant grace, and thinks, Great legs! and laughs guiltily to herself.

When he returns she is sitting with her back to him, staring out of the window, and he slides into the seat opposite and watches her.

'So tell me about the cottage,' she says casually. 'Do you really need another one?'

He leans back, stretching out his legs which touch her own, though he seems unaware of the contact. She sits quite still.

'I always need another one,' he answers lazily. 'It's what I do. When I've finished this one I shall simply pack up and move on to the next one, though it might take time to find it. It works very well. It takes times to feel what the house really needs, what it's all about, and to have the vision for what I want to do with it. It tells you itself if you give it a chance. This one has been a bit more of a challenge. I'm out of my comfort zone over here on the wild north coast and on the moor. Up until now I've stayed in the same area around St Mawes and I've got a trusty network of chaps who always work with me – a plumber, an electrician and an amazing carpenter – so this was a bit of a chance. I live in whichever cottage I'm working on until it's absolutely right. It's very exciting when you get just the right materials or design of some particular feature. Then I either put it into my renting portfolio or I might sell it, or put in a tenant on a long let, depending on the market. We did a whole barn complex once.'

She longs to ask how it worked with his wife; how she'd coped with such a peripatetic life, but she doesn't have the courage.

'I thought you might come and look at it with me,' he says. 'This cottage. It's not very far away. I'm meeting the agent there at five o'clock and I'd value your expert opinion. Why not?'

She tries to think of some reason why not. The pressure of his leg unsettles her and she is glad when the girl brings the tray of tea and so that she can move, sit upright and draw in her legs, without looking as if she's been conscious of the contact.

'I could, I suppose,' she says casually, 'if we're not too long. It might be fun,' and she smiles at the girl and thanks her, and begins to pour the tea.

Mo watches her go. She clips a few more stems and puts them into the wheelbarrow and then goes to sit on the wrought-iron seat on the flagstones outside the drawing-room windows. It's hot just here, out of the light north-easterly breeze, looking south-west across the garden and the fields to the low line of hills behind St Austell. John the Baptist comes to sit at her feet; sighing heavily he curls up, eyes closed. She nudges him very gently with her foot, just so as to acknowledge his presence without disturbing him, and he sighs again with contentment.

Mo sits quietly, ankles folded beneath the seat, but she frowns a little. What is Dossie up to? For a little while now she's been in an odd mood; scatty, effervescent, distracted. She's always been a cheerful, positive, outgoing girl. Even after poor Mike died in that ghastly motor accident she tried so hard to remain strong and positive for Clem. Dossie isn't the sort to whinge and mope around, though there were times when she found it very hard indeed to cope with work and Clem and widowhood.

Of course, she met other men but – rather like darling Mike – they were always . . . well, a bit off-centre. Mo frowns again, remembering Mike: tall and loose-limbed, just like Clem. They all loved him; even Pa was touched by Mike's warm-hearted extravagance. How he loved speed! Motor-bikes, Formula One, speedboats. It wasn't surprising that he'd come unstuck so tragically, given the way he risked himself. Mo shakes her head, sadly: poor Mike – and poor Dossie and Clem.

Then, later, there was the fellow who loved sailing. Dossie fell quite heavily for him, and little Clem adored him, and then, just when they were all wondering whether something might come of it, he announced that he was off to sail around the world. He asked Dossie to go with him, and Clem, too, but after a few weeks of agonizing over it she refused.

'I can't, Mo,' she said miserably, hunched on her bed, curled in the angle of the wall. 'How can I risk it? Clem starts school next term and we have no idea how long this voyage might last or how dangerous it might be. Anything might happen. I know people do take their children on long sea trips but . . . I simply can't bear the thought of any more accidents.'

Mo, sitting on the bed, watching her, felt so helpless. Her heart filled with anguish for her child but she simply nodded, agreeing, and then she lightly touched Dossie's knee as a gesture of comfort, and went away. And how relieved she and Pa were much later when they heard that the sailor had reached Sydney Harbour, and loved Australia so much that he abandoned the rest of his voyage and never returned.

There were one or two other relationships: Clem's history master, who was divorced with a large and complicated extended family; and a fellow who owned a string of restaurants – and a string of mistresses to match. Neither of these amounted to anything, but Dossie entered into them each time with hope and a great deal of naïvety.

'Why does she always get hurt?' Pa demanded after they discovered the true nature of the restaurant owner. 'Good grief! There must be an ordinary trustworthy kind of fellow out there somewhere. Why does she have to be attracted to nutters or to men who will hurt her?'

He thumped on the kitchen table with his fist, and John the Baptist flattened his ears and rolled an anxious eye at him.

'Dossie believes in love. She's an eternal optimist,' Mo answered at last, and Pa breathed in heavily through his nose and turned his eyes heavenward as if seeking patience, muttering, 'Oh, for God's sake!' under his breath. 'And it's no good making faces at this late date,' she added crossly. '*You* didn't see anything wrong with any of them either.'

He was irritated then, pushing his chair back so that its feet screeched on the slates, getting up and going out into the boot-room. John the Baptist struggled up, looking at her as if to say, 'Here we go again!' and followed Pa out, and they disappeared over the fields together.

Now, Mo closes her eyes and lifts her face to the hot sun. She is aware of the mower's engine stopping and the sudden silence, and then of other sounds: a robin singing in the escallonia hedge and the two notes echoing from the top of the ash tree where a great tit swings in its branches amongst the fat black sticky buds, which are bursting into leaf. She thinks of Dossie just now, running out to her car; of the way, lately, she checks and rechecks her mobile for messages; of her recent bright-eyed preoccupation. A shadow blocks the sun. Mo opens her eyes: Pa is standing looking down at her.

'All right, Mo?' he asks – and she is unnerved by the familiar enquiry just at this moment, wanting to share her suspicion with him but fearful lest he too should become alert to Dossie's behaviour and question her. It is impossible to swear Pa to secrecy and silence. Sooner or later he will speak out thoughtlessly and precipitate some kind of argument or action.

'Where did Dossie say she was going?' he asks, as though reading her thoughts. 'I thought she had a dinner party at Rock.'

'She has.' Mo speaks calmly. 'There's plenty of time. A client phoned, she said. Do you want a cup of tea after all that effort?' She gets up. 'It's so warm we could have it out here.'

'And when did you say Adam was coming?'

He trails after her, and her heart sinks at his question. She stops, staring down over the newly mown grass. It is foolish to be so fearful of Natasha and her two girls, yet every instinct warns her against this woman and her two sullen, uncommunicative daughters. The fact that she, Mo, still loves and misses Adam's ex-wife doesn't help the situation, and irritates him.

'Tomorrow morning,' she answers. 'In time for lunch. Dossie's got something special planned. If it's as warm as this we'll be able to eat in the garden.' She needs to be upbeat about it, otherwise Pa's antagonism might well spiral out of control.

'Why don't those girls ever speak?' he demanded after the last visit. 'No "please" or "thank you", no attempt at joining in, refusing to have anything to do with Jakey. Just glowering about and muttering to each other or plugged into those damned iPods. And those awful earrings and nail varnish.

Good God, they're hardly teenagers and they look like a couple of hookers!'

She remained silent. Adam had cornered her privately and suggested that it was time she and Pa downsized to a smaller house, and asked what Dossie's plans were if and when they were to do so.

'We've never discussed it,' she answered frostily.

'It's as well to be prepared for every eventuality,' he said coolly.

He didn't add, 'at your ages', but she knew that it was what he meant; that he is afraid that she or Pa might die with things left unresolved. Yet her heart rebels at leaving The Court or any part of their belongings to Natasha and her children.

'What do you think of her?' Pa asked, after that first visit just over a year ago when Adam and Natasha had come down from Oxford without the girls. 'Good-looking woman but a bit brittle. Not much heart to her. I felt she was sizing us up. Not just us, but the house and so on. Know what I mean?'

'Well, that's her job, after all,' Mo answered. 'She's an estate agent, like Adam. Country properties are their forte. It must be second nature.'

Later, she learned from Dossie that Natasha has no plans for any more children; she said that two were quite enough, she was well past coping with the baby stage, and Adam wasn't bothered. Mo isn't particularly surprised. She's long been resigned to Adam's complete lack of interest in producing children and she guesses that his reluctance was a contributory factor to the downfall of his first marriage. So there will be no more grandchildren for her and Pa. She tries not to mind too much. After all, they are lucky to have

Clem and darling Jakey not far away; and Dossie, of course, is a blessing.

Mo breathes in the sweet, evocative scent of new-cut grass. How wonderful if Dossie has met a man who can love her and support her in her work and share her life. Suddenly hopeful, she turns to Pa.

'Tea,' she says. 'We'll have some tea in the garden and then take the dogs for a walk in the field. Come on, you can help me carry,' and he slips an arm about her shoulders, and gives her a hug, and they go into the house together.

Sister Emily, arriving at the caravan door, finds a tea party already in progress. Jakey and Stripey Bunny are sitting at the small folding table watching Janna putting cakes onto a plate. Jakey beams with delight at Sister Emily and slides across the bench seat to make room for her.

'Come in,' cries Janna, always happy to dispense hospitality. 'We can manage another small one. We're celebrating the last day of term, aren't we, Jakey?'

'I'm having the Peter Labbit mug,' he explains. 'Janna's mummy gave it to her when she was small. I haven't got a mummy but Daddy gives me things instead.' He looks appreciatively at the small iced cakes. 'We've given up chocolate for Lent. And Janna has given up biscuits as well. But these aren't chocolate so we can eat them. What have you given up for Lent, Sister Emily?'

'I've given up getting cross with Sister Ruth,' she answers, squeezing in beside him. 'I do so hope that it will become a habit that will continue long after Lent is over.'

Jakey looks at her thoughtfully; he is considering it. 'Haven't you given up chocolate?' he asks rather wistfully.

Sister Emily shakes her head. 'It's much more difficult

giving up getting cross. Chocolate wouldn't have mattered much to me.'

Janna splashes a tiny amount of tea into the milk in the Peter Rabbit mug and passes it to Jakey. He perches Stripey Rabbit on the table, leaning against the window, and seizes the mug.

'I like tea,' he says happily.

'Where's Daddy?' asks Sister Emily. 'Isn't he invited to this tea party?'

'He's working. I'm going to stay with Pa and Mo after bleakfast because he's too busy to look after me in the holidays now that I don't go to nursery every day.'

Sister Emily glances involuntarily at Janna, who makes a sad little face; shrugs. 'All those guests arriving tomorrow,' she says. 'It's a bit difficult keeping an eye . . . you know. But you like going to stay with Pa and Mo,' she adds cheerfully. 'Don't you, my lover?'

He nods, setting down the mug and reaching for a cake. 'I like John the Baptist and Wolfie,' he tells them. 'Pa and I take them for walks. And I've got lots of toys there. Some of them used to be Daddy's. And sometimes Dossie takes me with her in the car to see people she's going to cook for.'

'Goodness,' Sister Emily says, impressed. Janna stirs a teaspoonful of honey into a mug of steaming raspberry and echinacea tea and sets it in front of her, and she smiles her thanks. 'It sounds great fun, Jakey. I think *I* should like a holiday with Pa and Mo.'

He gives her that same considering look. 'You could come too,' he suggests.

'But we have guests coming to stay,' she tells him. 'Chi-Meur will be full and I shall need to be here to help Janna.'

'I'm scared to death,' Janna admits. 'This is the first really big retreat that I've done without Penny.'

'You'll have lots of assistance,' Sister Emily assures her. 'These are some very old friends who are coming. They know their way around and will be only too happy to help out. They're family.'

Janna sits down opposite and takes a little cake. Jakey watches her anxiously.

'Daddy will help,' he tells her. 'Shall I stay and help you?'

'No, my lover, no,' she says, laughing. 'You have your holiday with Pa and Mo. You've been working hard at school all term and you deserve a holiday with John the Baptist and Wolfie. Eat your cake and after tea you can sing your new song to Sister Emily.'

By the time Clem arrives to fetch Jakey there are no cakes left but the party is a merry one. They all go out together into the early evening sunshine.

'The clocks go forward tomorrow night,' says Sister Emily joyfully. 'Spring is here at last!'

She and Janna go back to the house: Sister Emily to the chapel for Vespers and Janna to the kitchen to get supper. Clem and Jakey set off down the drive to the Lodge to pack Jakey's case ready for his holiday.

That night he sees Auntie Gabriel again, standing in the trees across the drive, looking up at the Lodge. He knows at once why she has come. It is because he is worried about Janna. Auntie Gabriel is there to tell him that she will be looking after Janna and Daddy while he is away at The Court with Mo and Pa. Jakey waves to her, really happy to see her there, and he holds up Stripey Bunny so that she knows how much they both love her.

Suddenly he hears Daddy's footsteps on the stairs and he gives one more big wave and hops quickly into bed.

Natasha drives them west. She hates being driven, and the girls say that they feel safer with her than with Adam. They know that he resents this but it is just one of many of the power games played out between them. The girls tolerate him but only for as long as he is useful. They sit together now, nudging with sharp elbows, making faces. Today they are in alliance, knowing that their mother is in sympathy with them. She has bribed them with promises of DVDs and new clothes if they will be good during this visit to Adam's parents. Nevertheless, they will push the boundaries to see just how far their powers extend.

'I wanted to go to Millie's party,' one of them begins in a whiny little voice.

'Cornwall's boring,' says the other. 'Bo-ring. Bo-ring.'

They watch as Natasha's back straightens, head up preparing for battle, as Adam gives a quick annoyed sideways glance at her. 'They are *your* children,' the glance says. 'Deal with them.'

Natasha's heart sinks: she really doesn't want to have a row with Adam just now. Her agency has sacked two of her colleagues because of the recession and she's doing three people's work; and doing it well, she reminds herself. She's tired though, very tired, and she could do without this long drive west. It's not the girls' faults that they don't want to go. There's so much going on in their lives and, to be fair, there's no reason why they should be thrilled at the prospect of a weekend with two old people and a four-year-old they hardly know.

'It's only for a few days,' she says quickly.

They note that she doesn't contradict them and that her voice is conciliatory, not yet irritated, and they nudge one another.

'It's not boring,' Adam says firmly. 'It's just different. Lovely beaches. Swimming. Sailing. Just wait until the summer comes.'

They make faces at one another. '*You* said it was boring,' one of them reminds him. 'Last time. You said to Mum, "I know it's boring but we've got to make an effort. We'll sneak out to the pub later."'

They watch the flush of blood under Adam's fair skin with interest. He can be quite scary when he's cross but they aren't really afraid of him. They've already assessed his place in the pecking order: Natasha is top dog, they share second place together, and Adam comes a poor fourth. But he's OK; they can handle him. Better the devil you know . . . for the moment. Soon they will eject him from their nest: they've managed it before.

'What I might say to your mother in private has nothing to do with it,' he begins. His voice is already irritated and they cover their mouths with their hands and roll their eyes at one another. They love it when he rises so readily to the bait. He has such a short fuse that he's easy game.

'You *did* say it,' they mutter sullenly, pretending to be hard done by, misjudged.

'Never mind all that,' says Natasha briskly – this, decoded, means that he is not to pursue any kind of criticism, and they writhe with delight – 'let's just try to enjoy it. Jakey will be there too.'

Cue for groaning: 'He's just a baby.'

'You don't seriously expect us to play with him.'

'That's enough,' shouts Adam. 'For God's sake, just try to

be civil for once in your lives. It's a pity nobody has ever taught you how to behave.'

They are silent, biting their lips with glee, hardly able to believe such luck.

'Thanks,' says Natasha icily. She really resents this. She's done a damned good job bringing up the girls with very little support after their father walked out. But it hasn't been easy and she can do without snide criticism. Also, this bickering is beginning to get her down and she's starting to wonder if she's misjudged Adam. He seemed very strong at first, very up together, but certain other less admirable traits are emerging.

'Oh, for goodness' sake,' he's muttering, 'you know what I mean.'

She's not prepared to back down quite so quickly without a proper apology. 'No, I can't say I do.'

'Look, all I said was . . .'

The girls subside, triumphant, plugging into iPods. They have won another tiny battle in the war for control.

'We are only a week away from Easter,' Mother Magda says into the telephone. 'I am sure that you understand that we cannot possibly enter into any discussions during Holy Week . . . Yes, I know, and we have talked about it, but we have not yet come to any decisions . . . Very well, I shall tell the community at the next Chapter meeting . . . I see. I am so sorry but . . . Yes, Mr Brewster, you've made that very clear. Thank you for telephoning.'

She places the telephone back on its stand and looks across the desk at Father Pascal.

'What is he saying?'

'I think it's what might be described as an ultimatum. He

says that he cannot hold the price he has offered for Chi-Meur indefinitely and that he must have an answer soon.'

They stare anxiously at one another.

'What do Emily and Ruth say?' he asks.

She shrugs; shakes her head. 'Not very much. They don't know what to say. Neither do I. I have written to the Sisters at Hereford, who would be glad to have us, though they are equivocal about Nichola. They are a quite small and vulnerable community, with elderly and ill Sisters of their own, and are worried about how they can manage any extra responsibility. This worries Ruth who says – quite rightly – that we should all move together. However, she feels that we should go if they will agree to have Nichola. Ruth is good friends with one of the Sisters there – they did their novitiate together – and she knows the community very well. She would be happy to go to Hereford. Emily, on the other hand, feels that this is not the solution for us. She believes that there is some other destiny for Chi-Meur but cannot quite see what it is yet.'

He stirs and smiles a little. 'I have great faith in Emily's feelings.'

'So have I,' Mother Magda says at once, 'but it is difficult simply to wait. If we move – and we may have to before very long – then we shall need the money, and an Elizabethan manor house, already partly converted for our peculiar needs, might not be as desirable to prospective buyers as it seems at first sight. I understand that Mr Brewster's offer is very generous, given the slump in the market. He tells me that anyone else in our situation would apparently "bite his arm off".' She raised her eyebrows at him. 'Not a particularly attractive idea – have you seen Mr Brewster? – but the gist of it is that we should accept his offer quickly.'

'I wonder if he's thought of the planning complications. Very tricky in an old grade-two-listed house. He wants it for an hotel, doesn't he?'

She nods. 'He already owns several, apparently, so I can only assume that he's thought about it very carefully.' She pauses. 'And, of course, it's not as if there are only ourselves to consider. There're Clem and Jakey and Janna, too.'

'Do they know?'

She shakes her head. 'Nobody knows but us. Mr Brewster has promised absolute confidentiality if we agree to a private sale. Emily believes that Clem and Janna, and Jakey too, are part of Chi-Meur and that they are here for a reason. We all do. This is part of her dilemma about moving.'

'I think I agree with Emily.'

She looks at him. 'My responsibility is to the community. We need to remember that although change can be inconvenient and uncomfortable it is part of the dynamic movement that ensures that we live as pilgrims. We should have no possessions; no resting place. We all understand that. Nevertheless, this proposed move is not necessarily God's will for us.' She hesitates. 'I suppose that I am afraid of missing this opportunity and finding that we should have seized it instead of simply doing nothing.'

'Praying for God's will to be revealed is not "doing nothing",' Father Pascal says, after a moment. 'Waiting is a terribly difficult thing to do. I think we should tell Clem and Janna. If Emily believes, as we all do, that they are part of your dynamic movement, then they should share in the responsibility of the prayer and the waiting.'

'Very well,' she says. 'I shall need to speak to Emily and Ruth, and Nichola, of course. It would be a mistake to assume that Nichola doesn't understand, even if there is no obvious response from her. The prayer life of a very elderly sister can be invaluable to the rest of the community.'

There is a little silence in the small panelled room, but it is a comfortable silence that stretches between them, each drawing strength from the other.

'So most of your guests have gone,' Father Pascal says at last, 'and Janna has survived it.'

Mother Magda laughs. 'She has been so good. There is such real warmth there; so much love. She's managed wonderfully well this week without Penny. Well, we all have. But, goodness, it's a strain. Emily is exhausted. She does far too much.'

'So much is expected of you all,' he answers soberly. 'Chi-Meur has always been a powerhouse of strength and prayer. Not long ago there were fifteen of you. Now there are four. Yet there is still that expectation.'

'So many people need us. As the world grows noisier and busier and greedier, the requirement for silence and peace grows correspondingly. We are needed here.'

He nods. 'I know it. And you have many good friends to help you, but it is not enough.'

She stands up and goes to the window. After a moment he joins her. Janna appears, walking quickly and lightly. She passes across the lawn and disappears from view in the direction of the path to the beach.

'Escaping,' says Mother Magda with a smile. 'And who shall blame her? Not I.'

'Nor I,' agrees Father Pascal. 'By the way, has this man who's staying with the Trembaths been bothering you? Apparently he's writing a book on the social history of north Cornwall, but old Jack is beginning to be suspicious of him.'

'Oh? Why? I haven't seen him, as far as I know, but why should Jack suspect him?'

'You know these people. They can smell fraud or inconsistency from miles away. They're not deceived by name-dropping, and Jack says he doesn't behave like an historian. He's met a few of those in his time and he says there's something wrong. Mr Caine doesn't ring true. I thought I'd mention it in case he turns up here.'

She laughs. 'Well, we have nothing here at Chi-Muir that a con man could want. But thanks for the warning.'

There are children on the beach, and two dogs. Janna watches them chasing a ball across the sand and then turns away, beginning to climb the cliff path from the village. Thrift is flowering in the shelter of the dry-stone wall that skirts the great cliff-top fields and she bends to touch the pink fuzzy-headed blooms: on the way home she will pick some to put into her little silver vase. Crouching lower she sees that there are hundreds of snails, piled together. Yellow and grey and striped, they cling like limpets to the rough, pitted granite.

Out on the cliff she braces herself against the strong, warm westerly, laughing with the sheer joy of it, looking away to Trevose Head, washed in brilliant golden sunshine and dazzling white sea-spray. Gulls tilt and balance on the wind, falling and rising beyond the cliff-edge, screaming in disharmony. She walks quickly, the sun in her eyes, her arms wrapped about herself as if to resist the plucking and pulling of the wind. Her heart is light, her spirits high. She has survived her first real ordeal at Chi-Meur, and now she is free to come out into these great wild spaces and be answerable to nobody.

Suddenly she longs to be travelling again; sitting up high, watching the countryside drifting by and not knowing where the journey might end. And yet she loves it at Chi-Meur with her little family: Mother, Father, Sisters, and Clem and Jakey. She loves her little caravan – her own cosy private space – yet there are memories tugging and pulling at her heart; a voice whispering restlessly in her ears: something to do with freedom, new horizons, change.

She guesses now that this is how her father felt: the sizzle of excitement in the blood at the prospect of independence and adventure, battling with the twist of terror in his gut when he realized that he had all the responsibility of fatherhood pressing in on him. On days like these she is able to forgive him – or, at the very least, understand him. This is better than resentment, and it takes the sting out of the knowledge that he didn't want her.

'After all,' Father Pascal pointed out, 'he didn't know you. The idea of an unborn baby is very different from the real person. He didn't give himself time to know you. That's his loss.'

The turf is soft and springy. She leans into the wind breathlessly, hurrying forward, whilst the sea surges and booms through empty caverns far beneath her feet and tugs and roars at the steep cliff-face so that the sound of its clamour is all around her. As she approaches Roundhole Point she sinks down into the shelter of the stone archway near the gateway to Porthmissen. It is here, when Clem and Jakey are with her, that they stop for their picnic. Jakey likes to climb on the stones and squeeze through the arch but, all the while, he'll be waiting for the moment when they'll walk together to the edge of the blowhole and, Clem and Janna holding his hands, he can lean forward and peer down into that great space; looking right through the cliff to the black rocks far, far below where the tide surges hungrily through a low archway in the cliff, licking the steep sides, and the spray is flung high into the air. She loves to feel the clutch of his hand as he leans perilously forward; his whole trust in her and Clem as he stares into the echoing abyss with wide, serious eyes.

She sits in the sunshine with her back to the rock, sheltered from the wind, and brings out her own small picnic: some nuts and raisins and a piece of chocolate. Clem carries a small rucksack with juice and a sandwich for Jakey and a flask of hot coffee to share with her, and perhaps some delicious treat that Dossie has made. Their picnics are celebrations.

Looking north to Gunver Head, watching the gulls soaring and diving, she thinks: How easy it would be if only I could fall in love with Clem.

She does love him; but she loves him as she loves Nat: as a sister might love an elder brother, yet with none of the sibling rivalries and jealousies. Her love for Clem is uncomplicated and precious. Like Nat, whose preoccupation was with his sexuality, so Clem's thoughts are fixed on his vocation: whether he should train for ordination and whether his belief in his vocation is a true one. Her love for Clem, and for Jakey, carries no weighty responsibilities: they have Dossie and Mo and Pa – and Father Pascal and the Sisters.

Janna finishes her chocolate, licking her fingers, thinking about them all. The Sisters, however, are rather different from Clem and Jakey. Without Penny, their dependence now rests upon her. Tough and self-contained though they are, yet they need her. Or, she argues with herself, they need someone. It need not necessarily be her. Yet she loves them too, and it will not be easy to walk away when the time comes.

She stands up and at once the wind buffets her and beats upon her as she moves beyond the shelter of the rocks. For a moment she stares longingly westwards towards Mother Ivey's Bay and Trevose Head, but knows that she should go back. She turns, and immediately the wind ceases to be a force to fight against and instead it lifts and hurries her along so that she leans back against it and allows it to carry her across the cliffs to Chi-Meur.

Mr Caine watches her pass and then moves out of the shelter of the rock. He takes out his phone, presses keys.

'Yeah, it's me,' he says. 'Look. Problems. We should've set up a website before I started on this writing-a-book stuff. Some clever little worzel's only gone and checked me out, hasn't he? "Can't find you on Google," he says, all cocky like, with his mates all staring at me, jostling and barging all round me. Scary. I tell you, it's seriously weird here. Anyway, I bluffed him. Told him I wrote under another name. "Don't tell me," he says. "You're J. K. Rowling in disguise," and they all yell with laughter. I pretended to laugh, too, and got out quick. But it's gotta be sorted straight away . . . No, I know we thought it might be all over by now but it isn't, is it? Let me know when you've got something up and running.'

He put his phone back in his pocket, stares out to sea. He's beginning to get a bad feeling about this one.

'He's right, of course,' Pa says gloomily. 'We need to bring our wills up to date, but I'm damned if I'll have Adam telling me how to do it.'

They walk slowly in the lane, the dogs running ahead with Jakey, who zigzags back and forth on his bicycle. Mo waves encouragingly to Jakey, who stops to look back at them.

'I know it's very wrong of me,' she says, 'but I simply cannot bear the thought of all our hard work being used in the end to support Natasha and those girls. And it *was* our hard work that kept The Court going. Without your pension and all the B and B-ers we'd have had to sell up years ago. And we could have done that, and lived very comfortably on the proceeds.'

'But we chose to do it,' he points out fairly. 'Nobody asked us to.'

He pauses to stare through a gateway, and Mo waits with him. She knows that these little halts along the way are simply an excuse to catch his breath and steady himself, but he would hate to admit it. Jakey comes cycling back.

'There was a labbit,' he calls excitedly, 'and Wolfie chased it and it went down a hole.'

'Good for the rabbit,' answers Mo. 'See if you can spot another one.'

He waves and pedals away, talking furiously to himself and to the dogs.

'Labbit!' says Pa. 'Should he still be having difficulty with his speech?'

'He's not five yet,' Mo answers defensively. 'And it's only with the "R"s and only then usually when they're at the beginning of a word, though there are a few words he can't quite manage, like "surprise" where the second "r" is quite strongly stressed. We've noticed that with some words. When he says "Stripey Bunny", for instance, he hardly pronounces the "r" at all. It's quite odd. We don't want him to get a hang-up about it but we're working on it.'

'He's a good little chap,' says Pa. 'Bright as a button, and very good manners. Clem's done well with him.'

'He *has* done well,' agrees Mo warmly; always ready to

respond to any praise of her beloved grandson. 'And that's the whole thing, Pa. Why should Natasha and those girls just waltz in and claim half of everything? Clem's got very little and he works so hard, not to mention how much Dossie does for us. I know we gave her and Clem a home, and Dossie's never had to find a place to live—'

'As Adam was so ready to point out to us,' mutters Pa.

'I know.' Mo walks for a while in silence. 'How horrid it is,' she says at last. 'I love Adam – of course I do – but . . .'

'But he's our son,' says Pa. 'And we have to be fair. Look, if I die everything comes to you, and if you die everything comes to me. That bit's easy. But if we pop off together . . .'

She takes his arm and they pause again to watch a pair of bullfinches flitting in and out of the hedge: the flash of a carmine breast and the flirt of a white and black barred tail.

'Bet they've got a nest here somewhere,' he murmurs, and then Jakey is back again.

'Is it time for our picnic, Mo?' he asks hopefully.

'Picnic?' repeats Pa. 'We've only been out five minutes. What's all this about picnics?'

Jakey watches him, eyes bright: 'You've got it in your pocket,' he says, jigging up and down on his saddle. 'I saw you put it in.'

'What?' Pa pats his jacket, frowning, shaking his head. 'No, nothing there.'

Jakey drops his bicycle and flings himself at Pa, reaching inside his coat to the big poacher's pocket and wrestling out the bag.

'Good grief!' says Pa, amazed. 'Look at that. Whatever can it be?'

'It's the picnic,' shouts Jakey jubilantly. 'Is there chocolate, Mo?'

'There's a biscuit,' Mo says, opening the bag. 'It might even be a chocolate biscuit. Here come the dogs. Now they'll want something too.'

They gather in a field gateway. Jakey perches on the top rung of the gate, while the dogs munch the biscuits that Pa always keeps in his pockets for them. Mo passes Pa a Kit-Kat.

'We could divide it into parts,' murmurs Pa, unwrapping it. 'No, not the biscuit. The estate. So many parts for Dossie, so many for Clem and Jakey, and so on. Doesn't have to be straight down the middle, does it? It could be split into four parts, if it came to that.'

'Oh!' She looks at him. 'Yes, I see. That's a good idea, Pa.'

He is staring over the field and he smiles suddenly, his face filled with joy. 'Look!' he says. 'See it?'

She turns and stares in the direction of his upraised arm. Skimming the new green shoots, swooping low over the field, there is no mistaking those long tail streamers, the gleaming bluish black feathers and pale breast. It is the first swallow of the summer.

Dossie is in Wadebridge. She's already finished her shopping and now she sits in the café, her mobile on the table beside her, waiting. She is allowing Rupert to be proactive, restraining herself from being pushy or keen, but she keeps her mobile close to hand these days: he is very good at sending quick, friendly texts.

This morning he texts that he's just been to Bodmin to collect some supplies – is she anywhere around, by any chance?

In Wadebridge, she texts. *Shopping. Having coffee in Relish in Foundry Square later.*

C u in 20 mins, he answers – and so here she is: waiting. Of course, she wasn't going to have coffee at all – she was thinking about getting back home to Mo and Pa and Jakey – but the opportunity is too good to miss. She's put the shopping bags into the car and then dashed round to Relish, and into the loo to tidy up a bit. And now she sits with her latte, pretending that this was what she meant to do all the time. And it is good, actually, to sit for a minute quite alone. The weekend was stressful: Natasha was friendly enough but the girls behaved as if they were there on sufferance so that there was a certain tension, and Jakey's exuberant presence wasn't helpful. Adam implied, privately, that Mo and Pa were too old to be looking after their great-grandson and she was rather sharp with him.

'I'm here most of the time,' she said. 'Or he comes with me. And he's nearly five. He's not a baby.'

'It occurs to me,' he said, very smooth, very barbed, 'that Clem should never have taken a job that puts so much pressure on Mo and Pa. At his age he should be self-sufficient.'

She stared at him. 'Now I wonder why you've never mentioned that before,' she said lightly. 'Can someone else have put the thought into your mind, I wonder?'

He flushed angrily. He blushed easily and as a boy it had always embarrassed him and made him cross. Later he realized that it could be used to good purpose. The fair fine skin flooded with bright blood; the light, rather frosty blue eyes: the whole effect was rather frightening. Dossie was not frightened, however. She continued to watch him.

'It's not a new idea,' he said. 'You know my feelings perfectly well. Things are becoming too much for them.'

'Pa and Mo love having Jakey, just as they loved having Clem. After all, they're only going to have the one grandson and great grandson, aren't they? At least, that was the impression Natasha gave me.'

'Are you thinking,' he asked softly, 'that you can go on living in The Court even after Mo and Pa die? Do you think that you can keep it as a home for Clem and Jakey, perhaps? Is that your plan? It won't work, Dossie. Not unless you can afford to buy me out. Can you? After all, you've never had to pay your own rent or your own mortgage, have you? You've just coasted along, using Mo and Pa as a support team, and that's what you want for Clem, isn't it?'

Jakey and the dogs came in then, and Adam turned away and went out of the room.

Now, Dossie glances at her mobile and then puts it away in her bag, and when she looks up Rupert is there. Her heart does some odd little jumps but she smiles quite casually and she doesn't speak until he's ordered coffee.

'You looked very serious,' he observes. 'Problems?'

'Yes,' she answers promptly, surprising herself. 'Yes, my wretched brother is being a problem and I don't know how to deal with him.'

He looks interested, sympathetic – and suddenly she begins to talk: to explain Adam and how he was born after several miscarriages and was a miracle baby: the longed-for son. As she talks, memories come rushing in: the places they lived in – South Africa, Western Australia – the long-haul flights back to school after the holidays.

'Granny was still alive then at The Court,' she says, 'and I went to school in Truro so that she could take me out for exeats and come to athletics day and plays and things. Adam was such a funny little boy, very self-contained, very poised. I wasn't jealous that he was still at home while I went off to school because I was six when he was born so I already had my own life going, if you see what I mean. I was old enough to be Mummy's little helper and all that stuff. But I always looked forward to a time when we'd connect. I imagined it would be fun, this special sibling relationship.' She shakes her head. 'It never happened. I suppose the timing was all wrong. Six years is a big gap. When he was twelve and I was eighteen, Pa retired. They were still quite young but I think they'd got fed up with the travelling. He was with Rio Tinto Zinc. Granny died and he and Mo decided not to sell The Court but to live in it and do bed and breakfast to supplement his pension. For some reason, Adam hated it. He simply hated other people around and Pa cooking breakfast when he'd been a top mining engineer, with people like De Beers consulting him, and he and Mo travelling all over the world. It was as if it were all below Adam's dignity. It got worse as he got older and he would never bring his friends home.'

She sits in silence for a moment, feeling slightly embarrassed at her outburst, wondering how Rupert will react or if he will tactfully change the subject.

'I suppose,' he says thoughtfully, 'that it was difficult to admit to his friends that his father was no longer living, by the sounds of it, a rather dangerous and glamorous life but simply running a bed and breakfast establishment. You can imagine how he'd describe it, can't you? Diamond mining; gold mining. For boys of that age status is everything, isn't it? Rather sad for Pa and Mo, though.'

'Well, it was,' Dossie agrees, grateful for his understanding. 'We all felt it, of course. It was as if he held us all at arm's length, judging us, and he was ashamed of us . . .' She says suddenly, and rather defiantly: 'He's a prig.'

Rupert begins to laugh. 'Fair enough. But what is he doing

just at this minute that is making him so particularly tiresome?'

She makes a face. 'He thinks that Pa and Mo should move out. Downsize while they're still young enough to cope with it.'

'And then what? How does this affect him?'

She shrugs, hesitates. She feels she is being disloyal, telling him all these family things, and she wonders if, by becoming more intimate about her life, he might feel that she is trying to involve him more deeply.

'Adam would feel safer if The Court was sold before Mo and Pa die. He's terrified of me still being there and having some kind of right to stay there. You know, squatter's rights or something. He'd rather they bought a much smaller place and tucked the money away somewhere.'

'And where would you go?'

This is the question she dreads. She fears that he might think she is trying to see how the land lies with him or whether they have a future together.

'Oh, I could always go to Clem while I got something sorted,' she says casually. 'That's not a problem. No, the problem is that Pa and Mo don't *want* to leave The Court. Pa grew up there; they both love it and it's been in the family for generations. We used to come back to The Court for holidays when we were posted abroad, and Clem grew up there too, when my husband was killed. I told you about that. It's a real family home. I want them to stay there but Adam suspects my motives and he unsettles Pa and Mo and makes them feel frightened. He's been down this weekend questioning them about their wills and making them miserable.'

'That's horrid. But surely he's crazy to suggest selling

anyway in this market. Didn't you tell me that he and his partner are estate agents? They must know that.'

'Well, he's cross they didn't do it a couple of years back when Pa had the stroke. The truth is that they're both so wound up about it now that it's become a matter of principle. Anyway, it doesn't matter. Sorry.' She smiles at him. 'It's just nice to talk to someone who isn't involved. I seem to spend my time with you telling you my life history.'

'But it's a very interesting history,' he says. 'And I spend my time with you showing you my houses. At least I'm hoping you'll come and see the cottage I'm working on sometime. I've put an offer in on the other one I showed you, by the way, so I'll have to get a move on in case it's accepted. Let me buy you another coffee and then we'll make a plan.'

Driving home, Dossie is in a complete turmoil of emotions. Partly she is cross with herself for making him a present of her past just as she did at the farm shop. Yet he is so amazingly kind, and – much more important – he is so *interested*. It is years since anyone responded with such immediacy and warmth to her feelings and thoughts. And this time, when they part, he drops his arm very lightly round her shoulders and touches his warm lips to her cheek. It is all so quick, over in a second, but her cheek seems to burn and now, once or twice, she touches it with her fingers, laughing at herself for being such an idiot.

She can't wait to see him again although she quite deliberately delayed the next meeting: she's got a lot of work over Easter; she's got Jakey to keep an eye on during the holidays; Mo and Pa . . . But they made a date and she is just so happy; she puts on her Joni Mitchell CD *Both Sides Now* and begins to sing along to 'You're My Thrill'.

Oh, God, she thinks. I'm falling in love with him.

*   *   *

Rupert gets into his car and checks his mobile: he's missed a call but there's a voicemail.

'How are you?' says Kitty's voice. 'It was a good weekend, wasn't it? I'll try again later.'

He phones back at once, waits for her to pick up. 'Hi,' he says warmly. 'Yes, it was a very good weekend. Are you OK?'

'Mmm. Just had coffee with Sally. She agrees with me that it's time we took a break from the development business. She says it's time we had some fun.'

Sally should mind her own business, but he doesn't say so. He knows the rules about criticizing his wife's closest friend and he knows too how much Sally and the tiresome Bill would love to make up a permanent four for golf and bridge and visits to the theatre. He shudders at the prospect.

'I'm sure,' he says cheerfully. 'Did you book the theatre tickets?'

'Yes.' She's distracted from the scent, as he hoped she would be. 'Yes, she and Bill are free that evening and we'll have supper together afterwards. I've organized the carer for Mummy.'

'Great. Look, I must get on . . .'

'Where are you?'

'Bodmin. Just picking up some stuff. Those lovely Italian tiles I ordered have just come in.'

A sigh. 'OK.'

He knows she wants to chat but he doesn't feel guilty. He's making real efforts just now to stay in touch, to dash up to Bristol midweek and at weekends, to keep her happy. Funny how he feels more energized when he's got a flirtation on the go. It was very early on, once the bars of marriage had closed down around him, that he realized that there were

113

still plenty of women out there who were quite happy to go along with a little bit of fun with no strings attached. They didn't want to break up his marriage or have his babies, they just wanted some excitement – and he was ready to provide it.

He could tell straight away who were the ones who understood the rules, and only once has he misjudged the situation. He had to do some very fast talking on that occasion. As he puts away the mobile in the glove compartment he makes a little face, remembering. The girl turned up at the cottage he and Kitty were renovating and made a scene. He wormed his way out of it somehow but it put Kitty on her guard and since then he's been careful, very careful. He loves Kitty and he doesn't want to lose her. She is his wife and everything else is nothing but a bit of fun. It has nothing to do with his marriage. The simple fact is that he likes women; he enjoys their company and likes to go to bed with them. Some men need to buy a new flashy car every year or wear designer clothes or a Rolex watch that's cost thousands. Rupert doesn't care about any of those things. He simply likes the thrill of the chase; the sheer fun of move and countermove, and the final capitulation – as long as both parties understand the rules.

As for Dossie . . . he smiles at the thought of her. She's a sweetie but not his usual kind of woman. The important thing is not to rush her; play it carefully. Usually he doesn't bother with women like Dossie. He leaves them well alone and goes for the easier option. The trouble is he can't quite get her out of his mind: she's under his skin. He starts up the engine, pulls out of the car park, humming the Cole Porter number, feeling happy.

PENTECOST

'What's happening?' Janna asks Clem. 'Why have we both been invited to the Chapter meeting this morning? Are we going to get the sack?'

'It doesn't seem likely that we'd get the sack when there's so much to be done and nobody else to do it.'

They stand together, near the caravan door; both of them puzzled and anxious. The orchard is full of bluebells, the ancient trees standing ankle-deep in a lagoon of shining blue. Somewhere above their heads swifts race, screaming.

'What would you do?' she asks. 'If we had to go, I mean.'

Clem takes a deep breath; he stares upwards between the leaves, wondering how to answer.

'It sounds crazy but it's not something I've ever thought about. Not in that way. I've wondered whether I should start my training again and hope to be put forward for ordination but I've been so busy thinking about that – apart from the work here – that it's never occurred to me that I might simply have to pack up and leave. I believed . . . that I was led here.' He hesitates but he knows that Janna will understand; she won't mock or deride his feeling. 'It seemed so right; everything fell so perfectly into place. It seems . . . well, impossible that we, Jakey and I, should be suddenly set adrift. Again.'

His jaw clenches and she sees the muscle moving in his cheek. He looks angry and confused, and she feels even more frightened.

'You could go to Dossie, couldn't you?' She speaks timidly. 'Just for a bit. And, anyway, it might be nothing. Just a kind of check-up on things. Like how we're coping and how we see things going forward.'

'It didn't sound like that, though, did it? I felt that Mother Magda waited until she'd got us both together at a busy moment so that there wasn't an opportunity for us to question her. She looked a bit fraught.'

Janna nods. 'And 'tis short notice, too.'

Clem looks down at her; suddenly his narrow blue-brown eyes crease in amusement and he seems to throw off his fear. 'She didn't want us to be doing this, that's why. Huddling together trying to guess what it's all about.'

Janna feels better at once. 'It'll be all right. 'Course it will. Father Pascal hasn't said anything, has he?'

Clem shakes his head. 'I'm not sure that means much, though.' He looks at his watch. 'Shall we go, then? It's nearly time.' He laughed. 'It's like having to go and see the Head, isn't it?'

She nods, biting her lips, taking courage from his cheerfulness. 'Come on, then. Let's hope 'tis only detention.'

In the library, chairs have been set in a semi-circle around a little table. Mother Magda puts some papers on the table and glances doubtfully at Father Pascal.

'It's quite right that they should be included,' he says, interpreting her look. 'It is the right decision. Sister Ruth isn't seeing it quite clearly. It's only fair that Clem and Janna know the score. You depend upon them – and they might have something valuable to add to the discussion. Maybe not immediately, of course, but Sister Emily has the root of it in her. We are all joined on this journey and each of us has a contribution to make towards it.'

She nods, reassured. 'It's just that Ruth says that Janna hasn't been here long enough to be consulted about such an important matter.' She hesitates, seeking for some tactful phrase. 'She has never been quite *comfortable* with Janna.'

Father Pascal snorts with amusement. 'Nor with Jakey.'

'No,' Magda agrees, smiling. 'She's not easy with children and yet she is so wonderful with Nichola. Caring for Nichola has brought out all her best instincts. It was the right decision yet we feared that she'd never manage. Ruth's always been so spiky; so sharp and so fearful of being undervalued. Do you remember how anxious we were?'

'God works with our brokenness, whether it's Nichola's physical and mental deterioration or Ruth's insecurities—' he begins – and stops as the door opens and Nichola and Ruth come in together.

It is clear from Ruth's face that she thoroughly disapproves of what is about to happen; but Nichola beams vaguely upon them all and is helped to her chair where she sits, looking about her. Sister Emily comes quickly in: she wears an eager, expectant look, as if great decisions might be made or wonderful truths uncovered. Father Pascal instinctively smiles, despite Magda's anxiety and Ruth's disapproval. Sister Emily's positive, almost childlike, approach always fills him with delight.

'Sister Emily is a "yes" person,' he said once to Clem. 'Everything is a possibility until proved otherwise.'

Even as he remembers saying it, there is a tap at the door, and Clem and Janna come in together. He sees at once their fear, their uncertainty, and his spirits sink again. As Magda hurries forward to welcome them and asks them to sit down he makes a little prayer for guidance. As yet he can see no way forward. Even if Mr Brewster's offer were not accepted it will not be long before the frailty of the community makes it necessary for a decision to be taken for its future. Surely it is better to jump than to be pushed – or is it? He tries to imagine Chi-Meur as a hotel: it would be themed, of course. The Tudor Experience, perhaps, or the Elizabethan Manor House Weekend. He tries to visualize the house with a bar and a gym and wonders what Mr Brewster would do with the small, perfect chapel. House yoga sessions?

He realizes that a little silence has fallen on the now assembled group. Sister Nichola is watching him. Half smiling, half frowning, she seems to be trying to read his thoughts. Her round pale face, freckled by the brown coins of old age, is surprisingly unlined; all cares and fears have been smoothed away as she's slowly been drawn into her parallel universe where she dwells in peaceful quietude. He nods at her, smiling, as if to say: 'All is well.'

'Silence,' she says sweetly, surprisingly, into the silence. Her voice is quite clear and unusually strong. 'The silence before and after music is as important as the music.'

The silence now takes on a new quality of surprise, almost trepidation, at what Sister Nichola might say next: she speaks rarely these days and her words are strange yet significant.

And she is so right, thinks Clem. Those amazing silences at the end of some great symphony, when the audience has been

Janna slips along to the kitchen to start preparing lunch and Clem follows her.

'So then. Now we know.' He closes the door and leans against the table.

''Tis awful. Oh, poor Mother Magda. She looks quite ill with the prospect of it all.' Janna goes to the sink and begins to scrub the tiny new potatoes Clem brought in earlier from the garden. Fresh-picked mint lies beside the saucepan.

'But I suppose it's not such a shock, in a way. They must have realized that they couldn't go on indefinitely like this. At the same time, it hadn't occurred to me that they might sell Chi-Meur.'

'Well, what did you think then?'

'I just assumed that they might bring in Sisters from another community. It happens all the time these days. I never thought that *they* might be the ones to go. Stupid of me.'

They speak very quietly as usual, but this morning both of them feel rather like conspirators.

'I'm the stupid one. I never thought about it at all. I just thought this was all quite normal, but they'd probably eventually have to bring in a few more helpers. After all, when we've got guests and the house is full it all feels just great. I know we're stretched but I never thought of them having to sell it and go. 'Tis horrible. They've been here for years and years. This is their *home*. And to turn it into a hotel . . .'

Clem can see that she is near tears but doesn't know how to comfort her.

'I thought it was brilliant when Sister Emily said that if there were one single nun remaining at Chi-Meur then there was a community here, didn't you?'

Janna dashes a hand across her eyes and nods, smiling a little at the remembrance of the valiant comment.

transported to another level of consciousness. How I hate it when people start shouting and clapping almost before the last note has been played, destroying the atmosphere that has been created. And the intensity of concentration at the beginning when the baton is raised and everyone is drawn into a breathless silence of expectation.

'And the silence before and after prayer,' says Father Pascal, taking his place at the table. 'Shall we wait in silence now before we pray for the wisdom to see God's plan for us here at Chi-Meur, and for the courage to follow it?'

In the churchyard, Mo is putting flowers on her parents-in-law's grave. Neither of them would have thanked her for hot-house blooms and, instead, she's picked a few of the pretty snowflakes that are still blossoming in the churchyard, and some red campion that grows wild on the big, old graves of other, long-gone, members of the family who have lived at The Court and worshipped in this beautiful little collegiate church.

'So what would you do?' she asks silently of their shades, as she takes out the withered stems of her last offering and puts the bright fresh flowers into the little holes in the metal holder. 'It was your house. You loved it and cherished it, as we do, and worked in the garden where there are the graves of all the dogs. Oh, the dogs! I remember them all so well. And how The Court was such a refuge to come back to after those foreign countries.'

She sits back on her heels, looking up into the dark glossy black-green leaves of the great yew tree, reaching out to touch the rough, grainy branches.

'You loved Adam so much when he was a baby. How proud you were of him. But what would you think now?

What would you want us to do? He doesn't want The Court. He doesn't value it. He hated it when we had the B and B-ers and he refused to bring his friends home in the holidays. He went away to them instead and we hardly ever saw him. I spoiled him, of course. After all those miscarriages, suddenly to have a son; we were overjoyed. And he was such a funny little boy, so cool and quiet. Always watching but never really joining in. So detached. Poor Dossie. She tried so hard to integrate him with whatever she was doing and with her friends but he was what the French call *insortable*.

'I was so happy when he married Maryanne. She was such a bubbly, warm, extrovert sort of girl. This will do it, I thought. She will make him really human, at last. But it didn't work. At the beginning she simply swept him along in the current of her energy but in the end his chilliness simply froze her out. It withered her until she had to leave so as to save herself. I could see that. She didn't really want to; she loved him but she simply couldn't connect. None of us could. Oh, I miss Maryanne. We stay in touch but it makes him angry. It was almost a relief when she took the job in Brussels. And now there's Natasha. She's another cold fish so they suit each other, and I'm sure that they are happy in their own way. I'm not judging that. I'm just wondering what to do with The Court. They don't want it. Those girls of hers hate it down here. They want shops, entertainment, noise. Adam and Natasha want to be certain that Dossie isn't left with any rights to stay in the house when we die. They fear that Clem and Jakey would move in too, and then there would be no money for them. I know it's wrong of us to feel this way if Adam loves her, but Pa said: "What if we leave it to Adam and then he dies unexpectedly soon and it goes to Natasha and those girls? We don't know them, and they

care nothing for us or The Court, and what about Dossie, then?" But Adam is our son and we love him. And if we leave it between them Dossie couldn't afford to buy him out and where would she go? It's her home.'

Mo gets up very slowly and painfully, dusting down her rubbed and faded navy-blue cords, looking with approval at the graceful, pretty arrangement of the flowers: the creamy white with the dark, rich pink. She stretches her cramped limbs and turns to look beyond the further wall to the distant gleam and dazzle of the sea. In the fields tall feathery grasses and bright yellow buttercups ripple before the wind, shining in the sunshine like the sleek pelt of a great healthy animal. The sun is hot on her shoulders and she breathes in the scent of the hawthorn and the new-mown grass. She is in some odd way consoled, as if those fierce, tough former guardians of The Court are still standing in the shadows ready to guide and protect. She picks up the wilted stems, folds them and crushes them, and puts them into a plastic bag, which she stuffs into the pocket of her Husky gilet. Under the great yew she passes, making her way to the gate, and there she smiles with pleasure because across the road at the end of the lane, with Wolfie and John the Baptist on their leads, stands Pa.

'Thought we'd come to meet you,' he says as she crosses the road towards them. 'The dogs were missing you.'

They turn back into the lane and he releases the dogs, and they jump about Mo with excitement as if she has been gone for days, and then they all set off home together.

The meeting is over. Sister Ruth goes out with Sister Nichola, Sister Emily behind them, whilst Father Pascal talks quietly with Mother Magda beside the table as she tidies the papers.

'But they've got to think ahead,' he goes on thoughtfully. 'Of course they have, yet there must be some way that Chi-Meur can survive.'

'How?' She looks at him hopefully. 'You could ask Dossie. She's always full of good ideas and plans. And Pa and Mo.'

'Nobody is supposed to know until the Visitor has been, Mother Magda said.'

'I'd never heard of the Visitor. Funny name.'

'It's Bishop Freddie from the Truro Diocese. Pastoral overview, advice, and all that stuff. He's always brought in when there's a really big decision to be made. Good job this hotelier is from upcountry, otherwise it would be all over the village by now. They're going to be really upset about it. That's probably why he's playing his cards so close to his chest. Doesn't want to upset the locals before it's absolutely necessary.'

Janna turns to him suddenly. 'D'you think it's that man that's been staying with Penny's uncle at the farm? He says he's writing a book but Penny says her auntie doesn't believe a word of it. Says he's writing a history about north Cornwall but never listens when you tell him anything. He's always talking on his mobile. I've seen him in the village and up on the cliffs. He's that man I saw in the grounds, ages ago. D'you remember? Penny's boy says he can't find him when he Googles his name. Perhaps he's just been spying on us.' Her eyes fill with tears again. ''Tisn't right. They belong here, the Sisters and Mother Magda. And you do too. You and Jakey down in the Lodge.'

'And what about you?' he asks softly. 'Don't you belong here?'

She bites her lips, slides the potatoes into the large saucepan and drops in the mint. 'Funny, isn't it? I've never felt I've belonged anywhere really before I came here. But 'tis like I'm not meant to, I suppose. I've always been frightened at the thought of settling anywhere and now it seems I shan't have to worry about it after all. I just wish it hadn't been so soon.'

'It hasn't happened yet,' Clem says.

He goes to stand beside her, wondering how to comfort her. Sister Emily comes gliding in and smiles at them, slipping an arm around each of them.

'Exciting times,' she says. 'Much to think about, and to pray about. What is for lunch? Oh, lovely lamb casserole and new potatoes. How delicious that mint smells.' She beams upon them, holding on to them very tightly for a moment. 'All will be well,' she murmurs.

She goes out again, and they turn to their tasks, but both feel oddly comforted.

Driving in the twisting, narrow maze of lanes at the edge of the moor, Dossie stops occasionally to check the map and to peer at slanting ancient finger posts.

'It was probably crazy to buy it,' Rupert said ruefully. 'Nobody will ever find it and I shall be having calls from desperate holiday-makers telling me that they're lost. Except that the mobile signal around here is a bit patchy. I shall have to get a telephone installed, of course. I'll email you a map and I'll be looking out for you.'

Luckily she knows roughly where she is, although it is definitely off the beaten track and she's already taken one or two wrong turns. She doesn't care: she is so happy. Marvelling at the glory of the spring, listening to Joni Mitchell singing 'At Last', she flees through the sunken byways; glimpsing the heavenly glimmer of bluebells in an oak wood that climbs a steep, rocky ridge; passing a farm gate where tender, fleecy lambs crowd, clamouring, against the bars. Stopping yet again to consult the map, and getting out so as to take off her jacket, she hears the yaffle laughing down in a valley hidden amidst creamy clouds of hawthorn blossom.

On she goes. The lane winds downhill and then, quite suddenly, she is there; and he is waiting for her. She pulls in just beyond the cottage, beside his Volvo in an old lean-to shed, and climbs out.

'Well done!' he cries, as though she's won some kind of marathon. 'Did you get lost?'

'Not really.' It is silly to feel like this each time she sees him: almost shy and not quite knowing how to behave. 'Not seriously lost. I made a few wrong turns but realized quickly afterwards. I see what you mean about your average tourist finding it, but it's utterly delightful.'

She stands in the lane looking at the small cottage basking in the sunshine. Wisteria climbs over the front door and she can hear the tinkling, gurgling murmur of water. The tiny stream runs at the edge of the square of lawn and disappears away down the valley. Rupert is watching her reaction.

'It's a bit gloomy in the winter,' he says. 'Not much sun then, but there's a good wood-burner and it'll be cosy. It's very small. Come inside and have a look.'

She sees at once that he is living quite comfortably and not simply camping. The inglenook fireplace, with its heavy wooden lintel beam, has been carefully cleaned and a book-case has been built into a recess. The two armchairs look shabby but comfortable.

'I try to keep areas of tranquillity,' he says, 'otherwise it's too depressing for words. It's not always possible, of course, in the early stages but I'm working upstairs now and keeping this room and the kitchen as couth as I can. Go and have a recce upstairs while I make some coffee. I thought we'd have it out in the sunshine. The staircase is very steep so be careful. I'm having a new rail made for it by an amazing blacksmith in Boscastle.'

The landing branches at the top and the floorboards are bare. One bedroom is clean and fresh, with new paint and sanded boards. She is impressed by the beautifully hand-built cupboards and the dark blue, folding linen blind in the small, deep-set window. A bathroom is being installed into what was a box-room, an elegant egg-shaped washbowl and tall shining taps plumbed cleverly into the deep slate of the windowsill so as to give maximum space. The third room – the bigger bedroom – is clearly in use. Although the floor is covered with an expensive rush matting and the uneven walls painted, there are no cupboards yet. Her quick, inquisitive glance takes in his belongings: a towelling robe flung across the bed, a book on the floor beside a radio. Some clothes hanging on a rail that stands in the corner. She turns, feeling as if she is spying on him, and comes cautiously down the steep stairs, one hand on the wall.

She stands in the narrow hall, listening, and then pushes open the door into the kitchen. It is clear that this has once been a living room with the kitchen in a lean-to behind it, and more hand-built cupboards and a dresser have been carefully installed in this bigger room. This is work in progress but still functional, and she is impressed by his vision and ability. She goes out again, passing through the hall and out into the sunshine. Rupert is unloading a tray onto the wooden picnic table on the little grassy space and she joins him. He glances up at her expectantly and she grins at him.

'I like it,' she says lightly. 'It's going to be really special.'

He gives a laughing little sigh of relief, as if her approval is really important to him. 'You really think so?'

'It's got everything,' she says, sliding onto the wooden bench. 'Character, charm, but with all the really nice modern bits. Glorious setting. Cosy in the winter.'

'Like to write the brochure for me?' he teases.

'At a price,' she says. 'Goodness. This is quite a feast! I approve. As a family we have a great picnic tradition.'

'I think I'd gathered that.' He pours some coffee. 'Anyway, you deserve it, having trekked right out here. So you don't think I was a fool to buy it?'

Dossie shakes her head. 'Not at all. I'm glad that you're moving the kitchen into the living-room, though. It must be a bit poky out the back there.'

'The old kitchen is going to be a wet-room . . .'

He begins to tell her his plans, his fingers sketching diagrams on the rough planking of the table, but she is only half listening to him; drugged by the warm sunshine, the music of the water, his voice. She drinks her coffee and eats some chocolate tiffin, and pulls herself together sufficiently to ask one or two intelligent questions. He pours more coffee and she turns to watch a bluetit on the nut-feeder, which someone has hung from the branch of an alder that leans above the stream.

'I had a crazy idea,' he is saying. 'It's such a fantastic morning I wondered whether we might have a walk. There's a path right through the woods beside the stream just over the bridge there. I think you'd love it. And then, perhaps, we could go to the pub in the village for lunch – if you don't have to dash off, that is.'

She looks at him, and then glances quickly away again.

'Yes, I think I could,' she murmurs. 'Yes, why not?' And then she looks at him properly and they smile at each other.

Later, Rupert phones Kitty. It's not that he's feeling guilty about Dossie, no, it's simply that he wants to connect, check that Kitty's OK. She answers after a few rings and her voice is unusually animated though a bit fuzzy. She's with Sally in her car, she tells him, whizzing back from Cribbs Causeway having had lunch and a retail therapy session at John Lewis. He can hear Sally saying something in the background and then Kitty reminds him that they're all going to the Ashton Court Club this weekend and that Sally says to tell him that she's looking forward to doing a tango with him, and then there's lots of girly laughing. He goes along with it all, making an outrageous remark about one of Sally's particularly daring outfits and there are more shrieks, and then he says that they're breaking up and shouts goodbye.

He puts his mobile in his pocket, breathes deeply. So that's good, then. It'll be a great weekend, he'll make certain of that, falling in with plans for shopping, a rubber of bridge, dinner at the Club: but still the prospect of this kind of future appals him. He cannot see himself as a retired husband: pushing the trolley around Sainsbury's whilst Kitty darts up and down the aisles, visiting the garden centre, 'doing' Badminton or making cosy foursomes with Sally and dull old Bill. He shrinks in horror from it. He'd like to have Kitty back with him, working together and having fun in their own way. Of course he could see that she had to go back to look after Mummy when Kitty's father died so suddenly – he'd absolutely encouraged it – but he hadn't anticipated that Kitty would have been so quickly reabsorbed into the social scene she'd once so cheerfully abandoned.

He goes into the cottage, thinking now about Dossie, and begins to whistle under his breath as he clears up the remains of their picnic.

Stripey Bunny has been very rude and silly, and he is sitting on the naughty step. The naughty step is the first at the bottom of the stairs and Jakey himself had been sitting on that step just a bit earlier. Now he sits at the kitchen table, running a little car to and fro, and wonders how Stripey Bunny is feeling. It isn't really fair to blame Stripey Bunny for not eating his tea properly because he hasn't got a very good mouth for eating things, but it made Jakey feel better to tell him off and plonk him down on the step. Earlier, Daddy did that very same thing to him because he was rude to Sister Ruth. It is unfair because everyone – the Sisters, Janna, Daddy, even Dossie – is behaving oddly and Jakey can't understand why. It is as if they aren't really noticing him or hearing him any more, and deep down it frightens him. They look worried and they frown, all except Dossie who is very happy and does funny things that make him laugh, but still worry him a bit too, in a different way.

And when Daddy met him off the bus he still had that same not-seeing look and said, 'Come on, Jakes, get a move on,' not smiling or asking him about school or anything and then Sister Ruth came through the gate, back from a walk, and said: 'Good afternoon, young man. So what have you learned today at school?' and he said, 'Nothing,' and turned his back, and Daddy grabbed him by the arm and made him apologize for being rude and then hurried him into the Lodge and plonked him on the step.

It wasn't long before Daddy came back and said that he could have his tea now and he said he didn't want any, and then he saw that it was his favourite Smarties cake and he thought he might like some after all but didn't want to give in because he still didn't think it was fair. But Daddy crouched down and gave him a kiss and said, 'All over now, Jakey. Come on. Let's have some of this nice cake,' as if he was sorry really, and so he climbed up on his chair and watched while Daddy cut the cake.

And then, just when he thought things were going to be all right again and Daddy was talking to him properly, his mobile rang and Daddy picked it up and went out of the room. So he finished his cake all on his own, feeling cross and disappointed, and that's when Stripey Bunny had been silly and he'd taken him out and put him on the naughty step.

Jakey drives the toy car to and fro, feeling muddled and upset. Then the door opens and Daddy comes in carrying Stripey Bunny and saying, 'Hey. Look who I found on the naughty step. He says he's sorry and may he come back now?' and he dances Stripey Bunny up and down on the table so that Jakey laughs and grabs him, and Daddy says, 'That's better. Listen. Why don't we walk down to the beach and look for stones for Janna?' This is a big treat in the week, because of being tired and having to get to bed on time because of school next day, and suddenly he's really happy again and he jumps up and down and shouts, and Daddy smiles at him so that he feels that some heavy thing has rolled away from his heart and everything is all right.

Janna puts her mobile down on the caravan step beside her and leans back against the doorway. Poor Clem; he sounded so remorseful.

'I feel such a pig,' he said gloomily. 'Mind you, he *was*

rude to Sister Ruth, but I think he's picking up my anxiety. Poor little chap.'

'Well, you made your point,' she answered. 'Now give him a real treat. Take him down to the beach and ask him to find me some more stones to put on the windowsill. He loves that. Oh, never mind bedtime and all that stuff just for once, Clem. It's such amazing weather and it'll be pouring next week. Be happy with him. I'll come down and see you later after supper.'

They are all feeling the strain. Even Sister Emily looks preoccupied. Janna pulls her skirt up around her knees and closes her eyes. Sister Nichola's remark about silence made her think about it and she's begun to realize that there are different kinds of silence. Sometimes she slips into the chapel and sits just inside the door. They offered her a place of her own, just behind Sister Emily, but she felt that this was too much; that she didn't quite merit her own place. Anyway, she likes the freedom of perching near the door: last in, first out. There is a silence in the empty chapel; not a scary, empty silence but the silence of a deep-down peacefulness that slows her breathing and calms her. If any of the Sisters are at Silent Prayer then the quality of the silence is a different one, though the other is held within it. This more human silence contains a sense of expectation; of waiting.

Now, sitting on the step in the sunshine, with the pretty banties pecking around her feet, she is aware of the rural silence: a silence that contains the drone of a bee, birdsong and, more distantly, the sea's unceasing whisper. Clem asked her to go with them to the beach – and she longed to go – but it would soon be time for Vespers and then supper. When she is with Clem and Jakey it is like having a family, but without any of the responsibilities. When Jakey sits on her lap and leans against her, and she rests her cheek against his small head, she feels a great longing: a deep, deep desire for a child of her own. Yet the prospect frightens her. She sees the relentless commitment that Clem makes to Jakey and she wonders if she'll ever have the courage to give herself totally to a relationship or to a child. Oh, but she loves Jakey. He has, by sheer force of character, finally carried away her *Little Miss Sunshine* book. He loves the story of the grumpy king who can't smile and lives in Miseryland and Little Miss Sunshine who teaches him how to laugh.

Sitting there, eyes closed, she remembers her mother saying to her: 'You're my Little Miss Sunshine. You can always make me laugh however bad things are.'

'I *need* the book,' Jakey would say, leaning against her knee, looking at her winningly. 'Then Daddy could read it to me at bedtime. I really do need it, Janna.'

'But isn't it nice to have it here as a treat, my lover?' she'd counter. 'Makes it sort of special.'

'But I could bring it when I come to see you,' he'd answer. 'Then I could have both.'

'But would it be so much of a treat?'

'It would be even *more* a treat. Twice-times a treat.'

Eventually she'd given way and he carried off the book triumphantly, though he still brings it back sometimes so that she can read it to him. Yet in the giving there has been real pleasure, as if she's passed on something precious, which now links her with Jakey in some way. Or perhaps it is more than that: in giving it away she's gained something more important in its place. Maybe that is what Sister Emily meant when she said: 'When you no longer need them then you will be free.'

'You shouldn't have given in to him,' Clem said. 'I warned

you about his arguing ability. You should have been firm. I can get it back for you.'

She shook her head. 'I want him to have it. He loves it. Don't worry, Clem.'

After all, she still has the Peter Rabbit mug and the shawl as reminders of her childhood and her mother: symbols to show that she has been loved. Perhaps, here at Chi-Meur, these symbols are less important – but how would it be if she had to leave? And where would she go? Janna opens her eyes and folds her arms around her knees, filled suddenly with a sense of panic and loss.

'Mother Magda's trying to find another group who could come here to Chi-Meur to make it more viable,' Clem told her. 'It's a rather last-ditch effort. In the last year two Sisters have died and the novice who was here decided she would be more useful if she were to take Holy Orders. Losing three people in twelve months is a big deal in a small community. After all, Mr Brewster has merely hastened an inevitable process. Something has to be done. There might be another community somewhere, in the same position, that could join us here.'

Janna stands up and her long scarlet cotton skirt swishes around her slender ankles. She gathers the thick, wiry, lion-mane of her hair into a great bunch on top of her head, stretching her back and breathing in the heady scent of the bluebells. Suddenly a new sound is introduced into the silence: the sweet high note of the bell ringing for Vespers.

'They're thinking about it,' says Mr Caine. 'Not a good time to ring. I've told you before it's best I call you. People about.' He smiles at a few locals as he edges out of the pub and crosses the road to the sea wall. 'Look, it's no good swearing at me and Phil. We're doing our best and they're thinking about it . . . The dit is that they might get other nuns to join them. That's the latest thing . . . No, it's common gossip in the village. I don't need to creep around, spying. I told you, they love these old dears. Nobody wants a hotel, I can tell you that . . . One of the old ducks was born round here and she's still got rellies in the village . . . OK. Just warning you. Anyway, nothing to report . . . No, I'm stuck here now, aren't I? Ear to the ground. Poor old Phil has been doing his stuff but he can't put the frighteners on 'em. You just don't get it, do you? They're not like the poor little people you usually bully. These old girls have different values . . . Yeah, yeah, whatever, but you're not here, are you? I'll keep you up to speed.'

He snaps his mobile shut and slips it into his pocket. He nods to a couple of young men who lean on the sea wall, pints in their hands. They stare back at him.

'I love you too, baby,' he mutters, and goes back into the bar.

The thrush wakens her. The clear distinctive thrice-repeated phrases evoke other springs and half-forgotten emotions connected with youth and restlessness. She knows that it will be impossible to sleep again now and she turns carefully, so as not to waken Pa, and tries to see the little bedside clock: a quarter-past five. It is quite light and she slides quietly out of bed, pushing her feet into slippers, gathering up her dressing gown.

The dogs raise their heads, watching and waiting. Is this simply a bathroom break or something more? Mo opens the bedroom door and gestures them to follow her. They come at once, tails wagging, across the landing, down the stairs and into the kitchen. Mo closes the door, lest either of them is tempted to sneak back upstairs to look for Pa or Dossie, and pulls on her long dressing gown and ties its belt firmly. Then she lets them out through the boot-room and into the garden where the thrush is still singing.

She changes her slippers for gumboots and follows them, wandering over the dew-drenched grass, pausing to break off a spray of the sweet-scented yellow azalea as she waits for the sun to rise. A blackbird hops ahead of her, pausing to eavesdrop on a worm. The garden is full of rosy light; the clear pale sky streaked with crimson and scarlet. The thrush, perched high in an ash tree at the field's edge, continues to sing; she can just see his pale speckled breast between the light green leaves.

Now, away in the east, the world's rim flames and dazzles and suddenly the whole landscape burns into brilliance as the sun rides up clear of the earth. The garden is a magic place: trembling with a soft radiance; flashing with jewelled brightness; filled with the pure, unearthly sound of mounting notes and trills and cadences as other birds join the thrush to welcome the morning.

The dogs come back to her, pushing against her cheerfully, eyes bright, and she bends to stroke them.

'Much too early for breakfast,' she murmurs, ignoring John the Baptist's hopeful gaze. He sits down and offers his paw. 'Well,' she relents, 'perhaps a tiny biccie each while I have my tea.'

Back in the kitchen she leans against the Aga waiting for the kettle to boil, thinking about Dossie. Every instinct tells Mo that there is a new man in Dossie's life: she can recognize the signs and she is anxious. At first it presented itself as a wonderful prospect – Dossie is so happy, almost effervescent – but now, with Adam asking questions about wills and their future plans, she can see complications. Just supposing Dossie *has* found the right man at last, and she suddenly decided to set up a new home with him – or move in with him – then Pa's newest idea, that The Court should be left to Dossie, might not be such a good one after all. If Dossie doesn't want to live at The Court then there is no good reason why it shouldn't be left equally to her and Adam.

Mo spoons tea into the tea-holder and puts it into the large blue and white Whittard's teapot. But just supposing the relationship doesn't work out? After all, none of the previous attempts has been successful. Well, then: if she and Pa died Dossie could still use her share of the proceeds from the sale of The Court to buy a place of her own. And if one of them or both of them were still alive then she can simply come home again. But how terrible if, by then, The Court had already been sold and Dossie couldn't come back to it; and, of course, it wouldn't be there for Clem or Jakey if they should need it.

The kettle boils and Mo makes the tea, caught up again in the tangle and anxiety of her indecision. Pa is getting tired of these endless discussions. He wants to leave The Court to Dossie and all other disposable assets to Adam, and that is that. The trouble is, she doesn't dare tell Pa that she believes that there is a new man in Dossie's life. He would charge in at once, questioning her. If only she could tell what lay ahead then they could make this final important decision. Leaving The Court to Dossie only makes sense if things go on exactly as they are now.

John the Baptist's tail begins to beat upon the floor; the door opens and Pa comes in.

'So there you are,' he says. 'Woke up and wondered where you'd gone. It's a bit early for you, isn't it?'

'It was the thrush,' she says, reaching for a mug from the dresser so as to pour him some tea. 'Its singing was just so beautiful and the sunrise was magical. I simply couldn't stay in bed. And, anyway, we used to be up early with the B and B-ers, didn't we? Six, at the latest.'

He sits down opposite, yawning, hair on end. 'God, I miss it,' he says. 'All the coming and going. Kept us young, Mo.'

'I don't miss certain bits of it,' says Mo more cautiously, 'but I agree that it seems very quiet sometimes.' She watches him compassionately: he is alert and fit. Only the tremor in his right hand – a legacy from the stroke – betrays the fact that he is not as young as he looks. 'We'll invite a few of the old chums down again this summer. Dossie'll fix it.'

'I know she will.' He picks up his mug, holding it with both hands, elbow on the table to give him security and disguise the shaking. 'So what's she up to, Mo?'

She starts, almost spilling her own tea, and he snorts derisively.

'Did you think I hadn't noticed? Dashing about like a demented chicken that's just won the lottery. Never letting that damned mobile phone out of her reach. Always peering at it and checking it. Hurrying out when she gets a text. I'm not blind. It's a man, I suppose.'

'I hope so,' says Mo drily. 'It usually is.'

They look at each other anxiously.

'Not very good timing,' he observes, 'in view of our new plans. Of course, it might be nothing.'

'It's never "nothing" with Dossie. She's always so whole-hearted when it comes to men,' says Mo, resigned. 'But there's nothing we can do until she's ready to tell us.'

'We can ask her,' Pa says. He brightens at the prospect. 'Why not? It's normal to take an interest in one's child.'

'She's not a child,' says Mo at once. 'That's just the point. Just because she lives with us doesn't mean that we shouldn't respect her privacy.'

'But you worry about her,' he says cunningly, 'don't you, my darling? Isn't it best to make certain that she's not doing anything foolish?'

Mo looks at him narrowly. 'Don't try to wheedle me. And don't you dare to say a word to her.'

'Oh, really!' Pa rolls his eyes; sighs weightily. Suspecting ructions, John the Baptist struggles into a sitting position and watches him warily.

'Look,' Mo says, 'I know we want to make the decision: get it all settled. I want it just as much as you do. It's just that it's a bit tricky leaving The Court to Dossie, only to find that she's about to settle down somewhere else. After all, if we leave it to Dossie and her new man, why not to Adam and his new woman?'

'Exactly my point!' Pa exclaims in a kind of whispered shout. They've both instinctively lowered their voices, leaning across the table towards each other. 'That's why we should have it out with her.'

John the Baptist's tail begins to beat against the table leg and Mo and Pa instinctively turn towards the door. Dossie comes in. She wears pretty flowered pyjamas, her fair hair is fluffed up around her head and she looks radiantly happy.

'What are you up to?' she asks brightly. 'Bit early, isn't it, for plotting over the teapot?'

'Plotting?' begins Pa, flustered by her sudden entrance. 'How d'you mean? Plotting?'

Mo kicks him, not gently. 'You're up early too,' she says to

Dossie. 'Was it the thrush singing? He disturbed us and then we simply had to get up to see the sun rise. It was wonderful. We were just making plans for today, weren't we, Pa? Deciding what to do.'

She stares at him, daring him to contradict her. He breathes in through his nose and pours some more tea, his lips tightly compressed. John the Baptist goes to sit beside him and lays his heavy head consolingly upon Pa's knee.

'So, then,' says Dossie cheerfully, fetching a mug, pouring tea. 'What are these plans for today?'

'Yes, indeed,' says Pa blandly. 'How far had we got with the plans, Mo?'

Mo sits up straighter. Her eyes sparkle challengingly. 'We decided that we'd go over to Chi-Meur, and have a chat with Clem, persuade him to make us some coffee, perhaps, and then go to the Eucharist. It's so peaceful and the Sisters always love to see us. That was as far as we'd got, wasn't it, darling?'

Pa, who has already decided on a delightful pottering sort of day in the garden, is silenced.

'Sounds great,' Dossie is saying. 'And then you can have a pub lunch and take the dogs for a walk on the cliff.'

'And what about *you*?' asks Pa suddenly, ignoring Mo's look of warning. 'What are *your* plans? Anything exciting?'

'Take some freezer meals over to a holiday cottage at Port Gaverne,' she answers. 'Make some phone calls to clients. Work out a menu for a lunch party. Catch up on a bit of paperwork. Usual sort of day. I thought you were working in the garden today, Pa, rather than going off on a jolly.'

'So did I,' says Pa grimly.

'Plenty of time for both,' says Mo brightly. 'You can easily get a couple of hours in before we go off to Chi-Meur. Better hurry up and get some clothes on, though.' She beams upon him. 'You can take first go in the shower. What luck that the thrush woke us so early, wasn't it?'

'I wonder now,' says Clem, 'whether I got it all wrong. I should have continued with my training.' He glances at Father Pascal, hoping for a response but the old priest remains silent. 'The problem was,' he continues almost defensively, 'it just seemed utterly crazy with a baby. Even with a nanny, and I'm not sure how on earth *that* would have worked in a theological college. The distractions would have made studying and working impossible.'

There is a longer silence. Sunlight slants through the cottage window, picking out the colours of the books on the shelves and sliding over the paintings on the walls.

'Why, then,' asks Father Pascal placidly at last, 'do you feel that you got it wrong?'

Clem sighs; a kind of angry, groaning sound. 'Because I can't see where I'm going. I love it here, actually, but I've never seen it as my life's work. I thought something would evolve out of it. Something to show me clearly where I should be going.'

'But how do you know it won't?'

Clem leans forward in his chair, staring at his hands clasped between his knees. 'I suppose all this worry about what will happen at Chi-Meur is unsettling. I thought that I'd have the time, you see, to make a plan rather than just waiting for the blow to fall.'

'But waiting is essential to the spiritual life. And waiting on God demands patience. But it need not be a passive patience as if you're waiting for the rain to stop, or a bus to come along. We wait in expectation, living each moment fully in the present. You know that as disciples we are always waiting. During Advent we wait for the birth of Jesus, at Easter we wait for the Resurrection and now, during Pentecost, we wait for the coming of the Spirit. You know this, Clem.'

'It's not just me, though,' Clem protests. 'I have to think about Jakey too. I don't intend to stay on here if Chi-Meur becomes a hotel, even if Mr Brewster were to offer it. I think I'd like to go back to college but I don't know how I'd manage it with Jakey.'

'Would you consider leaving Jakey with Dossie and Mo and Pa during the term-times? Would they be able to cope?'

'I don't know. He'd have to change schools, of course, but he'd have to do that anyway if I went back to Oxford. And I couldn't afford a nanny for him this time.'

'And afterwards? How do you see your ministry?'

Clem sits back in his chair. He relaxes; his attractive bony face brightens. 'Well, what I *have* discovered is that I love Chi-Meur best when it's packed with guests and retreatants. The vibes are terrific. And people talk to me, you know, when they see me around and it's utterly amazing to talk to people who regard a conversation about God as normal. Some of them are just so strong in their faith and others have been shaken by some disaster and are dithering, and they sometimes wander round with me as I work and we discuss it.'

Father Pascal studies him thoughtfully; he knows that some of the guests have spoken with great respect of Clem. 'Have you ever considered being a chaplain?' he asks.

Clem stares at him. 'What, in the Services, d'you mean?'

Father Pascal shrugs. His shrug is a Gallic one: shoulders, hands, even his face shrugs. 'Not necessarily. There are other kinds of chaplaincy. Universities, prisons, hospitals, retreat houses. They all have chaplains.'

Clem thinks about it. 'A retreat house,' he answers at last. 'That would be really good. Are there many? You mean like Lee Abbey over on Exmoor?'

'That kind of thing. I'm not certain how many there are but I know one or two that are attached to monasteries . . .'

The thought occurs to them at exactly the same moment: they stare at each other.

'A retreat house,' Clem says softly. 'Why not? Could it be done?'

Father Pascal can hardly speak; his heart hammers. 'It must be done. This . . . *this*, Clem, is what we have been waiting for, I feel sure of it.'

Without being aware of rising they are on their feet, almost breathless with excitement.

'But how does it start?' asks Clem. 'Who would actually run it? What has to be done?'

'Much,' is the answer. 'But it's so right. You feel it too?'

Clem nods. 'Will the Sisters agree?'

Another shrug. 'If it is right. Go away now, Clem. I need to be alone. To think and to pray. You do the same. I shall be up to the Eucharist later and we'll speak again then.'

Clem nods, glances at his watch. 'Pa and Mo are coming over,' he says. 'I must dash anyway.' He hesitates. 'But it will be OK, won't it? I mean, it's just such a perfect answer.'

He looks almost beseeching, and for a brief moment Father Pascal is reminded of Jakey pleading for some treat. He touches the tall figure lightly on the shoulder.

'Go and see Pa and Mo,' he says gently. 'Come to the Eucharist and pray for guidance but don't speak of it yet to anyone.'

He opens the front door. Clem ducks beneath the low beam, exchanges one last excited look with the old priest, and hurries away up the steep hill to Chi-Meur.

'Butterfly cakes,' Dossie says, 'because I've been doing a children's party. But I thought that we needed a moment. We haven't had one for ages, have we? Gosh, the lavender smells wonderful.'

She gives the cake tin to Janna and bends to run her fingers through the lavender's scented spikes. The caravan seems to rest amongst a flowerbed: pots of varying sizes and shapes containing herbs and flowers are piled around its base. Dossie touches first this one and then that, pausing to sniff luxuriously at her fingers. Janna watches, delighted to see her: in her faded jeans and baggy white cotton shirt Dossie looks young and pretty and happy.

'I love butterfly cakes,' Janna says. 'And the timing is just right. We've got some oblates staying and they're giving me a bit of a holiday by taking on some of the work, so I've got a day off. Cuppa?'

'Mmm, yes, please. Camomile and lemon would be good with the cakes.' She straightens up and looks at Janna. 'How are you?'

'Yeah, I'm fine.' She tries to conceal her anxiety about Chi-Meur, about her future, knowing that Dossie has no idea of what is happening. ''Tis good to have a bit of help. The people who come here are just amazing, you know. 'Tis like they're part of the community. Like family. 'Course, they've been coming for years so I suppose they *are* family. Hang on, I'll get the kettle on.'

She brings out a little folding canvas chair, sets it beside the lavender for Dossie, and goes back inside to make the tea. After a few minutes she reappears with a tray, which she puts on the grass, and then sits down again on the caravan step.

'I love it here,' Dossie says dreamily, eyes closed in the sunshine. 'It's funny, isn't it, that the grounds have exactly the same atmosphere that you have in the chapel. It's like there's some kind of spell over the whole place. You're not frightened, sleeping out here on your own?'

Janna shakes her head. 'Sometimes I even leave the door open when 'tis hot at night. The top half, anyway. I've felt more frightened in a street full of people than I've ever felt here on my own. It'll be difficult—' She stops, biting her lip, reaching for her mug.

'What?' asks Dossie idly, eyes still closed. 'What'll be difficult?'

'Nothing. Just thinking about managing when the oblates go home. Some of the women come up from the village to help when they can, though, so it's fine really. So what about you? You look fantastic.'

Dossie opens her eyes. 'Do I?' she asks, delighted. 'Really? I feel rather good at the moment.'

'So what's it all about then? Got a new fella?' teases Janna, and is taken aback when Dossie turns her head to look at her and says, 'Actually, I have.'

She laughs at Janna's expression. 'Crazy, isn't it? But, listen. Don't say anything, will you? Nobody knows yet. It's just I'm not ready yet to talk about it. Pa will start questioning me – you know what he's like – and Mo will fuss. And Clem . . .' Her voice trails away. 'It's always a bit tricky explaining to your son that you're . . . Oh, well.'

'I can see that. But Clem would be pleased if you're happy, wouldn't he?'

144

'Yes, I'm sure he would, but the truth is I haven't got a very good track record for picking men. That's why I'm not telling anyone, even my old friends. They always want to remind me about the last time. It's never quite worked out, you see, and I always feel such a prat afterwards. This time, though . . .'

She sips her tea and Janna casts about for something to say that will be encouraging without seeming nosy.

'He's nice, is he?' she asks lightly. 'Does he live locally?'

Dossie shakes her head. 'He's rather peripatetic. He's got a portfolio of properties including some holiday cottages, mostly on the south coast. He lives in the one he's doing up at the time and then buys another and moves on. He's never long in one place.'

'Sounds good,' Janna says enviously. 'Does he need a mate?'

Dossie laughs. 'I'm hoping so.'

Janna grins. 'I didn't mean like that. What was that word you said? Perry-something? It means moving about, does it? Sounds better than being a traveller. I'll remember that one.'

'Peripatetic. Really, it means living on the edge. He seems very happy, anyway.'

'And would you like that?' asks Janna curiously. 'Moving about and never having a real place of your own?'

Dossie frowns. She puts her mug down on the grass and selects a butterfly cake, peeling off its paper cup. 'Sometimes the thought of it seems like heaven. No responsibilities. Now here, now there. Seeing each place come together must be very satisfying. And then again . . .' she shrugs. 'I've lived at The Court for nearly all of my life, and I'd miss it dreadfully. I can't really imagine living anywhere else. I suppose a change would be exciting, though I've no idea how on earth

I'd tell Mo and Pa. And how would they manage? I'd feel so selfish.'

'Maybe,' Janna suggests, 'if you get together, this man might decide to settle down somewhere near to them. He could still do places up, couldn't he? He doesn't *have* to live in them?'

'His name's Rupert. I've thought about that too. I just wish I knew how he really feels.'

'About you, d'you mean?'

'Mmm. I mean, we get on really well, and he seems keen. Phones up and texts, suggests pub lunches, and he's shown me the place he's working on and another one he hopes to buy, but we seem to be a bit stuck, if you know what I mean. He's really easy to be with, and great fun, and he's affection-ate and . . . well, he says nice things, but we're not moving on very quickly.'

Janna takes a cake too. 'It could be that he's had a bit of a bad time and he's being cautious. Is he divorced?'

'His wife died not that long ago. He doesn't talk about it, just goes a bit grim and silent. Someone else told me.'

'Well, then. That could be it, couldn't it? He might just be feeling guilty about falling for you. Sort of callous when she's died, poor thing. I can understand that.'

Dossie brightens. 'I'd wondered about that too.'

'Perhaps he just needs time to sort of fix it with his conscience.' Janna pauses, feeling anxious in the role of confidante. After all, what does she know? 'So Mo and Pa haven't met him?'

'Heavens, no!' Dossie speaks vehemently. 'It's all so dif-ficult because of living with them. I always feel like a kid taking home a boyfriend. Obviously they'll have to meet him sooner or later but just for now I'm trying to be low key about it, and Rupert doesn't ask. He knows the situation and I think he'd be as embarrassed about it as I am. I'm hoping that it will happen sort of naturally, somehow. You won't say anything, will you?'

''Course I won't. I promise. I'm just glad you're happy. The rest'll sort it itself out.'

'I know.' Dossie finishes her cake. 'So how about you? No gorgeous men coming on retreat?'

'Actually, it does happen sometimes. Generally, though, they're married priests, although there have been one or two others. Widowers, generally.'

Dossie raises an eyebrow. 'Bit old for you, I should have thought.' She hesitates. 'Pity you can't fall in love with Clem, that's what I think.'

Janna chuckles. 'I couldn't agree more. I love him but just not like that. He's the same about me.'

'Funny, isn't it, this old chemistry business? You simply can't manufacture it, can you?'

Janna shakes her head. 'I don't think I've ever really been in love. I don't just mean the sex thing. That's easy. But the real passion; I've never known that one. Is that what you're feeling now?'

Dossie blushes and Janna laughs. 'No need to answer. I can't wait to meet him.'

'You may have to,' retorts Dossie. 'I'm not going to introduce him to a gorgeous young creature like you until I've got him well and truly hooked.'

Later, walking down to the beach, Janna wonders what it must be like to be Dossie: to be in love but unable to talk about it. She can imagine how hard it would be for Dossie to tell Mo and Pa that she would be leaving them, and to explain such emotions to Clem. It is so sad, though, that she has to hide her happiness instead of sharing it. It seems that everyone has secrets just at the moment. As she begins to climb the cliff path, Janna wishes that she could share her own secret with Dossie; but the fate of Chi-Meur isn't just her secret. Clem and Jakey are involved, and Dossie would be anxious about them.

The lark's song, bubbling up and up and followed by the swift descent into silence, distracts her. Here, on the sheltered path, plump pink cushions of thrift flower; above them, on the rough granite walls, delicate white rockroses clamber amongst clumps of red valerian. She crouches down, gathering her red cotton skirt around her knees, so as to examine a nest of scurrying ants who work busily in and around the base of the wall by the root of a mallow. How organized they are; how committed: fetching and carrying and guarding their home. She teases them for a while with a long grass stalk, smiling to herself but impressed, too, as they rear up and wave their pincer-like forelegs fearlessly at this intruder.

Out on the cliff the strong wind seizes her, battering her; still cold despite the sun's warmth. As she draws nearer to the cliff's edge she can hear an unusual sound: a high-pitched noise like the crying of a thousand babies. Curious, she looks out to sea where a white sail thrashes on the turquoise-green and inky-purple water, and tall, white-topped waves race in to smash themselves in flying spray against the steep, glittering-grey walls of the cliffs.

The crying is coming from somewhere below her and, looking down, she sees a strange sight: hundreds of seagull fledgelings are crammed in rows in the rocks' crevices, all screaming for food. The parent birds dive and plunge below the rocks, landing and taking off again in a frenzy of providing. Suddenly the gulls are all around her in a whirling white storm of beating wings, and Janna steps back, instinctively raising her arms to ward them off. She moves away from the cliff's edge, half frightened, half exhilarated by the encounter, struggling against the force of the wind and turning on to the path again. It will be better down on the beach. Tucked into the shelter of the rocks, she can sit in the sunshine and sleep.

'Surely,' Sister Ruth is saying, 'surely it would be more sensible for us to go to the Sisters in Hereford rather than open Chi-Meur to strangers. To move out of our own quarters into the Coach House would be an enormous upheaval. How would we manage?' She looks at Sister Nichola, who seems to be listening intently to something that nobody else can hear. 'How would she cope? She's been very restless again lately, disappearing on her own, and I'm sure it's because of all this worry.'

Ruth feels the situation is slipping beyond her own control. She knows that Sister Emily will welcome it – she's always been a radical – and that Magda will dither anxiously, trying to make certain everyone is happy. Can't they see, she asks herself crossly, the unsuitability of cramming themselves into the Coach House?

Father Pascal waits for Mother Magda to speak but when she remains silent, he says: 'Any change is going to be an upheaval. Surely, if it could be arranged, it would be less of an upheaval to move across to the Coach House than to go to a completely strange place. I know that you communicate regularly with the Sisters in Hereford but, even so, it would be a very big change.'

'I think,' says Sister Emily, eyes shining, 'that it is a *wonderful* idea. To stay here and to see Chi-Meur still used for the spiritual comfort and guidance of many, *many* people. Even to have a small part in it. Oh, what a gift it would be.'

She opens her cupped hands, as if already receiving the gift, and Father Pascal tries to suppress the uprush of affection and joy that she always invokes in him.

'But,' says Sister Ruth rather desperately, 'surely this would all take time? It seems rather a risk. And if it doesn't work? What then? We might still have to move, and think what a toll that would take on Sister Nichola.'

'I think, if we were able to ask Sister Nichola, she would want to stay here if it were at all possible,' says Sister Emily. 'She was born and brought up here, after all. Her relatives visit her regularly. Think how much she would miss them.' She raises her chin, in the imperious way she has, and beams upon her old adversary.

Sister Ruth stares back. She would like to smack Sister Emily very hard. This is not a new sensation and she wills herself to sit still, reluctantly acknowledging that it is an important point. The fact that she has been trying to ignore this aspect of the move to Hereford simply makes her feel guilty about Nichola and even more resentful towards Emily.

Father Pascal watches them, aware of Sister Ruth's muddled emotions; still he waits for Mother Magda to speak. He knows that she is very taken by the idea of Chi-Meur becoming a retreat house, though she is anxious – Mother Magda is always anxious – about how it is to be done.

'Try not to worry about the nuts and bolts of it,' he said, when they first talked about it. 'Just try to think about it as a whole, and pray about it, and then we can speak to Emily and Ruth and Nichola.'

'It sounds a wonderful solution,' she said cautiously. 'We could remain a community but still have a part in this greater movement.'

'Exactly!' He was barely able to contain his excitement. 'You could live in the Coach House and keep the orchard for your own use. You'd still be quite private and self-contained. Naturally there would have to be some small changes to the Coach House to make it easier for Nichola – perhaps a stair-lift – but I'm sure it could be sorted out. And Chi-Meur could continue its tradition with people coming on retreat and on courses, and you could still be part of that but not responsible for it.'

Now, as he waits, she gathers herself to speak, her thin, lined face intent with the need to say the right words: to convince, to encourage. Suddenly he remembers the young Magda who looked after the small herd of dairy cows in the days when the convent was much more self-sufficient. How she'd loved those quiet, gentle creatures; she'd hurry from the milking parlour, coming in late to the early Office with wisps of straw on her habit, boots kicked off at the chapel door, her face rosy and peaceful. How sad she'd been when keeping the farm had no longer been an option.

'I believe that this is something we must think about most carefully,' she says now. Her fingers nervously pleat and repleat the skirt of her habit. 'It could be a very great opportunity to see our community growing rather than shrinking. We've been unsuccessful in finding any other group to join us and some of us are unwilling to leave Chi-Meur and allow it to become an hotel. Who knows? Out of the retreat house we might find vocations being discovered and novices wanting to join us . . .'

'In the Coach House?' Sister Ruth speaks sneeringly, and Mother Magda is silenced.

'Yes, if necessary.' Father Pascal is firm. 'All things are possible with God. And this kind of movement is much more likely to attract young women than the older, more retired ways would. You must be prepared for change.'

Sister Emily takes a deep, happy breath. 'And Clem and Jakey and Janna could stay with us.'

'If they wish to, and I feel certain that Clem will.' Father Pascal hesitates, choosing his words carefully. 'You all know that Clem was selected for training and hoped to go on to ordination. It was only the tragic death of his wife that made him postpone it so as to bring up Jakey. Perhaps, now, he could start his training again. In my opinion he would make an excellent priest and warden. Of course, I would still be here, and so would you. It is you who would be laying the foundation stones.'

'And if Janna would stay we would be very grateful to have her,' adds Mother Magda.

'We'd certainly need her,' says Sister Emily bluntly. 'We'd need someone who knows our ways and whom we trust and feel safe with.'

'And Jakey?' asks Sister Ruth sarcastically. 'I suppose we need him too?'

'He balances us,' answers Sister Emily. 'We who are so old and Jakey who is only four. It is refreshing to see things through his eyes and to hear his thoughts and ideas. Yes, I think that Jakey could be contained within it all, don't you?'

'If Clem stays, then Jakey stays, and we certainly need Clem,' Father Pascal says strongly. 'They could stay in the Lodge, of course. Nothing need change there.' He looks around at them. 'We have much to think about and to pray about, I know that, but it gives us a fresh hope and the prospect of a new beginning. I am reminded of that verse from Isaiah: "Arise, shine; for your light has come, and the glory of the Lord has risen upon you . . . Nations shall come to your light, and kings to the brightness of your dawn."'

'As long as we can manage it all. If only we were younger . . .' Mother Magda still looks anxious; Sister Emily is radiant and Sister Ruth judicious. Sister Nichola gets up from her chair and shuffles across the room to stand beside Father Pascal. She bends towards him.

'"Have you not known?"' she quotes softly. '"Have you not heard? Those who wait upon the Lord shall renew their strength: they shall mount up with wings as eagles, they shall run and not be weary, and they shall walk, and not faint."'

They sit for a moment in silence and then Father Pascal smiles up at her. 'You do right to quote Isaiah, too,' he says. 'A prophet of vision and of great faith. Shall we have a prayer to close?'

'I like butterfly cakes,' Jakey says contentedly. He sits on the grass outside the caravan door. Stripey Bunny is propped against the leg of the canvas chair and the Peter Rabbit mug stands beside him on the picnic rug. 'Shall I have another one?'

'Why not, my lover? You should eat Stripey Bunny's. I don't think he likes them much.' Janna is stretched out on the grass beside the rug. 'Is Daddy coming back for a cuppa?'

'He said he would.' Jakey peels away the paper carefully and licks some crumbs from it. 'He's happy again now.'

'Is he?' Janna shades her eyes with her hands and looks across at Jakey. 'That's good, then.'

Jakey nods, eating his cake. 'Auntie Gabriel came in the night and then Daddy was happy again.'

'Auntie Gabriel?' Janna half sits up, propping herself on her elbow. 'Isn't she the angel you had at Christmas standing on the bookcase?'

Jakey licks his fingers and wipes them on the grass. 'She comes and watches us in the night. She looks after us.'

'Watches you?'

'She stands outside but I can see her when I look out of my bedloom window.'

'And then what happens?'

'I wave to her.'

'And does she wave back?'

Jakey shakes his head. 'She has her hands together like *this*.' He clasps his hands. 'She's holding her heart so she can't wave back.'

Janna sips her tea thoughtfully. She remembers the large, delightful angel with her string hair and fragile crown; and now, too, she remembers the red satin heart that Auntie Gabriel holds between her hands. Janna guesses that it must have been a particularly vivid dream.

'As long as you weren't frightened,' she says.

'No. I love her,' he says. 'She's not flightening. She watches over us. Look! Here's Daddy.'

Clem comes striding towards them through the orchard, the pretty grey and gold banties scattering before him; he looks strong and confident and purposeful. Janna watches his approach with a mixture of surprise and wariness: it is clear that he's heard some news. Instinct warns her that great change is imminent for all of them and her heart beats faster in trepidation.

'We saved a cake for you,' Jakey is crying to him, delighted to see him. 'You can sit there, in the chair.'

Clem folds himself into the small chair and smiles at them both. Janna stands up, still wary, examining the excitement that shines in his eyes.

'You look like you've won the lottery,' she says lightly. 'Want a cuppa?'

'Oh, yes, please. Just ordinary stuff, if you've got some.' He accepts the cake that Jakey presses upon him and looks again at Janna, who hesitates at the bottom of the caravan step. 'I've just seen Father Pascal.' He speaks quietly. 'Good news. It seems we might not have to go, after all. Can you come down and have some supper after I've put Jakey to bed?' She nods and he smiles at her reassuringly. 'It sounds really good,' he promises, and then Jakey flings himself upon him, wanting attention, and Janna climbs up into the caravan to make the tea.

TRINITY

After two weeks of cold winds and heavy rain, which beat down the remaining frail blossoms from the azaleas, the last week in June is sunny and hot. In The Court's gardens, baby woodpeckers sporting their bright red caps cling nervously to the nut-feeders, trying their new skills, still hoping to be fed by their watchful parent. From a corner, beneath the stone wall, a bronze slowworm slithers silently into the dank warm safety of the compost heap.

Mo, weeding the long border, sits back on her heels. She feels tired and anxious. Earlier, Adam, Natasha and the girls left to go back home after a weekend of tension, and she and Pa are suffering from the strain of it. The girls were un-communicative, as usual, whilst Natasha seems to condone their behaviour, shrugging, smiling apologetically, but doing nothing to suggest that they might answer questions or be polite.

'I suppose,' Pa said, 'that we are utterly irrelevant to them. They have a father, even if he is estranged, and aunts and

156

uncles and grandparents, and we are just a tiresome pair of old biddies that they don't need to bother about.'

'But even so,' Mo answered, 'that doesn't excuse rudeness. It doesn't matter who we are, surely common politeness is still necessary, especially whilst they are our guests.'

He raised his eyebrows. 'Clearly not.'

And now he is determined to speak to Dossie; to tell her that they want to leave The Court to her and to ask if she knows of any reason why this wouldn't be a good plan.

Mo climbs rather painfully to her feet and puts a handful of weeds into the wheelbarrow. Her heart pounds unevenly and she steadies herself by grasping its handle.

'So,' Adam said casually when they were alone together. 'Anything decided yet? Any plans for the future? I thought that Pa was looking a tad stretched. He's OK, is he? No more keeling over sideways?'

'No,' she answered, shrinking distastefully from his callous words. 'No, none of that. He's very fit at present. And so am I.'

Adam glanced around the garden and up at the house. 'Just as well,' he said lightly. 'I can't think how you manage it all.'

'No, I don't suppose you can.' She turned away from him, not liking him, and horrified at herself for such a feeling.

He followed her, catching at her arm. 'It's no good being upset, Mo,' he said, almost angrily. 'It's got to be sorted out. I'm wondering if I – and Dossie – ought to have power of attorney, just in case. It's all very well being proud, but things can happen suddenly at your ages.'

'Or even at your ages,' she responded sharply. 'You might have a heart attack, mightn't you? What then? What are *your* plans? Does everything go to Natasha? After all, you've known her for little more than a year and you're not married. Do you intend to get married?'

He flushed: that odd, familiar yet almost shocking reaction, which suffused his fair skin with such vivid colour that his eyes looked frostily cold and rather frightening. She stared at him, fascinated.

'It's none of your business,' he said shortly, turning away from her, so that it was she, this time, who followed and grasped his arm.

'Why not? Why are you allowed to question us but we are not allowed to know your plans?'

He shook himself free and went quickly into the house, and she had to wait for several minutes to control her uneven breathing and the odd pain in her side. She thought, wryly, that it was quite the wrong moment to – how had he put it? – keel over. Suddenly she was determined to go with Pa to their lawyer and get it sorted out: The Court must go to Dossie.

Now, standing quietly, breathing deeply, she prays that Dossie still wants it; wonders if this new man might yet set all their plans awry. As she lets go of the wheelbarrow, she hears Pa calling her and the dogs appear, as if to collect her. She turns towards the house and he waves to her and she raises her arm in response.

'All right, Mo?' he asks as she approaches, and they sit down on the wrought-iron seat together.

'No,' she says crossly, when she's got her breath back. 'I am *not* all right. I feel angry and frustrated and, oh, lots of other things.' She looks at him as he turns towards her and lays his arm along the back of the seat. 'Where did we get it wrong, Pa? We loved him so much, didn't we? The longed-for son.

We were so proud. All those miscarriages. Do you remember in Jo'burg? God, it was so hot and you getting called away on some emergency and me losing the baby. It was like a miracle, having Adam. Yet it's as if he's a changeling.'

'Yes, that's exactly it.' Pa nods. 'Somehow I've never really *recognized* him. Dossie's a mixture of you and my mother, and a bit of me mixed in too, which helps us to understand her, doesn't it? And old Clem . . .'

'I worried about Clem for a bit when he was at that adolescent stage. He became a bit distant. Dossie calls it "austere" and I feared that he might turn out like Adam. But he didn't. He *is* austere but he's also got a tremendous capacity for compassion. And a great sense of humour. Adam just doesn't have that, does he?'

Pa shakes his head sadly. 'I can't reach him. I disappointed him when I stopped being someone he could brag about.'

'We got it wrong for him when we came home and settled here. I thought he'd be pleased, which was stupid of me. I suppose it's more fun for a teenage boy to be travelling across the world for his holidays than having his parents close enough to be able to turn up for athletics days and rugby matches. And he'd got used to us being so far away. He'd had to learn to manage without us and then he found he could. We can't blame him for that.'

'But it was exactly the same for Dossie,' Pa argues. 'She was older, of course, but she'd been away to school, too. Dossie loved us all being together.'

'I've often wondered if Adam takes after my father,' Mo says. 'After all, I was only five when he was killed at Dunkirk, and he was a professional soldier so I hardly remember him at all. His photographs are all so formal. And black and white, of course, so it's a bit difficult to see much of a resemblance, though his very fair colouring is right for Adam. My mother rarely spoke about him except in a kind of respectful way but never with great passion or huge regret.'

'Well, it wasn't a generation that let it all hang out, was it? Grief was a private thing. Stiff upper lip.'

'Even so.' Mo sighs. 'I cannot connect with him. Adam, I mean. And it just breaks my heart. I can't connect with Natasha, either, or those girls. Whatever shall we do?'

'Whatever we do, I don't intend to leave Dossie without a home. If she wants to stay here, then that's what I want for her. I know they could sell and split the money and she'd have enough to buy a little place of her own but Dossie loves The Court. It's her home.'

'But could she afford to live here on her own?' asks Mo anxiously. 'We're all chipping in, aren't we, at the moment? But without our pensions, especially yours from RTZ, could she manage?'

'She could do what we did,' he says.

Mo looks at him, puzzled. 'What we did? Oh! B and B-ers?' She is silent for a few moments. Then, 'Actually,' she says slowly, 'that's not a bad idea. And she'd be so good at it. But would she even consider it?'

He shrugs. 'She might get tired of all this driving to and fro. Making food, catering for dinner parties, dashing round the county.' He grins at Mo. 'Wouldn't it be great?'

She smiles at his enthusiastic optimism. 'It would be just wonderful.'

'So when are we going to ask her about this man?'

Panic seizes Mo's heart again. 'Oh, good grief,' she groans. 'However can I ask her? How would I start?'

They sit together, considering ways and means, whilst the dogs doze at their feet in the sunshine.

✝   ✝   ✝

In the car, travelling back to Bristol, the girls sit in silence. They know that they have behaved badly but they also know that, though Natasha's loyalty is to them and not to Adam's parents and that she refuses to hear a word against her children, she is secretly embarrassed by their behaviour.

Natasha *is* humiliated but refuses to acknowledge it: she implies that the old dears must put up with it. Adam is cross and as she drives she is wondering how she can keep these tiresome visits to a minimum without Adam losing his in-heritance. It's not really fair to the girls to introduce another set of elderly people into their lives, especially when Adam is not even particularly close to his parents. And she simply cannot bring herself to call them Mo and Pa: she said so to Adam right from the start. It's ridiculous to use such silly names; she'd feel a fool.

'It's not important,' Adam said. 'Get over it. Everyone calls them Mo and Pa.'

Nevertheless she insists on calling them Mollie and Patrick. The girls, taking her lead, refuse to call them any-thing at all – which they know she finds a bit difficult, and annoys Adam – and she says defensively that she can see their points of view.

'It's not as if they're grandparents,' she said to Adam. 'The girls have got two sets of those already. They don't need any more.'

The girls agreed: they certainly don't. But they could see he was annoyed.

'So what will they call them?' he asked. 'They can't call them Mollie and Patrick.'

She didn't answer. Sometimes she finds this is the best way: silence is a very useful weapon.

The girls have made a note of this and use the same trick themselves. They have agreed between themselves that their mother is more malleable if she has a man around. Adam's presence ensures an ongoing conflict of loyalties and by clever manipulation they are assured of more treats and attention than when Natasha is managing alone and expects more cooperation from them and is often touchy, tired and short-tempered. However, they do not regard him as a permanent fixture in their lives – he is too irritable, too selfish – but they are experts in control and they will choose their time to evict him. Just now they want to put an end to these trips to Cornwall. So they wait.

'So,' Natasha says. 'Did you manage to say anything?'

'Yes,' he says shortly, staring out of his window

Watching from the back seat the girls can see that his body language is telling her that he doesn't want to talk right now. Probably he doesn't want them to hear. He hunches away from her, scowling out, and they wait in breathless silence to see what she will do.

'What then?' she insists, though she lowers her voice. 'Did she see your reasoning? About you having power of attorney?'

He sighs heavily. 'She says they haven't made any plans. In fact, she turned the tables on me and asked what *our* plans are? She said that I might die suddenly and, if I did, would everything go to you?'

She gives him a quick sideways glance. 'How d'you mean?'

'Well.' He shrugs. 'I suppose she's got a point.'

'What point?'

'Oh, come on,' he says crossly. 'They don't like the idea of you and the girls inheriting half of their property if anything happens to me.'

162

The girls nudge each other: here it comes.

'That's hardly fair, though, is it?' Natasha says. 'You're their son, after all. And we're your family now. Which means *their* family.'

'In that case,' he mutters, 'it might be wiser to act like it. You doing your patronizing "Patrick and Mollie" act, and your children behaving like louts . . .'

Natasha's grip tightens on the wheel; she prepares to defend her corner: 'I resent that. We've given up another weekend to drive all this way . . .'

The girls grin at each other: result. They sit back in their seats as a bitter little argument develops.

'I hope you don't mind,' Dossie says rapidly. 'I sent a text but you didn't answer and I wondered if it was just the signal playing up again. But I wasn't far away so I just thought I'd dash down to say "Hi" and to see how you were getting on . . .'

She looks around her, smiling, still keeping up the jolly, casual approach, but she is feeling embarrassed. Rupert's welcome hasn't been one of unconditional joy and she is cursing herself for seizing this chance and taking him by surprise. Yet why shouldn't she? Surely they have known each other long enough for her to make such a move. It occurs to her that, up until now, it is he who has been the proactive one; suggesting meetings and times and places.

'Of course I don't mind,' he's saying, 'except that I've no picnic this time, nothing prepared for you. In fact, the place is a bit of a mess.' He begins to laugh, looking a bit shame-faced, regaining his composure. 'The truth is I made a bit of an effort last time, so as to impress you.'

'That doesn't matter,' she cries, relieved. 'Don't be silly. It's

163

just you said something about having to dash upcountry for the weekend so I thought I'd come and say goodbye.'

She feels a complete fool now. All the way here she's imagined this meeting: how his face would light up when he saw her and that he might even take her in his arms, and she hoped that the unexpectedness of it would precipitate something exciting; something physical. She's been playing Joni Mitchell's 'At Last' again as she drove over, feeling light-hearted and happy and full of love for him; and wanting to feel his arms round her. Instead, his reaction has made her feel as if she were taking liberties.

'Look,' he's saying now, 'come and sit in the sun. I'm sorry I was a bit off. It's just that I'm not looking forward to this trip. I'm going to see my bank manager to try to sort out a bit of extra finance for that cottage we saw. The owner's holding out on me to raise my offer. It's been a very slow season for the rental market and I need to reassess one or two things. I may have to put this place out on a long let, for instance. Or put it back on the market when I've finished it, though it's not the best time for trying to sell.'

She is sympathetic at once; sitting down at the little table, looking at him with concern.

'I'm really sorry,' she says. 'I wasn't thinking . . .'

'Why should you?' he asks quickly. 'I'd got myself into a bit of a state. Look, I'll go and make us some coffee. Only instant, I'm afraid. And, like I said, no picnic.'

'That's fine,' she says warmly, anxious to reassure him and to comfort him. 'Of course it is. I just wanted to say "Hi", that's all.'

'Bless you,' he says, smiling now. 'Shan't be a minute.'

He goes away into the cottage and she slumps a little with relief. Poor Rupert, no wonder he is looking a bit stretched and preoccupied. This might not be the moment for passion but at least she can support him; make him laugh. It's hard, when you're alone, to deal with all the problems of running a business and earning a living.

Slowly, as she sits quietly, she grows aware of the noise of the water. The little stream is full to overflowing after the heavy rain of the last two weeks, and the grass is sodden underfoot. No chance of a walk today, or lunch at the pub, as she's hoped; she won't suggest it. She'll play it by ear.

He comes out looking more relaxed, carrying two mugs. 'You've caught me out, you see,' he tells her cheerfully. 'I had it all off perfectly last time, hoping to impress you, and now I'm reduced to two mugs of instant coffee.'

'You don't need to impress me,' she answers. 'Surely you know that by now.'

He reaches out and touches the back of her hand with one finger, running it lightly up and down.

'You're a darling,' he says. 'You know that, don't you?' He stops stroking her hand and picks up his mug. 'But how are you? Didn't you say that your brother was down again? How did it go?'

She can't speak at once; his touch has unsettled her and she wants to take his hand. She drinks some coffee to cover her reaction.

'It's difficult,' she says at last, marvelling at the calmness of her voice. 'He wants Mo and Pa to make all these decisions about The Court. Well, I told you, didn't I? I suppose it would help if we all had a crystal ball and knew what the future held.'

She falls silent, waiting. Rupert raises his eyebrows and draws down the corners of his mouth; a facial shrug.

'Wouldn't it just?' he agrees lightly. 'I'd give a great deal to know what my bank manger is going to say this afternoon, for instance.'

It isn't the answer she hopes for but she rallies. 'This afternoon? Where are you meeting him?'

He hesitates very briefly. 'In Bristol. I've had my account since I was at university there. I shall stay on for a few days and see my mother.'

Somehow she hasn't expected a mother and for some reason she can't quite understand it makes her feel more cheerful. He glances at his watch and she finishes her coffee and sets down the mug.

'I'd better let you get on,' she says, getting up. 'Have a good journey.'

He gets up too, and they walk together to her car. She smiles at him, not quite knowing what to say.

'Thanks for the coffee.'

Quickly he put his arms round her and kisses her passionately, taking her by surprise. She responds instinctively, holding him tightly.

'Darling Dossie,' he mutters. 'I wish I didn't have to rush away. I'll text you. Take care.'

He lets her go just as suddenly and, shaken and confused, she climbs into the car, fumbling with the keys, hardly knowing what she is doing. He has already walked away and now stands by the door, watching her. She backs the car out and turns, and pauses to wave to him. Rupert raises his hand in response and she drives quickly away.

Rupert takes the mugs inside and rinses them under the tap, runs upstairs to finish packing his bag and, twenty minutes later, is driving in the opposite direction. He curses under his breath, regretting the missed opportunity with Dossie simply because there is too much evidence in the cottage to support his supposedly single status. He'll remember that, just in case there is a next time, though he generally prefers to play away rather than at home. The real problem is that Dossie isn't the sort to mess around. He suspects that if she finds out that he's married she'll drop him – and he's got rather fond of her. He wonders if he's read her right and whether she might after all be prepared for a little fling: she fancies him, he knows that. He remembers the kiss. She'd been ready for it then, he'd swear to it. Perhaps she doesn't want a permanent relationship and he's being a fool in not seizing the chance. It's a pity that she should turn up just as he's on his way to Bristol: to Kitty.

And what about Kitty? Since meeting Dossie he's been quite enjoying his double life and he doesn't want to spend all his weekends in Bristol with the wretched Sally and Bill always on the doorstep, making up foursomes. And Mummy, tottering on her frame between her little sitting-room and her bedroom, or in her wheelchair, not even able to make it into the garden now. Though actually Mummy's still up for a bit of a laugh, poor old darling: wheezing away, gasping for breath, tears of mirth filling her eyes when he teases her outrageously. The prognosis isn't good. Six months at the most now, the doctor says. She's still very with it mentally, but she suffers from angina attacks, shortness of breath and she gets very dizzy and even faints if she overdoes things. He understands why Kitty feels she must be there, but they argue so much of the time now about whether or not she will ever be able to face returning to the life she once enjoyed.

'You loved Cornwall,' he reminds her. 'We've had such fun. You said you never wanted to live in a city again.'

'I *know* I did,' she cries. 'I know! So OK, things have

changed. Perhaps *I've* changed. It's just that I'm enjoying being back in civilization. I'd forgotten what it's like to be able to go to the theatre or the cinema almost on a whim, or to text a girlfriend and have lunch. I was born and brought up here, remember. It's my home.'

'But not in a flat, even if it is in Sneyd Park looking down the River Avon,' he answers. 'I feel suffocated here. You know I do.'

Her face turns sulky then, and she stops trying to jolly him out of his determination.

'You don't have to go on with this renovating work,' she says. 'We could afford for other people to do it. We've got a big property portfolio now, and poor Mummy will leave me very well off. We'll be able to sit back and enjoy it.'

'I don't want to sit back and enjoy your money,' he shouts. 'I love my work. I love the planning and designing and making an old place beautiful again. I thought you liked it too. You were pretty keen about it at the beginning. You said you loved the independence, the freedom and the wonderful satisfaction when we'd finished a cottage. You said you loved all that. Do you really see us sitting here in this flat with no purpose to our lives? What the hell would I do? Go with you to have coffee with Sally and her boring, horse-mad husband? Take up a tidy little hobby? For God's sake! We're not fifty yet.'

Then she walks out, banging the door, and there will be a period of non-negotiable silence, warming very gradually into monosyllabic interchanges, followed by a hasty reconciliation before he goes back to Cornwall. He's begun to dread these weekends and just lately he's allowed them to become less regular, pleading an excess of work or sudden problems. He's also beginning to see the advantages of having a bit more freedom: perhaps a compromise can be reached after all. He envisages a scene where Kitty is close but not necessarily too close: far enough away to give him a little more scope.

Kitty and Sally are having coffee. Kitty is faintly irritated – Sally has turned up unexpectedly – but she tries not to show it. Sally is quite aware of Kitty's irritation and is quietly enjoying it. She likes to control their friendship – always has; ever since they were two little new girls at Clifton High.

'You can be my new best friend.' Sally has the important air of someone who knows the ropes. Indeed, she has two older siblings at the school – one of whom is a prefect – and Kitty is dazzled by her good fortune. And so it is through all the years of growing up: Sally leads and Kitty follows.

'Like the new haircut,' says Sally now. 'At least . . . is it a tad short? A tiny bit? You have to balance your jaw line. Anyway, it'll grow out. No, no, it looks great. Honestly. So Rupert's on his way. He hasn't made the last couple of weekends, has he? I expect he's hurrying to get the cottage finished. You simply mustn't let him buy another one, lovey. It's madness, him being away like this. You must be so worried, well, not worried exactly, but edgy. Well, he's such a charmer, isn't he? Not that he'd *do* anything, of course, but the mid-forties is a dangerous age, isn't it? Even dear old Bill is beginning to fear time's winged chariot is hurrying a bit too near. Did you see him at the Club last time we were there with poor Claire? Of course, she played up to him. Honestly, I did laugh. I said to her afterwards, "Just ignore him." Still, I'm really sorry to hear that your mum is worse again. You are such a saint. Bill was only saying last night, "Kitty is an absolute saint to put her marriage on hold for her mother. And old Rupert all on his own in Cornwall." Look, I must dash away. I know you've got lots to do and I'm having lunch with Claire. See you soon . . .'

She whirls out on a trail of scent and a flutter of scarves and a clattering of heels. Sally still looks amazingly young: her longish, bobbed, ashy-blonde hair is more ash than blonde but she doesn't care.

'Dyeing the hair is so ageing, don't you think,' she says occasionally, glancing with a little secret smile at Kitty's dark – rather darker, these days – short hair.

Kitty slams the front door behind her and peers in the hall mirror, turning her chin slightly. Is her hair too short for her slightly square jaw? She can see now that it is, and some of her confidence trickles away. Sally's observations have roused other fears. Of course, Sally always fancied Rupert herself; still does. But she's simply not his type: she's much too managing, much too bossy.

'I had a sergeant-major just like her,' he said just after they met – and they'd laughed together, though she'd felt guilty. Guilty, but pleased.

Sally was there when she first met him: they'd been taking a mid-term break together from their university office.

'Dishy,' Sally said, after Rupert had shown them round the cottage and given them a key. 'He fancies you.'

They had a fit of giggling, just as if they were still schoolgirls, but now, as Kitty stares at her hair – it *is* too short – she can still remember the little jolt in the diaphragm when she looked at him that very first time. He told her his future plans for the restoration of old properties over a pint in the pub one evening. His vision and passion thrilled her and she knew quite simply and clearly that she wanted to be with him every minute. And she had been: camping, laughing, working together.

So why not now? It isn't that she doesn't want to be with him; it is simply that she's got used to city life again, and the prospect of going back to remote cottages and painting walls has suddenly lost its appeal. Even the days she's spent down at the cottage haven't reignited any enthusiasm. She prefers it when he comes to Bristol. If she's fair she has to admit that, if she were living with him, the cottage would be much more comfortable but she doesn't want to be fair. Just at the moment it is rather good having a big, roomy flat to live in, with the city on her doorstep. Even with Mummy in her confined state and needing supervision, she manages her moments of freedom.

She's still hoping that without her there, Rupert, too, might be tiring of this peripatetic way of life, and that he'll be pleased to take it easier, but so far he's made it clear – very clear – that such a future does not appeal to him at all. Of course, it's a bit tricky with poor Mummy ill – she can understand that – and Rupert's not the kind of man to function at his best in the sick-room atmosphere. That's why he's not getting back quite so regularly; nothing to do with playing around. Sally has always liked to imply that he's not quite to be trusted – and, to be honest, there have been a couple of moments when she's had to be very watchful – but she's always been able to tell when he's being distracted. He seems to almost shine with contentment, eyes bright, and he's even more up for it than usual.

Kitty turns away from the looking-glass, that firm jaw set pugnaciously. She's not about to give in over this one. No more camping, no more renovations: this is to be the last one. She might just consider a terraced house in Bristol, for students' use, perhaps, which Rupert can oversee perfectly well from this comfortable sunny flat.

Sally's right: it's time to make a stand.

When Rupert arrives Kitty's waiting for him. She studies him closely but can see no signs of anything out of the ordinary: he's cheerful, affectionate and clearly quite happy with his life. Somehow this irritates her.

'You look on good form,' she says: it's almost an accusation. He agrees readily.

'Tired, though,' he adds quickly as though he's given away a point. 'Bushed, actually. I've been working very hard this last couple of weeks.'

'Well,' she can't resist such an opportunity, though instinct warns her against it, 'what have I been saying about slowing down?'

'Oh, come on, love,' he says, half laughing, half impatient, dropping his overnight bag on the floor. 'Let me get in the door before you start.'

Immediately she feels aggrieved and some of her good intentions vanish. 'I'm not starting anything,' she snaps. 'Do you want some lunch?'

'That's usually the form at this time of day,' he murmurs sarcastically – and she suddenly wants to shout at him, to kick his bag in a childish fit of anger, but the cleaner puts her head round the kitchen door and says, 'Can I have a word, Mrs French?' and Kitty quickly rearranges her face and tries to smile. Rupert is greeting the cleaner as if she is some dear old chum, and the cleaner is beaming and bridling, and Kitty is able to grab her temper and calm down.

But the weekend is not off to a good start.

*   *   *

Two days later, Rupert parks the Volvo outside the cottage, climbs out and stands in the afternoon sunshine. He feels quite limp with the relief at being back again. Without taking his bag out of the car, he walks onto the little lawn and looks about him with delight; listening to the water's clear ringing song mingling with the soft insistent murmurings of an unseen dove. He breathes deeply, aware of the thick sweet scent of the honeysuckle that winds its intricate clinging way over the thorny hedge. This, *this* is where he is most at home; most himself. And once Kitty would have felt the same, he tells himself. She professed to love the tranquillity: the slow, inexorable rhythm of the quiet places. He can imagine her here: eating breakfast at the picnic table, still in her pyjamas, watching for the dipper bobbing on his midstream boulder, listening to the robin's cheerful song. Or in the long midsummer evenings: sitting with a glass of wine, waiting for the full moon to rise above the trees' leafy canopy and hearing the owl's shrill scream down in the woods below.

He broached the prospect of buying another property to restore but she prevaricated and he grew impatient. His cheerful mood was disseminated into the chill and brittle atmosphere that he was beginning to know and dread, and which lasted right through Sunday.

Surely she must see that he can't simply give up his work and sit in a flat in Bristol whilst someone else runs his business. Even though he could afford to retire he would feel miserable with no projects and no challenges: surely, knowing him as she does, she can understand this.

Standing in the hot sunshine, he thinks suddenly about Dossie: cooking, planning, dashing about in her little car. She understands how he feels. He needs someone to chat to about the day's work, about suppliers' incompetence and the idiosyncrasies of his clients. Dossie understands and sympathizes about all these things and it is good to share a meal, have a pint together, and simply relax with her. It's a bit tricky that she seems to think that his wife has died. Possibly Chris at Penharrow is unwittingly responsible for that, having heard some rumour and muddled the fact that Kitty went back to Bristol to look after her mother when her father was taken suddenly ill and died. He doesn't know Chris very well, and they've never discussed anything of a personal or private nature. Anyway, it's too late to go into it now with Dossie. He has no intention at the moment of rocking the boat by telling her the truth. He works on the 'need-to-know' basis with women.

As he gets his bag from the car and unlocks the cottage door he is acknowledging to himself that it would be good to see Dossie; really wishing he hadn't been quite so edgy during that last meeting when she'd taken him by surprise. He glances at his watch: twenty past four. He'll send her a text.

He drops his bag in the hall and goes into the kitchen. There are a few things, one of Kitty's scarves and some fashion magazines and a pair of her walking shoes, that he feared Dossie might see – and ask about – when she turned up unexpectedly. Luckily, there was no need for her to go into the cottage but he reminds himself that he'll have to be much more careful. Taking his mobile phone out of his pocket he goes back outside to the picnic table where the signal is strongest and begins to text, wondering where she is.

She is on the beach at Peneglos with Jakey. A few local families are grouped about in the narrow cove whilst seagulls perch on black spiny rocks and watch them with yellow glass eyes. The tide had turned and the sea retreats placidly, sending little white-fringed wavelets across the smooth yellow sand where three children play at the water's edge. Even now, on this hot afternoon in late June, the sea is icy cold and Jakey is happier paddling in one of the sun-warmed rock pools whilst Dossie wanders close at hand, keeping a lookout for pebbles or larger stones that might do for Janna's collection. Jakey's big red plastic bucket stands nearby containing a few selected pebbles and Stripey Bunny, whose long legs hang over the edge of the bucket.

Jakey lies down in the shallow water and splashes and kicks and pretends that he is swimming.

'Look at me,' he shouts. 'Look, I'm nearly swimming, Dossie,' and she laughs and claps her hands and holds up Stripey Bunny so that he can see too.

Jakey comes out all in a rush and a scatter of water, and stands before her; his warm sun-browned skin glitters wetly in the sunlight. He shakes himself like a dog and drops of water fly around him, bright as a rainbow.

'Is it time for the picnic now?' he asks hopefully. 'Stripey Bunny's hungry.'

She picks up the big soft towel and wraps him in it, rubbing him dry and hugging him at the same time, and his narrow blue-brown eyes sparkle as he wriggles and protests and chuckles as she tickles him. She pulls his navy-blue hooded towelling jersey over his head and puts the towel on a rock to dry in the sunshine.

'OK,' she says. 'Let's see what we've got. Honey sand-wiches, I think. And some rice cakes and some grapes. And there's a Fruit Shoot.'

'No chocolate?'

175

She shakes her head: 'This is one of Daddy's healthy picnics,' she says, and puts two small sandwiches on a little paper plate beside him on the rug. Just now, sitting cross-legged, his gilt-blond hair ruffled by the breeze, he is so exactly like Clem was at the same age that she is transported back across the years to the beach at Rock, and she and Clem picnicking in just this same way. Even as a tiny stab of nostalgia and sadness pierces her heart, her mobile makes its little bleeping sound that signifies the arrival of a text.

She opens her bag and lifts it out, heartbeat quickening, eyes narrowing against the bright light as she tilts the phone to read the message.

Back home. All well with bank and mother. Hope u ok.

Dossie takes a deep relieved breath: all is well. He is home and all is well. Ever since she last saw him, some deep-down anxiety has troubled her and she's regretted that sudden impulse that took her down to see him unannounced. A tiny voice tells her that she has every right to take the initiative occasionally but she smothers it with sympathetic considerations for his situation: she must give him space and time to recover from his grief. She doesn't want their relationship to be haunted by ghosts of his former life. Because it is never discussed between them she is free to be herself and to approach him happily without sighs and sad looks for his loss. One day it will be right to speak of it, but not yet.

She hesitates, rereading the message, and then decides not to answer it immediately. It is better to stay cool; not to look too keen.

'Who is it, Dossie?' Jakey has finished his sandwiches and is watching her. 'Is it Daddy?'

She shakes her head, reaching for the wipes and rubbing

the honey from his fingers. 'Just a friend. Tell you what, why don't we build a lovely sandcastle and have some more picnic afterwards? What d'you think?'

Jakey considers and then nods. He scrambles up and goes to fetch his spade whilst she takes Stripey Bunny and the pebbles out of his bucket and puts them together on the rug. As she watches Jakey digging, busy and preoccupied with his task, she remembers that kiss. She smiles inwardly and happiness expands her heart. Suddenly, dispensing with caution, she fishes her mobile out again and taps out a short message. *Glad all is well. Same here.*

She hesitates, wondering whether to add something more encouraging, but decides against it. It's up to Rupert to make the next move. She sends the message, tucks her mobile away and kneels down on the sand to help with the sandcastle.

Waiting patiently, sitting at the little picnic table, Rupert reads the message with relief: all is well. He considers the week ahead and decides to take a chance. He texts quickly: *Meet here coffee on wed? Lunch at pub?*

While he waits for her reply, he scrolls down to the Bristol number. Kitty answers at once.

'Hello? Are you back? How was the journey?'

'It was a good one. No hold-ups.'

He notes that her voice is bright, willing him to be cheerful, and he responds to it readily. It is as if he's come to some kind of decision and it is important now for her to be reassured. She's chattering on, telling him about some plan she's got for the theatre when he comes back again.

'But not this weekend,' he reminds her. 'The plumber's coming in on Saturday morning . . .'

'I know, I know,' she says. 'I remember you told me about

it, but the weekend after that, perhaps? Look, I'll phone and check the ticket situation and let you know. We can have dinner afterwards.'

It is very clear that there has been no change of heart on her part. She isn't missing him that much and is determined to pretend that their only life together is in Bristol.

'Sounds fine,' he says lightly. 'Look, I'd better unpack and get some supper sorted.'

'Take care, then,' she says.

She hesitates, as if she might say something more, and her voice is suddenly slightly anxious but he presses the button quickly and sits quite still for a moment, staring out over the little stream. It is as if some kind of Rubicon has been crossed but he doesn't quite know why or how. He feels elated, excited, free. His mobile beeps and he scrolls quickly to Dossie's answer.

Love to. C u 11-ish Wed.

He sighs with relief and pleasure, puts the mobile in his pocket, and goes into the cottage.

It is very hot. The dogs lay stretched at full length on the cool flagstones in the boot-room; Pa walks them early and late in the cool of the day. In between he watches Wimbledon, where people are passing out with the heat and there is no requirement, *none at all* – he repeats with enormous satisfaction – for the new roof.

'Pa is *such* a Luddite,' Dossie says. 'He hates change.'

'Roofs,' he snorts with contempt. 'The whole point of Wimbledon was that the weather sorted out the men from the boys.'

Mo watches too, but her mind is elsewhere. It is too hot to work at anything. In the little parlour, with the windows wide open, there is no breath of air. The garden lies drenched in heat and there is no birdsong now: no thrush to waken her at dawn. As she watches white-clad figures racing hither and thither over the balding tennis court she broods on the conversation they had with Dossie, remembering her surprise, almost shock, when Pa told her that they want her to have The Court.

'But what about Adam?' she asked. 'What will he have? How does that work?'

'We've thought about it carefully,' he answered, 'and Mo and I aren't particularly happy to think of Adam having this house and simply leaving it to Natasha and those girls.'

'No, no. I can see that,' she said, 'but surely the fair thing to do is to leave it between us.' She looked from one to the other, frowning a little. 'Isn't it?'

'Not necessarily fair,' Mo put in quickly. 'The point is that your work has helped to keep us all going here, especially once the B and B-ers stopped. I know Pa's pension is very important but we wouldn't be managing here without you, Dossie. And we think that you look on it as your home in a way Adam never has. We'd like you to go on being able to do that, if you want to. And Clem and Jakey, too.'

Mo recalls Dossie's expression: she looked shocked and touched and fearful, all at the same time.

'It's true, Doss,' Pa said. 'You've made it possible in many different ways for us to go on here. We all know that.'

'But if you leave it to me, won't Adam contest the will? I mean, it's a big thing, isn't it? He'll be . . . well,' she looked alarmed, clearly imagining Adam's reaction, 'he'll be incandescent. And, to be fair, I wouldn't blame him.'

'It's quite fair.' Pa was stern. 'Adam has never cared about the place. You have. He has no children of his own to inherit it. You have. He has a home of his own with Natasha. You haven't a home other than this one.'

Mo, remembering, saw Dossie struggling with this, thinking out the weaknesses.

'The thing is,' she said at last, 'that I don't know how I'd manage to keep it running all on my own. And I can't guarantee that Clem or Jakey would ever be able to, either. Look, don't think I don't want it – I love this house and it would be very sad to leave it – but I can't promise anything. And then how would Adam feel if I had to sell it anyway?'

She gazed at them anxiously and Mo felt compassion for her, and fear. Pa was ready for that one, though.

'We were thinking, Mo and I, that there might come a time when you'd want to give up all this dashing about the country and settle down a bit. And we wondered, didn't we, Mo, whether you'd consider going back to the B and B-ing.'

Now, recalling Dossie's expression, Mo almost laughs aloud.

'B and B-ing.' Her lips framed the words but she made no sound. After the first shock her eyes held an inward, considering look. Slowly, very slowly, she began to smile.

'Do you know,' she said carefully, 'that's not as mad as it sounds.'

Pa was so relieved and delighted that she didn't simply laugh in his face that he made no protest about the suggestion being mad. Instead, he waited with hopeful, anguished patience whilst Dossie considered it.

'May I think about this?' she asked at last. 'Don't be hurt that I'm not grasping it with both hands, but I'd be the one left facing Adam and I'd want to be confident that I could deal with him.'

'Of course you must think about it,' Mo said quickly, before

Pa could exert any pressure. 'We quite understand that you need notice to consider it from all angles. We just want you to know how we feel.'

'But you'll think about the B and B-ers?' Pa added quickly.

Dossie laughed; she still looked almost shell-shocked, but excited too. 'I promise,' she said, and Mo nudged Pa's foot with her own to warn him to leave well alone.

Now, watching Federer's graceful, athletic performance, Mo wonders what Dossie is up to. She's still made no mention of any new relationship though it is clear that something is going on. Yet she seems to think that her future might be at The Court. Perhaps this new fellow, whoever he is, might move in with them. Mo tries to imagine it, how Pa might react and how it would work, and shakes her head. It is impossible to speculate on such a prospect. Meanwhile they must wait for what Dossie will say. Pa seems content, now he's spoken out, to wait for Dossie's decision – and, anyway, he's absorbed as usual with Wimbledon.

Mo stirs restlessly. She's never been as committed to the tennis as Pa is. Glancing about for her book she sees a leaflet advertising the St Endellion's Summer Festival lying on her small bureau: there will be concerts and music and events to go to in the little collegiate church, and it is time that she booked tickets. She hopes that the swine flu scare – 'bacon fever,' Pa calls it – won't affect it. Reaching for the leaflet and her spectacles, Mo settles down to study it.

Her eyes widen with delight. The festival opens with a wonderful Choral Evensong including music by Mendelssohn and Holst and then, on Sunday morning, a Eucharist sung to Haydn's *Missa Brevis*. There is to be a performance of Britten's *Death in Venice* with James Bowman, a chamber music concert with pieces by Tchaikovsky and Mozart, and the festival ends with a performance of *Twelfth Night* on the rectory lawn.

Mo begins to mark certain events with a pencil. Presently she dozes.

A few days later Clem and Janna sit facing each other across the caravan's little table. They can hear the whisper of soft rain falling beyond the open door where the drenched banties peck disconsolately. A gang of squirrels marauder in the apple trees, and delicate sweet peas flower under the window.

'You've made up your mind then.' she says. 'I can tell. You look really happy.'

And he does. His eyes gleam their narrow smile at her and his lips are pressed tightly together as if he fears that he might smile too much and give away a secret. Jakey looks like this sometimes when he brings her a stone and says, 'Close your eyes and put out your hand . . . *Now* you can look,' and when she opens her eyes he'll be watching her with just this same expression.

Clem nods. 'If we can show that it could work and it goes ahead then I shall stay and train for ordination. I don't have to go away for two years this time, though. I can do a much shorter course while I'm still carrying on working here. Father Pascal and I have been talking it through with Bishop Freddie. He's really excited about it. Well, they both are.'

Janna watches him. She's never seen him so animated, so alive – or so attractive. He wears an old, faded blue cotton shirt with its sleeves rolled up over his brown arms, and his silver-fair hair, damp with rain, is a striking contrast to his deeply tanned face.

'What about you?' he's asking. 'You'll stay too, won't you? The Sisters will need you more than ever.'

She looks away from him, drawing little patterns on the table-top with her fingers, shaking her head evasively.

'I don't know yet. I'd like to know a bit more about it, see. I mean, it's OK now because we're like family. Even the guests are lovely and friendly and I feel I can manage. But this'll be different, won't it? Father Pascal says that it'll have to be more businesslike than we are at the minute.'

'Well, that's true. But we shall have full-time staff to help rather than the way we go on now. I was thinking of you being with the Sisters rather than actually working in the retreat house itself. They'll need continuity when they move into the Coach House; someone to be looking after them. Just like you do at the moment. Wouldn't you be happy doing that?'

'I'm thinking about it,' she says defensively.

It seems that only she and Sister Ruth are not completely in favour of this new plan and she feels almost guilty that she can't enter wholeheartedly into the excitement. She looks out through the door into the damp orchard, fearful and confused. She doesn't want to leave Chi-Meur but nor does she want to be too heavily relied upon. The Sisters seem to believe that she is part of their family now; committed to the future with them.

Clem is watching her, but when she meets his eyes reluctantly she is immediately calmed by the understanding she sees there.

'I wouldn't be able to stay in the caravan,' she blurts out. 'They need the orchard for their private garden. Anyway, they'd like me to be in the Coach House so as to be close at hand as they all get older. 'Tis just . . . I feel happier out here.'

He nods and they sit for a minute in silence. 'The Coach

House is going to be rejigged,' he says tentatively, 'so it's possible that you might still be able to be a bit private. We need to look into that.'

She crosses her arms, as if to defend herself from any persuasion. 'It seems all wrong,' she tells him, 'for me and Sister Ruth to be on the same side. She's never liked me much and I don't get on with her anything like as well as I do with Sister Emily or Mother Magda.'

'She's frightened that they'll all be swallowed up by the new venture. She can't quite believe that their work will be carried forward and expanded and that they'll still have a vital role to play. She's terrified of being sidelined and undervalued. Her insecurity and fear make her aggressive.'

Janna is puzzled. It's never occurred to her that the sharp-tongued Sister Ruth is either insecure or fearful.

'Promise me,' Clem is saying, 'that you won't just disappear, Janna. Even if you feel you don't want to be part of it, promise that you'll say goodbye.'

She stares at the table, unwilling to make such a promise, knowing her deep-down need to be free; shrinking from the prospect of saying goodbye to all these people whom she loves. She swallows and bites her lip, and then nods almost imperceptibly.

'I'd never be able to explain it to Jakey,' he says quietly. 'D'you see how hard it would be for him – let alone all the rest of us – if you just vanished overnight? He loves you, Janna.'

Her lips tremble as if she might cry but she shakes her head, denying it. 'He's got you,' she muttered, 'and Dossie and Pa and Mo . . .'

'That's irrelevant,' he says impatiently. 'Yes, he's got all of us but that's not the point. You are important to him, Janna.

What would I say to him? If you go you must say goodbye to him.'

'I love him, too,' she protests. Tears stand in her eyes and she blinks them away. 'You know I do. And that's one of the problems. He comes here to see me, the dear of him, running through the orchard, calling out to me. And we sit here or outside on the grass, and we have silly picnics and stuff, and we laugh and sing songs.' She leans towards him, across the table, the tears falling down her cheeks. 'And how will that be in the Coach House? How will they cope with that? They won't have it. Specially Sister Ruth won't have it. I can tell you that now.'

Clem is silent and Janna leans back and takes a deep breath.

'Let me think about it,' he says at last, 'and, meanwhile, please promise that you won't do a runner.'

She wipes her cheeks with the backs of her hands. ''Tis time for the bus,' she says. 'Jakey'll be getting wet,' and Clem glances at his watch and gets up quickly with a muttered curse. He gives her one long last look, and hurries away through the orchard. She watches him go, trying to hold back the tears and wondering if it would be possible to lie to Clem.

TRANSFIGURATION

We have come before the throne of God
To share in the inheritance of the saints in light.

Ever since wakening, the Canticle for the Festival of the
Transfiguration of Our Lord has been running through Sister
Emily's head. It seems appropriate now that so many people
are being transfigured with new hope. Clem is happier than
any of them have yet seen him; Father Pascal is brimming
with plans and ideas. Even Mother Magda – now that Bishop
Freddie is so enthusiastic – has cast aside her habitual cloak of
anxiety and is entering into this new climate of expectation
with a positive determination. She has even written to Mr
Brewster explaining why they will not be accepting his
offer. Only Sister Ruth refuses to be swept along on the new
transfiguring tide of excitement; Sister Ruth . . . and Janna.

*We have come before God's holy mountain . . . the city of
the living God . . .*

The words sing in her head as she goes about her tasks of
dusting and polishing. Passing through the rooms lightly,

like a little fragile-boned bird, Sister Emily flourishes her yellow duster and rubs industriously, and ponders on Janna. Father Pascal and Clem are worried about her too.

'Janna's inner angel has been packed about with fear,' she said to Father Pascal. 'Its light shines out – we can see it – but is obscured and fogged by her need to belong and her terror of commitment.'

He smiled at the imagery: 'Odd, isn't it,' he mused, 'to be driven by two such conflicting forces.'

He'd gone on to speak of genetics, of nature and nurture, and she said rather impatiently at the end: 'Yes, yes, but we must *hold on* to her. If she leaves us now it will be disastrous for her.'

He understood her. 'But how can we make her stay? We can't forbid her to go.'

'I know,' Sister Emily answered wretchedly, 'but we can pray that her inner angel might have a chance of being un-packed at last.'

Father Pascal smiled and nodded. 'And what about Sister Ruth's inner angel?' he asked teasingly.

She laughed with him. 'Sister Ruth's angel is not so deeply buried. In all the years since her profession her angel has had many shining moments, some longer than others, before the wrapping goes back on – but at least we know it's a strong and healthy angel.'

He hadn't asked about her own angel – or his – but had gone away, still laughing, waving his hand.

We have come before countless angels making festival . . .

Still singing the canticle Sister Emily whisks onwards, unable to prevent an uprush of joy, even with her fear for Janna so much in her thoughts. After dreary days of rain, of thick soft cloud from the Atlantic rolling over the

187

headlands and lapping at the windows, the sun is shining again.

'I suppose,' she said tentatively to Mother Magda, 'it would be impossible for Janna to remain in her caravan once we move into the Coach House.'

The anxious little frown returned between the feathery brows. 'Is it a problem?' Mother asked. 'Oh, yes, I see. How foolish of me. Yes, dear Janna must be feeling a little bit nervous at the prospect of living with us. And I know that Ruth isn't keen on it either, though she's been used to having a nurse or a carer in our wing when we've had problems with sick and elderly Sisters.'

'Janna is neither a nurse nor a carer officially,' Sister Emily pointed out, 'though she'd make an excellent one. But we've agreed that she is necessary to us and *we* are necessary to *her.*'

'I quite see that,' Mother Magda answered gently, and Sister Emily felt relieved; not that she really doubted Mother's great wisdom and insight, but it was good to be assured that they were all thinking – and praying – along the same lines.

'But,' Mother Magda went on, 'we shall need the orchard for our private use. It is essential that we are able to retain some kind of privacy. You do agree?'

'Yes,' Sister Emily answered reluctantly. 'I do agree, but we need some solution to Janna's fear.'

'We shall pray for it,' Mother answered with that quiet, gentle spiritual certainty that springs from her own inner angel when she allows the veils of anxiety to be drawn back from it.

We have come before God . . . we have come before Jesus . . .

Peace flows into Sister Emily's soul as she finishes dusting the library and opens a window wide to the blustery sunny day. She can see Clem mowing the grass and, beyond him, the flick of scarlet on the path to the beach: Janna escaping to the freedom of the cliffs. Yet this does not make her anxious now. The peace continues to hold her heart in quietude. She closes the door behind her and goes through the hall and along to the kitchen where breakfast has been cleared and lunch is already prepared: a special lunch for the Feast.

Sister Emily smiles in anticipation, puts away the polish and prepares to wash out her duster.

We are receiving a kingdom that cannot be shaken: so let us give thanks . . .

Out on the cliff Janna wanders in the golden blowy air. Below the wall, adders are hatching: writhing gold bootlaces are side-winding away over the sandy grass. The mallows and the thrift have finished flowering but pale pink convolvuli climb amongst the granite stone, and there are bright red poppies growing amongst the rain-drenched barley on the wide headlands. The great gull-spaces of clear blue sky are empty but she can see the flocks wheeling down low over the sea: shining white against the bright green, then black against the brilliant dazzling surf. If she were to lie on the grass with her ear to the ground she would hear the booming echoes of the sea-tide surging and retreating in the secret hollow chambers far below.

Walking quickly, with her face to the west, she tries to grapple with the problem of the future, but she is simply too tired to think clearly. She feels herself being drawn inexorably along on a great tide of change and just at present she has no strength to swim against it. Nevertheless, she has no intention of letting herself be carried away by it. When the moment comes she must harden her heart and fight for her freedom.

A middle-aged couple come striding towards her, dressed in shorts and T-shirts and sunhats, and carrying rucksacks. They greet her cheerfully. 'Glorious, isn't it?' they cry, gesturing to the sun, the sea, the dramatic stretch of coastline, and she nods and answers in return that yes, it is glorious; wonderful. They all beam approvingly at one another and pass on their separate ways. Beside a smooth grey boulder is the man whom she knows now is called Mr Caine and is supposed to be writing a book about the north Cornish coast. He sits staring out to sea, his mobile clamped to his ear, and she slips past him unnoticed.

On the cliff above Trevone she looks down at the children playing on the beach, at their parents tucked behind gaily coloured windbreaks; at the surfers, crouched and swaying on their boards as they skim the long steep rollers that pour in between the headlands. She wonders if she might know any of them, whether they are the same group with whom she cadged a lift from Padstow that day last autumn when she first went to Chi-Meur.

She stands watching them, seeing their cars and vans parked on the beach, with other surfers changing, drying themselves, talking. Suddenly she longs to be down there with them, idle and easy, following the surf – yet she knows that they won't remember her. She always sat too loose to the people she met to make real friends; here one day, gone the next. Even with Nat, whom she loves, she guards her freedom. This is the first time she's had anything like a real home and a family who truly love her: Father, Mother, Sisters: Clem and Jakey . . .

Janna hesitates. She can go down the cliff path to the

beach, chat to the surfers, make friends, cadge another lift, or she can return to her family. Suddenly it seems that she hears Sister Emily's high clear voice in the blowing wind. She is singing the grace that she always chooses when it is her turn, emphasizing certain words in her own inimitable way:

> God bless to us our *bread*
> And give food to those who are *hungry*
> And a hunger for *justice* to those who are *fed*.
> God bless to us our *bread*.

Today is a Feast Day and Sister Emily, as usual, is looking forward to her lunch. Janna draws a deep sighing breath. She hears Clem's voice saying: '. . . please promise you won't do a runner' – and she turns away from the beach and the surfers, and begins to walk home.

'You have got to be joking,' Mr Caine is saying. 'You mean she's actually written to you saying, "Goodbye and thanks for all the fish"? Jesus! His Royal Highness will go ballistic when he hears this. And what's a retreat house, anyway? . . . Bloody hell, Phil, how am I going to tell him? He thought it was in the bag . . . Yeah I know that's what I get paid for. Thanks for that. There's no possible doubt, I suppose? . . . Where are you now? London? Well, lucky you. . . Nah, I'm still stuck in this wilderness. I get away when I can, mind . . . I'd better do a bit of earwigging before I phone him; see what I can find out. It might not be absolutely cut and dried.'

He sees the girl from the convent go whisking past and slips down a bit lower behind the boulder until she's out of sight. He'll go back down to the village and see if he can pick up any odds and ends. The old priest might be in the pub for a lunchtime pint; they've got quite matey now and he might get something out of him. He stares out to sea: he's still got that bad feeling and he wishes he was anywhere but here.

Dossie walks in the lane with the dogs; last outs before bed. She keeps her hand over her mobile phone in her pocket, hoping and waiting for a message from Rupert. Tomorrow he is away again for the weekend, checking out his properties on the south coast, and she is hoping that he might have time for a quick moment on his way. John the Baptist chugs along beside her, pausing briefly to check out a scent here and there, but Wolfie is far ahead on a rabbit's trail and she follows him, her brain busy with ideas.

Ever since Pa's conversation about having B and B-ers again at The Court she's been thinking of little else. Almost at once she could see the advantages: she knows that it might be some time before Rupert can be persuaded to change his way of living but he might, in future, look at properties to convert near at hand so that they can spend more time together. She'll be able to keep her weekends and evenings free, instead of dashing about doing weddings and dinner parties, and one day, way ahead, perhaps he might live with her at The Court.

She pauses in a gateway to give Jonno a breather before the long plod back, and stands looking out across the pale stubble of the new-cut fields. One small star is tangled in a long fleece of cloud and she can see a ghostly illumination running like pale fire along the black edge of the distant horizon. The moon's bright curved rim appears above the long low hills and it seems as if she can feel the movement of the earth as it tilts towards it. Holding her breath, she watches as the moon rises: full and mysterious and magical. The deep silence is broken only by the querulous cry of an old ewe, the settling and stuttering of small birds in the hedges, and two owls calling.

When her mobile vibrates with its double ring, her hand closes on it with shock. She stands for a few moments, still entranced, before taking it from her pocket and reading the message:

Early picnic midday my place?

She smiles with relief and anticipation, sends a reply and puts the mobile away. Calling to Wolfie, patting old Jonno's head, she turns back towards home.

That night Jakey sleeps restlessly. He's spent the day with Pa and Mo, making a little house in the garden which he can have for his own during the summer holidays. It was once a wood store but the logs got damp so Pa keeps them in the barn instead and now the little lean-to shed is almost falling to pieces. He and Pa worked very hard, making it dry and tacking some felt on the sloping roof, and Mo found a little stool and an old card table to make it look like a proper house. John the Baptist was persuaded to come inside and lie down on an old blanket but Wolfie simply wouldn't. He barked and got silly and dashed round in circles on the lawn.

Jakey dreams fitfully: the house has grown much bigger and all his friends have come to tea but Wolfie stays outside barking and barking . . .

He wakes suddenly, surprised at how bright it is and thinking it is morning, and then realizes that it is moon-light streaming into his bedroom. He climbs out of bed, a certainty in his heart, and goes to the window. She is there, as he knew she would be: Auntie Gabriel, standing amongst the trees across the drive. She is looking up at his window with her hands clasped as usual, though he can't see the red satin heart that she holds. He can see her white dress, though, gleaming in the moonbeams that shaft down like tiger-stripes between the smooth boles of the trees.

Jakey raises his hand and waves to her. She doesn't return the wave, she never does because of holding the heart, but he knows that she is smiling at him. He sees that she bows her head a little, in acknowledgement, and he waves again. He wonders whether to go out to her but he knows that Daddy will be cross if he goes outside without telling him. He watches her hopefully, wishing that she would come inside, and then he gives one last wave with both hands to show that he loves her and climbs back into bed, clasps Stripey Bunny, and falls asleep.

Kitty stands at the sitting-room window watching Rupert getting into the Volvo. It is a dull, drizzling day and the trees look weighty with the burden of their leaves. As she waits while he puts his bag in the car she is prey as usual to a whole muddle of emotions: sad that he's going, yet certain that she mustn't allow herself to be coerced. Rupert slams the tailgate and opens the driver's door. He glances up and raises his hand in a last farewell. The car disappears and Kitty moves back into the room, arms crossed, trying to will away her feelings of anxiety and guilt. For the first time in their married lives, a real battle is joined and she knows that she must continue to fight her corner.

She stares up at the large, gilt-framed oil painting that hangs above the fireplace: an atmospheric seascape full of drama, and evoking memories of her gypsy life with Rupert. A bank of thrift on a stony headland bows before the wind that carries the sea birds on its thermals and whips up long curling breakers to crash upon the sandy shore. Just for a moment she can hear their cries above the restless sighing of the sea and her heart contracts with pain, as if she's lost something precious, and then her mobile rings and she runs to answer it, longing for it to be Rupert, knowing it isn't.

'Kitty.' Sally's voice. 'I expect Rupert's just gone and I wondered if you were feeling a bit miz and if you'd like me to pop in. I'm just down in Whiteladies Road.'

'Oh, Sal, I'd love it.' Kitty seizes on this distraction with relief. 'Honestly, it's so weird. Rupert was really sweet this weekend, and now I feel guilty. It sounds crazy but it's almost easier when we argue about it all. No,' she pushes her free hand through her hair, 'no, I don't mean that. Oh hell . . .'

'Hang on. I'll be with you soon.'

Kitty hurries about, tidying, checking on Mummy, who is dozing in her chair in the little sitting-room, making coffee.

'It's a waiting game.' When Sally arrives she is firm. 'You simply can't give in and go back to living like a gypsy. He's got to compromise a bit. He doesn't have to do it all himself, does he? He could still keep his hand in a bit and spend much more time with you here.'

'I don't think he likes the flat much. I think Rupert still feels like a guest, especially with Mummy in the state she is now. It's OK for a weekend but it's not really home.'

'But that's the whole point, lovey, isn't it? You and Rupert never *had* a home.'

'I suppose not.' Kitty heaves an irritated sigh. 'It could be such fun to think that at some future point we could relax and enjoy ourselves but I just wonder if he'll ever be happy doing that.'

'At least he could give it a try,' her friend cries. '*You* were prepared to fall in with *his* way of life, to follow him around and never have a settled place of your own. Well, now it's *his* turn to give *you* a chance, for a change. At least he could try it out before he denounces it.'

Kitty is silent: she feels slightly uneasy when Sally is so forceful. Sometimes she wishes that she hadn't been so open about the ongoing problem between her and Rupert. Sally has never quite believed that her dear old friend could have been quite as happy as she's always claimed in such uncertain and peripatetic circumstances. It is as if, now, those fears have been justified and Sally cannot quite hide her glee.

'He's got to finish the cottage,' Kitty says at last. 'He's talking about buying another one . . .'

'What? Not in Cornwall, I hope?'

'Yes, well, not necessarily.' Kitty stares down at her coffee. 'He needs to be doing something, that's the point. I thought maybe a property here in Bristol, but he was a bit wary about it.'

'Why?' Sally pounces at once. 'Why wary?'

Kitty shrugs. 'How should I know?'

'Look, lovey.' Sally's voice takes on its silky note: the old school chum caring about her best friend. 'There isn't anything going on down there, is there?'

'What d'you mean?'

'Well, you know. Another woman. We all know that Rupert is an absolute pushover for a bit of flattery. He loves women, doesn't he? Plays up to them, flirts. Well, that's nothing new and we all know that he wouldn't actually *do* anything, but Bill was only saying last night that he was surprised that Rupert doesn't get back a bit more. We've hardly seen him in the last few months.'

'It's always a busy time just at the end of getting a place together,' says Kitty. She can hear the defensiveness in her voice and her stomach churns at the mere thought of what Sally is suggesting. Her mind quickly ranges back over the weekend: Rupert was on top form and ready to fall in with anything she suggested. He was sweet with Mummy, really patient, and made no attempt to discuss the future. Kitty mentioned her idea of doing up a house as a student let but he simply said, 'Let's leave it a bit and see what happens.' She thought he meant with Mummy but now she isn't so sure.

'Don't be silly,' she says. 'I'd know at once if Rupert was being unfaithful to me.'

She sees Sally raise her eyebrows and would like to smack her. She feels slightly sick and suddenly frightened but she won't admit it to her dearest, oldest friend.

'Want some more coffee?' she asks brightly.

Rupert drives westward. No hold-ups today: no delays. It's still raining a dank, mizzling rain. He too is thinking about the weekend, confident that it's the right decision to step back and let things develop naturally now: no more persuading and cajoling and arguing, just allowing himself to go with the flow. He is pleased that he managed to maintain a cheerful attitude – and Kitty responded to it with relief, and everyone had a good time instead of engaging in the bitter little arguments and sniping that have been the hallmark of the last few months.

As he drives past Exeter and turns onto the A30 he feels almost elated. Even the dismal sight of Dartmoor shrouded in cloud, or the overgrown faded hedgerows where the leaves are already beginning to turn, hasn't the power to depress him. Maybe, he tells himself, he should be more anxious but, just for now, he simply can't imagine his two worlds colliding: Kitty in Bristol and Dossie in Cornwall. He can simply coast for a while, finish off the cottage, and give Kitty a little longer to get this easy life in Bristol out of her system. After all, she's already grown tired of it once.

He can remember when he met her in that very first cottage he converted and the instant buzz that passed between them. She was bored with her predictable life, with her wealthy parents in their big house in Clifton; with their photographs in *Country Life* and the regular round of social and charity events. She was bored too with her work as a PA at the university and, when he showed her the future they might have together, she simply took wing. Soon, he has no doubt, she'll be as bored again with city life as she was back then.

Perhaps he ought to be feeling a bit guilty about Dossie but – he shakes his head – Dossie has her own agendas: she's thinking of resurrecting her parents' bed and breakfast business and it's clear that she's very excited about it. He's encouraging her, of course. It sounds a very good plan and he's glad to think that her life is taking a slightly different direction; more new challenges and less dashing around in that little Golf. Funny that she and Kitty have identical cars; even the same dark blue.

It's good, talking things through with Dossie, taking time off with her, making love occasionally. She's such fun – and she has so many people to love and cherish; she isn't lonely or needy . . . Rupert frowns a little: he's glad though that he's decided not to buy the cottage near St Endellion. Perhaps some kind of self-protective instinct warned him that it might be just a little too close to The Court for comfort – and, anyway, the owner is still holding out on him. It isn't a problem. He still has his own cottage to finish and there's always plenty of work to be done on his existing properties through the winter months. At the same time the familiar creative urge is stirring. He needs new projects, new challenges.

He decides, as he passes over the River Tamar into Cornwall, that he won't text Dossie just yet. He told her that he was going down to check over his properties on the south coast so he'll have to watch what he says; let a few days elapse, perhaps. He hates lying – of course he does – but just sometimes it's necessary to stretch a point or two to cover his tracks. At the same time he longs to see her. Odd how Dossie has captivated him . . .

When he arrives at the cottage he feels the same sense of relief and release he experiences each time he comes back from Bristol. He gets out of the car, stretches and looks around contentedly. A bedraggled pheasant pecks disconsolately beneath the seed feeders on the little lawn, the stream brims at its banks and the valley is full of the sound of rushing water. Rupert takes a happy breath. He'll light the wood-burner; give the cottage a real warm through. Then he'll wander up to the pub for lunch.

Ever since lunch Dossie has been on edge; wandering around aimlessly, continually checking her mobile, preoccupied. Mo watches her thoughtfully, wishing she could ask Dossie outright about the new man in her life. It is perfectly clear that there *is* someone who is making Dossie exalted or anxious or distracted. Yet still Dossie makes no move to talk about him or introduce him. It's been several months now since she began to behave differently, and the big fear for Mo and Pa is that the man is married.

'Dossie wouldn't do that,' Pa said uncertainly, whilst John the Baptist sat beside him, head on knee, exuding comfort.

'I'm not accusing her of being a home-breaker,' Mo said irritably. 'It might simply be that the man is just coming out of the relationship and there are complications.'

'What kind of complications d'you mean?' he asked, puzzled, and she felt even more irritable and said, 'For goodness' sake use your imagination.'

Mo fetches the secateurs and potters out into the garden. At least, during the weekend, they all had another conversation about restoring The Court to its old status, and Dossie agreed to give it a go. Pa was exultant.

'In which case,' he said privately, while Dossie was out, 'I've made up my mind, Mo, and I hope you'll agree with me. I'm going to gift the house to Dossie outright. If she's prepared to start bed and breakfast again then I'm going to make sure she's secure here.'

Her heart jumped and banged with anxiety. 'What about Adam?' she asked fearfully. 'What will he say?'

'Shan't tell him,' Pa answered. 'No. Wait.' He held up his hand in magisterial mood. 'Look, Mo, this sounds a bit heavy but I can't help that. This house has belonged in my family for generations. My father left it to me and I'm leaving it to Dossie. That's it. End of story. And I'm doing it now in the hope that I shall live another seven years so she'll be free of death duties *and* before we go back into business. It needs to be gifted to her before we take in any revenue and I shall go and see Glyn about it first thing Monday morning.'

She was speechless with shock.

'Adam doesn't need to know,' he said. 'Come to that, nor does Dossie. Luckily old Glyn is her lawyer too, so that makes it nice and simple. Nice surprise when Glyn reads the will.

Obviously it'll mean Dossie could throw us out if she wanted to, but no need to be anxious about that . . .'

Mo shrugged away his remark; she had no fear of Dossie throwing her out of her home – only of Adam's anger.

'But what shall we say to him?' she said. 'He's our son.'

'I've made up my mind,' Pa answered. 'This is not something we can discuss with him in any sensible way, and if Dossie wants to live here and make her living out of this house then I'm going to back her. You never know, Jakey might take it on when the time comes. He loves it here. Adam has never given a single, solitary damn about The Court or about us either, if it comes to that. Oh, I know, I know. He's our son and we love him but I feel strongly about this, Mo, and it's not a subject for negotiation.'

And this morning he went dashing off to Truro, leaving her to watch Dossie working herself up into some kind of state, and still wondering how on earth they could keep this from her or from Adam.

John the Baptist appears beside her, pushing his head against her thigh, and she strokes him gratefully, glad of his company.

'What shall we do, Jonno, old fellow?' she murmurs. 'Whatever shall we do if Adam finds out?'

But he can give no answer to her questions; he can only give the comfort of his presence.

Clem straightens up and stretches his aching back, looking back along the hedge-line to see how much he has accomplished. The grass is still wet after days of rain but it's looking tidier now. He lays the strimmer on the grass and picks up the rake. There is a glimmer of blue in the dappled shadows of the buddleias and Sister Nichola comes

201

slowly forward, leaning heavily on her stick. She is wearing her working habit and two hats: a wide-brimmed straw and a cotton sunhat perched on top of it. Clem glances instinctively around for Sister Ruth, who is usually never far away, but today Sister Nichola is alone. She stands watching him, smiling almost shyly, and he smiles back at her.

'Hello, Sister,' he says. 'It's good to see the sun for a change, isn't it?'

She nods, rather unsteadily, and takes a firmer grasp on her stick. Clem puts down the rake and goes to her and guides her to a nearby bench. She accompanies him quite willingly, peering up at him from beneath the brim of the ancient straw hat, and sits down beside him. There is a little silence; very peaceful, not in the least awkward. Butterflies float and flit over the dark purple spikes of the buddleias, and a squirrel runs across the grass and flees swiftly up a tree. Clem looks down at her, eyebrows raised, wondering if she's seen it.

She nods, as if in answer to his unspoken question. 'Tree rat,' she says clearly.

Clem almost jumps with surprise; then he laughs. 'They do a great deal of damage,' he agrees. He smiles to himself, at his assumption that she'd see the squirrel as a fluffy Nutkin kind of creature. He feels an odd affinity with her and they continue to sit in an amicable silence; she leans heavily against his arm.

'So why do you wear two hats?' he asks, wondering if she might have begun to doze and whether he should escort her back to the house.

'One has a hole in it,' she answers.

'Ah.' He nods.

She looks sideways at him, a searching look that slightly

embarrasses him, and then she reaches out and takes his hand in her own. She turns his hand and studies it whilst he sits quite still, waiting.

'Do you forgive me?' she asks, very low. 'Do you? I couldn't help it, could I?'

Her hand tightens on his, and he presses it in return, though he is suddenly anxious.

'Of course I do,' he hastens to reassure her, looking into her brimming eyes. 'Come, Sister. Let's go and ask Janna to make us some coffee, shall we?'

He stands, bending over her, trying to help her up; and she stares up at him, her eyes still full of tears, trying to obey him and get to her feet.

'*There* you are!'

The cry startles both of them, and they turn together. Sister Ruth comes at a run across the grass; her expression is a mix of relief and irritation.

'I couldn't think where you'd got to,' she says to Sister Nichola, nodding to Clem. 'We were picking beans for lunch,' she explains, 'and suddenly she'd gone.'

She is still breathing hard and Clem senses her very real anxiety. 'We've been sitting in the sun,' he says, smiling at Sister Nichola – who now looks vague but calm – hoping that she's recovered from whatever had upset her. 'All is well.'

Sister Ruth takes the older woman's arm. 'Come on,' she says. 'Let's go back. You've had your little adventure.' She glances again at Clem, giving him a brief, tight-lipped smile and a nod, and they walk away over the grass together.

Clem gives a little shrug and turns back to his strimming and raking. He wonders what has upset Sister Nichola and for what she might need forgiveness – and from whom.

*   *   *

Dossie drives Jakey back to Chi-Meur in the early evening. There is purple loosestrife growing in the long faded grasses beneath the thorn hedges, and some melilot, but it is clear that summer is nearly over. The stubble glimmers beyond the ragged hedgerows, bleached and pale, and a flight of house martins swoop and turn above the fields.

'I'm five now, Dossie,' Jakey says suddenly.

'So you are,' she agrees. 'You're a big boy now.'

'How old is Stripey Bunny?' he asks.

'Well.' She hesitates, wondering how old Jakey would want him to be. 'Is he five, too?'

'No, of course he isn't,' Jakey cries derisively. 'He can't walk yet.'

Dossie makes a face to herself. 'Fine. OK. So how old d'you think, then?'

'He's nearly two,' Jakey answers.

They drive in silence for a while; passing through Crugmeer and out towards the coast, beneath a wide empty infinity of sky that indicates the proximity of the sea. That sky and the sudden gleam of water on the horizon always raises Dossie's spirits; she glances in her mirror. Jakey has put his thumb in his mouth and is staring out of the car window.

How lucky we all are, Dossie thinks, that he is such a good child; that he fits in so well and is so adaptable. Gran'mère and Gran'père have visited from France, spending a week with them all and they've had such fun.

She wonders how they will manage once Chi-Meur has become a retreat house; whether it will make a great deal of difference. Jakey will continue to spend most of his holidays with her and with Pa and Mo and, in between, he will grow used to the changes.

'It won't be very different,' Clem said. 'Some retreat houses are run by young couples with families and the guests enjoy having children around. Of course, there will be certain rules but Jakey's already used to that. We shall stay in the Lodge so we've got the garden for him to run around in and, between us all, we shall make certain that he's looked after. I shall start training this autumn but I shall do most of the course work at home, though I shall have to go away for a few weekends. Father Pascal will still be the chaplain here until after I've been ordained, and we're hoping that I can do my curacy here in the parish but I shall be heavily involved with it all, of course.'

He was so excited that she didn't raise any negatives; Jakey is happy to be at The Court and now, with her new plan for B and B-ing, she will soon be able to be there for him whenever necessary. And she will have more time to spend with Rupert. She thinks about Rupert and is energized and excited by the joy of having him in her life. She slightly wishes that he'd be a bit more ready to talk about the future, but she can wait. There's so much to plan for; so much to enjoy.

'I think that Stripey Bunny should have a birthday party when he's two,' Jakey says unexpectedly.

Dossie smiles. Jakey enjoyed his own birthday party enormously – a boat trip with three small friends, followed by fish and chips in Padstow – and is clearly angling for a replay.

'That's a good idea,' she agrees. 'Where would he like it, d'you think?'

'In Janna's caravan,' he answers, surprising her. 'To cheer her up.'

Dossie frowns, peering at him again in the mirror. 'Why does she need cheering up?'

He shakes his head, puts his thumb back in, and Dossie,

worried now, turns into the narrow lane and drives between feathery tamarisk and trailing blackberry down to the gates to the convent.

'The whole difficulty about loving,' Father Pascal is saying, 'is that it opens us up to the pain of rejection, and the fear of losing someone – or something – we value.'

'I feel I can't win,' Janna says wretchedly. ''Tisn't that I want to be difficult, but I can't see myself in that Coach House with the Sisters. I shall feel like a prisoner. And then I shan't be any use to anyone, however much I love them.'

He watches her, praying silently for guidance, thinking of a very similar conversation with Sister Ruth.

'Janna doesn't know our ways,' she said. 'That's not her fault. Why should she? But to live enclosed with us is very different from the way we manage now.'

'The important thing,' Father Pascal said gently, 'is to try to do what we can to continue to embrace all of you at Chi-Meur. There must be compromises; changes. Janna is a very unusual girl. She doesn't want to give parties nor have friends round. She is by nature solitary; she loves the wild empty silent places. You could say – in fact, Sister Emily *does* say – that she is heaven-sent.'

He saw by the tightening of Sister Ruth's lips that it was unwise to mention this.

'Sister Emily has always been avant-garde,' she murmured. 'It was she who introduced the Taizé courses. I suppose there will be a great deal of that kind of thing with this new retreat house idea.'

'Probably.' He refused to be drawn into this long-held argument. 'The fact is, Sister, that you will need someone with you in the Coach House to care for you all. Why not Janna?'

She was unable to answer without displaying her preju-dices: that Janna was not an educated girl, that she was not even a Christian.

'Janna lives Christ,' Sister Emily said firmly when this charge was levelled against Janna at one of the Chapter meetings. 'She is loving, giving, kind, and she has the great gift of humility. She is not asking to become a postulant; only to serve us.'

Now, looking at Janna's face, Father Pascal is filled with frustration.

'I can see why the caravan wouldn't work for much longer,' she is saying. 'They need someone close at hand in case there's an emergency. They're all so frail, aren't they, and that's not going to get any better? But wouldn't it be better to have someone qualified, like a nurse or something? I mean, what do I know, if anyone is taken ill.'

'The crucial thing is love,' he says, 'and trust. They feel safe with you. We can always call an ambulance or find a carer or a qualified nurse, if that should be necessary. They love you.'

'Sister Ruth doesn't,' she says bluntly, and then suddenly she laughs. 'Sorry, Father,' she says contritely. 'I don't mean to keep coming down here and droning on at you, honestly. It's just I can't see how it's going to work out between her and me. Can you?'

'No,' he answers honestly. 'I can't. The initiative is with God. I shall continue to pray for an answer.'

She looks at him, still smiling. 'It's a big ask.'

He smiles too. 'He's used to that,' he says cheerfully.

Stripey Bunny's birthday party is held a few days before Jakey goes back to school. The wet, dreary August has given way to a warm blowy September; gold and red nasturtiums tumble across the grass at the bottom of the caravan steps, and Janna's silver vase is full of late sweet peas.

Dossie mooted the party to Janna, who responded with enthusiasm.

'Jakey says he thinks you're sad,' she said in her usual direct way. 'Not Sister Ruth getting you down, I hope?'

'Sort of.' Janna shrugged. 'But it's not her fault. It's me, too. I can't quite see myself as part of this new set-up. That's all. Never mind that.' She changed the subject. 'How's it going with Rupert, then . . . ?'

Now, as she puts out plates of tiny salmon sandwiches and sausage rolls on the rug outside the caravan, Dossie is still worrying about Janna.

'Father Pascal's on the case,' Clem said. 'We all are. She's promised me that she won't do a runner.'

The mere thought of Janna doing a runner shocked Dossie and filled her with a kind of dread. By now she knows a little of Janna's dysfunctional past, her fear of commitment battling with her need to belong. As she goes about her own work and begins to prepare to open The Court again to B and B-ers, Dossie has a growing horror of Janna disappearing; of being set adrift again. Even more worrying is Janna's refusal to be drawn on the subject; to be open. Lately she's begun to turn aside all discussions about her own feelings and Dossie fears that she is already moving apart.

She's relieved by Janna's ready agreement to use the caravan as the venue for the birthday party. One thing has not changed: Janna's love for Jakey.

'There, my lover,' she is saying to him. 'I've brought Stripey Bunny a present. D'you want to open it for him?'

Jakey takes the package, surprised into silence. He hasn't

thought of actually giving Stripey Bunny a present. Jan na winks at Dossie above the gilt-blond head, and Dossie smiles at her with love and appreciation. Janna is wearing a T-shirt printed with the words 'Jesus loves you but I'm his favourite'. Sister Emily has said, smiling, that it's probably true. Dossie wonders how any of them will manage now without Janna.

'You'd better wait for the rest of the guests to turn up,' Dossie tells Jakey. 'Look, here come Sister Emily and Father Pascal. Oh, how lovely. Sister Nichola is with them.'

Janna looks round quickly, almost fearfully, but Sister Ruth is not with the little group who are advancing beneath the boughs of the ancient apple trees.

'Apple-picking soon,' cries Sister Emily gleefully, who is passionate about any kind of gleaning. 'What fun. You'll be able to help, Jakey. Sister Nichola has come with us. Is there a chair for her?'

She is helped into one of the deck chairs that Dossie has set around the rug and she sits smiling happily. Jakey goes up close and stares into her eyes. He knows Sister Nichola quite well, though mostly at a distance, but seems struck by something new in her peaceful, sweet old face.

'Did you bring Stripey Bunny a plesent?' he asks her.

She looks at him as if he delights her, but doesn't answer.

'We have brought nothing but ourselves,' says Sister Emily regretfully, and Father Pascal shakes his head sorrowfully.

'But we've made him a lovely tea,' says Dossie quickly. 'Look at his cake.'

The cake indeed is a masterpiece: rabbit-shaped and striped with coloured icing, red, blue, green and yellow. Everyone exclaims with delight; even Sister Nichola stares at it with puzzled pleasure.

Jakey is tearing the paper from Janna's present: a truck to go with his train set.

'I know how much Stripey Bunny likes playing trains,' she says, smiling at Jakey's glowing face. 'You'll have to help him with it, though.'

He places the truck carefully on the rug before Stripey Bunny, who sits with his plate in front of him as well as the Peter Rabbit mug, which he's been allowed as guest of honour. Sandwiches are passed around and Dossie pours tea. A game of I-spy is started which the birthday boy is allowed to win, with Jakey speaking for him. The strong warm wind blows the wrapping paper from the rug and bowls it away between the trees with Jakey in pursuit. Sister Nichola smiles and shivers a little, and Janna gets up from the top step and goes inside. She brings out her precious Indian shawl, pale silk with frayed gold threads, and puts it around the old nun's shoulders. It is faded and thin, but Sister Nichola strokes it softly and draws the long silky fringe through her fingers.

Jakey comes panting back with the wrapping paper. 'Is it time for the cake?' he cries. 'Can we light the candles?'

The two candles are lit, and Jakey helps Stripey Bunny blow them out, and the whole party sings 'Happy Birthday to You'.

It is only much later, when the party is over and Janna is alone again, that she realizes that Sister Nichola has taken the shawl away with her.

Clem finds her at dusk, sitting on the steps, listening to the robin, with the banties pecking round her feet. He sits down in one of the chairs and smiles at her.

'Funny, isn't it?' she says. 'The birds seem to stop singing in July and August and now they've started again. You always think of birds singing in the summer, don't you? I've never noticed it before.'

'I think it's because they moult,' he says. 'They disappear into hedgerows because they can't fly so quickly. And they're not defending territories any more because their babies have flown. Something like that. I hear the party was a great success. Dossie's bathing Jakey so I thought I'd dash down and say thanks. He had a great time.'

'Jakey or Stripey Bunny?'

Clem grins. 'Both of them.'

They sit in a companionable silence for a moment, listening to the robin. Clem reflects on the vulnerability behind Janna's happy-go-lucky façade: her need to be loved, to be part of a family, and the fear that drives her from just such a commitment as soon as it begins to make demands upon her. He is working up his courage to suggest a solution to her fear.

Janna draws up her feet and laces her fingers around her knees. 'Want a cuppa?'

He shakes his head. 'I wanted to show you something, actually, over in the Coach House. There's nobody around and it won't take long. Come on, before I shut the banties up for the night.'

She gets up slowly, reluctantly, and goes with him through the orchard and round to the front door of the Coach House. He leads her along the hall and up the stairs, branching left at the top, away from the main bedrooms, and passing along a short corridor to a room in its own wing at the end. He opens the door and lets her go ahead of him. She goes in slowly, looking around at the large, light room that was once full of lumber. It has a big window looking west across the fields and the village out to sea, and a roof-light facing north. She goes at once to the big window.

'I've never been in here,' she says. ''Twas never used for guests, was it?'

'It's never been needed,' he says, trying to hide his eagerness. 'There's so much space here, isn't there? We thought, Father Pascal and I and the Sisters, whether you might like it as your own room . . . if you were to move in here.'

She stands at the window, staring out, and he can feel her unwillingness to be persuaded or coerced into any immediate decision.

'It's just an idea,' he says quickly. 'It's on its own here at the end, and there's a room below it that's been used as a bed-sitting-room by visiting priests on silent retreats, which you could have as a living-room. It's got a tiny kitchen and a door out into a little courtyard so you could have your own outside entrance and, when the other alterations are being done, we thought that we could put in a spiral staircase from the corner over there directly down to it. That way you'd have doors connecting you to the rest of the house but you could move freely within your own quarters.'

Clem waits whilst she turns and looks around the room and finally at him. He raises his eyebrows hopefully and she smiles rather doubtfully.

'Just think about it, that's all,' he says. 'Now, come and have a look downstairs.'

'Phil?' Mr Caine is on the cliff path, looking down on the beach where a few of the locals are playing football in the dusk. 'Have you heard the latest? . . . Thought you hadn't. Listen. His Serene Bloody Highness is only over the moon, that's all . . . I know, I know. We thought it was all over and then the solicitor boyfriend says that if it's a retreat house then it isn't a convent. And even better, the nuns, so I hear, are moving out of the house and into the Coach House so even more ammunition . . . Yeah, that's why I'm still here, well, some of the time. You never know what crumb you might pick up in the pub or in the shop . . . He's well pleased, I can tell you . . . So you're back in the frame, mate. He wants you to get a letter from the old duck in charge . . . Yeah, yeah, I hear you. I know you've had one already but that was just mooting the possibility of the retreat house. He wants you to write asking her if she's really certain about these plans and if she'd like to reconsider your offer. We're hoping she'll come back with something really positive this time. It might not be necessary in the long run but it might speed things up a bit. See? . . . Get on with it then, and I'll tell him it's all in hand. Might get a bonus for this one, mate.'

He's reached the bottom of the path and suddenly he's surrounded by yelling, shouting boys, who jostle and push him so that he has to duck and dive and fold his arms around his head to protect himself. It seems that they are trying to snatch his mobile and he shouts then, gripping it tightly in his hand, lashing out with the other. And just as suddenly they are gone again, racing across the sand with their ball, screaming harshly like the gulls above them.

'Bloody lunatics,' he shouts, heart pounding, and then glances round quickly to see if he is being watched. His cover is wearing thin, he knows that, but he must keep up appearances a little longer. He walks quickly through the village to where he has left his car, and climbs in and sits still for a minute, regaining his poise before he drives back to the farm.

*   *   *

'I'm sorry, sweetie,' Rupert says, 'but you know how it is, don't you? There's simply nothing I can do about it. I'll definitely be up the following weekend. Look, the plumber's just arrived. I'll phone again this evening. Must dash.'

Kitty slams her mobile down on the table. Sally, who has popped in to bring Mummy some flowers, raises an eyebrow.

'Problems?' she asks sympathetically; hopefully.

'No, not really,' snaps Kitty. She would like to scream with frustration but she won't let Sally see any cracks in her relationship with Rupert. There is something about Sally's watchfulness that is wearing her down, but she can't bring herself to let off steam or to voice her tiny fear that Rupert is less keen to get home these days. She doesn't want to see the flash of triumph in Sally's eyes; to hear the satisfied note in her voice. Sally has always resented the fact that her best friend escaped the round of ordinary married life by disappearing to Cornwall and living an almost gypsy existence with a deeply desirable man and having a really good time, while her contemporaries were juggling with jobs and babies and childcare.

Sally has always predicted that payback time will come for the evasion of such responsibilities, and now she asks, 'So he isn't coming home this weekend?'

'No,' answers Kitty brightly. 'No. Crucial things are happening and the plumber's booked in for Saturday. He'll be up for Mummy's birthday, though.'

'Why don't you pop down to see him?' suggests Sally. 'Take him by surprise.'

Kitty stares at her. 'I can't leave Mummy,' she begins uncertainly.

Sally smiles. 'I can look after your mum,' she says. 'Or you can get that nice carer in. You went before, ages ago, when the weather turned nasty and you got snowed in. And once or twice since, just for the day. This time you could just dash down unexpectedly. Give him a nice surprise.'

They look at each other.

'Go on, lovey,' says Sally softly. 'It might do you both good. After all, he's always on your territory here, isn't he? Much more romantic down there, I should think, in all this wonderful sunshine and no dear old Mummy down the corridor. Why don't you give it a whirl?'

'I might,' says Kitty uncertainly, wondering why her stom-ach clenches with anxiety at the thought. 'I just might do that.'

'Just imagine how he'd feel if you were driving up this minute and getting out of the car and he's working away like mad at whatever and suddenly sees you. Imagine how thrilled he'd be.'

'I'll definitely think about it,' says Kitty. 'Are you staying to lunch?'

'This weather is amazing,' Dossie is saying to Rupert, sitting at the picnic table with the remains of a shared lunch between them: pâté and fresh rolls and cheese. They've just made love and she feels energized and relaxed all at once. 'After all that dreary rain it's so wonderful to feel the sun on my back again. I feel I can manage anything if the sun is shining.'

She is so happy; so full of hope. She's got The Court a listing on the West Country Tourist Board website, and Pa and Mo have sent emails to some of their special old B and B-ers. Already they've had delighted answers back from couples who loved to walk the coastal paths and explore the beaches and the pubs, booking up for the spring and summer. The Court is back in business.

'And what about you?' she asks Rupert, having told him all her good news. 'What will you do when you've finished here? What a shame that you couldn't get your offer accepted on that cottage we saw.'

This is the one little flaw in her happiness: that Rupert won't be nearby working on another cottage. He's frowning a little, pursing his lips regretfully.

'They keep telling us that it's a buyers' market but it's not true,' he says. 'It was way over price but the old devil wasn't giving an inch and I simply couldn't risk it.' He shakes his head, shrugs. 'Something else will come along. It always does.'

'And meanwhile you'll stay here?'

'Through this winter, probably. I shall finish it and then I might let it on a short-hold tenancy next spring. It hasn't been a brilliant summer for holiday letting and I'm thinking that this might be the way to go forward.'

She nods. 'It's probably crazy going back into B and B-ing after a terrible summer like this but we're lucky that we've got a long list of people who will be happy to come back to us. At least, that's the theory.'

'I feel absolutely certain you've made the right decision,' he tells her. He smiles his sexy smile and grips her wrist for a moment and gives it a little encouraging shake. 'I can just see you all. You and Mo and Pa. Sounds magic.'

'You must come and meet them,' she says lightly, heart knocking in her ribs. She's made a little plan to move things along a bit and now she broaches it.

'It's Pa's birthday at the end of the month,' she says. 'We're having a tea party so that Jakey can come, and Sister Emily thought she'd rather like a little outing. There will be some of Pa's friends too, and Clem, I hope. Perhaps you'd like to come along?'

He nods. 'Sounds great.'

She is so relieved she feels quite faint. 'Good. That's good.'

They both turn at the sound of an engine: a van comes slowly down the lane and pulls into the verge. Rupert gets to his feet, a hand raised in greeting.

'Damn. It's the plumber,' he says to Dossie. 'Bloody awful timing. Sorry, love. I'm going to have to get on.'

'It's fine.' She stands up, picking up her bag. 'I ought be on my way. See you soon.'

'Very soon, I hope. I'll text you.'

She wonders if he might kiss her and he does, holding her tightly, though briefly. Then he is away across the little lawn to meet the man who's climbing out of his van. Dossie hesitates and then calls, ''Bye then,' and goes to her car. She drives away with a cheerful little hoot on the horn but Rupert is deep in conversation with the plumber and doesn't seem to hear it.

Sister Emily and Janna are blackberry picking in the meadow below the house. Wasps crawl, heavy and slow, on the ripe fruit, drunk on the sweetness; thorny brambles trail over the grass, catching at the skirts of Sister Emily's blue working habit. As they reach cautiously for the blackberries, stretching up as high as they can, other luscious globes dislodge and fall just beyond their grasp. Each time this happens Sister Emily cries out, vexed at losing even a single delicious berry.

Janna groans in sympathy. 'Why are the best ones always out of reach? Look at those whopping great big ones up there on that bramble. Look, pull him down with your stick; easy now, nearly got them. Ooooh . . .'

And they cry out together in frustration as the black-berries drop into the thicket of thorn hedge. Picking up their big plastic containers, they move a little further along the hedge where clouded indigo-blue sloes ripen in the September sunshine.

'Sloe gin?' Janna suggests. 'What d'you think?'

Sister Emily pauses, her eyes sparkling with the prospect of more gleaning.

'But will you be here to share it with us?' she wonders, and Janna turns quickly away as if she's been stung by a sleepy wasp or pricked by one of the sharp thorns.

'It's going to be so exciting.' Sister Emily drags a particularly clinging bramble from her skirt; the blue cloth is already snagged, threads pulled, from other past excursions. 'Courses, workshops, Ignatian retreats. We're getting feedback from other retreat houses now and there's so much to learn and look forward to. We shall all be very busy. Is it being needed that frightens you?'

Janna is silent, trying to define her own feelings, and then speaks honestly.

'I s'pose it does a bit. But it's more than that. Sister Ruth and I just don't get on and I can't see it working at such close quarters.'

'And have you always got on with the people you've worked with? If so you've been very lucky. Of course, there's no place like a community for generating misunderstandings and quarrels but that's simply a symbol of the general failing of one human person to understand another. Is it really all to do with Sister Ruth? I have seen great changes in you, Janna; a growth of confidence.'

'Have you?' She is pleased – and puzzled. 'I'm not sure *I* feel it.'

'Didn't I see Sister Nichola wearing the shawl your mother gave you?'

'Oh, that.' Janna picks a few more berries. 'Well, I wrapped it round her at that party we had for Stripey Bunny and she sort of went off with it. I haven't had the heart to ask her for it back. She seems to wear it rather a lot.'

They both smile at the incongruity of the faded Indian shawl, with its glittering gold threads, wrapped about Sister Nichola's ample shoulders over her sober habit.

'But once,' hazards Sister Emily, 'I think that you'd have wanted it back, wouldn't you? You cherished it and needed it. It was an important symbol.'

Janna does not answer immediately but continues to pick the fruit. The slanting afternoon sun is hot. Velvet-winged butterflies – meadow browns and tortoiseshells – flit and settle on the fruit, whilst shimmering clouds of midges dance in the still air; above them a pilgrimage of swallows cluster on the telephone wire, discussing routes in high sweet voices.

'She seems to get some sort of comfort from it,' Janna admits unwillingly at last. 'Just now she needs it more than I do, that's all.'

'We all draw comfort from you, with the possible exception of Sister Ruth,' says Sister Emily softly. 'Commitment is hard, isn't it? Commitment to God in a community can mean that *we* might be crucified by proximity or by loneliness, and so it is not to be undertaken lightly. But *you* need make no such undertaking. *You* can still walk away whenever you feel like it.'

'I don't *want* to walk away,' Janna cries. 'I love it here. If only we could have gone on as we were.'

'What is the difference?'

Janna hesitates: what *is* the difference in living in the caravan or in the rooms Clem has shown her? Slowly she fumbles towards the truth.

'When I first came to Chi-Meur you had Penny taking most of the responsibility for the cooking and that. I was happy just doing what was needed round the outside and helping her out, and then, when she was ill, it was like an emergency. You step in, don't you? You cope somehow and then you find you're OK with it. I'm used to that. Turning up for a job, filling in, helping out, moving on. That's what I do. Now,' she takes a breath, '*now* it's got to be deliberate. There's all these new ideas, new plans. And I'm part of it. I've got to take a proper role from the beginning. So, yeah, like it's a total commitment to the future here and I don't want to think that I can walk out on it. That's not what it's about, that I can go if I don't like it. I've got to really want to do it, haven't I? 'Tis like you said just now about being crucified. You chose that. You took a vow. Now, it's like *I've* got to take a vow somewhere inside me and I don't know if it's right or if it's what I want. I just don't *know*!'

She looks suddenly as if she might cry, and Sister Emily puts an arm about her shoulders.

'It's never clear,' she murmurs. 'Sometimes it has to be a leap of faith. And it is never easy or perfect, just the best we can do at the time. But we are vouchsafed people on the journey to sustain and encourage us. We value you and feel that you have a special role here with us so we are reluctant to let you go simply because, just at the moment, you can't see clearly. That's all.'

There is a cry, a shout of greeting, the wild ringing of a bell, and they see Jakey wobbling over the meadow on his bicycle with Stripey Bunny in the basket on the back and Clem striding behind. Janna swipes away the tears from her eyes and waves back.

Sister Emily chuckles. 'Saved by the bell,' she says.

MICHAELMAS

Sister Nichola squeezes through the half-open door and waits for a moment. If she were to sit here, right at the back, just inside the door, nobody will see her. She likes to do this; slipping into the chapel just as Compline begins and watching the Sisters at Night Prayer. The sanctuary light glimmers in its stone niche, and candles have been lit in the terracotta bowl at the feet of the statue of Our Lady.

Mother speaks the familiar opening words: '"The Lord grant us a quiet night and a perfect end."'

There are owls calling and the faint scent of Michaelmas daisies mingles with the traces of incense. Sister Nichola breathes deeply, happily. How pure and sweet is the face of that young novice in her stall beside Our Lady, half hidden in the gathering shadows: how happy she looks and how clear the voices are as they begin to sing the evening hymn together.

'Before the ending of the day, Creator of the world
  we pray,

That you with steadfast love would keep Your watch
around us while we sleep.'

Sister Nichola closes her eyes and her thoughts drift.
Memories shift like smoke: 'I would never make a nun! I'm
far too passionate, too greedy, too intolerant. But I should
like to live in the little stone lodge by the gates at the end of
the drive, working in the big, walled garden and helping in
the kitchen. Simply living on the edge of the community: I
might manage that much and, perhaps, some touch of grace
would rub off on me. I could slip into the chapel, like this;
sitting just inside the door, joining in with the psalm.'

That girl, that young novice, how wise she looks, how
single-minded. How wonderful it must be to be so confident.
She must be sure that she's been chosen. God has touched
her on the shoulder and said, 'You are Mine!' Watching her
and listening to the owls remind Sister Nichola of Con;
darling Con.

'Live at the convent gates if you must, Nicky,' he'd cried. 'I
don't care where it is as long as we are together. I'll work in
the gardens, too. I'll grow the best vegetables the nuns have
ever tasted.'

Sister Nichola smiles, remembering as clearly as if it had
been only yesterday. He would, too: he could do anything,
could Con! He is so strong and cheerful and single-minded
– and so good-looking. Yet there is some barrier between
them: something holding her back.

I love Con, she thinks, confused. Of course I do. Who
wouldn't love Con? He's so exciting – but there's something
I want even more than I want Con and the little lodge at the
end of the drive.

The chapel is the heart of the convent. She loves the big,

busy kitchen with the delicious smell of home-made soup simmering on the range and bread baking in the oven; and she loves the high, cold refectory, too, with its long polished table and a lectern set at every place. The library, with its shelves of books and mullioned windows facing south and west, always seems full of sunshine, but the chapel, simple and clean, with its plain stone altar, is the very heart of the community; drawing her back again and again to listen to the Word in the silence.

It is very strange but the novice in her shadowy stall has disappeared: quite gone.

She thinks: I must slip away now, quickly, quickly, before I am seen. How heavy the door is tonight. I can hardly push it closed behind me, but I must hurry now. Too late! I know this nun who approaches and takes me by the arm.

'It's very naughty of you, Sister Nichola,' Sister Ruth says reproachfully. 'You're supposed to be in bed. You'll catch a chill, just in your nightgown.'

And when she looks down she sees that indeed she is in her nightgown, though she has a soft, silk shawl too. Her hands are mottled with freckles, an old woman's hands, and suddenly she feels shaky and frightened. Where is the young girl who loves Con but not quite enough to marry him; who can't believe that she could become a nun but wants to live in the little lodge at the end of the drive so that she can come into the chapel and sit in the shadowy stall near the statue of Our Lady?

Sister Ruth puts an arm about her, wrapping her warmly in the pretty shawl, and they go out together.

'We feel rather anxious about Sister Nichola,' Mother Magda says.

She stands in Father Pascal's room, looking about rather vaguely as though she is wondering why she is there. He notes the familiar lines of anxiety drawn in the thin face and remembers once again the much younger Sister Magda and how she feared the responsibilities of being Mother Superior. Even now she prefers to be called 'Sister' rather than 'Mother'.

'I don't often see you here,' he says warmly, taking her elbow in his hand and guiding her to an armchair. 'Have you time for some coffee? Or tea?'

She subsides into the chair with a sudden sigh, as if she is abrogating all her worries.

'I should love coffee,' she says gratefully. 'Yes, please. And I am here because I want to speak in complete privacy and confidence without anyone seeing us and jumping to conclusions.'

He goes to make coffee, calling back through the open door to her: 'Sister Ruth?'

'Yes.' She sighs, almost guiltily. 'I am anxious that Sister Nichola is getting too much for her but she simply won't have it. She becomes defensive and angry if the subject is even broached. You heard how Sister Nichola came down to Compline in her nightgown? Well, what can one do? We can't lock her into her room, after all, but it has been decided that it is simply too late for her to be up at night now. After all, she is ninety-two, and not strong.'

Father Pascal comes back into the room whilst the kettle boils. He leans against the doorjamb. 'Now this is an instance where it would be better if you were in the Coach House with Janna. She could keep an eye sometimes, couldn't she?'

'She could,' agrees Mother Magda. 'In fact, she already does. Sister Ruth has her own work and duties, and then the rest of us step in, but she is like a hen with one chick. She feels that nobody is quite as capable as she is.'

'Surely this little escapade has shown her that she must accept that she's not quite managing?'

'She was humiliated.' Mother Magda gives an involuntary snort of amusement, remembering. 'We heard a noise and there was Sister Nichola in her nightie and Janna's shawl, wrestling with the chapel door. Poor Sister Ruth was almost apoplectic.'

Father Pascal makes a pot of coffee and carries it in. 'Perhaps she's aware of the excitement,' he suggests. 'Maybe it's unsettled her. Next year she will be celebrating seventy years of her profession.'

Mother Magda watches him pouring the coffee, smiling a little. 'And all of them here at Chi-Meur. She was born in Peneglos. She told me once how she was in love with a local farmer's son and she wanted to marry him and live at the Lodge, but then she realized that she loved God more than the young man and she broke off the engagement. Apparently he took it very badly and went out to New Zealand. You probably know that? It isn't a secret.'

He nods. 'I know the story. It seems half the local people are related to her and were very hot under the collar at the prospect of her not ending her days here. They're all thrilled that you're staying on. They told me that he used to send her photographs of him with his new love and their children so as to underline what she was missing.'

'And she used to show them to everyone so proudly. She was simply relieved that he was happy. "Yet I loved him so much," she used to say, gazing at his picture. And, in a way, I think she still does.'

'But not enough,' says Father Pascal, passing her a mug.

Mother Magda shakes her head; she sips her coffee appreciatively: real coffee is a luxury in which the Sisters do not indulge.

'So what is to be done?' he murmurs. 'We need a tiny crisis, not too serious, which will enable Sister Ruth to accept Janna's help.'

'That would indeed be a miracle.'

'Surely Sister Nichola's need is greater than Sister Ruth's pride?'

'Oh, yes, but it will take something more than this to help her acknowledge that it is her pride that is causing the barrier.' She watches as Father Pascal pours his own coffee.

'Then we must pray for another miracle.'

She smiles at him and raises her mug as if in some kind of toast or pledge. 'After all,' she says, 'in our line of work it is our job to expect miracles. By the way, I've had another letter from Mr Brewster urging us to reconsider his offer. I think it's quite in order for us to tell him that the retreat house is not just a hope but a very real possibility, don't you?'

'I think it will be quite in order,' Father Pascal says. 'It would have to be some very great disaster to stop us now.'

Sister Emily and Jakey are picking apples. Stripey Bunny is perched in the fork of a low branch, watching them. The higher branches have been shaken from a vantage point a few steps up on the ladder and now Jakey approaches each windfall cautiously, turning it with the toe of his shoe lest a wasp should be lurking. He places each apple carefully into Sister Emily's basket whilst she reaches into the lower branches to pick any remaining ripe apple with a quick, deft twist of the wrist.

Janna, who has done the shaking – 'Not too hard,' cries Sister Emily, 'we don't want bruising' – has retired to make refreshments for the workers and now appears at the caravan door to call them.

'We've done thlee tlees,' says Jakey contentedly as he climbs the steps. 'There are lots and lots of apples. Can we be outside, Janna?'

'Not today, my lover,' she answers. ''Tis too wet after the rain last night.'

'What a gift to have this sunshine.' Sister Emily appears at the door and beams up at them. 'This is a proper St Luke's little summer.'

'Why is it?' asks Jakey, eyeing the picnic with professional approval. 'What is St Luke's little summer?'

'It's when we have unusually warm weather in October. St Luke's special day is next week, you see.' She beams at Janna. 'A lovely Feast Day.'

Janna shakes her head. 'She's a terrible lady for her food,' she says to Jakey.

He scrambles up onto the little moquette-covered bench, not really understanding but simply happy to be with these two people, reaching for a scone.

'Oh!' He puts his hand over his mouth. 'I've forgotten Stripey Bunny. He's still in the tlee.'

'He'll be fine,' Janna says. 'He can watch over the apples while we have our picnic.'

Jakey hesitates, considering, then shakes his head. 'He needs some tea too,' he says, and climbs down, squeezing past Sister Emily and running out into the orchard.

Sister Emily nods approvingly. 'He is faithful to his friends,' she says.

Janna puts milk into the Peter Rabbit mug and stands it

by Jakey's plate. Sister Emily sits down gratefully; she loves apple-picking but it is hard work.

'Clem'll be along in a minute,' Janna says. 'He can do some picking and carry the baskets. It's a really good crop. Obviously your apple trees like nice wet summers.'

Jakey reappears, clutching Stripey Bunny, and wriggles up beside Sister Emily.

'He's been stung by a wasp,' he announces, holding him up for inspection, checking to make sure that they are properly horrified. 'On his poor leg. Look.'

He holds out the long stripey leg, while Janna and Sister Emily cluck and commiserate, and then he seizes the Peter Rabbit mug.

'He needs some tea,' he says, putting the stripey arms around the mug, pretending that Stripey Bunny is holding it himself; but somehow it slips between the knitted paws, bounces on the table and falls to the floor, spilling the milk and cracking the handle from the mug.

There is a horrified silence. Jakey stares from the broken mug and the spilled milk to Janna's startled face, his eyes wide with shock. Sister Emily waits, holding her breath.

'It's bloken,' Jakey says miserably. 'The Peter Labbit mug. I've bloken it.'

There is one brief, silent second before Janna slides out of her seat; her concern is for Jakey: 'You couldn't help it, my lover,' she says gently. ''Twas an accident.'

He looks at her tearfully, his cheeks scarlet. 'It was your best mug,' he says.

She shakes her head, touches his cheek. 'Not any more,' she says. ''Twas once but not now. Not for a while. Let's get that milk cleared up.'

He picks up the mug and the handle, trying to fit them

together. 'Daddy could mend it,' he suggests hopefully. 'He mended my mug when it got bloken.'

'Of course he can,' says Janna cheerfully. 'Mind your feet now while I wipe up. Sit up by Sister Emily, that's a good boy, and have a bit of scone.'

He wriggles back onto the seat, looking at Sister Emily anxiously. 'Stripey Bunny's very sad about it,' he says. 'He didn't mean to do it. He liked the Peter Labbit mug too.'

'We all liked it,' she says soothingly. 'But, in the end, it is only a mug. Janna has many other precious things now. Things that won't break so easily or vanish in the face of reality.'

Janna, crouching by the table, looks up at her questioningly, almost fearfully; Sister Emily looks back at her challengingly. Suddenly, quite unexpectedly, Janna bursts out laughing.

'Don't overdo the sympathy,' she says.

'A much overrated reaction, I always think,' says Sister Emily calmly. 'Rather disabling, especially in large doses.'

And Jakey, feeling relieved by this odd exchange, reaches for a scone and is happy again.

'We were wondering,' Mo is saying, 'whether you and Natasha and the girls would be coming down for Pa's birthday. Dossie's planning a bit of a gathering, just a few friends. I mentioned it a couple of weeks ago, if you remember, and you said that you might manage it. We thought tea, because of Jakey being able to come to it, but we'll have a family supper later, of course, if you—'

'Hang on,' Adam says. 'Just a sec.' He puts down the phone and shouts, 'Turn that music down!' The music ceases suddenly and there is a burst of mocking laughter. He picks up the phone again. 'Sorry. Yes, I remember you mentioning it, and I did talk about it to Tasha, but it's a bit tricky, actually. One of the girls has got something on that weekend. You know how it is. Makes it a bit difficult, but I'm sure Pa will understand. I mean, it's not a big one, is it?'

'How,' asks his mother, 'do you define "a big one"? Anything after one's three score years and ten is a big one, I suppose. Especially if you've had a stroke. Pa will be seventy-three.'

'Well, of course, I didn't mean . . .' He feels irritated. She's just trying to put him in the wrong. 'I was thinking if it was his seventy-fifth, for instance . . .'

'Oh, I see. That's "a big one", is it? Well, perhaps you could pencil in his seventy-fifth so as to be sure you get down for it.'

'Come on, Mo. No need to be like that. It's difficult juggling everybody's needs . . .' His voice heavy with irritation and self-pity, he reminds her that he and Natasha both work full time, and the girls have lives too, and that it is unfair to make him feel guilty . . .

'I do understand,' she breaks in. Suddenly her voice is warm, friendly. 'Of course I do. And it doesn't matter a bit. Goodness, it's only a little birthday party. Now, I must hurry away. Wait, though. Did we tell you that we're starting up the bed and breakfast again in the spring? So much to do and lots of bookings pouring in. It's so exciting. Pa's got a second lease of life but then don't they say that seventy is the new fifty? Well, then . . .'

'Hang on; hang *on*!' He's almost shouting. 'When did all this happen? You haven't said anything to me about this. It sounds like utter bloody madness. How can you possibly cope with all that again?'

'Well, it's Dossie who will be doing most of the coping, and she says that cooking breakfast for six or eight people is a doddle after catering for dinner parties and weddings. She's really excited about it and so are we. It'll be so good to see all the old faces again and so many of them are keen to come back. It's rather touching. Of course, the house is still virtually all set up for it so there's hardly anything to do but take the bookings.'

'I just can't believe this,' he says quietly. 'One minute we're talking downsizing—'

'No, no,' she interrupts him. '*You* were talking downsizing, Adam. *We* never were. This is our home and we love it. Because of Dossie we're able to stay in it and so is she. For as long as she needs to. What's wrong with that?'

'Wait,' he says, as though he is speaking to a fractious child. 'Now just wait. First you imply that Pa is getting old and we ought to be coming down for his birthday because, having had a stroke, he might keel over at any minute, and the next minute you say that you're opening up The Court for business again. Isn't this a bit irrational? Can't you see the strain it'll be on you and Pa? Never mind that Dossie's cooking the breakfasts, just having people there, coming and going all the time, is enough to give anyone another stroke.'

'You don't understand,' Mo says. 'You never have. We love having people here. Pa adores having someone to chat to, to have a drink with; and we've known some of these friends for more than thirty years. It's not a stress for us, especially with Dossie doing the real hard work. It's giving us something to look forward to and to plan for and enjoy. Can you try to understand that, Adam?'

'I think it's a terrible mistake,' he says stubbornly. 'It's like trying to regain your lost youth; it's simply bound to end in disappointment. I know that Natasha will agree with me.'

'Well, that's good,' Mo says affably. 'As long as someone does. Now, I really must go. Sorry we shan't see you at the party but we quite understand. 'Bye, darling.'

She puts the receiver down and he waits for a moment and then slams the phone on the table.

'What is it?' Natasha has come into the room. 'What's going on?'

The girls are close behind her and he wonders if it will ever be possible to have a conversation without these two listening in; watching; giggling in corners.

'You'll be glad to know,' he says vindictively, 'that your behaviour has finally done the trick. Because of your refusal to go to Pa's party you and your children have done me out of my inheritance once and for all.'

'Oh, honestly.' Whatever next? She is getting really, really tired with these silly dramas. 'What's that supposed to mean?'

'It means that because you never ever do anything you don't want to do they've given up on me. They've decided to go back to doing bed and breakfast with Dossie in control, and I suspect that this will be the end of it.'

Natasha frowns incredulously, and then laughs; the girls move closer to stand one each side of her.

'Are you seriously telling me that because we can't go down for your father's birthday he's disinheriting you? You must be joking.'

'No. I'm not joking, and it isn't just that and you know it.'

'You didn't want to go either,' says one of the girls. 'It wasn't just Mum.'

'It's no good trying to blame us,' says the other.

He loses his temper. 'I'm not talking to you,' he shouts. 'For God's sake just clear out, will you?'

The girls move closer to their mother, as if they are afraid of him, and she puts an arm around each of them. She has made her decision, she's known for quite a while that she and Adam don't have a future together, and now he has played into her hands. She and the girls can manage very well without him.

'If there's any clearing out I think you'll be doing it,' says Natasha calmly. 'Maybe you've forgotten that this is my house and these are my children. Since you seem to imagine that we are rotting up the brilliant relationship with your wonderful family then I suggest you clear out now.'

The girls stare at him. Their eyes are bright with malice and triumph as he storms past them, out of the room and up the stairs.

Through the window she can see Wolfie playing on the lawn whilst John the Baptist watches him. She sees that Wolfie has got old Jonno's bone and he is racing round in circles with it, dropping it temptingly, and then seizing it again before Jonno can grab it, and dashing away with it.

Dossie comes in behind her. 'So what did he say?'

'They can't make it.' Mo doesn't turn round. 'He's cross about the B and B-ing.'

'Well, that's hardly a surprise.' Dossie stands beside her. 'What else?'

'Nothing else. He thinks we're crazy trying to regain our lost youth.'

Dossie laughs. 'He simply doesn't get it, does he? But then he never did. I simply don't know where he came from. Weird, isn't it?'

Mo nods. 'Weird, and very sad. We love him; he's our son. And he's a complete stranger. It seems impossible to connect and I can't see what we did wrong.'

'Why do you think you did anything wrong? It's just a genetic cock-up, that's all. There's nothing any of us can do about it. Look, we still speak, we stay in touch and he can come down any time he likes. We simply have to accept that it's all we're going to have.'

'But try to imagine how you would feel if it were Clem. Or even Jakey. That you'd given birth to someone you can't recognize, and who doesn't understand you, and yet you still love him terribly even if you don't like him very much.'

'Sorry.' Dossie puts her arm round Mo's shoulders and gives her a hug. 'I didn't mean to be clever about it. Really I didn't. It would break my heart, of course it would. It's just that he makes me cross and I hate it for you.'

They stand together watching the dogs. John the Baptist has made an attempt to retrieve his bone from Wolfie and the two of them are rolling together, play-fighting, barking with excitement.

'I must go and rescue poor old Jonno,' says Mo. 'That will be doing his arthritis no good at all, though he seems to be enjoying himself. Perhaps he's trying to regain his lost youth, too.'

Dossie watches Mo as she crosses the lawn, shouting to get the dogs' attention. She persuades Wolfie to give up the bone, drops it into a bag and disappears out of view with both dogs at her heels. Dossie continues to stand at the window, staring at the empty lawn, wondering how Rupert will get on with Mo and Pa. She spent ages planning just how to raise the subject with them and in the end she did it rather clumsily, standing up from breakfast and saying: 'Oh, by the way, I thought I'd bring one of my Fill the Freezer clients to your birthday bash, Pa. He's rather nice. Recently widowed. I think you'll both like him.'

They both looked up, Pa from the Sudoku and Ma from a letter she was writing, and stared at her. She knew at once that only rigid discipline was preventing them from nodding at one another and saying: 'I told you so.' There was no surprise; she detected only a certain amount of relief in their reaction.

'Well, good, that's good,' Pa said vaguely, whilst Ma smiled and said: 'We'll look forward to that. What's his name?'

She felt rather foolish, as though she were a teenager again, and mumbled an answer and then said she must go up and check emails. Neither of them has mentioned it since.

Dossie can't decide whether she is pleased that her announcement has been received with such a startling lack of interest or whether she'd rather there were a few animated questions: 'So where did you meet? Where are his holiday cottages?' or, 'So what is he like and how old is he?'

The truth is, she guesses, they've suspected that there is someone in the background – it's a bit naïve to think otherwise – and they are simply relieved that they're going to meet him at last and that he isn't married. She is sure that they would like him – how could they not? – but much more to the point is how he and Clem will get along. She hasn't yet mustered up the courage to tell Clem about Rupert; she can't quite find the words to explain their relationship. And this is a real problem because she doesn't quite know how to define it even to herself. For instance, they aren't an item; neither takes the other for granted or assumes that a date or plan can be made without consultation. There remains a slight formality between them that she's been unable to break down. One of the difficulties is that she has no place of her own where she can invite him for supper or for a barbecue, or any casual date. They have the cottage, of course, but it means it's always his call. At least she's made the big step of inviting him to meet Pa and Mo – and he's perfectly happy about it.

Rupert is on the phone to Kitty.

'. . . And I know you can't get home this weekend,' she is saying, 'but I've got the next one planned round Mummy's birthday on the Sunday. She's really thrilled about it. Of course we all know it's going to be the last one so it's got to be special . . .'

She chatters on but he isn't listening. Leaning forward to look at his diary he's just seen that next Saturday is Pa's birthday and he's promised he'll be at The Court for tea. He's been dreading it, wondering how he'll handle it but now it looks as if he'll have to cry off. He can't cancel a second weekend with Kitty, and though a part of him is deeply grateful for this excuse he has no idea what he will say to Dossie. She still thinks he has a mother in Bristol and he'll use her as the excuse. After all, it's not too far from the truth . . .

Kitty, sensing his distraction, is asking him if he is OK; whether something has turned up.

'Just looking at the diary,' he says. 'I was supposed to pick up some stuff this morning in Bodmin and I'd completely forgotten it. Look, I'd better dash, sweetie. I'll call you later. 'Bye.'

He lays his mobile down and curses below his breath. He can't disappoint Kitty or her mother, but he needs some very good excuse to get out of this one. Dossie is going to be upset. It's getting difficult, trying to keep his two worlds separate, but he's reluctant to give up on either. Dossie has become important to him; she's the perfect companion just now and he sees no reason why this particular boat should be rocked. He'll have to be careful, though, to keep an important date with his 'mother' at the root of his excuse. He's learned that it's always best to have a seed of truth in the middle of a lie. And anyway, dear old Mummy has indeed been like a mother to him since his own died, so it's a kind of truth. He'll have to box clever, though. After all, he'd hardly forget the date of his mother's birthday. No, it needs to be some other kind of celebration; some kind of family event involving his sister, perhaps. He'll think of something – and meanwhile he has to tell Dossie.

Sister Ruth gives the flowers a last twitch and glances round the small West Room. Guests are being asked to bring their own sheets and towels these days, but there are one or two exceptions that include elderly visitors of very long-standing. This is one of those cases and so the bed has been made up and towels hung beside the basin, and the little room looks clean and fresh and inviting.

She's picked the last of the sweet peas and some purple hebe for the green pottery vase that stands on the well-polished table, and is pleased with the effect. It is good to be hospitable, though she can never quite let herself go as Sister Emily does, and Mother Magda, welcoming their guests with hugs and kisses. She was taught to be restrained and self-effacing and she's never been able to be demonstrative. Only very occasionally with Sister Nichola can she relax a little and give her the good-night kiss that the elderly Sister expects and looks for, or to hold her hand sometimes when they sit quietly together. Caresses and overt affection have never come naturally to her as they do, for instance, to Janna with Jakey.

Sister Ruth runs her duster once more over the wooden framed armchair. Of course, her own upbringing was a strict one; children were kept firmly under control. To be fair, Jakey is a good child but in some odd way she feels threatened by him. She fears that if he were to be disobedient or rude she might not have control over him, which frightens her. He is so quick and determined, unhampered as yet by social mores. The others love this childlike spontaneity and find it funny: only *she* finds it threatening. It's always been the same: she needs to feel that she has control over events and people or she is overcome by panic and by fear.

When it was suggested that she should be Sister Nichola's 'carer' she'd been torn between pleasure – and surprise – that she'd been chosen and anxiety lest she should fail. Sometimes it seems that Sister Nichola is the one in control because the elderly nun's calm sweet temper is like a balm on the fretted edges of her own nervousness, gently enabling and smoothing her into her carer's role. She is grateful for it, encouraged by her ability to 'manage' Sister Nichola so successfully, proud of her special status, and the suggestion that this privilege of caring is now to be shared with Janna fills her with dismay and jealousy.

Folding the tartan rug and placing it at the foot of the narrow bed, she is aware of a tensing of the muscles and a twisting of the stomach at the mere thought of Janna. Like Jakey, the girl is an unknown quantity. Neither of them is bound by the natural rules of a good upbringing and a formal education: Jakey because he is too young to have yet acquired them properly and Janna because she's never been exposed to either. And now there is the daunting prospect of all this change: moving to the Coach House, and Chi-Meur becoming a retreat house. Panic flutters her heart and she sits down on the edge of the bed, pressing her hand to her breast. Perhaps it would be best simply to go to the Sisters at Hereford where she trained as a novice all those years ago. Even back then she'd been fearful; keeping herself to herself and suspicious of her fellow novices.

'I expect we'd all prefer to have a relationship with God on our own terms,' the Novice Mistress said to her once. 'He requires us to mix with the oddest and most unsuitable people, doesn't he?'

She stands up and bends to smooth the duvet cover and pick up the duster and polish. With one last glance around the room she goes out onto the landing and down the stairs. There are several guests in the hall and she passes them quietly with a little nod and heads for the kitchen, where Janna is making lunch and looking after Sister Nichola. The old nun smiles with delight as she comes in and holds out a hand in her easy affectionate way and Sister Ruth takes it and holds it for a moment, smiling back at her.

'She misses you,' Janna says warmly, observing the little scene, and Sister Ruth mutters, 'Nonsense,' but she is pleased. Janna is wearing the T-shirt that has 'Jesus loves you but I'm his favourite' printed on it. Sister Ruth finds this almost offensive: we are all equal in the eyes of God. However, when Janna offers her some coffee she fights down all the usual antagonism and says that perhaps she would like just a small cup, thank you.

*   *   *

Later, Janna slips away. She crosses the courtyard to the Coach House where work is in progress to adjust it to the Sisters' requirements. The kitchen needs modernizing, a stair-lift put in, and an interconnecting door to the chapel, as well as the spiral stairway in the end room. The bedrooms, with their small en-suites, are larger than the nuns are used to, a definite improvement. One of the sitting-rooms next to the kitchen will make a very satisfactory refectory and the other a good-sized library and parlour combined. This leaves two smaller rooms and Janna's rooms at the end of the building.

The workmen have gone home and she stands for a moment, simply listening and letting the atmosphere take hold of her. It is a happy place, she decides. The guests who have stayed here have left an impression of friendly goodwill and there is a homely feel. She goes swiftly along the hall and into the room that Clem showed her. To her surprise – and alarm – the spiral staircase has already been installed. She stands at the bottom, her hand on the wrought iron, staring upwards. She feels an uprush of anger; as if Clem has forestalled her by acting so swiftly though she knows that, if she were to leave, whoever has these rooms will need a certain amount of privacy and that the alterations would have been made anyway.

Nevertheless, the changes unsettle her, and she climbs the staircase, almost reluctantly, rising into the bedroom above it, which is bright with the glow of the sunset. She goes straight across to the window, drawn as usual by the great expanses of cliffs and sea and sky, and stares westward. Immediately the peace and the sense of the infinite calms her, and she tries to imagine standing here with the Sisters in the house around her, working, reading, going to and fro to the chapel and to the house for meetings and courses.

The caravan has been her first real home; somewhere that is hers alone and where she can be truly independent. She'd had live-in jobs in pubs and hotels, and dossed on friends' sofas and, for a while, she'd used Nat's cottage as a bolt-hole when things were really tough; but the caravan was her first taste of privacy. It delights her to offer her own particular brand of hospitality and to come and go as she pleases. After having a beer with her friends in Padstow, or popping into the pubs to see old mates, it is good to come back to the isolation and peace of the caravan.

She leans her forehead against the cold glass, wondering why the quietness of such an existence holds no terrors for her; why she isn't worrying about missing out on the life her contemporaries are leading.

'We're alike,' Clem said once. 'Sometimes I get a bit frustrated but I don't miss London or Oxford. I'm very happy here with Jakey and with lots of work to be done, especially now with the new challenge of the retreat house. It sounds as if the drink and drugs scene was never quite your thing any more than it was mine, and we're a bit oddball but very content to be so. And what's wrong with that? We see our friends; we can surf and swim and sail. Why not simply accept that we're where we are supposed to be, if we're content with it? What else would you be doing?'

Janna straightens up: what indeed? She goes down again into the room below, which has a compact kitchen corner and a breakfast bar, a very small wood-burning stove and a French window that opens on to the courtyard. It is charming; hardly any bigger than the caravan but offering her a certain amount of independence. She could still welcome her friends and have Jakey to tea and, after all, where else would she go and what would she do?

She knows that it is the prospect of responsibility that irks and frightens her, and something more: something that presses in, gently but firmly, demanding some kind of commitment that she can't quite understand.

The bell for Vespers is ringing and she has a sudden longing to be there, in her little corner in the chapel, absorbing the deep-down peace and listening to the quiet voices of the Sisters at prayer and worship. She goes out, shutting the door gently behind her, and hurries across the courtyard.

Later again, after Vespers and supper, she is slipping down the drive to the Lodge, opening the door very quietly and calling out 'Hi' to Dossie, who is doing the early baby-sitting shift whilst Clem is at an evening training course.

By now, Jakey has had his bath and is in bed, and Dossie is watching a cookery programme. She stands up and switches it off as Janna comes in and gives her a hug.

'Eight o'clock and all's well,' she says. 'He was fast off when I had a look just now.'

'How are you?' Janna looks at Dossie critically. Her face is strained, her eyes darkly shadowed. 'What's wrong?'

'Nothing,' Dossie answers sharply. She shakes her head, as if Janna doubts her. 'Nothing,' she repeats. 'Why?'

'You don't look right,' Janna says. 'Come on. You can't fool me.'

Dossie takes a breath, looks around as if for guidance, and then shrugs. 'It's Pa's birthday. I'd got it all planned and then Rupert tells me he can't come after all. He said he would be there and I'd told them and everything, and, well . . .' She shrugs.

'No! What? Why not?' Janna cries indignantly – and immediately puts her hand to her lips and glances upwards. 'What's he saying, then?'

She speaks more quietly and Dossie answers in the same way, both of them conscious of Jakey asleep in the room above.

'He said that he hadn't really taken the date on board when we made the arrangement and his mother's planned a family event involving his sisters and their children. He says he simply can't disappoint her and it's been arranged for ages and he simply forgot. His mother isn't terribly well and he feels there's nothing he can do.'

Janna looks sceptical and Dossie makes a face. 'Well, I can see the problem,' she says reluctantly, 'and he was really sorry but . . . oh, I don't know. I'm just really gutted about it and I don't quite know why.'

''Tis a bit more than that, though, isn't it?' Janna asks shrewdly.

Dossie looks so disconsolate that Janna's heart is wrenched. 'Bloody men,' she says. 'He's still holding out on you, isn't he?'

Dossie nods reluctantly. 'He is a bit. I still can't quite get beyond first base. He's sweet and kind and fun, but there's some kind of invisible barrier that I never manage to cross.'

Immediately Janna is reminded of Nat. 'He's not gay, is he?'

Dossie stares at her in surprise. 'No,' she says at once. 'No, he was married, I told you.'

Janna grimaces. 'So? Lots of married men are gay. No children?'

'No, but that doesn't mean anything.'

'Not necessarily, but it's just interesting.'

'Is it? Anyway, I'd be able to tell if he were gay.'

'Would you? Nat's mum never guessed. Most people didn't. We made love, just once, and I wouldn't have known if I hadn't known, if you see what I mean. He would've liked to have been straight if he could've. But he just couldn't cross that barrier.'

'No, no. That side of things is fine, really good, I promise you. It's just he won't commit in any way to a settled relationship. It's like we're stuck and I can't see why. Look, I must be off. You'll be OK?'

''Course I will. No problems.'

Dossie goes out quietly and presently Janna hears the little car pull away. She sits down, heaving a frustrated sigh. She hates to see Dossie looking like that yet she has a horrid suspicion that something is wrong and the sooner Dossie knows what it is, the better it will be for her. She channel-hops for a while and then turns the television off, feeling restless. Clem has lit the fire and she gets up to put on another log from the basket beside the grate.

She glances at the clock: Compline is over and the convent will be in silent mode with the nuns in their rooms, writing or reading or already getting ready for bed. Their day is a long and busy one, and their guests will have retired too, lights shining out from their bedroom windows. Clem's little sitting-room reminds her of Father Pascal's parlour: bookshelves lining the walls, a few paintings, the table beside the sofa overflowing with newspapers, more books – some of them Jakey's – and a few magazines.

Janna sits down again at the end of the sofa and picks up a couple of small books. Presently she is absorbed by Little Grey Rabbit, Squirrel and Hare. The charming Margaret Tempest illustrations fill her with delight: the indigo blue of the night sky with its brilliant stars, Fuzzypeg in his tattered smock with his hedgehog spikes sticking through; the cosy interiors. She's read these stories many times to Jakey but she reads them again, almost able to taste on her tongue the delicious chill of sucking long icicles on a winter morning and experiencing the thrill of horror as the skating party return home to discover the terrible Rat asleep in Squirrel's bed. Jakey especially enjoys that bit: 'And he's eaten up all their picnic supper!' he cries, round-eyed with horrified delight, willing her to be properly shocked. The Alison Uttley stories have not been a part of her childhood and now she loves these books, which once belonged to Dossie, as much as Jakey does.

She has no idea how long she's been absorbed when she hears the patter of footsteps in the room above. She raises her head, listening. Jakey doesn't call out; there is simply silence. She gets to her feet and swiftly climbs the stairs, all her senses alert. Gently she pushes his bedroom door more fully open and peers inside. He's drawn back the curtains and she can see him on tiptoe at the window, outlined in the moonlight, looking out.

'Jakey.' She barely more than whispers his name, frightened of scaring him and wondering if he is sleepwalking. 'Are you all right, my lover?'

He turns towards her quite naturally, fully awake, pleased to see her.

'Has Dossie gone?' he asks.

She nods. 'Shouldn't you be in bed in the warm?'

'It's Auntie Gabriel,' he says, gesturing towards the window. 'She often comes when the moon shines. I knew she'd be here tonight.'

Janna moves quickly to the window, slipping an arm

around him, looking out but keeping in the shadows. She can see the figure, pale and rather bulky amongst the silvery trunks of the trees.

'She never waves because she's holding her heart. See?' He waves but the figure doesn't move, simply an inclination of the head, which reminds Janna of something. Her own heart beats fast and she wonders what she should do: she mustn't frighten Jakey.

'I want her to come in so that I can talk to her and see her ploperly,' he is saying. 'Will you go and ask her to come in, Janna?'

'No, no, my lover,' she says quickly. 'You can't treat angels like ordinary people. 'Twouldn't do at all. She'd simply disappear. She's just come to make sure you're all right and to wish you sweet dreams. Now give her another wave and get back into bed. You'll get cold.'

He waves obediently but rather sadly, and pulls the curtains together. 'I wish she would, though,' he says. 'She'll be cold out there and we could make her some tea.'

She tucks his quilt round him. 'She wouldn't want any tea. Angels are funny like that. Can you go to sleep?'

He nods, pulling Stripey Bunny close, putting his thumb in, whilst she crouches beside him and smooths the pale blond hair. Presently his eyelids droop and his breathing grows slower and more regular. Janna stands up and takes a few steps away from the bed, still watching him. He doesn't stir and very gently she lifts the corner of the curtain: the figure is still there.

Janna goes swiftly downstairs, into the kitchen and out by the back door. She passes noiselessly around the corner of the house, crosses the drive in the shadows by the gate and approaches the figure from the side. Gently she takes

Sister Nichola by the arm, embracing her and murmuring to her, and the old nun looks surprised and pleased to see her, though she still holds her stick firmly between her two hands, leaning on it and gazing at the Lodge.

'Come,' murmurs Janna, glancing anxiously at Jakey's window. 'Come with me, Sister. You know me, don't you? 'Tis Janna. Come on now, but very quiet.'

Sister Nichola seems reluctant to approach the cottage but Janna persuades her, talking gently, helping her along, until she is safely in the kitchen.

'There now,' she says, weak with relief, praying that Jakey won't come downstairs. 'There, Sister. That's better, isn't it? I'm going to make you a cup of tea. How about that? We need one, don't we, after standing about in the cold?'

Sister Nichola draws Janna's shawl more closely around her and smiles vaguely. She seems puzzled but content. Janna makes the tea and they sit at the table, clasping their mugs, with the teapot between them. They are still sitting there together when Clem arrives home.

'Hi, Phil. Hang on, mate.' Mr Caine leaves the bar and goes to stand outside in the darkness. 'Sorry. In the pub. Thanks for getting back to me. The good news is that the dear old Rev Mum has come up with the goodies with that letter. The bad news is that the boyfriend is now bottling out and wondering whether it'll stand up in court, after all. Seems he's taken advice and the fact that the nuns are still there and operating, as it were, means it could be a long-drawn-out expensive business . . . Hang on. Someone coming out . . . Yeah, so that's how it stands. Legally, he reckons he can use the terms of the old will to get them out but it might take time and money . . . I wouldn't want to be in his shoes if he succeeds, mind. He won't be popular round here, I can tell you that. Hello? You're breaking up . . . Lost you. If you can hear me, I'll try again later.'

He puts his mobile in his pocket. Beside the wall a shadow seems to swell and shrink again and he peers into the darkness. He's holding his breath. Is there someone there? He feels oppressed, fearful. Suddenly a car pulls up and there are footsteps and voices out in the road, and he breathes again. Christ, he'll be glad when he's out of this place for good. He goes back into the brightness and warmth of the pub.

'I simply don't know what we can do,' says Sister Ruth despairingly for the third time. 'Several times she's appeared at Compline and we've agreed that we cannot lock her in her room. But to think that she's been going out at night . . .'

She picks up her mug of camomile tea and sets it down again, her expression anguished.

Janna looks at her with compassion, the shock at finding Sister Ruth standing at the bottom of the caravan steps subsiding a little.

'It was good of you,' Sister Ruth says, 'to come to find me last night instead of going to Mother Magda. Not that it should be a secret, of course.'

'Why not?' asks Janna. 'Nobody need know except you and me and Clem. Jakey will continue to think it was Auntie Gabriel, like I told you, and the others don't have to know what happened.'

Sister Ruth is silent. She picks up her mug and sips a little of the tea. She was almost indignant to find Janna knocking softly at her door last evening but, before she could demand a reason, Janna drew her along to Sister Nichola's room and explained privately what had happened. Her relief that nobody else knows is just as great as her horror that the elderly nun has been roaming the grounds at night, and this knowledge makes her feel ashamed. And that it should be Janna who found Sister Nichola simply heaps coals of fire upon her shame.

'The important thing,' Janna is saying now, 'is that we stop her opening that back door. But I see your point about needing to get out if there should be a fire in your wing. If the key is taken out and put somewhere safe it could be a real problem in an emergency. And, anyway, everyone would want to know why. 'Tis a pity she can reach the bolt.'

She is aware of Sister Ruth's dilemma and feels very sorry for her. She remembers the look almost of outrage on her face last night when she opened her door, and the shock that swiftly replaced it. It was a shock for Janna, too, to see Sister Ruth in an ancient plaid dressing gown and her hair free of its veil. Her hair was the biggest shock: thick and dark and curling round the well-shaped head. She looked much younger, more vulnerable without the veil, and Janna for the first time saw her simply as another woman, and a woman who was frightened and at a loss.

She followed Janna quickly, gazing at Sister Nichola, who was now tucked up in bed and deeply asleep, listening to Janna's story in disbelief.

'But how often has Jakey seen her? Anything might have happened to her. She might have fallen or wandered into the lane. Thank goodness the evening was warm and dry.'

'I think 'tis all to do with the full moon.' Janna tried to reassure her. 'Jakey says she comes when the moon shines. It probably wakes her, as it does him, and she gets up and goes down to the Lodge. Wasn't there something about her being engaged to a local boy and they were planning to live there?'

Sister Ruth nodded, her frightened eyes still fixed on the recumbent form. 'It was so long ago but her memory plays tricks.'

'She'll sleep now. I'm sure of it. We'll think about what can be done. Clem won't talk about it and neither will I unless you say so.'

Sister Ruth nodded again, biting her lips, and Janna knew that the nun wouldn't get much sleep but would remain alert to the sound of a door opening and footsteps in the long passage.

Now, looking at her unhappy, weary face, Janna feels another surge of compassion. She can't forget the sight of that same face – vulnerable and younger-looking – with its short cap of dark curling hair.

''Twill be easier in the Coach House,' she suggests gently. 'You'll all be upstairs, for a start, and you could put one of those children's gates across the stairs at night. Everyone knows that she wanders so 'twould simply be a sensible precaution. And if she has a room between yours and mine at least there'd be two of us on watch.'

Sister Ruth looks at her quickly, eyebrows lifted. 'You'll be staying then?'

Janna takes a firmer grip on her mug. 'Sounds like it, doesn't it?' she asks ruefully. 'I don't know what to do, to tell the truth.'

She waits for some negative response but Sister Ruth remains silent. Outside the banties bicker in the warm sunshine and the old orchard is filled with soft golden light.

'I love it here, see,' Janna continues, moved to say more, to reveal something of herself – albeit reluctantly – to the woman who sits opposite at the little table. 'I feel a bit independent. People can come and see me and I don't feel we're disturbing anyone else. I've never lived in a place that's really private like this. It's been quite special.'

Another little silence. Sister Ruth stirs, staring down into the mug.

'But those rooms in the Coach House – your rooms – wouldn't there be privacy there?'

Janna shrugs. 'Sort of. They're really lovely and I'd be lucky to have them but 'tisn't the same. When Jakey comes we sing and play and make a bit of noise and nobody can hear us. 'Twouldn't be quite like that, would it?'

'Perhaps,' Sister Ruth says with an obvious effort, 'perhaps we might like to hear you and Jakey singing.'

Janna laughs. 'Come off it,' she says cheerfully. 'You know we drive you mad. Both of us.'

To her amazement, Sister Ruth raises her eyes and smiles at her. 'I deserved that,' she answers honestly, 'and it's quite true. I am uneasy with children. I don't know how to behave with them, and I have no experience of them. No younger siblings, no nephews and nieces. I was brought up to be seen and not heard. Actually, Jakey is a good little boy and I was very touched when you told me about Auntie Gabriel and how he wanted her to go inside and have some tea to warm her up. It's a wonder that he didn't recognize Sister Nichola.'

'She was standing among the shadows of the trees and he wouldn't be expecting any of the Sisters about at night. And she was always in that cream-coloured dressing gown and a shawl and no veil.'

'And he wasn't afraid?'

Janna shakes her head. 'He expected an angel and that's what he saw.'

251

Sister Ruth smiles again and finishes the last of her tea. 'Perhaps that should be a lesson to us all,' she says.

'A miracle.' Sister Emily is waiting at the vestry door, beaming with delight. 'A miracle has occurred. It seems that Janna has almost definitely decided to stay with us.'

Father Pascal gives a little cry of pleasure. 'Oh, but that's wonderful. Did she tell you so?'

'She told Sister Ruth.'

His expression changes almost ludicrously. 'Sister *Ruth*?'

Sister Emily nods, enjoying the drama. 'That's the real part of the miracle.'

'She told Sister *Ruth*?' He still can't believe it. 'But why? I mean, how did it happen? I believed that they never communicated at that kind of level. There's usually too much antagonism between them to imagine such confidences.'

'Something has happened,' Sister Emily says. 'So far it is only a hint that Sister Ruth dropped by mistake. We shall find out in due course when she is ready to tell us the whole truth.'

He frowns, puzzled. 'What do you mean?'

'I don't quite know,' she answers serenely. 'That will be the final part of the miracle.'

He shakes his head. 'You're talking in riddles today.'

She smiles mischievously. 'Those inner angels are being unpacked; layer by layer they are being revealed.'

She whisks out of the vestry into the chapel and Father Pascal, baffled, begins to prepare himself for the Eucharist.

Pa's party is being a great success. The continuing warm weather allows the tea party to be held in the garden, and he is enjoying himself enormously, surrounded by old friends and by his family. Sister Emily, looking oddly Bohemian in smart narrow navy trousers and a loose cream linen shirt, with a small scarlet cotton handkerchief tied gypsy-fashion over her fine white hair, converses eagerly, totally at ease.

'You look great,' Dossie told her when she arrived, driven by Clem, with an excited Jakey in the back of the car. 'It's so odd to see you in ordinary clothes.'

'Mufti.' Sister Emily regarded her outfit with pleasure. 'I've put that nun away in the cupboard for the afternoon.'

She turned away to greet Pa and Mo, and Dossie found Clem beside her, wearing his usual enigmatic expression.

'She has a niece,' he murmured, his eyes still on Sister Emily, 'who lives in London. It's a wealthy family, you know, and the niece passes on one or two rather smart bits of designer-label gear to her old auntie.'

Dossie grinned. 'She looks smarter than Mo.'

Clem grinned too. 'Wouldn't be difficult. She's never been a dresser-upper, has she, our Mo? So. Are you OK?'

He continued to stare out at the people milling about in the garden, but she was aware of his attention focused on her. She felt moved by his caring, and tears pricked the backs of her eyes.

'Of course I am,' she said. 'Absolutely. Just a bit tired getting all this organized.'

'Mmm.'

He didn't sound convinced, though he still didn't look at her, and she had a childish longing to burst into tears and tell him everything.

'Go and mingle,' she ordered him. 'Be a good grandson. Jakey can hand round. He likes that.'

Clem gave a snort. 'People telling him how good and

clever he is. He revels in it. He's in danger of becoming a spoiled monster.'

She laughed. 'Good luck to him,' she said. 'It'll soon pass. Let him enjoy it while he can.'

He was smiling as he went down to join Pa's friends, and she watched him go, her heart full of love for him, suddenly seeing his father in Clem's tall, long-limbed grace. She bit her lips, the tears coming quickly now, and turned away into the house, hurrying into the kitchen.

Now, she closes the door behind her and stands holding the Aga rail, trying not to weep with the sensations of loss and frustration. It is odd how Rupert's excuses have hurt her. She tries to believe him, to make allowances for the explanation of a former arrangement with his mother, but it has simply brought to the fore the things she's been trying to ignore. Perhaps he's just using her and has no intention of considering any kind of future with her apart from this present friendship.

Dossie picks up a tea cloth, twisting it to and fro, trying to decide what she should do about Rupert. She hears footsteps running across the hall and quickly wipes her eyes with the cloth. Jakey bursts in, eyes gleaming with excitement and importance.

'Mo says we need more tea. More *tea*, Dossie,' he shouts gleefully.

She takes a wavering breath, trying to smile brightly, but he comes closer, his own smile fading a little.

'What's the matter?' he asks anxiously. 'Are you clying, Dossie?'

'No, my darling, of course not,' she says, though his concern makes her want to weep even more. 'No, I just burned my hand a little bit on the Aga and it made my eyes water. Isn't that silly? I'm absolutely fine. Go and tell Mo that more tea is on the way. I'll put the kettle on.'

He hovers, some instinct telling him that she isn't being truthful, but she swiftly picks up a plate of small cakes and turns to him.

'Now,' she says seriously. 'Do you think you could carry these out into the garden without spilling a single one? What d'you think?'

He grows solemn at once, taking the plate carefully and going out with them, his eyes fixed on the plate. Dossie watches the small earnest figure and is obliged to quell another urge to burst into tears.

'Honestly,' she mutters. 'What is the *matter* with you? Get a grip, for God's sake!'

It's a relief that Janna hasn't been able to come to the party; there are rather a lot of guests staying at Chi-Meur for St Luke's Day tomorrow and she is just too busy. Dossie knows that she wouldn't have been able to hold on to her composure under Janna's sharp, compassionate gaze.

John the Baptist comes wagging in, panting with the exertion of being fussed over by so many people and having been given rather too many little treats. He seems almost to be laughing with the fun of it all and she can't help smiling back at him; tugging at his ear and smoothing his head.

Quickly she takes her mobile from her pocket and checks it for messages: nothing. She's sent a couple of texts to Rupert but has had no reply: obviously he is far too busy with his mum. Her heart weighs like lead in her breast and she makes a little face at John the Baptist.

'No go, old chap,' she murmurs.

The kettle is starting to sing and she picks up a big teapot and makes the tea.

Mo watches her come out onto the terrace and put the big teapot on the table. Her heart aches too. She knows that Dossie is unhappy, that her explanation for Rupert's absence has been much too brittle and bright, and her heart is wrung with pain for her daughter.

'Parents are only as happy as their saddest child'– she's read that somewhere recently and has been struck by the truth of it. Her gaze wanders over their guests. Pa is in his element: nothing he loves more than being surrounded by friends and dispensing hospitality. Presently the gin and tonics or wine will be poured, and Dossie's delicious little nibblies will appear, and the party will trundle on into the evening; some of the guests will inevitably be invited to supper. Dossie has planned for that too.

Mo sighs: oh, how she longs for Dossie to be truly happy. And she believes that she *has* been happy with this Rupert, but something has gone wrong. She watches Clem, tall and elegant, laughing with an elderly couple, and is sharply reminded of his father. How often this must happen to Dossie; and how does she cope with this constant reminder of her loss? And there is little Jakey, weaving his way in and out of the chattering groups, pausing to offer cakes and to receive praise and pats on his head, as if he were old Jonno. How does Clem manage to contain the pain of his wife's death whilst bringing up their child?

She drops her hand and feels old Jonno's head beneath it; she strokes him gratefully, accepting his silent comfort. Pa glances around, spies her, and raises his arm in a cheerful gesture that says, 'Come here. Come and join me,' and she steadies herself and makes her way across the grass with the old dog plodding behind her.

Dossie takes a step back from the little group, and then another, and stands alone though ready to smile or nod if required. She looks around at the familiar scene. The sun is still hot and the sweet scent of new-cut grass lingers in the heavy, warm air. Scarlet fuchsia blossoms hang delicate and bell-like on their arched stems and the leaves of the sumac trees burn like fire against the faded blue October sky. Michaelmas daisies, smoky blue and pinky-purple, stand in tall clumps against the grey stone walls.

'Isn't the weather heavenly?' Sister Emily is beside her. 'St Luke's little summer is lasting a long time this year.' Her eyes twinkle at Dossie. 'His Feast Day tomorrow. What fun!'

Despite her heavy heart, Dossie bursts out laughing. 'And don't I know it, what with Janna pestering me for something special for you all to eat.'

'Don't tell me,' says Sister Emily contentedly. 'I do enjoy a surprise.'

'And how will poor Janna manage when the new retreat house opens for business?' asks Dossie, still smiling.

'Our dear Penny is coming back.' Sister Emily rises onto her toes and falls back again, as if she is unable to contain her pleasure. 'She is quite recovered from that debilitating shingles disease and she will be back in the kitchen, and her married daughter is going to help with the other work. We're hoping to involve the village more fully as we progress – to find jobs, that kind of thing.'

'I see.' Dossie watches her affectionately, comforted simply by her presence. Even in her unfamiliar clothes she remains essentially Sister Emily. 'But there must be quite a lot of other things to think about. I know that Clem will be fully involved once he's trained but who actually runs the show and deals with the nuts and bolts?'

'We shall all work together,' Sister Emily answers. 'That is Chi-Meur's way, but we are fortunate to be supported by a wonderful group of oblates and alongsiders. One of our oblates, a widow who lives in Padstow, has offered to be our secretary and administrator. It will be organic, of course, and we shall make mistakes, but we have plenty of helpers to whom we can turn. We are very lucky.'

'Yes,' says Dossie. 'Yes, but you have earned it.'

'And you?' asks Sister Emily.

'Me?' says Dossie. 'How d'you mean?'

'I hear that you are starting a new venture, too. Or, at least, taking up where Mo and Pa left off. That's very exciting.'

'Yes,' she answers rather dully. 'Yes, it is, isn't it?'

Sister Emily watches her for a moment, then touches her lightly on the arm. 'Thank God for work,' she says gently. *'Courage, ma brave.'*

She goes away, smiling first to one group and then another, and then Pa appears at Dossie's shoulder and says: 'I think it might be drinks time, Doss. What d'you say?' and she goes with him into the house.

ALL SAINTS AND ALL SOULS

Janna stands watching the thick golden mist drifting on the invisible surface of the sea, moving inland, obscuring the further headlands and the cliffs. The crying of the sea birds is muffled, indistinct. Yesterday there was a seal pup on the stony beach, far down beneath the steep cliff near Trevone, and she fears that the mother has gone and that the helpless pup will not survive. She sees in her mind's eye the cruel, stabbing beaks of crow and gull, and shivers. There is no point in attempting to see whether the pup is still there. The soft mist is rolling in now, lapping at the cliff's edge, drifting across the fields and enveloping her in its chill clamminess. She turns away and begins to walk back. No picnic today, no sitting in the sunshine; yet she is not depressed as she so often is when the clouds cover the sun. She sees someone on the path but is past before she recognizes him as the man who is researching a book. Through the grapevine she's heard that the locals believe he's behind the man who wants the convent for a hotel and that he isn't writing a book at all. It doesn't matter any more: Chi-Meur is safe.

She walks quickly with her hands in her pockets, trying to come to grips with an odd experience she had in the chapel before Compline last night. This is the time for Silent Prayer, the chapel lit only by candles, and Sister Emily was in her stall in her usual attitude of contemplation. A priest, at Chi-Meur on a few days' retreat, sat on a chair near the altar gazing up at the big carved crucifix. Another guest kneeled in the visitors' pew, head in hands. Janna noted them before slipping into her own corner. Closing her eyes, breathing deeply, she sat simply absorbing the silence, enfolded in the atmosphere of peace. And then, quite suddenly, she had been utterly ravished by a sense of joy. Her heart seemed to flame and burn with it and for a while – nearly ten minutes, she discovered afterwards – she was totally unaware of anything but this overpowering exaltation.

When she opened her eyes, shocked into consciousness by the clicking on of the chapel lights by Mother Magda for Compline, she was dazed, bewildered. She could feel that her mouth was smiling of its own accord and she was still filled with a fading awareness of the joy. Sister Ruth, coming in and seeing her, raised her eyebrows hopefully and Janna gave a little nod and hurried out to keep vigil over Sister Nichola until Compline was over. This is the arrangement just for now.

This morning, as she walks swiftly in the ever-thickening mist, Janna remembers the joy and her heart beats a little quicker; it is as if she is in love. She shakes her head, mocking herself, but still pondering on what has happened.

'What's all this praying about then?' she once asked Sister Emily.

'Prayer unites the soul with God,' she answered. 'That's what Mother Julian tells us.'

Janna didn't know this Mother Julian but she remembered what Sister Emily said, and now she broods on it. She does indeed feel as if she's been united with something or someone; bound in delight and sharing and love. When Mother Magda switched on the chapel lights she'd felt as if she were dropping from space – as if she'd briefly transcended the earth's gravity – and she really understood the phrase 'coming back to earth with a bump'. Maybe she'll speak to Clem about it, or Father Pascal.

She wonders how Sister Ruth is managing at night to keep an eye on Sister Nichola. The elderly nun has forged a link between them, and Sister Ruth is appearing more often in the kitchen with her and leaving her in Janna's care.

It is odd, Janna thinks, how much she enjoys the almost silent companionship of Sister Nichola. Sometimes she might speak but her words are strange to Janna, and she guesses that they are texts or quotations. She thinks about them afterwards and tries to read some meaning into them. She makes her coffee or a cup of tea, which is drunk with great relish. In this way she is like Dossie and Sister Emily: everything is a celebration.

And now it seems that at some deep level she's taken the decision about staying at Chi-Meur and had more or less committed herself with those words to Sister Ruth, of all people. Afterwards she panicked: the old terrors returned. Then, last night in the chapel, she'd known that extraordinary sense of peace and belonging.

The mist is swirling about her now and she keeps close to the thorn hedge that borders the cliff-top fields. How easy it would be to miss her step; to plunge over the edge of the cliff onto the rocks below. It is with relief that she turns onto the path that leads across the field to Chi-Meur.

*   *   *

It's crazy to come up here in this weather, though the sun was shining when he set out. Trouble is, he's getting paranoid: seeing things that aren't there; hearing noises. Still, it's nearly over for him; another twenty-four hours and he'll be out of it. He and Phil will have done their stuff and it'll be up to the legal team. Just one more call, out here where there's nobody about, and he'll be packing his bag. He passes the good-looking bird from the convent and nods a greeting. The mist is creeping in now but he'll be quick. He gets out his mobile, scrolls down, presses the button.

'Listen,' he says, 'just want you to know that the nuns know about that old will . . . Yeah, according to the gossip, I gather they've been told it's OK because they'll still be within the messuage. Something like that. The wording is very important, apparently, but they've obviously got someone who knows his onions . . . No, that's all I know. It's all Chinese whispers round here, but that's the gist . . . Look, I'm outa here first thing tomorrow. Then it's up to you and your solicitor friend. Just hope he's got the balls for it, that's all . . . I've told you what it's like round here. You'll have a fight on your hands with the locals if you win, but that's your problem . . . Yeah, OK. I'll call in later on.'

The mist drifts over the cliff-top and he turns to go back, but suddenly the mist thickens, rolling in thick moisture-heavy clouds so that he can no longer see clearly. He can hear feet on the path below him; footsteps that grow faster, break into a run. They are purposeful, heavy, and strange cries accompany them, echoing and eerie. It sounds like a group of savages hunting a wild animal and suddenly he is filled with an atavistic terror. They are all around him now,

262

corralling him, guiding him, and instinctively he turns and runs, away from the village, into the thickening mist towards Trevone.

'I know that I should have told you at once,' Sister Ruth is saying. 'It was my pride that held me back. I thought that I'd failed in my duty as carer. I can see now that this was wrong and that Sister Nichola's safety is far more important than my pride.'

She looks round at the shocked faces: Father Pascal, Mother Magda, Sister Emily. Sister Nichola is watching her too but with great affection and a warm smile. Sister Ruth takes courage from the smile.

'I simply can't manage to watch all night,' she says rather desperately. 'So I have to ask for your help.'

Mother Magda is the first to speak. 'But it was never part of your duties to have to do so,' she cries. 'How frightening for you it must have been. None of us would ever have imagined that Sister would go out at night. It doesn't bear thinking about.'

'How lucky that Janna saw her,' says Father Pascal.

'Very lucky.' Sister Ruth raises her chin almost defiantly and looks at them all in turn. 'She brought her back to me, as I told you, and between us we've been more watchful. But the nights are too much for me.'

'It will be easier in the Coach House,' Sister Emily says thoughtfully. 'Or . . . will it?'

'Janna has suggested that Sister Nichola occupies a room between hers and mine.' She ignores the surprised reaction, the uplifted brows. 'And that at night we put a gate across the top of the stairs to prevent accidents.'

'That sounds a splendid idea,' Mother Magda says warmly.

'So, does this mean that Janna has decided to stay with us? She hasn't mentioned it to me.'

She glances around enquiringly but Father Pascal and Sister Emily remain silent, with little shakes of their heads, merely looking surprised and pleased. Sister Ruth's cheeks are bright with colour.

'We simply talked of it in passing,' she says quickly, 'when we were trying to think of a solution. I wouldn't want to pre-empt Janna's final decision. The idea of the gate was hers, not mine. Clem used one for Jakey.' Her blush deepens. 'I have no wish to denigrate Sister Nichola by implying that . . .' She hesitates, flustered. 'I know that she is not a child but . . .'

'But it sounds a very practical idea.' Father Pascal helps her out of her confusion. 'We need to make her feel safe and I agree that locking doors is not an option if we can avoid it. And I think you need feel no shame for something that was quite beyond your remit.'

'Indeed not,' agrees Mother Magda. 'This rests with all of us. And I quite see what you mean about removing the key. If there were to be an emergency it could be disastrous. What-ever can we do?'

'Move into the Coach House straightaway,' suggests Father Pascal. 'There's nothing to prevent you now that the kitchen is done and the new door into the chapel is in place. The rest of the work is simply making the orchard secure for you and laying a proper walkway around the house so that you can get into it easily from the back. If you are happy to move in then your quarters here can be made ready for guests.'

They all exchange glances. Sister Ruth, it is clear, is only too ready now to make the move and share the load of her responsibility; Sister Emily has her usual positive enthusi-asm for a new project. Even Mother Magda, less confident and more anxious, recognizes that the moment has come. Yet between the three of them passes a tremor of regret, of sadness, and of a backward glance to other times. Only Sister Nichola remains impassive, her lips curved in a half-smile, as she waits placidly.

Father Pascal watches them: this is not the time for platitudes and reassurances. They are drawn together, these three survivors, in a shared moment that belongs only to themselves. It is Mother Magda who makes the first move.

'This has happened in so many other communities,' she says quietly, 'but for us it is much more than moving to another house. We are beginning a whole new project of our own in which we are deeply involved. We have already supplied the foundation stones and now we must build on them with Christ as our cornerstone. This is the very first step. We should make it wholeheartedly.'

She reaches out and takes Sister Emily's hand, eagerly stretched to her, and Sister Ruth's, who responds with a slight embarrassment. Just for a moment they remain, united, and then she releases them and turns back to Father Pascal.

'We are ready,' she says.

'I'm sure Clem will be at your disposal,' he says, 'and it needn't be done all in a moment. It will take time to decide what you need in your own library, for instance, and the kitchen.'

'And Janna?' asks Sister Emily. 'Will Janna be prepared to move too?'

'She certainly shouldn't be in that caravan for another winter,' Father Pascal answers firmly. 'But whether she is ready fully to commit . . .' He shrugs and looks at Sister Ruth. 'Shall you speak to her? She has implied to you that she will stay. Could you, d'you think, ask her what she intends?'

Sister Ruth looks uncomfortable. 'She *did* speak of staying, but she was anxious about it. And about retaining some kind of privacy but, more importantly, not disturbing us. I tried to reassure her but I was probably clumsy. Janna and I have not always been . . . easy together. I have to tell you that she very kindly agreed to keep Sister Nichola's visits to the Lodge to herself until I was ready to speak to you all. Nevertheless, I think Sister Emily would have a more open and truthful response from her.'

There is a little silence during which Father Pascal carefully refrains from meeting Sister Emily's eye. He almost believes that he can hear the beat of angel's wings, newly released from captivity.

'Would you be prepared,' Mother Magda is asking Sister Emily, 'to approach her for us? It's very sensitive, we all know that, but it seems that perhaps Janna has decided to throw in her lot with us and you have always had a special relationship with her.'

'Of course I will speak to her.' Sister Emily's natural ebullience is slightly subdued. She gives Sister Ruth a little smiling nod of approval. 'Nevertheless, you must have won her confidence since she was so ready to say even that much to you.'

'Shall we say a prayer, then,' suggests Father Pascal, 'asking for the courage and wisdom for these new undertakings? Let us be silent for a moment.'

When Sister Emily arrives at the caravan, however, in the quiet hour after lunch, she receives a shock. Janna is sitting at her little table and in her hands is her old tote bag, which she is turning reflectively; shaking it out and smoothing it. She gets up quickly at Sister Emily's knock, hurrying to let her in. The mist has become a heavy rain and it drums on the caravan roof and drips in rivulets down the windowpanes.

'Come in,' she says, pulling Sister Emily inside. 'Quick. You'll be soaked. Whatever are you doing wandering round in the rain?'

'I'm not wandering,' she protests. 'I'm paying you a visit. Are you planning a holiday?'

Janna smiles and shakes her head. She folds the tote bag and puts it on the floor. 'Just thinking about things,' she says. 'I haven't got much to put in it now. All my treasures are gone.'

Sister Emily sits down at the table. 'I hope not all,' she says. 'Sister Ruth has been telling us an extraordinary story about Sister Nichola going out at night and you finding her and bringing her back. She was very grateful that you haven't spoken of it until she was ready to tell us.'

Janna shrugs. 'It was a shock to both of us. And I knew that she'd feel she'd failed in her duty and needed time to tell you in her own way. It was very scary.'

'She says she's been very anxious ever since and, of course, so are we all now. We have decided that it's time we moved into the Coach House so as to be able to keep a better watch on Sister Nichola. After all, we were going to do it quite soon anyway.'

Janna fills the kettle and turns on the gas. 'Well, that sounds sensible,' she says. 'I couldn't see how Sister Ruth was managing at night. She was really frightened. So was I. But there isn't much I could do about it over here.'

'She said,' says Sister Emily carefully, 'that she'd gained the impression that you might have made up your mind to stay with us. It would be helpful if we knew whether you've made the decision.'

Janna leans against the bulkhead, staring at the kettle. 'It's been odd,' she says reflectively, 'the last week or two. First, that night when Sister Nichola went walkabout and then when Sister Ruth came here to the caravan the next morning to talk things over. I kind of saw her differently. We talked. And I saw, just a bit, that it might work after all. And then, well, just other things have made me feel that I sort of belong here.'

Sister Emily watches her, almost too frightened to speak lest her great joy might put pressure on Janna. 'You know that we all think so too,' she says at last. 'I, for one, firmly believe that you were guided here for a reason. Perhaps many reasons.'

The kettle boils and Janna makes tea – raspberry and black-currant – and spoons in honey. She puts the mugs down on the table and sits opposite Sister Emily. The rain beats down harder, tattooing on the roof, and the wind gusts through the orchard and shakes the caravan's fragile sides.

'Shall you come with us tomorrow, then? Into the Coach House? We shall make an early start. Perhaps do some pack-ing this evening but, like you, we haven't too many treasures to take with us. It will be hard for us to leave Chi-Meur, after all the years we've been there in the house, even though we're only moving across the courtyard. We shall be glad to have you with us on our new adventure, Janna. You have become very dear to us.'

Janna looks at her, biting her lips, tears in her eyes. ''Course I'll come,' she says. ''Course I will. I really finally decided this morning out on the cliff.'

Sister Emily breathes a deep, grateful sigh. Having been at Silent Prayer the night before she has a very good idea why, finally, Janna has made her decision; she saw her exaltation and knows that some great gift has been vouchsafed her. Thankfully she takes up her mug and raises it to Janna in a toast to their future.

Janna smiles back at her and lifts her own mug. 'Good job I got the old tote bag out then,' she says cheerfully. 'I'd better start packing.'

'Tommy. It's me, Phil . . . No, I know. Listen. Really bad news. Jim's dead . . . Listen, just listen. He drowned. Fell off the cliff, well, sort of. Same thing, anyway . . . That's just it. Thick fog, lost his way. That's the dit but I'm not sure. Did he tell you how it was down there? . . . Yeah, he had a really bad vibe about the place, poor old Jim. Look, the thing is, the police were crawling around and I just wondered if they've found his mobile and got the SIM card. See what I'm saying? . . . Quite. That's why I've got a new phone and you didn't recognize the number. I don't want the Old Bill asking me what my connection is with Jim Caine, and neither do you . . . No, I'm right out of it. I just hope there wasn't anything on his laptop. We did everything by mobile. Thank God, we did Pay as You Go! You were right about that . . . Yeah, we'll be in touch when you've changed your phone. Make a note of this number. See you.'

Mummy dies quite suddenly, quite quietly; it is pleurisy that defeats her at the last and quenches the long struggle for life. Rupert comes up for the funeral, all Kitty's friends surround her, but now she is alone again in the flat with Mummy's ashes in a container that looks like a sweet jar.

'Honestly,' she says to Rupert, 'you'd think they could do better than that,' and he hugs her sympathetically and comforts her but he has to go away again, back to Cornwall.

Kitty stands at the sitting-room window staring out at the rain. It's odd to be here alone, without Mummy somewhere in the background. The structure of her day has gone and she feels odd and lonely and sad.

'Of course you do, lovey,' Sally says. 'It's only to be expected. You should think of the future now. But for goodness' sake don't give in and go back to Cornwall. Stand firm, for once in your life.'

Kitty turns away from the window. She is beginning to form a plan, a plan that Sally suggested once before: a visit to the cottage. It might be fun to go down to see how it has come on; to take Rupert by surprise. He's been so sweet since poor Mummy died that she's almost forgotten that she was getting suspicious about his not getting home. He told her that he'd been thinking it best to let out the cottage after all and he's been really working at it to get it absolutely right. She really wants to believe him. In her state of sadness and grieving for Mummy she's coming to the decision that they need to be together, but not in Cornwall. She's definitely made up her mind about that. She can understand if he doesn't want to stay in the flat – he's always found it claustrophobic, and Rupert is a man who needs to feel free – but there are some very nice properties around here or just across the Suspension Bridge in Leigh Woods, and she's still holding on to her idea about buying and renovating houses for student lets. He needs a project, she can see that: he hates to be idle and confined. That's why he was always so sweet with Mummy.

'Poor old Mummy,' he said once. 'If I had to be so restricted I'd top myself.'

Tears overwhelm her at the thought of poor Mummy. She always loved Rupert and he made her laugh with his terrible teasing. Weeping bitterly now, Kitty texts him: *Hope ur ok. Looking fwd 2 w/e xx*. She puts the phone on the table and dries her eyes, wondering where he is.

Rupert is driving through the narrow lanes, cursing the rain, one eye on his watch. It is just his luck that the weather should change so drastically when he's arranged for someone to come and see the cottage with a view to taking it on a long let. Heading down the hill, windscreen wipers slicing the rain away, he tells himself that it is foolish to worry about the weather; this couple have been coming to Cornwall on holiday for many years and they know the score where the weather is concerned. Even so, it is a stroke of luck that they should have phoned to ask for his advice about renting.

'I suppose,' the wife asked jokingly, 'that it would be too much to expect that one of your lovely holiday cottages might be available but we thought you might know of something.'

He explained the location of the cottage at the edge of the moor, and they were rather excited at the prospect, so the meeting was arranged, and now it is pouring with rain and he's been held up and is going to be late if he doesn't step on it a bit. He hears the mobile beep in the glove compartment but decides to ignore it for the moment. He'll check when he gets to the cottage. After all, if Kitty has a serious problem she'll ring rather than text.

And there is another source of anxiety. Ever since he had to chuck Pa's party, he's been trying to make it up to Dossie and she's going to be upset when she knows that he's decided to let the cottage after all and they'll have nowhere at hand to be together. At the same time he knows that if he stays at the cottage then he'll have to commit in some way to Dossie. This is a perfect let-out for him. He'll spin some story about another property not too far away that's too good to miss . . . something like that. The trouble is he's been confused about his feelings for both women, wanting to have his cake and eat it.

And, as for Kitty, well, since Mummy died they've drawn closer again. Poor old Kitty is really devastated and he hasn't the heart to be anything but loving towards her. During the weekend things were better and set them back into a happier relationship again. Not that they got quite so far as discussing the future but much of the tension was gone. Even so, sooner or later, some decisions are going to have to be made. Whistling under his breath he drives down the hill, making a plan. He'll go to Bristol at the weekend and see if he can't persuade Kitty into some new ideas for the future.

He glances at his watch again: he'll just about make it. He swings the car into the low, long, lean-to and scrambles out. As he lets himself into the cottage he glances around, checking that the room is tidy. He hears a car engine approaching, slowing to a halt, and he hurries out to meet his prospective tenants.

'So what's happened to this Rupert fellow, then?' asks Pa.

Mo, perched on a chair with Wolfie on her lap, vigorously drying him with a towel, shakes her head.

'I have no idea,' she says impatiently. 'I've told you a dozen times that I simply don't understand what's happening. When I mentioned him to Dossie she nearly bit my head off.'

John the Baptist stands, his own towel draped over his back, waiting for Pa, who is kicking off his boots. His wet paws make little puddles on the slate floor and he gives a half-hearted shake, which is hampered by the towel. That youthful passion he had for water is rapidly diminishing and his ears droop disconsolately as he waits for his turn for a rubbing. Then he will be allowed into the kitchen, as close to the Aga as he can get, with a consolatory biscuit for staying out of the puddles.

Mo puts Wolfie on the floor, hangs the towel to dry and pulls off her hat.

'Come on, Jonno,' she says. 'Let's get you dry.'

'Leave him,' says Pa. 'I'll do him. God, I hate rain.' He rubs Jonno's undercarriage briskly. 'There was simply no redeeming feature about that walk. The weather was utterly vile. And if it weren't for you,' he adds to John the Baptist, 'I wouldn't have had to be out there in it this morning.'

'And you wouldn't be as fit as you are now,' retorts Mo sharply, opening the door into the kitchen.

Pa breathes in heavily and self-pityingly, and Jonno flattens his ears in sympathy though his attention is focused on the kitchen now, and the sound of the biscuit container being opened. Pa gives him a pat, hangs up the towel and Jonno hurries eagerly into the warm room where Mo has put his biscuit on his rug by the Aga. Wolfie sits in his basket, crunching appreciatively, with one covetous eye on Jonno's biscuit.

'The trouble is,' Pa says, following him in and closing the door, 'we shall never know unless we ask. About Dossie, I mean.'

'I *did* ask,' says Mo. 'I said, "Oh, what a pity Rupert couldn't make it. Why don't you invite him over for lunch? Or tea. Or whatever." And Dossie suddenly went all prickly and muttered something or other, and that was that.'

'Well, I just don't like all this secrecy and silence,' he grumbles. 'It makes for a tricky atmosphere just when we're getting the business up and running again.'

'You know what I think about it.' Mo starts to root about in the fridge. 'I've said all along that my instincts tell me that he's a married man. When Dossie said he was coming to the party I thought that perhaps things were sorted out and he was free. Now I'm doubtful again. Shall we have some soup? Or cheese on toast?'

Pa watches her glumly. He is out of sorts: grumpy and anxious and irritated. He feels that they should all be happy now that the B and B-ing is starting up again and bookings are coming in for next season. And instead there is all this anxiety about Dossie and this tiresome fellow. Poor old Dossie. He wants her to be happy – of course he does – but he knows that this is all wrong and he simply longs to tell her so; to have it out with her. Mo is looking at him, frowning, waiting for his decision about lunch.

'Let's go to the pub,' he says. 'Why not? It'll take our minds off things and the dogs will be quite happy for an hour or two. Come on, Mo.'

She smiles in spite of her own irritation and anxiety. 'Why not? Wait while I get my bag. Have you got the car keys?'

They go out together, shutting the kitchen door. John the Baptist lies down, head still raised, ears cocked. He listens to the sound of Mo coming back downstairs and the car engine starting up while Wolfie nips out of his basket and does a quick hoover round for crumbs, and then settles down close beside him. The front door closes, a car door slams, and the sound of the engine fades away down the lane. At last he puts his head down on his paws and sleeps.

Janna's rooms do not yet reflect the full impact of her personality but there are promising signs: pots of pink and purple cyclamen are ranged in brightly patterned saucers on the breakfast bar and a large piece of soft, plum-coloured velvet is thrown casually over the comfortable old chair beside the little wood-burner. The silver vase that Clem and Jakey gave her stands on a drop-leaf table folded back against the wall. She's put a spray of berries in the vase and its reflection gleams in the sheen of the smooth rosewood.

'That's a very pretty table,' Dossie says appreciatively. 'Was that here already?'

Janna shakes her head mischievously. 'I nicked it from over in the house,' she admits. 'Mother Magda said to take what I needed and I wanted a table we could all sit round. You know, like when we have our picnics. There was just a little round table and the breakfast bar, so I went and had a forage. I couldn't have anything too big in here and this is just perfect 'cos I can drop the leaves down when I'm on my own. It *is* pretty, isn't it? Clem helped me bring it over. We took the round table back to replace it. Chairs are a problem, though. There are these two,' she indicates the two cane-seated chairs at either end of the table, 'and there's another up in my bedroom I can bring down, but if there were lots of us I'd be a bit stuffed.'

'We'll find some folding ones,' Dossie says, 'and keep them somewhere handy. Don't worry, we'll manage somehow. So how are you feeling now? About moving and being here.'

'Yeah, OK.' Janna stares round her new quarters. Once the decision has been taken and the move got under way she's begun to enjoy herself; she is surprised that she's already feeling at home. 'There wasn't much to move, and Clem's been great. And Jakey approves of it too. He wasn't sure he was going to like it as much as the caravan but he thinks 'tis fun, perching up at the breakfast bar, and he loves the spiral staircase.'

'And you don't feel too hemmed in after all?'

'Not as much as I thought. I think 'tis because these two rooms are in this little wing on the end and I can look right out. Especially from upstairs. The view's amazing. Go up and have a look.'

While Dossie makes her way up the winding wrought-iron staircase Janna slips behind the breakfast bar and switches on the kettle. It is good to have Dossie here; each visitor makes it feel more like home. Sister Emily has already popped in for a coffee break and so has Father Pascal. Clem and Jakey have come for tea so that Jakey can show Stripey Bunny the funny staircase and let him sit on one of the tall stools with his stripey arms propped up on the little counter.

'It's like being in a café,' he said delightedly, 'and you're our waitless, Janna. We'd like two cups of tea, please, and some cakes.'

She pretended to be a waitress and served him and Stripey Bunny, and then gave them a bill on the back of an old receipt. Clem paid and she put the money in a little pottery bowl to give to the Air Ambulance.

Dossie reappears, coming down carefully. 'What a view!' she exclaims. 'You can see right across the cliffs. It's utter heaven, Janna.' She hitches herself up onto one of the stools. 'But wasn't it awful about that man falling down the blow-hole in the mist and you having to say that you'd seen him up on the cliff path only just before?'

Janna pushes the mugs across the counter and comes round to sit beside her. 'It was awful. The coroner was really nice, though. Accidental death. Lost his way in the fog. He's been around for months, on and off, researching a book, he said, though Penny never believed it. She said he was all tied up with making the convent into a hotel. Anyway, he must've just completely lost his bearings.' She shudders. 'Imagine how terrible it must've been. Stepping into space and crashing down and down, smashing against the rocks. Tide was coming in too. He didn't have a chance.'

They sit for a moment in silence, thinking about it.

'Anyway,' Janna says, 'how about you? How's it working out with you and Rupert?'

Dossie shrugs, nods. 'OK, actually. He's had to rent out the cottage which is a bit of a bore, but he's thinking of buying one not that far away, so it should be OK. But he's still playing a bit difficult to get. When I talk about his meeting Pa and Mo he hedges a bit. I just wish I had the nerve to ask straight out where he thinks we're going but I can't quite summon up the courage. He's still running it all, if you see what I mean. I don't feel I can take anything for granted. I still don't feel I can just drop in on him.'

'Bit odd, isn't it?' agrees Janna. 'I wonder why he won't commit? I mean, it's no great deal, is it? Meeting your parents. You're not kids any more. Your dad's not going to ask him his intentions. Perhaps you should take him by surprise at the cottage. I mean, what's he got to hide? I wonder why he's so twitchy.'

As Dossie drives home she wonders why, too. It is beginning to affect too many people: Pa and Mo are feeling the strain, she can see that. At the same time it is impossible simply to be truthful with them. She can't find the right words to describe the relationship and, if she were to try, she can imagine all too clearly their expressions: puzzled, sympathetic, anxious. And then there is Clem. Clem is happier than he's been since before Madeleine died: loving his training, confident about his future, and Jakey's, at Chi-Meur. She has no wish to embroil him in explanations about Rupert unless she can be certain that he is going to be a real part of her own future.

As she passes through Crugmeer she feels the familiar sensation of despair at having to face the fact that this might be just another failed attempt at love. She seems fated to pick men who, for one reason or another, just don't stand up to making good partners. Except for Mike: Mike was the exception. And Mike died.

Swiftly, as if avoiding the familiar descent into introspection, Dossie presses the CD button: Joni Mitchell singing 'Both Sides, Now'. Dossie smiles bitterly to herself. This CD has seen her right through the relationship, and now the words of the title track seem depressingly apt. It is true, thinks Dossie, that she really doesn't know love at all: it is love's illusions that she recalls each and every time. The CD finishes, there is a pause, and the first track begins: 'You're My Thrill'. With a tiny stab of pain to her heart the song reminds her of how she reacted when they first met; how she felt each time she saw him.

She won't give up yet; not yet. As she drives through the narrow lanes towards The Court she begins to make a plan.

Father Pascal passes down the steep cobbled lane between granite, herringbone garden walls and cottages, armour-plated against the weather with grey slates. Hydrangeas – wine-red mopheads and delicate creamy lace-caps – still flower in small sheltered gardens, along with the hardy fuchsias, scarlet and pink. Overhead, the wild warm wind whirls the fine wrought-iron weathercocks dizzily perched on stone chimneys, and flees down narrow alleyways with ginger and golden leaves scurrying before it. Out at sea, framed briefly between two tall gateposts, a white sail slices across the choppy water, sharp and fast as a shark's fin.

As he walks he ponders on the homily he might give next Sunday: the Feast of Christ the King and one of the most important days in the convent's calendar. Fragments of the readings and the intercessions are in his mind, along with the memories of the past few weeks, all jostling together. Under his breath he murmurs the antiphon for the psalm: '"He will be called the Peacemaker; and his throne will stand for ever."'

This year the celebration will be especially important, given all the changes and the exciting prospects ahead. How different it was last November. Back then he wondered whether the fragile little community would still be together in twelve months' time. So many miracles have come to pass that his heart is full of joy, though there is much yet to be accomplished: Clem's training and ordination, as well as the establishment of the retreat house. How crucial this next year will be for them all, and for the willing team of people who have gathered to support them.

Lord Jesus Christ gather your flock from every corner of the earth . . .

It is a blessing that Sister Nichola's nocturnal visit to the Lodge has precipitated the move to the Coach House. What might have been a painful, reluctant, drawn-out transition has become an immediate necessity, and the Sisters have welcomed it as a solution to the problem. Once in, they've begun to enjoy the extra space and comfort of their rooms, and Janna and Clem between them have made the move as painless as possible.

Father Pascal silently gives thanks that this November he will be celebrating the Eucharist for Christ the King in Chi-Meur's chapel with the community on the brink of a whole new life, when they might so easily have been scattered, the Sisters taken in by other houses, Clem and Jakey and Janna set adrift again, whilst Chi-Meur itself waited to be converted into a hotel.

Let us take a possession of the kingdom prepared for us since the beginning of the world.

Father Pascal turns into the narrow passage that climbs up towards the church and the cliffs, still thinking of his friends – and of his homily. To Sister Emily, the move and the opening of the retreat house represents an exciting adventure and she has readily embarked upon it; Mother Magda sees it as a challenge to be overcome and is bracing herself accordingly; as for Sister Ruth, who has spoken so strongly against it, she is simply too relieved to have such a ready-made solution to her worries about Sister Nichola to be anything other than cooperative about the whole project. Sister Nichola, herself, is confused but cheerful, and as for Janna . . . He is so proud of Janna: she has risen to the occasion, hiding her own fears and doubts so as to support the older women during the move. Using her strength and her humour she has made the event seem like one of her picnics, full of fun and laughter, and now she too is installed with the others and already beginning to settle in. And there is a new confidence about her, which is enabling her to approach the Sisters on equal terms at last.

By speaking the truth in the spirit of love, we must grow up in every way to Christ . . .

He lets himself into his little cottage and goes up to his study to put down on paper some of these thoughts and prayers that have begun to come together in his head.

ADVENT

Sister Emily is writing a letter. Sitting at her small table, her papers and letters in neat piles, she is finding it difficult to concentrate her mind. She is not yet accustomed to the view and she is secretly shocked by her lack of discipline and by the frequency with which she gets up from the table simply to stare out across the grounds to the cliffs and the sea. Hitherto, their ground-floor rooms looked into the kitchen garden and there was little temptation to stand dreaming. Now, the huge expanse of sea and sky draws her back again and again to gaze out on the constantly shifting light. Light: the word occurs so often in the scriptures, and even now she is writing to a woman whose son is struggling against the darkness of drugs and addiction and fear.

Instinctively, Sister Emily puts down her pen and goes again to the window for inspiration. The sun is already setting, balanced at the sea's rim, splashing the choppy surface with gold and crimson fire. As it sinks, the fleecy clouds glow briefly, rose pink and creamy yellow, and then fade as the shadows grow more dense. Evening settles gently

281

on the land, drawing its wings of darkness inexorably across the brightness in the west. The light is being extinguished; but, even as she watches, a tiny pinpoint of light flickers over the cold grey glimmer of water, and then another, and another. The stars are shining in the darkness.

Texts flicker like the starlight in her mind.

The light shines in the darkness and the darkness has not overcome it . . . Let your light so shine before men . . . I am the light of the world . . . We are the children of light . . .

She goes back to her table, switches on the small lamp and continues to write.

> . . . Yes, I agree. The hand-to-hand battle between good and evil, between darkness and light, is constant. It doesn't let up for a moment, but isn't it encouraging that he is talking to you about it and trying to let you help him? Joyful news that you can come to us next week for a few days! You will be able to rest and allow Chi-Meur to support and refresh you . . .

She continues to write whilst it grows quite dark outside, and she finishes with a phrase from the Collect for Advent: *Let us then lay aside the works of darkness and put on the armour of light.*

She puts her pen down with a little sigh of frustration at her inadequacies. This poor woman, who has been coming to Chi-Meur for twenty years, is watching her beloved son being drawn down by addiction. How can she help them? Suddenly she remembers a conversation between Father Pascal and Clem regarding a counselling course being given on this very subject, and how such courses could soon be held at Chi-Meur.

Sister Emily makes a note about it on a long list of things to do and picks up the next letter to be answered. The bell begins to ring for Vespers and she looks at her bedside clock with surprise. Remonstrating with herself for wasting time at the window, she adjusts her veil and hurries out. Alone on the landing, unable to resist, she sits down on the little seat of Sister Nichola's stair-lift, presses the button and is whisked down to the hall. It reminds her of sliding down the banisters as a child, only rather more sedate. As she stands up, straightening the skirt of her habit, Janna comes out of the kitchen. Two spots of guilty colour burn in Sister Emily's cheeks and Janna grins sympathetically.

Silently, in spiritual harmony, they go along the hall together to the chapel.

Kitty is packing an overnight bag. Everything is prepared for the next day. She will set off after an early lunch, hoping to arrive at the cottage by about three o'clock. She doesn't want to be driving through the lanes in the dark. For the third time she checks that she has the cottage key; Rupert always insists that spare keys, one for each of the properties, are kept at the flat in case of emergencies, each with its name printed on a small luggage label.

She tucks Rupert's birthday present into the corner of the bag and stands up. He hasn't guessed that she intends to surprise him, even though she tried to find out, when she phoned him earlier, what his movements will be tomorrow. He is almost certain that he's got tenants for the cottage, he told her, and he will be taking them out to lunch after they've had another look around the cottage in the morning. He was very confident, very cheerful, and she longed to tell him that she'll be down in time for tea; instead she hugged the surprise to herself, imagining his face when he sees her.

He was so sweet the last time he was home that she broached her idea about moving into a house they both really love within easy distance of Clifton, whilst buying something suitable to renovate for student accommodation. She was absolutely firm about staying in Bristol but ready to compromise about his having some project that he would really enjoy.

Now, Kitty switches on the television for a weather report and opens the map book to recheck the route. She's made her point and he hasn't rejected it. She thinks that she can make the trip to Cornwall without feeling that she is giving in, and it is going to be such fun.

Rupert, having spent the day rebuilding the stone wall at the edge of the lawn, is feeling tired. It's rained, gently but persistently, all day and he was soaked through and covered in mud by the end of the operation. He wants to get the wall finished and tidy up the garden before his new tenants arrive in the morning to measure up, and he's very ready now to take a shower and drink a beer. As he worked he thought about Kitty's proposition: move to a bigger house just across the Suspension Bridge and buy a terraced cottage in the city that he can work on gradually.

As he pulls on clean clothes and goes down to the kitchen to pour his beer he is experiencing a faint sense of excitement at the prospect, though he refuses to consider letting any house he has lovingly restored to students: that's just not on. But an old Georgian terraced house, for instance, might be a worthy challenge. Anyway, it was a good weekend and he is beginning to feel ready to meet her halfway.

He's seized with a pang of guilt. He wishes he hadn't told her that he's taking the new tenants out for lunch tomorrow. It was a stupid thing to do and he doesn't know why he said it. After all, Kitty won't know what he'll be doing at lunchtime. He supposes it's because he's feeling guilty that he's meeting Dossie. He told her that it was his birthday and she said, 'Well, in that case we must celebrate. What about lunch?' and he couldn't see any reason why they shouldn't. He still can't, except that he knows that he's leading Dossie on in allowing her to believe that there might be some kind of future for her with him.

Feeling irritated and anxious, he goes into the sitting-room to light the wood-burner. He'll leave it on overnight so that the cottage is warm and welcoming for his tenants in the morning. As he lays the kindling and searches for matches he tries to rationalize his relationship with Dossie; to reassure himself that he hasn't actually misled her. Of course he should never have allowed her to believe that he was a widower, and the moment has come when he should have it out with her. He is very fond of Dossie, they've had a great summer, but he knows that the time has come to ring down the curtain on their little show.

Rupert lights the fire-lighter and stands up, watching the flames take hold, blue and orange tongues licking hungrily at the kindling and the logs. Tomorrow he will tell Dossie the truth. She deserves to hear it from him, and he must face up to it. But his heart is weighted with anxiety and his gut churns at the prospect.

'Happy birthday.' Dossie raises her glass to Rupert. 'I won't ask how old you are.'

He smiles but doesn't answer, touching her glass lightly

with his own. She is aware of a tension, a look in his eyes, which is making her uncomfortable so that the ease that usually flows between them is missing. The pub is half empty on this gloomy, wet afternoon and the atmosphere is rather hushed and solemn, though the fire in the big inglenook is blazing cheerfully. On one side of it two late-season holiday-makers in their walking boots study maps whilst their dog, some kind of collie-cross, lies quietly at their feet, occasionally rolling a hopeful eye at their plates.

Dossie has already made friends with the dog. She bags the other table on the opposite side of the fire and then crouches down to talk to him whilst his owners beam approval. They start a conversation – where they come from, where they are staying, their proposed walks – so that, by the time Rupert arrives, a relationship of a kind has sprung up and now one or other addresses a remark or a question to Dossie from time to time, which is making any kind of intimacy with Rupert even more difficult.

'Oh, I never admit to my age,' he is saying now with an attempt at jollity, but his response hangs heavily between them and Dossie, feeling quite desperate, smiles back at him and pushes her plate aside. She knows that the proximity of the friendly couple is inhibiting him and this is odd; he is usually quite capable of taking such a pair in his stride, happy for them to be part of the moment – but not today.

He goes up to the bar to order coffee and she watches him with misery in her heart. His mobile bleeps and he takes it out, glances at the screen and presses the button.

'Hi, mate.' He turns away from her and the girl behind the bar, as if shielding himself from them, and Dossie tries to pretend she isn't interested, though she is listening. He comes back to their table wearing an expression of irritation and relief.

'Problems,' he says briefly. 'I'm going to have to go down to St Mawes. Damn nuisance.'

'What, now?'

'The damage assessment bloke's turned up unexpectedly. Remember I told you that a holiday-maker had fallen over on the path and was claiming damages? That was Trevor, my manager. I'm going to have to go and sign some forms. Look, I'm really sorry, Dossie. D'you mind?'

'Of course not.' She makes a huge effort to smile naturally. 'I quite understand. Will you bother with the coffee?'

He hesitates and then shakes his head. 'Sorry, I'd better get a move on. Look, thanks for my birthday lunch. I'll be in touch.'

She can see that he is trying to decide whether he should kiss her or not, and then the coffee arrives and she says, 'Yes, text me,' to him and, 'Thanks,' to the waitress, and he stands indecisively for a moment and then nods and goes out.

The friendly couple send commiserating little smiles and she smiles back but, even as she smiles and drinks her coffee, she is making her mind up. It is too painful to continue like this, too humiliating to be the one who loves too much yet is allowed no rights or privileges. She will take a chance and make her own investigation.

She stands up and collects her things, pays for the lunch, and with a smile to the couple and their dog, she leaves.

She drives slowly to the cottage with Joni Mitchell keeping her company, singing 'You've Changed'. It is after three o'clock when she arrives and parks in the lean-to. She knows where Rupert keeps the key hidden, just in case unexpected deliveries or the plumber or the electrician should turn up whilst he is out somewhere, and she goes round the side of the cottage to the back door. The key is under a stone behind the dustbin.

'It's such an obvious place,' she said to him, and he shrugged. 'There's nothing worth breaking in for,' he answered. 'And hardly anyone ever comes down this lane, anyway.'

So now she picks up the key and comes back again to the front door and opens it, leaving the key in the lock. All the while her heart is beating very quickly and she is breathing fast, as if she's been running. Supposing Rupert were to come driving down the lane now; what would she do?

Dossie shrugs, bracing herself to courage. She has nothing to lose. She stands in the little hall, staring up the steep stairway, letting the silence fill her ears and slow her breathing. She peers in through the doorway of the sitting-room, trying to take it in: the comfortable old armchairs and the small portable television; a table standing under the window with a book and some newspapers stacked tidily on it; no pictures on the walls. She can see a flickering of flame through the wood-burner's glass doors, and the room is warm but impersonal. She remembers that Rupert told her that he'd keep the fire on overnight so the cottage will be warm when his tenants come round: that's why the room is so tidy.

She goes back through the hall and into the kitchen. Some birthday cards are piled on the table. Dossie moves them gently, pushing them apart to look at the pictures, and then opening them to see who has sent them. Several are signed by couples – probably his sisters and their husbands – and inside one is a photograph. She picks it up, her heart jumping:

Rupert is standing with his arm around the shoulders of an attractive dark woman, whose arm is round his waist. They smile out at the camera looking easy and happy together. Another couple stand beside them: a fair, pretty woman with a stocky, cheerful-looking man. Dossie turns the photo over but there's is nothing on the back. The card, however, carries its own message: 'We thought you might like this photo of us all at the club a few weekends before Kitty's mum died. Kitty says you're back this weekend so we're hoping to see you to drink a belated birthday toast.' The card is signed 'Sally and Bill'.

Dossie stares at the photograph: is the dark woman Kitty? Has he been with Kitty at the weekends when he's been unavailable, unwilling to commit himself? Clearly he has a separate life in which he and Kitty go to clubs with Sally and Bill – and it is to Kitty that he is going this weekend to celebrate his birthday. She looks at the other cards. One is an amusing cartoon from the *New Yorker* and inside a more personal message: 'Happy birthday, darling. I shall be keeping your present for the weekend! All my love, Kitty.'

Kitty. There is no point in looking any further. Feeling sick and angry and unhappy, Dossie closes the card and goes out into the hall. Her stomach is churning. So, all this time that she and Rupert have been meeting, there has been this other person: someone who is missing him and to whom he was going at weekends.

As she opens the front door she can hear a car's engine. Heart thudding, she closes the door behind her, takes the key out and runs round to the back, pushing the key under its stone with trembling fingers. She's just reached the path again when a small car pulls up in front of the cottage.

The woman who gets out is thin and dark and elegant:

Kitty, the woman in the photograph. She reaches back into the car for her bag, slams the door and approaches Dossie with a frowning smile that is almost arrogantly interrogative. Her attitude is so confident that Dossie's legs can barely support her. There is no doubt that the newcomer believes she holds all the rights of ownership.

'Can I help you?' she calls. Her voice is clipped and cool, and Dossie has to summon every ounce of courage to smile back, quite calm and collected.

'Hi,' she answers casually. 'No, not really. I was wondering if Rupert was around.'

'Oh?' The sharp question is almost offensive. 'I'm his wife. Is there anything I can do?'

'Wife?' Dossie is shocked out of her fragile composure. 'But Rupert's wife is dead. At least . . .'

It's clear that the woman is as shocked as Dossie now. 'Dead?' She falters over the word, looking almost frightened, as if something terrible has happened; as if Dossie has cursed her. She looks so appalled that Dossie somehow needs to reassure her. She tries to regain some kind of control.

'It was just some rumour I heard when a mutual acquaintance told me about him,' she says, pushing her trembling hands into her pockets. 'I'm sorry. I had no idea whether it was true or not.' She tries to think quickly, unable to scream the truth at this woman with the white, horrified face. 'I've been trying to contact him but without success. Maybe his email's down. I've been doing a Fill the Freezer option for people who have holiday homes and I've done a few for Rupert. I'm giving it up as of now and I wanted to let him know.'

The woman still looks shocked and hostile, but Dossie's

anger suddenly flares again. 'Perhaps you can tell him? Dossie Pardoe. He'll know the name.'

She steps round her to reach her own car, desperate to get away now. She climbs in, has a moment of panic when she can't see her bag – has she left it in the cottage? – and then picks it up off the floor and fumbles for the keys, which are still in the ignition. She backs out, manoeuvring around Rupert's wife's car, and drives away much too fast and shivering violently with reaction.

Kitty watches the car out of sight before she goes in and shuts the door behind her. She is shaken by the encounter. The sight of the woman has given her a shock. Blonde, pretty, shapely, she is the sort of woman Rupert likes, though he always denies it. Kitty stands in the hall, biting her lip, hardly taking in her surroundings. Why has the woman come here to the cottage? How does she even know about the cottage? There are no visitors here who might want her Fill the Freezer facility. And all the while the word tolls like a bell in her mind: dead. Why should she think Rupert's wife should be dead? Who would have said such a terrible thing?

Dossie Pardoe. Dimly Kitty recalls Rupert mentioning the Fill the Freezer idea way back but he hadn't talked about the woman. She pushes open the sitting-room door. She's glad that the fire is alight. She needs comfort and warmth, and she opens the door of the stove and puts on some more logs.

Crossing the hall she goes into the kitchen and immediately sees the birthday cards and the photograph. Clearly Rupert has not been hiding them from the sight of any pretty, blonde visitors. Even so, her anxiety and horror will not go away. She goes upstairs, checking out the work he's done and keeping a sharp eye for evidence of any other kind, but there is nothing. Nevertheless, all her instincts are working overtime and her suspicions are aroused, but it is much worse that that. Dead. Could Rupert possibly have told that woman that she, Kitty, was dead? The horror of such a thought affects her oddly. She feels weak, as if she has been dealt a fatal blow, and shocked even beyond anger.

She glances at her watch, wondering where Rupert might be. She will make some tea and sit by the fire, waiting for him and planning her reception.

When he pulls in, much later, he is alarmed to see the small Golf parked in the lane and lights on in the cottage. He peers at the car in the darkness, his stomach somersaulting with apprehension, trying to remember whether Dossie's car is this dark colour. The front door swings open as he reaches the porch and with a shock that is part horror and part relief he stares at Kitty.

'Good God!' he says, trying to laugh. 'Are you trying to give me a heart attack or something? I wondered who the hell had broken in.'

She smiles briefly, stepping back and opening the door wider, but he knows at once that something is wrong. This ought to be a moment of excitement on her part; she should be enjoying his surprise. Instead he sees the brittle quality of her smile and feels the tension in her shoulders as he embraces her.

'Happy birthday,' she says coolly. 'I thought I'd come and celebrate with you.'

'That's wonderful.' His mind leaps to and fro, wondering if there has been anything she's seen to make her suspicious. 'I just wish you'd told me. Terry phoned at lunchtime and I had to dash down to see him. It was to do with that claim.

If I'd known you were coming I'd have tried to put him off somehow.' He thinks guiltily of Dossie; he would have put her off, too, if he'd known.

'I wondered why you were so late.' She goes ahead of him into the kitchen. 'Let's have a drink.'

He silently gasps a breath, still recovering from the shock. 'Thanks.' He takes the glass of wine she gives him. 'And thanks for coming down.'

She raises her own glass and says again, almost ironically, 'Happy birthday.'

He is puzzled by her contained, cool behaviour. 'What a great present.' He sips, sets the glass down and puts his arms out to her. 'And I thought you said you were keeping it until I got home.'

She moves into his arms, still holding her own glass, and he knows that something is very wrong. He kisses her, but she draws away quickly, still on edge and smiling the same brittle smile.

'I brought some supper with me,' she says. 'I hope you're hungry. Or were you planning to go out?'

'No,' he answers. 'I'd probably have made myself a sandwich. I had lunch at the pub.'

'Oh?' she says quickly. 'I thought you were lunching with the new tenants?'

'Yes,' he says. 'That's it. At the pub. And then Terry phoned. What time did you arrive?'

'About three o'clock. Earlier than I'd allowed. There was a woman here.'

'*What?*'

His reaction is too extreme and she looks at him, eyes wary, chin raised. 'A pretty blonde woman. She was looking for you.'

His heartbeat almost stifles him. Dossie, here, looking for him when they'd only just separated and she knew he was on his way to St Mawes? He shrugs, manages a little chuckle.

'Really? Well, lucky old me. Pity I missed her. Who was she?' He takes another sip from his glass, trying to look indifferent. His brain clicks busily from one possible scenario to another.

'Her name is Dossie Pardoe. She said she'd been trying get in touch with you.'

'What about?'

'The Fill the Freezer thing.' A pause. 'Or so she said.'

He knows at once that Kitty's instinct has gone straight to the truth of the matter and it is with great control that he frowns slightly and says, 'Dossie Pardoe? But why on earth would she come out here? She phones or emails usually.'

He sees that his calmness has thrown her just a little, cast a tiny doubtful shadow on the searching beam of that infallible instinct of hers, and he makes haste to build on it. 'She came out here once, way back in the spring,' he says. 'We had coffee on the lawn and she showed me her menus. She's been quite useful, actually. The punters love it.' He drinks some more wine, makes a face, half puzzled, half indifferent. 'Wonder what she wanted.'

'She said that she was stopping it – the Fill the Freezer thing. She said she'd tried to get in touch and couldn't, and that she didn't want to let you down over Christmas.'

'My email was down for a bit,' he says idly, hiding his relief. 'It might have been that. But it was good of her to come over in that case. We *have* got some people in for the New Year who were asking about it, and it could have been embarrassing.'

His brain seethes: what on earth has Dossie been doing? And what if she comes back?

'It just seems odd,' Kitty is saying, arms crossed over her breast, glass held up in one hand, 'for her to come here.'

'It's a pity she's giving up,' he muses, trying to deflect her. 'I expect those batty old parents of hers have persuaded her back to the B and B-ing.' He laughs. 'I've never met them but Dossie's parents are one of those old Cornish families who have lived for ever on the peninsula and they've been running a bed and breakfast, which they had to stop when they got a bit creaky. And they're always trying to persuade Dossie to give up her own catering thing and run it again. She lives with them, apparently, in this big old house over Padstow way. She's a widow.' He pauses. 'Her son's a local priest,' he adds casually, 'widowed very young too, and there's a grandson. Goodness, it's like some soap opera. They all sound mad as hatters.'

'You seem to know a lot about her from just one meeting.'

'Oh, I've met her a few times, obviously, when she's taken things down to St Mawes. She's a great favourite with Terry, actually, but I've seen her there a few times and she's talked about her family.'

'But you've never told her about yours?'

'What?' He is taken aback. 'What d'you mean?'

'She said she thought I was dead.'

For a moment he cannot speak. He feels the blood beating in his cheeks, his chest is constricted, and he knows – absolutely knows – that he has given himself away. Kitty's eyes are bright and cold, but her mouth shows that she is in pain.

'So you *did* tell her that?' Her voice is corrosive with contempt, her look tells him that he disgusts her, but still she cannot disguise the pain.

'No,' he cries. He sets down his glass and holds out his arms, but she steps back from him with a gesture of rejection.

'You've been having an affair with her.'

'Look,' he says, dropping his arms. 'Wait.' Desperately he tries to muster some measure of control. 'It's exactly like I said, honestly, only Dossie's one of those women who enjoys a bit of a flirtation with their work and well, you know what it's like, love.' He spreads his hands, puts on his naughty-boy expression; a 'how can I help it if women fancy me?' look that expects understanding, forgiveness.

She stares at him. 'So you told her I was dead.'

'No,' he shouts. 'No. I *told* you . . .'

'OK. You allowed her to believe it.'

'No. How do I know what she believed? We never talked about it.'

'Have you been to bed with her?'

'What? Oh, for God's sake . . .' His blustering isn't working. She turns away, picks up her bag. 'What are you doing?'

'I'm going back to Bristol. I can't bear the sight of you another moment.'

He bars her way. 'Don't be so silly, darling. This is crazy. Please, just listen for a moment.'

'I don't want to hear any more. You disgust me. And I don't want you at the flat.'

He stares at her, shocked. 'What are you saying? For God's sake, Kitty. I'm telling you that nothing happened. There was nothing except one of those silly flirtations that often spring up when you work with a member of the opposite sex. Ask anyone. I flirt with Sally and you don't mind that.'

She hesitates just for a moment, and he knows that he's

touched a nerve. What will she say to Sally? How will she explain this to her best friend?

'Look,' he says rapidly, 'just don't get this out of proportion. I can see it's a shock, Dossie turning up here. But I promise you that she means less than nothing to me. You can't destroy our marriage on the strength of a silly flirtation.'

'I'm not destroying anything,' she says. 'You are the destroyer. I'm going now and I don't want you following me.'

She slams out and he hears the engine start up and the car draw away. He stands still, knowing that it would be foolish to follow her and to force another confrontation. He must give her time to cool down, to get over it. He has admitted nothing and, clearly, neither has Dossie. His gratitude is tinged with shame and he wonders what she is thinking and what she will do.

He goes back into the kitchen and refills his glass: 'Happy bloody birthday,' he mutters. 'What the hell happens now?'

Dossie can't stop crying. It is shock, she tells herself, rubbing her cheeks with tissues, doubling up again with the pain. Shock and humiliation and disappointment squeeze her heart, forcing the tears into her eyes.

Pa and Mo are out with the dogs when she arrives home and she simply shuts herself in her room, still shivering with shock and reaction and, sitting down on her bed, she begins to cry. It is so demoralizing to know that he's simply been treating her as a kind of stop-gap, a comfort break, while he is away from his wife. From Kitty. She speaks the name silently, bitterly in her head. Kitty.

So he was married all the time and he'd allowed her to believe that his wife was dead. Liar, she thinks fiercely.

Cheating, lying bastard. She is suffused with shame and humiliation, burning with this overwhelming sense of being betrayed. He knows – of course he knows – that she loves him, and he's just played her along and then gone back to Kitty at weekends. How he must have laughed up his sleeve at her readiness to accept the position of waiting and hoping; how he must have congratulated himself on her willingness to take what she was given and not ask for more.

She weeps again with loss and fury. And now there is nowhere to go – and nothing to look forward to any more. No more dates and meetings; no more plans and picnics and unexpected texts. The future stretches emptily ahead.

Exhausted, Dossie pushes her hair back from her wet cheeks. Still slumped on the edge of the bed, she hears the car returning and Pa and Mo getting out, releasing the dogs and coming into the house. Hastily she gets up and goes to the little basin in the corner of the room. She turns on the cold tap and, bending over, she splashes water onto her hot cheeks. She is filled with resentment that she is not to be allowed even an hour's grace to recover; that she must pull herself together so as to face them. Fresh anger seizes her, but the moment passes.

Raising her head, she stares at herself in the glass above the basin. She's been here before and she knows the score. Deep in her heart she is glad that there was someone to go downstairs to; people to talk to, for whom she must make an effort to cast off the pain and the self-pity. Mo and Pa will ask no questions; they are too wise for that. They will simply be there.

She picks up a towel, blots away the signs of weeping and begins to repair the damage. There is a little scratching at the door. She stands quite still for a moment, and then goes to open it. John the Baptist is waiting for her, tail wagging very slightly and ears flattened, as if guessing her mood and doubtful of his welcome. She strokes his head gratefully, swallowing back more tears, and allows him to escort her downstairs.

On a bright cold morning a few days later, Mother Magda is checking through the articles for the *Advent Newsletter* before they are sent down to the village, where a kind friend who organizes the parish magazine will assemble the contributions into a coherent whole and print it off. The most important news, of course, is the plan for the retreat house. She and Father Pascal have collaborated over this and she is very pleased with the final result. Clem has contributed a piece about his new training, and Sister Emily has been very conscientious over creating a diary of the events that have taken place at Chi-Meur over the past year. There is a charming photograph of Janna's caravan garden at its prettiest to be included, and another of a group of oblates taken in the orchard during the special oblates' weekend in October, and a copy of Father Pascal's uplifting and thought-provoking homily for the Feast of Christ the King.

Mother Magda shuffles the pieces of paper into the right order and then writes a last important note for inclusion on the back page:

> Although we are very appreciative of your kindness at this season we would like to remind any of you who are thinking of sending chocolates, biscuits or sweets to the community that we now number only four, one of whom is diabetic!

'Don't,' warns Sister Emily, 'discourage the delightful fellow who sends the case of claret each year. That Château Labat was very, very good. Father Pascal really appreciated it. And so did Bishop Freddie.'

Mother Magda chuckles to herself, remembering: Sister Emily had appreciated it too. She pushes all the pieces of paper into a large envelope and goes out to find Janna, who will probably enjoy a walk down to the village on this sunny winter morning. She finds her in the kitchen with Sister Nichola who, wrapped about with Janna's shawl, is sitting at the table carefully cutting up old Christmas cards – nothing is wasted at Chi-Meur – and pasting the pictures on to plain white cards on which the sisters will write their own greetings. She works painstakingly, and very slowly, and Mother Magda suffers a little pang as she remembers the beautiful little pots and bowls and candle-holders the older nun used to make, and how deft and clever she was.

Janna, who is making a fish pie, smiles a welcome, points questioningly at the coffee jar. Mother Magda hesitates – it is rather luxurious to be stopping to drink coffee when there is so much to be done – but she gives a little sigh of acceptance and relaxes into a chair at the table. She watches Janna moving about and wonders if she has any idea how much they all value her youth and strength and cheerfulness. Today she is wearing an apron on which is printed: 'Hard work never killed anyone but why take the chance?'

Mother Magda sits peacefully, drinking her coffee, watching Sister Nichola cutting and pasting, making Christmas cards that will be sent out to the community's vast number of friends and supporters. Presently she holds up the big brown envelope.

'Do you think you could take this down to the village,

Janna dear? It's the *Advent Newsletter*. We're a little bit late this year, I'm afraid.'

'I'll be finished in a minute,' Janna says, 'and Sister Ruth will be back soon. I'll enjoy a walk.'

They smile at each other in complete understanding and then Mother Magda stands up, takes her mug and washes it up, and goes back to her work.

'So it really is all over. Whatever it was,' says Pa. 'Well, I can't say I'm sorry, though I'm just so sorry for poor old Dossie.'

Mo is silent. 'It's all over,' Dossie told her. 'He was married but I didn't know, and I'm gutted and I don't want to talk about it.'

It is very cold. The ghost of a new moon hangs low in the sky and the sunset light is dying rapidly. The dogs potter ahead, noses to the hard, frozen ground; their paws crunch in the thick frost beneath bare thorny hedgerows where small birds roost, shifting uneasily and twittering anxiously.

'Anyway,' Pa is saying, 'at least she'll be able to concentrate now. She's been away with the fairies these last few weeks. Poor old Doss.'

Mo's heart aches for Dossie and she slips her hand under Pa's arm as if seeking comfort in its warmth. He presses his elbow against her hand, responding to her gesture.

'She'll get over it,' he prophesies. 'She always does. Thank God I took that decision about The Court. She's got a home, Mo, and she's told us how much she's looking forward to making a change and not having to dash about all over the county. And Christmas will be fun. We'll see to that. It's good that there are some extra people coming. Always a sound move to have friends as well as family at Christmas. Keeps everyone civilized. Pity about Adam, though.'

They walk for a while in silence. Both are reluctant to talk about Adam. Adam has told them that he won't be down for Christmas. He and Natasha have split up, he tells them, it just hasn't worked out, and his company is transferring him to London. He's got a lot to sort out in his new office, and then there's the move into the flat he'll be renting. Perhaps in the New Year he'll get down to see them . . .

Mo agrees to everything, sad that he won't be with them but not sorry that they'll never have to see Natasha and her children again. He refuses to disclose the reasons for the break-up, although he says he doesn't think he's cut out for fatherhood, and that he'll be in touch. The now familiar guilt surfaces and she struggles to remain cheerful. She concentrates her mind on Christmas Day. It will be fun to have guests, and Jakey and Clem will be coming to lunch, and afterwards they'll listen to the Queen and have presents from the tree. Clem will be his usual comforting source of strength, and Jakey will certainly keep everyone in good spirits. Yet still she thinks about Adam, longing for him to be happy.

'After all,' says Pa, 'he can always come back to us if ever he needs to.'

They turn for home, calling to the dogs, trying to feel more hopeful.

'All right, Mo?' Pa asks as they near the gates to The Court, and she is able to answer truthfully.

'I'm fine,' she says firmly. 'It's going to be a good Christmas. Come on, let's get in and light the fire. I'm frozen.'

Kitty wanders from room to room in the flat, moving small ornaments, staring out of windows. Her feelings of anger and pain occasionally give place to a sense of loss and loneliness.

Mummy's spirit still inhabits the flat and Kitty misses her terribly; now, when she remembers her, all she can think of is how much Mummy loved Rupert and how he joshed with her and teased her. What would Mummy have said to all this? Once, she remembers, way back when Rupert was being a bit silly with a rather attractive acquaintance, and Kitty had complained about it, Mummy had said: 'Well, you wouldn't want a man nobody else wanted, would you?' It had been a bit of a shock, frankly, and Kitty had felt almost as if she'd been silly to mind.

But this is different; quite different. How can she possibly ever forgive him for allowing that woman to believe that she, Kitty, was dead? It's almost as if he were wishing that she were – and she can't forget it or forgive it.

'Can you get it into your head that we never discussed you at all?' he shouts during one of the telephone conversations that have taken place during the last few days. 'We talked about work . . . Just listen, will you? That rumour came from Chris at Penharrow. He completely misunderstood that you'd simply gone back to Bristol when your father died so suddenly and he'd got it into his head that it was you . . . Yes, I *know* it's horrible, but you can't blame me if Chris heard some kind of rumour and elaborated on it. He must have mentioned it to Dossie Pardoe when she checked up on me after I asked him about the Fill the Freezer thing when I saw it on his website. He was the link. For God's *sake*, Kitty . . .'

Rupert is lodged in one of their cottages at St Mawes. He has nowhere else to go. Perhaps he is seeing Dossie Pardoe – but no, Kitty shakes her head. Remembering the shock on Dossie's face, Kitty instinctively knows that whatever was going on between them is over. Such deception is unforgivable.

Kitty raises her chin and hardens her heart. She is prepared now for Sally, who has been away visiting her daughter and is now home, and who is arriving any moment for a cup of tea and to catch up on the news.

Sitting over the tea cups – Mummy's lovely delicate old Worcester – Kitty summons all her courage and tells Sally that she thinks that Rupert and she might be going their separate ways. Sally is utterly shocked.

'He simply can't face the idea of living in the city,' Kitty says bravely, 'and I can't face going back to scrubbing down walls and camping. It's a complete impasse and neither of us will back down.'

'But I thought you were going to buy a house out near us in Leigh Woods and Rupert was going to renovate old properties for student lets.'

Kitty is ready for this one. 'He says that doing up houses for scruffy students simply isn't his idea of restoration. He needs to be creative.'

'Well, yes, I can understand that when you look at his work. But, Kitty! You can't seriously be considering giving up on your marriage over this. There must be other compromises.' She looks at Kitty, a 'come on, you can trust me' look. She leans forward a little. 'It's not just that, is it? What's happened?'

Beneath the caring expression Kitty sees a glimpse of the dreadful glee and she knows very well that her dear old friend has sniffed at the truth. For a terrible moment Kitty imagines the gossip – 'You'll never guess . . .' 'Well, we all know old Rupe, don't we . . . ?' 'Poor old Kitty. Imagine how humiliating . . .' – and she has to stiffen her spine and stare down Sally's spuriously sympathetic gaze.

'It is exactly that,' she says firmly. 'I've realized that those years with Rupert were like having a long holiday, though it was hard work too, and when I came back to look after Mummy I suddenly felt that I'd come home. It's wonderful to be back in the city and in this lovely flat. To be able to go to the theatre or see a film and have a social life again is heaven. If Rupert wants to be creative out in the sticks then he can do it all on his own. We've both learned to live apart over the last year and now we find we rather like it. After all, it was you who said I shouldn't give in on this one.'

'Well.' Sally sits back in her chair, startled, put out, now that Kitty has challenged her. 'Yes, I know I said that . . . but even so. Still, if it's what you both want . . . but I think you're being rather extreme.'

Kitty suspects that Sally doesn't really believe her, and that she will say as much to Bill, but suddenly she doesn't care. Having spoken the words she is filled with a terrible desolation and she wants to be alone so that she can burst into tears.

'Bastard!' Janna says. 'I can't believe it. Honestly!'

Dossie tries to smile. 'Your language hasn't been improved by living with nuns,' she says.

Janna makes a face. 'Can't make a silk purse out of a sow's ear, but Sister Emily's working on it. Honestly, though, Dossie. I'd've stayed there that evening and made a big row.'

Dossie shakes her head. 'No you wouldn't. That's not your style any more than it's mine.'

'No.' Janna looks sombre. She is remembering just such a scene that she unwittingly precipitated between Nat and his mother. How hateful it had been! 'No,' she says again. 'You're right. I hate rows. But what will you do? Apart from taking him off your Christmas card list.'

'What *can* I do? I suppose I just forget him and pretend it never happened. I've dumped him very explicitly by text though it seems there's nothing to dump.'

'And you haven't heard anything?'

Dossie shakes her head. 'Nothing. I thought he might at least text back.'

'Coward!' Janna says fiercely. 'Wouldn't I love to tell him what I think! What about Mo and Pa?'

'It's just as well they never met him. I've told Mo that it's all off, and both of them are being painfully tactful. Luckily they're being distracted by excited people writing or email-ing to book their holidays and making plans for next year. And then one of Pa's old chums has been recently widowed and he asked if he could come for the New Year. We weren't going to start until around Easter-time but we talked about it and then asked him if he'd like to come for Christmas. He was so grateful it was really touching. And we've got one of Mo's cousins coming too, as well as Gran'mère and Gran'père, so I foresee it working up into a very big jolly by the time we've finished.'

'Well, that's good,' Janna says. 'Isn't it?'

Dossie nods. 'I'll be busy and it'll be fun . . . But I still miss him. I can't seem to stop the way I feel about him. Apart from anything else I was such a fool. I should have guessed.'

Watching her downcast face, Janna is filled with rage and compassion. She hates feeling so helpless when Dossie is suffering. Not knowing what else to do, she gets up, refills the kettle and rinses out the empty mugs.

'Let's have some more tea,' she says. 'What about Clem? What does he say?'

'Nothing,' says Dossie firmly. 'He never knew anything about it. It's just you, really. You're the only person I can talk to. Sorry about that. Anyway, let's forget about Rupert for a while. How's it going? Are you really settled in? It all looks very comfortable and you seem very relaxed. No regrets?'

'You know 'tis weird, but I feel really happy here. Having taken the decision all those awful terrors kind of melted away. I'm really busy, mind, but I like that, and I still get time to get out on the cliffs or down into Padstow to meet up with a few mates. I just feel I've dropped into a ready-made family but without the in-fighting real families seem to have. And 'tis great having you and Clem and Jakey. You're all part of it.'

'And Sister Ruth?'

Janna laughs. 'Sister Ruth needs me just now so we're OK. She's not so bad really, and Sister Nichola is there like a . . .' She hesitates, searching for a word.

'A buffer state?' suggests Dossie.

'Yeah! That's it. She keeps us nice and polite to each other.'

'Sister Emily and Mother Magda must be thrilled to bits with you.'

'I shall get a gold star,' Janna says contentedly. 'It'll be my Christmas present. Talking of which, I shall need some ideas from you for a very special Christmas Day lunch. Sister Emily is already dropping hints.'

Rupert sits in the pub, staring at his pint. He's just had another totally fruitless telephone conversation with Kitty and he's feeling at the end of his tether. She's told him flatly that she can't see a future for them, that she certainly has no intention of moving from the flat or of buying any other properties. She's in a position to call all the shots. Now that Mummy's dead, Kitty is a wealthy woman.

He picks up his glass and sips reflectively. If they separate she will be entitled to half of his properties and income –

but, by the same token, he will be entitled to half of hers. He thinks about it: pretty much six of one and half a dozen of the other. Neither of them will lose financially but he feels angry and hard done by: nothing much has happened, after all. Yet Kitty is quite happy to walk away from their marriage without giving him the benefit of the doubt. She is prepared to wreck it all because of Dossie's chance remark.

Rupert thinks about Dossie. He's had a furious text from her, which he has not answered. He doesn't blame her for sending it but for the last few days he's been trying to convince himself that there's a very faint chance that she might be able to forgive him. If he's honest, he knows in his heart that he's completely finished as far as Dossie is concerned, but he hasn't wanted to face it. Even if Kitty is really serious – and he still can't quite believe that she is – he knows that he doesn't have any future with Dossie.

He finishes his pint. Suddenly he doesn't give a damn about either of them. He has property, money, and he can find himself a new exciting project: something that will thoroughly occupy his thoughts and his imagination, something he can work on and to which he can give all his mind and his energy. He imagines his future – if he has one – in Bristol, endlessly paying back for his little lapse by humbly following Kitty around to her parties and bridge clubs and being patronized by Sally and Bill. Kitty will demand retribution and he shudders at the price he will have to pay.

If Kitty's father hadn't died so suddenly, if they hadn't been apart so much during this last year, perhaps none of this would have happened. All those arguments and wasted weekends, during which they bickered about whether he should give up his work and move into the flat, have weakened them. The separation has shown up cracks in the relationship. Kitty values city life and her friends more than she values her marriage. If there was ever a chance of compromise it is over now, and he knows that she will never return to their former life together.

As for him, he is certain that he cannot live a life with no mental challenges, no work, no structure to his day – and especially not in a city. He remembers his relief each time he returned to the cottage; his satisfaction at the end of a productive day. Clearly they have reached an impasse.

Unexpectedly he is seized with a terrible sadness. He thinks of Dossie, of her generously loving approach to life, and how he belittled and demeaned her to Kitty in an effort to protect himself. He remembers Kitty, his exciting, enthusiastic companion of those early years of their marriage – how happy they'd been – and how he has implicitly denied her to Dossie. Now he has lost them both.

He sets down his empty glass. His anger has passed and he feels diminished, ashamed, and very lonely.

In her room, Sister Emily is packing Christmas presents. During the year the generosity of the guests and friends of Chi-Meur is manifested in gifts. Some send practical things that they know the Sisters will enjoy using: packets of pretty notelets and postcards; scented soap; pens and pencils; warm socks. The Sisters share these gifts, putting the contents of a parcel on the table in the library and each carrying away one or two objects – depending on the largesse of the parcel – to use or hoard to give as presents in their turn. The Sisters are given individual Christmas presents, of course, and from these the wrapping paper is carefully taken and smoothed out, Sellotape neatly sliced off, tags removed, so that the paper can be reused.

Now Sister Emily examines her little cache of possible gifts. For Sister Nichola, who has a sweet tooth, there is a box of sugared almonds; for Mother Magda, who suffers with arthritis, she has set aside a pair of knitted fingerless mittens. Sister Ruth is more difficult: she is rather a Puritan when it comes to the giving and receiving of gifts and it must either be especially practical or have spiritual properties. Sister Emily's hand hovers over a simply framed postcard: a print of Rublev's painting of the Holy Trinity. They have recently had a study day on this icon, led by a Benedictine, and Sister Ruth was much taken with the large print of the painting, which was placed on an easel during that day.

There is a knock at the door, and she swiftly covers the little hoard with her old black shawl before she turns and calls, 'Come.'

Sister Ruth is standing there with a parcel in her hand. She looks rather awkward, defensive even, and Sister Emily is intrigued.

'What is it?' she asks. 'What can I do for you?'

Sister Ruth closes the door behind her and holds up the parcel.

'My cousin has sent me this,' she says, 'and I've been wondering if it might do for Janna's Christmas present. It's much too fine for me.'

Sister Emily's eyebrows shoot up in surprise and a small spot of red burns on each of Sister Ruth's cheeks. She pulls aside the tissue paper and a pashmina the colour of blackberries, and threaded through with fine strands of scarlet and gold, flows over Sister Emily's outstretched hands.

'Oh,' she cries softly. 'Oh, how beautiful it is.'

Her old thin hands tenderly smooth the soft fabric whilst

Sister Ruth watches, her habitually guarded expression softening into a faint smile.

'I thought it would be from us all,' she says, 'since Sister Nichola has appropriated Janna's own shawl. Janna need not know where it has come from. I hope you approve. Mother thinks it's quite in order.'

'It's perfect,' says Sister Emily, 'and completely solves my problem of what to give Janna. She's working so hard for us all and this will utterly delight her. It's a wonderful and generous gift. Your cousin won't mind?'

Sister Ruth flushes brightly and in that moment Sister Emily knows that, whilst it is no doubt true that the cousin has sent the pashmina, it has been at Sister Ruth's request.

'It's perfect,' Sister Emily repeats quickly. 'Thank you very much. Do you have some paper to wrap it in?'

Sister Ruth folds it back into its tissue and glances at Sister Emily's little pile of Christmas wrapping paper.

'Perhaps you might do it? I think I shall have to beg some paper this year.'

'Of course I will.' Sister Emily hesitates; if this had been Mother Magda they would have had a little hug and a shared pleasure in the prospect of Janna's delight. This is impossible with Sister Ruth, who would be embarrassed by transports of joy and awkward to embrace. She gives a little nod and glides out, and Sister Emily watches her go with affectionate exasperation. It's sad that they cannot celebrate such a generous idea but she must respect Sister Ruth's feelings.

Eagerly she begins to select a suitable piece of wrapping paper.

The Christmas tree has been brought home to the Lodge and put in a large ceramic pot. Clem has strung it about with the lights which, by some miracle, are in working order and Dossie has driven over amidst snow showers so that she and Jakey can decorate it together. By lunchtime there are two or three inches of snow and Dossie says that it is time to get back to The Court. She checks the freezer, kisses them both and drives away very slowly and carefully.

As she peers through the windscreen, the wipers sweeping little piles of snow before them, she is aware of the dull ache in her heart; the emptiness where once there had been the prospect of Rupert.

The car slides a little, skidding on the bend in the snow and she grips the wheel more tightly. She switches on the CD and Joni Mitchell: 'I Wish I Were in Love Again'. She makes a little sound that is a mix of a groan and a kind of sob, and makes an effort to fix her mind on all that she loves and values: Pa and Mo at The Court; Clem and darling Jakey at the Lodge. And Janna. Odd how the positions have reversed and that it is Janna, once so insecure and uncertain, relying on her treasures and terrified of commitment, who is now the comforter, the strong one.

She is glad to get home at last, to turn in through the gates, and to see Pa hurrying out into the snow to meet her with John the Baptist at his heels, tail wagging furiously.

'Thank goodness you're back,' Pa is crying. 'Mo was worrying. More snow to come, they say. It's going to be a white Christmas, Doss,' and she shuts the car door and they all go into the house together.

Jakey is rapt with joy that it should be snowing just in time for Christmas. He waves goodbye until Dossie's little car is out of sight and then goes back inside to admire the tree and all the familiar decorations: the little carved wooden figures the drummer boy, the snowman and the small boy with a lantern – and the fragile glass baubles: the owl, and the clock and the bell. Clem follows more slowly, thinking about Dossie and hoping she'll recover from her heartbreak. Of course, he's said nothing about it – and neither has she – but he's been well aware of her heightened emotions through the summer and autumn, and he hopes that something good might come out of it all.

Watching Jakey staring up at the tree, he wonders whether either he or Dossie will ever find that special person. It seems unlikely to have such luck twice in a lifetime. Jakey crouches down to examine the brightly wrapped parcels that Dossie has put under the tree and Clem feels all the usual emotions: love, pride, sorrow and responsibility.

'Look,' he says silently to Madeleine. 'Look at him. Am I making a good job of this without you?'

Jakey glances round, sees him standing there and immediately looks guilty.

'I'm not touching them,' he says defensively. 'I wouldn't.'

'I know,' Clem says. Loneliness smites his heart: he will never be able to share the joy of their son with the girl he loved so much. 'Of course you wouldn't. Look, shall we get out the Holy Family and put them on the table? I know we don't usually get them out until Christmas Eve but there're only a few days to go. Would you like to do that?'

Jakey beams with delight. 'I'll do it,' he cries. 'I can do it on my own. Oh! And Auntie Gabriel.' His eyes shine as he remembers her. 'Can I do Auntie Gabriel, Daddy?'

'"May I?"' mutters Clem automatically. 'Yes, of course. I'll get out the stable for you. Hang on a minute.'

He goes to the merchant's chest, opens the heavy bottom drawer and takes out the open-fronted stable. Beside him,

Jakey reaches for the old linen shoebag. Clem stands the stable on the low table beside the tree.

'There you are,' he says. 'Can you manage?'

Jakey nods, clutching the bag. 'I'll do it on my own,' he says, 'and then you can come and look when I tell you. It'll be a surprise for you, Daddy.'

Clem is fighting an uncharacteristic urge to burst into tears. 'OK,' he says lightly. 'I'll be doing some work while you're at it. Call me when you're ready.'

He goes out into the kitchen, pulling the door closed behind him. There are times even now, with his future full of exciting challenges, when he longs for more certainty, more conviction; a strong, unquestioning faith in the mysterious ways of God. Fighting his sense of loss, he sits down at his computer and opens it. His tutor has given him a title for an essay and he stares at it thoughtfully. It is a quotation from *The HitchHiker's Guide to the Galaxy*: 'Who Is This God Person Anyway?'

Jakey slowly draws open the neck of the shoebag and looks inside. They are all there: the Holy Family and their attendants. As he takes the small figures from the bag he remembers how they fit into their stable. Gently he places them: the golden angel standing devoutly behind the small manger in which the tiny Holy Child lies, swaddled in white. His mother, all in blue, kneeling at the head, opposite a shepherd who has fallen to his knees at the foot of the crib, his arms stretched wide in joyful worship. Joseph, in his red cloak, with a second shepherd – carrying a lamb around his neck as if it were a fur collar – both standing slightly to one side, watching. A black and white cow curls sleepily in one corner near to the grey donkey, which stands with its head slightly bowed. And here, just outside this homely scene, come the Wise Men in gaudy flowing robes, pacing in file, reverentially bearing gifts: gold, frankincense and myrrh.

And all the while, as he is setting out the Holy Family, he is thinking about Auntie Gabriel; remembering her clumsy wooden shoes, and the white papier-mâché dress and golden padded wings; her hair that is made of string and her scarlet, uptilted thread of a smile that is compassionate yet joyful. The clumpy feet might be set square and firm on the ground but when he places the golden wire crown upon the tow-coloured head then there will be something unearthly about her. And, held lightly between her hands, the red satin heart: a symbol of love, perhaps?

At last, filled with happy anticipation, Jakey lifts the big bundle out of the drawer and puts it carefully on the sofa. Kneeling down, he begins to unpack the angel.